GRATERFORD CORRECTIONAL FACILITY, 1974

He had arrived by bus, wearing chains and linked to thirty-five other men. The four-story-high cellblock to which he was led was a giant room containing hundreds of households, and the accumulated din of male voices, soul music, blaring television sets, and slamming steel doors was deafening. Fourteen years of this noise ahead of him.

As he walked in line, Frost stared up at the vast area of the cellblock—listened to the racket and smelled the stink of men living closely together, like rats in a hole. He thought of the detective sergeant who had put him here with lies and planted evidence. Frost closed his eyes and called up Murphy's features. He fixed them in his mind. Rhino Frost planned to think about Frank Murphy a lot in the coming years. He planned to dream of Murphy every night.

What he did not plan to do was forget.

ACTION ADVENTURE

SILENT WARRIORS   (1675, $3.95)
by Richard P. Henrick
The Red Star, Russia's newest, most technologically advanced submarine, outclasses anything in the U.S. fleet. But when the captain opens his sealed orders 24 hours early, he's staggered to read that he's to spearhead a massive nuclear first strike against the Americans!

THE PHOENIX ODYSSEY   (1789, $3.95)
by Richard P. Henrick
All communications to the USS *Phoenix* suddenly and mysteriously vanish. Even the urgent message from the president cancelling the War Alert is not received. In six short hours the *Phoenix* will unleash its nuclear arsenal against the Russian mainland.

EAGLE DOWN   (1644, $3.75)
by William Mason
To western eyes, the Russian Bear appears to be in hibernation — but half a world away, a plot is unfolding that will unleash its awesome, deadly power. When the Russian Bear rises up, God help the Eagle.

DAGGER   (1399, $3.50)
by William Mason
The President needs his help, but the CIA wants him dead. And for Dagger — war hero, survival expert, ladies man and mercenary extraordinaire — it will be a game played for keeps.

Available wherever paperbacks are sold, or order direct from the Publisher. Send cover price plus 50¢ per copy for mailing and handling to Zebra Books, Dept. 2187, 475 Park Avenue South, New York, N.Y. 10016. Residents of New York, New Jersey and Pennsylvania must include sales tax. DO NOT SEND CASH.

A KILLING FROST

DANIEL LYNCH

ZEBRA BOOKS
KENSINGTON PUBLISHING CORP.

ZEBRA BOOKS

are published by

Kensington Publishing Corp.
475 Park Avenue South
New York, NY 10016

First printing: October 1987

Printed in the United States of America

PROLOGUE

"What are your plans for yourself?" Zanfani asked.

The big man shrugged his shoulders. "Maybe head West. I never been to California."

"I've been out there," Zanfani said, going through the big man's file one last time. "I went out there on vacation a couple of years back. L.A. is Jersey with palm trees. And the palm trees aren't native, either. They were brought in. Actually, the whole place is a desert, like Arizona or somewhere. It's warm all the time, though. You might like it."

"I might. I hope so."

Zanfani leaned back in his worn city-issue chair in his worn little city office. *He* was a worn-looking man of forty with a perpetually sad expression on his face. He had been born with that expression, but it might well have developed on its own, given the nature of his work. Zanfani had been a Philadelphia probation officer since he got back from Vietnam. Vietnam had been easier than this work, he often reflected.

This meeting was no more than a formality. The big man was not one of his cases. The big man was one of Clyde's cases. Only Clyde was out with a heart attack—

5

the result of too many cigarettes, too many western omelets, and too little relaxation for too many years. Clyde routinely carried the heaviest caseload in the office—sometimes as high as eighty guys at once—and he also got the worst ones, the ones nobody could really be sure about.

This guy was one of those, and Zanfani had him on fill-in. Now it was the big guy's last visit, and Zanfani was just going through the motions. They were going to let the big man off parole. He'd been a good boy for a solid year now. What were you going to do? The worst part about it was that Zanfani hardly knew him, except through the file he had in front of him. Clyde knew him, but Clyde was out, and Zanfani had over sixty cases of his own to worry about, and that was tough enough without taking over for Clyde.

"I'm running out of questions," Zanfani said finally.

"That's okay. I'm running out of answers." The big man smiled as he said it. He was trying, Zanfani could tell. He was really trying. This guy wanted off probation in the worst way. All those years in the slammer and then probation after that—meeting with Clyde every month, having Clyde check up on him, knowing that if he just looked at somebody cross-eyed Clyde would violate his ass and ship him back to Graterford. He wanted off, all right. Who could blame the guy?

"I'm going to give you my little speech now," Zanfani said, closing the file. "You ready for it?"

The big man sat up somewhat straighter in his chair. "Tell me what you got to tell me."

"You did a lot of hard time, Mr. Frost. You're not a kid anymore. You know that if you get nailed again

6

with your record, you're going back there for a long time. You know that."

Frost nodded. "I know."

"You don't want that, do you?"

Frost shook his shaggy head.

"You've got a new chance now," Zanfani told him. "You go out there and do it right this time. Put all this behind you and start again. It's all up to you now. Nobody beats the system for long, and you pay real hard when it catches up with you."

"Yeah, I know."

That was all Zanfani could do. He stood up and extended his hand. "Good luck, Mr. Frost. Just remember, TCOB."

The big man stood up. No, he wasn't big. He was huge, immense. Zanfani, who stood just a shade under six feet, was dwarfed by him. Frost took his hand, enveloped it in his own huge hand, which was roughly the size of a Hormel ham. Zanfani felt the power of the man as their fingers grasped. It made him somewhat uneasy, being in such close quarters with somebody this big, somebody this strong, somebody who had done what this guy had done so many years before.

"TCOB?" Frost said.

"I always say that," Zanfani told him. "TCOB. That means take care of business, Mr. Frost. If you do that, you'll be fine."

A slight smile played around the giant's bearded lips. "TCOB. Yeah, I'll do that. I'll take care of business."

7

CHAPTER ONE

From the moment he had awakened, Murphy had known it would be a bad day—a truly rotten day, a suckola day of epic proportions. He had a sixth sense about these things.

After a late night of too much pasta and red wine with friends at a South Philadelphia joint with the stylish name of Ralph's, he had been dragged into wakefulness this morning by Winston Churchill lying on his chest and licking his face, urging Murphy to get his ass out of bed and take Winston for his morning walk. It had been brutally hot even at seven in the morning, the sun beating down through the oily skies hovering like a shroud over Center City. Murphy—bloated with tomato sauce and more or less hung over as he walked briskly behind the big English bulldog—had begun sweating even before he had finished his first Camel.

Then, back in his apartment, he had managed to take a nice slice out of his chin while shaving with his new plastic Bic razor from the Rite-Aid drugstore on the corner—a razor he had used out of sleepy habit instead of the new, battery-powered electric number he had recently come into possession of. And after that—on the way to work—he had tripped on the marble steps outside his brownstone building, falling and ripping a nice hole in the pants of a brand-new pin-striped suit that he had bought because it made him look almost thin. Swearing and seething, he had rushed upstairs and put on an old suit with a cigarette burn in the trousers. Muttering creative curses, he had then gotten himself, without breakfast, to City Hall, where he had met his client, Sorino, in the hallway outside the courtroom.

"Ready?" Murphy had asked.

"Hey," Sorino had grunted to his lawyer.

Murphy took that for a yes. Murphy had realized early on, when Sorino had first come to Murphy's office, that the word "hey" was Sorino's primary mechanism for communicating with the rest of humanity. So you want me to represent you? Murphy had said. Hey, Sorino had replied. Can you pay me my fee up front? Hey. Are you guilty of what they charged you with? Hey. Does that mean yes or no? Hey.

Now they were ready to begin the trial, and Murphy was faced with the prospect of the prosecution putting Sorino on the stand. Terrific, Murphy had thought, studying his client. Sorino was about thirty, a gorilla of two hundred and thirty pounds wrapped in a lime green double-knit suit. He was up on charges of aggravated assault and battery—a small matter of Sorino's allegedly having broken the wrist of a Center City real estate guy who had fallen behind on his payments to Sorino's employer, a South Philly loan shark. Sorino's defense was that the attack on the real estate guy had taken place at night, that the real estate guy had made a faulty identification and that, anyway Sorino had been at home with his wife watching a rerun of *Little House on the Prairie.*

Would the wife back up that story?

Hey.

In his heart, Murphy knew the truth. But a lawyer had to make a living—especially a lawyer who had been in practice precisely five months—and Sorino had paid Murphy's fee up front, a luxury to which Murphy wasn't accustomed and which he found strangely appealing. Sorino might be a slug, but he was entitled to his day in court. Charles Manson had been entitled to his day in court. And was Sorino worse than him? Was he worse than Richard Speck? Was he worse than John Hinckley? David Berkowitz?

Hey, Murphy wasn't sure.

Even slimeballs were entitled to representation, though. That was the way Thomas Jefferson and John Hancock and all those other guys had planned it. On the other hand, Murphy had to admit, Thomas Jefferson and John Hancock had never met Sorino, who had elevated slimeballing to an art form.

Be that as it may, however, the primary difference between those other slimeballs and Sorino was that Sorino had chosen Murphy as his lawyer. Surely, that should count in Sorino's favor. Something should, Murphy thought.

As they walked into the courtroom and took their places at the defense table, it occurred to Murphy that a crucial element was missing.

"Where's your wife?" he asked. "She is going to be here this morning, right?"

"Hey," Sorino said.

"All rise," the tipstaff ordered.

They did. Joe Luce, the judge, came into the courtroom and settled behind the bench. He looked at Murphy and nodded in recognition. Then he looked at Paul Toddman, the first assistant district attorney, who was prosecuting this case himself only because the legislature, in its limitless wisdom, had cut back on the district attorney's budget. Moreover, Toddman was obligated, after all, to give vacation time to those incompetent young assistant DAs fresh out of law school. And somebody had to try the case.

Actually, Toddman didn't mind doing this one himself. He and Sorino had met before. The last time Sorino had done thirteen months in Graterford, which was why he had found himself a new lawyer this time around.

"Is the prosecution ready?" Joe Luce asked wearily.

"We are, Your Honor," Paul Toddman said.

"Is the defense ready?" Joe Luce asked Murphy.

"The defense is ready, Your Hon—"

Then Sorino reached up and caught Murphy's arm.

"Hey," Sorino said, "we gotta talk."

"Excuse me, Your Honor," Murphy said. He leaned down to Sorino and whispered, "Talk? What talk? The trial is starting."

"Hey, we got a problem," Sorino said. "My old lady just came in. In back there."

Murphy looked up and saw Sorino's wife in the rear of the room, wearing a light dress and sunglasses. She was a pretty woman, small and dark and shy. During his pretrial interview with her, she had promised she would support her husband's story. She said it none too convincingly, but there was little Murphy could do about that.

11

"We had this little disagreement last night," Sorino whispered hoarsely. "The bitch said she ain't gonna do it for me. I told her to stay away then, but she's here this morning. That means she's gonna spill it if somebody puts her on the stand. She's just been looking for a chance like this."

Murphy looked back at Sorino's wife. She took off her sunglasses, and he saw that one eye was blackened. Mrs. Sorino's other eye was an angry slit. Murphy decided that this was not a good witness.

"What do you want me to do?" Murphy said.

Sorino shrugged. "Hey, cop me a plea. See what you can do for me, okay? Be a good guy."

Murphy sighed deeply. He stood up. "Your Honor, may I speak briefly with the representative of the district attorney's office?"

Joe Luce looked slightly amused. "You may."

Murphy and Paul Toddman huddled in the court-room, away from the jury.

"Well?" Toddman asked.

"I think I can talk him into making a deal, if you're interested."

"Fuck him," Toddman said. "We already spent two days empaneling a jury."

"Come on, Paul," Murphy insisted. "He just gave me a sign that he's getting weak knees. I think I can talk him into going along with a deal under the right circumstances. Look, I might get him off, you know. You know how juries are. I've got some other clients, though, and I wouldn't mind getting out of this one. This guy is willing to go to trial if you push it, and I just barely got him to consider a plea bargain. I don't know how long I can hold him."

12

Toddman frowned. He didn't like being in court. He wasn't at all sure that Murphy had better things to do, but he knew he did.

"I don't know, Frank," he said finally. "The DA's office has got a fair amount of time and effort invested in this."

That was certainly true, Murphy reflected. He and Toddman had fought tooth and nail all week over the jury, with Murphy coming out on top, he figured. Then Sorino had blown it all by beating up his wife. Tax work, Murphy thought. It he could just get some tax work and forget this criminal crap.

"Three months," Murphy said. "I think I can get him to take an assault two. Otherwise, you'll have to take it all the way."

"Eight months," Toddman said.

"Five," Murphy shot back. "Paul, this guy's sister is a nun. She'll tell the jury he's always been a great guy. I've got her on standby. And she's a Carmelite, too. They still wear the uniform, you know. I could always put on his mother, too, but we might have some trouble getting her wheelchair into the elevator, and at her age and with her heart con—"

"Fuck you," Toddman said. "Six months. That's as good as it gets."

"Be back in a minute," Murphy said. He looked up at the bench. "Your Honor, may I consult for a moment with my client?"

"So consult," Joe Luce said wearily.

Murphy went back to Sorino. "Six months," he said.

Sorino frowned. "Too fucking long."

"That's as good as it's going to get, believe me. You want your old lady on the stand?"

13

Sorino sighed and shrugged. "Hey."

Murphy went back to Toddman. "Deal," he said.

"Okay," Toddman said. "Your Honor? May we approach the bench."

Joe Luce yawned. "Be my guests, gentlemen."

At the bench, Murphy said, "Six months, Your Honor. Otherwise we go to trial."

Luce looked at Toddman. Toddman shrugged. "It'll keep him off the street for a while."

"Stand away, please, gentlemen," Joe Luce said.

Murphy and Toddman, as if in military formation, stepped back.

"Your Honor," Toddman said, "the people moves for a reduction in charge to aggravated assault second."

"Defense concurs," Murphy said.

"So moved," Joe Luce said, slamming down his gavel. "Augusto Sorino, please stand."

Sorino didn't move. Murphy leaned over him and whispered, "Stand up, asshole."

Sorino stood up.

"Augusto Sorino," Joe Luce said, "do you understand the charges against you and the modification in them so suggested?"

Sorino stood before Judge Luce wearing an expression of utter mystification.

"Say yes," Murphy said.

"Hey," Sorino replied.

"Does he mean yes?" Judge Luce asked Murphy.

"He does, Your Honor," Murphy said.

Joe Luce slammed down his gavel. "Guilty of assault two," he said. "Six months. Augusto Sorino, you are hereby ordered to surrender yourself at 9 A.M. next

Thursday to the custody of the county sheriff, who will transport you to Holmesburg Prison to serve your sentence. Do you understand the sentence of this court?"

"Say yes," Murphy told his client, "and this time make it yes."

"Uh, yeah," Sorino said.

"Close enough," Joe Luce said, slamming down his gavel once again.

Toddman caught up with Murphy outside the courtroom. The fleshy folds of his usually mournful face were formed into a rare grin.

"Well, Frank, is the practice of law so far what you had in mind?"

Murphy shook his head wearily and pulled out a Camel. "Got a light?"

Toddman produced his lighter and one of the huge cigars he so adored. He lit both smokes.

"It's about what I figured, yeah," Murphy said. "I'd been hoping for more civil work, but I guess I got this reputation after all those years as a cop. And working for you for three years got my name around to a lot of slimeballs, so that's who's looking me up."

"Well, I don't want to give you a swelled head, but you know you were a damned good chief investigator," Toddman told him. "The office hasn't been the same since you left."

Murphy shrugged. "Maybe I'll come back if Fletcher ever gets voted out."

Toddman frowned at the very mention of Fletcher Lake's name. The district attorney had been the primary reason Murphy had finally taken the bar exam and escaped from more than twenty years of public service into private practice. Toddman detested Lake every bit as much as Murphy did. The difference was that Toddman loved being a prosecutor, had devoted his life to the work, in fact. So, for him, private practice wasn't an option. He would work for the DA no matter how annoying a fool he happened to be. Right now, the DA happened to be Fletcher Lake—thanks to the continuing stupidity of the voters, who seemed to like Lake's smile. Toddman's respect for the democratic process had been badly savaged by having to work for this DA.

"Fletcher is the best argument for a military dictatorship I've ever come across," Toddman grumbled to Murphy.

"Why don't you run against him yourself next time?"

"I might, one of these days. If somebody who looks like Ed Koch can get elected mayor in New York, somebody who looks like me might have a shot at DA here."

"You'll have to get funnier, though," Murphy advised. "Compared to you, Koch is Buddy Hackett."

"Fletcher gets laughs enough for both of us," Toddman replied, "but only when he goes into court. Well, I've got another case in front of Desiderio. Call me for lunch one of these days, okay?"

"That's a deal," Murphy said, "and the city can buy."

Toddman headed back into the courtroom, cigar jammed between his teeth. "Have a good one, Frank."

"I already have a good one," Murphy told him, "I just don't get to use it very often."

It was eleven o'clock and already past ninety degrees

when Murphy left City Hall and walked the four blocks down South Broad Street to the Fidelity Bank Building, where he rented a small office and the part-time services of a secretary from another attorney, Harold Warren. The secretary Harold let him use on a part-time basis was a luscious black woman in her mid-twenties who looked like Lena Horne would have liked to look forty years ago. Her name was Esmeralda Bright, and every time Murphy saw her he felt like rubbing his antlers against a tree. When he'd left the DA's office, he'd toyed briefly with trying to bring his city secretary, Beverly Kavanaugh, with him. But he couldn't afford to pay her what the city was paying her, and he had made a mental note that when things were looking up he'd make her an offer. As for now, there was Esmeralda, who made beads of sweat break out on Murphy's forehead.

"You had two phone messages," Esmeralda told him. "One was from your wife, and the other was from Mr. Warren."

Murphy took the messages and his mail—which was all bills. "Get my wife, okay?"

He went into his little office. It had his name on the door—Francis P. Murphy, Attorney-at-Law—and it overlooked South Broad Street and the Bellevue Stratford Hotel across the street, where Murphy liked to eat lunch when he wasn't eating at the Harvey House next door. The office was furnished with Harold Warren's leftovers, which made it vastly more plush than Murphy's City Hall office had ever been, although he missed the big old city-issue desk he'd had there. He missed it primarily because when he'd moved out he'd forgotten to take with him the three-quarters-full

17

bottle of Jim Beam he'd kept in the bottom drawer.

Esmeralda buzzed. "Your wife is on line three."

Murphy picked up the phone. "Hello, Mary Ellen."

"Hi, Frank," the familiar voice said over the phone. "No support check so far this month. Just thought I'd nudge you."

He groaned inwardly. "It's only the fifth."

"And it's due the first," she pointed out.

"You're right. I'll send you a check this afternoon. Don't cash it until the end of the week, though. Friday, maybe."

"Frank," she said in the same tone that had prompted Murphy to leave her, "what's the point in having a support check due on the first if I can't cash it until the tenth or so? I mean, what's the point in that?"

"Did I or did I not pay Patricia's first tuition payment?" he asked her, annoyed now. "And in advance, too."

"You did," she told him.

"Have I ever—I mean ever—missed sending you a support check the month it was due?"

"You have not," she conceded.

"Then could you get off my back for a minute or two?" Murphy demanded. "You know I'm just into a new practice. You know that this isn't like working for the city. You know that I don't get a regular paycheck every week. You do know that, don't you, Mary Ellen?"

Mary Ellen said, "Frank, your business affairs are all a matter of monumental disinterest to me, if you want the truth. If you want to leave a steady paycheck after twenty-two years of municipal service because you can't stand your boss, that's your decision, and you're

18

welcome to it. All I care about is money to feed and clothe and educate Patricia, and you're late with it again."

"It'll be in the mail today," he told her, fuming.

"Thank you, Frank," Mary Ellen said. "Oh, and a happy forty-fifth."

"My birthday's not until next week."

"Yes," she said, "but I don't plan to speak to you again until you miss another support payment."

Then she hung up.

Murphy took a moment to swear viciously, then he called Harold Warren.

"Got a minute?" Harold asked him.

"Is there some money in it?" Murphy demanded.

"Touchy, touchy," Harold told him. "I have an ex-wife too, Frank."

"Yeah, well, I'm still married to this one."

"Poor Irish Catholic bastard," Harold said consolingly. "Still married to a woman you don't have sex with."

"We didn't have all that much sex when we were living together, if you want the truth," Murphy observed.

"Listen," Harold told him. "I've got a client I think could use your services more than mine. I'll split the fee with you, fifty-fifty."

"Seventy-five, twenty-five," Murphy said.

"It's my client."

"Fuck you and sixty-forty."

"My kind of guy. I'll send her in."

Carol Highland turned out to be in her late twenties, pretty in sort of an antiseptic way. Tall and sandy blond and just a little too WASPy for Murphy's taste.

His daughter had told him repeatedly that it was wrong of him to notice first how sexually attractive a woman might be, but Murphy was very much a creature of habit, and his habits were such that women struck him first as women, secondly as human beings. Also, he thought in his own defense, compared to guys like Sorino he was Phil Donahue.

"How do you do, Mrs. Highland?" Murphy said in as gracious a fashion as he could muster.

"I've been better," she told him. "Mr. Warren said you might be able to help me."

"I'll try," Murphy said, and smiled. "What's your problem?"

"My first problem is your cigarette. I hope you don't mind putting it out. I'm allergic to tobacco smoke."

Murphy looked at his freshly lit Camel, thought about Mary Ellen's phone call, and stubbed out the cigarette with reluctance. The things you had to go through to make a living in the real world.

"I'm sorry," he said. "Go ahead, please."

Carol Highland looked somewhat awkward, which pleased Murphy. "I don't know quite where to begin," she said.

"Try the beginning."

She took a deep breath. "All right. I'm from Fanwood, New Jersey. That's a suburb of New York. I've lived here six years. I came to Philadelphia to go to college."

"Where'd you go?" Murphy asked.

"Temple."

"That's where I went," Murphy told her. "I went nights for a lot of years, getting my B.A. and then my law degree while I worked as a cop."

20

"I went days," Carol Highland said in businesslike fashion. "I took education. In my sophomore year, I met a man named Hank Kirby. We got married, and we split up after eighteen months. Hank was a doper, among other things. Later, I got word that he'd died in New York City. The word came from a woman he'd been living with, and she asked for money to bury him."

"How'd he die?" Murphy asked her.

"Supposedly from an overdose. I sent the woman the money, and I counted myself lucky to be out of it. Hank wasn't a nice man, believe me."

"So what's the problem?"

Carol Highland sighed. "After I graduated, I started teaching at Girls' High. Later I moved to another school. I took some graduate work at Penn, in sociology. I fell in love with my professor. We dated for a while and he asked me to marry him, which I did. We've been married not quite three years."

"Are you happy?"

"More or less."

Murphy pursed his lips. He would have liked to have lit up another Camel. "How should I take that?" he asked.

Carol Highland looked uncomfortable. "I take it that this conversation is covered by lawyer-client privilege, that you'll keep this to yourself?"

Murphy nodded. "What we say is confidential."

"Ev is happy. That's my husband, Everett Highland."

"But you're not, I take it."

"Not entirely."

Murphy got the message. "Is there another man?"

Carol Highland looked at him levelly. "I've been

having a relationship with my boss."

"Who is?" Murphy asked.

"His name is Bob Waterson. He's the principal of the school where I teach now."

"Is it serious?"

"Reasonably so," Carol Highland said.

"And you want a divorce?" Murphy said. "That's why you're here?"

She shook her head vigorously. "No. I most emphatically do not want a divorce. Bob is married and plans to stay married. He has children. That's not my problem at all. My problem is Hank."

Murphy was nonplussed. "I have to admit to some confusion. If he's dead, Mrs. Highland, what's your problem?"

Carol Highland sighed, a ragged sound. "It turns out that he's not dead. He's very much alive, I'm afraid. He called me about a month ago. He's back in town, and he wants money."

"Have you gone to the police?"

"No. I never told Ev about my marriage to Hank. I didn't see any reason to tell him at the time. Hank was dead. He was a closed chapter in my life. You know what all this means, I take it."

Murphy pondered the matter for a moment. Then he said, "I think so. You have a husband and a lover. That much I think I grasp. But more important . . ."

". . . I'm not legally married," Carol Highland said, her voice shaky now. "Not if my first husband is still alive. Now do you see? Do you see the horrible situation I'm in?"

Murphy sat back in his chair. So this was what lawyers did, the sort of story they listened to. He was

22

more or less amazed at it all. Murphy had thought his own life was a mess, but this beat the living shit out of his own problems. No wonder Harold had sent this woman over to him. Thanks, Harold.

"And your husband knows about none of this—not about Bob or the earlier husband?"

Carol Highland was near tears. "No, none of it. Mr. Murphy, all I want out of this is my husband. That's all I want."

"I see," said Murphy, who didn't—not entirely.

Carol Highland began to weep quietly. "And there's more than that."

"Oh?" said Murphy, wondering what more there could be.

She nodded, tears streaming down her face. "My husband's mother is a very strange and difficult woman. She's a born-again Christian. She's been one ever since her husband got religion some years ago, before he died. And he left her very well off. She's hated me since the day Ev and I started dating. Ev's only gesture of rebellion was his marriage to me. If she finds out I was married before, that this marriage isn't binding—"

Ah-hah, Murphy thought. Now he suddenly grasped Everett Highland's attraction for his wife, who clearly didn't love him. Everett Highland was rich. Women were just wonderful, Murphy thought. "I get the picture. I understand, Mrs. Highland. You're right. You definitely have a problem."

And it's a weird one, Murphy thought. He'd taken contracts in law school. He understood as much about the uniform commercial code as most general practice lawyers. He'd taken torts and criminal procedure. He'd taken constitutional law and civil procedure. A born bullshit artist, he'd been a whiz at mock court. Murphy had, because of his natural intellect and the fact that he'd been a grownup when he'd gotten to law school— in marked contrast to the fuzzy-cheeked kids fresh out of undergraduate school with whom he'd gone to law school—been a terrific student, law review every year. But nobody had ever covered this kind of shit in law school. There was nothing in his class work to cover a case like this. On the other hand, being an ex-cop had its advantages.

"I don't know what to do," Carol Highland said.

"How did you happen to come to Mr. Warren?" he asked.

"I was in an auto accident a few years ago, and Mr. Warren got me some money for it. I don't know any other lawyers. I didn't know who else to go to."

Murphy sat back in his chair. "Where's your husband now? Your first husband, I mean. What's his name—Hank?"

"He's staying at a motel out on Roosevelt Boulevard."

"Do you have the address?"

"Yes."

"Well," Murphy said, "the first thing you need is to have somebody tell him to get lost. That seems the most sensible course of action to me."

"That's why I'm here," Carol Highland told him.

Murphy smiled. "I'm your man," he said.

CHAPTER TWO

Coming out of his office building at the end of the day, Murphy was preoccupied.

It was abundantly clear that several factors had prompted Harold Warren to send Carol Highland down the hall to him. One, she was the victim of a crime, blackmail, and Murphy—as an ex-cop—had vastly more experience in dealing with crime victims. Harold's background in such matters involved only sympathetic dealings with the perpetrators of crimes, not the victims. Two, she didn't want to report the crime to the police, which posed a problem for whoever was her attorney. Three, this meant that whatever action that could be taken in her behalf would have to be taken outside routine legal channels. And, four, the woman herself was guilty of having broken the law. She was—technically, at least—a bigamist.

In no way was this Harold Warren's kind of case. He and his associates did high-priced general legal work for profitable companies. They handled lucrative negligence cases. They offered tax advice to people who suffered under the adversities of high incomes. And Harold had several clients who were rather successful and prominent in the criminal community for whom he performed a valuable and profitable service—he kept their jail time to a minimum. Clearly, he had listened to what Carol Highland had to say and had said to himself: who needs this? So he had shipped her off to Murphy, who needed the work and the money and was grateful.

In the end, the only service Murphy could think of to perform on her behalf was to go see Hank Kirby and try to scare the hell out of him—to menace him enough to make him go away, if possible. He got from Carol the address of Kirby's motel and told her he'd keep in touch. After she left, he phoned Kirby's room and let it ring ten times before giving up. Throughout the day, he phoned four more times, with no success. Meanwhile, he sent Esmeralda out to a deli and ate a chopped liver and onion sandwich on rye with a side of potato salad and a beer while he did paperwork at his desk. He finished off a will he was writing. He did the preliminary paperwork on two real-estate closings. He spent most of the afternoon taking depositions in a divorce case.

By the time he got out of there at five, Murphy was looking forward to going home, walking the dog, doing some drinking and reading, maybe catching part of the Phillies night game on TV, then crashing hard for the night. His plan was to be at the door of Hank Kirby's motel room at seven in the morning. From Carol Highland's description, Kirby was not an early riser, so Murphy would have a better than even chance of finding him in. Murphy also would prefer to take the man by surprise, early in the day, when he would not be fully awake and would be a likelier candidate for

26

intimidation than he might be later, when his faculties were in full operating order.

Surprise counted for a lot in such matters, Murphy knew. Mostly, when you scared somebody, it wasn't because you were tougher; it was because you were smarter and you had made it a point to catch the other guy off guard. Murphy was a big believer in preparation in such matters, and he was a big believer, too, in having the deck stacked in his favor as much as possible. It was one of the reasons that, as a cop, he'd never engaged in a fair fight if he could avoid it. His job in a fight had been to win, and no sportsmanship awards had ever been at stake as best he could recall. Consequently, Murphy had always been a big believer in certain physical combat aids—like brass knuckles and saps and shoes with steel-tipped toes.

Murphy approached the practice of law with much the same philosophy. When he had to try a case, he wanted a completely fair, impartial, and intellectually honest jury—if that was the best he could get.

All this was on his mind as he walked out onto South Broad Street, and it had been some time since Murphy had actually worked as a cop. So he could be forgiven for not seeing the huge, shaggy man until they were almost nose to nose.

Or, rather, nose to chest. Murphy was not quite six feet tall, but his nose got no higher than the top of the big man's chest. Sensing an immense object in front of him, Murphy looked up suddenly from the *Daily News* he was scanning as he walked. Recognition flashed in his eyes, and he felt his stomach do a back flip. He swore silently to himself. He'd left his pistol at home.

"Hello, Rhino," Murphy said softly, his heart

27

beginning to thump as he tensed to defend himself.

"Recognized me right away, Sergeant. Good for you. It's been a while."

What was not to recognize? Rhino had gotten his nickname for good and sufficient reason. He was roughly six foot eight and weighed in at about two-fifty. He wore biker boots, jeans, a tank top, and a headband. He was wearing his hair in a ponytail and his beard was braided today into little ropes. Except for the gray strands in the hair and beard and the gold hoop dangling from his left ear, Rhino Frost looked much the same as he had so many years ago.

"You don't look much different," Murphy said, eyeing the huge man carefully and wondering if there was a cop around. "A little grayer, maybe."

"You sure look different, Sergeant," Frost said gesturing idly with an enormous bare arm at Murphy's gray hair, his mustache, and his paunch, none of which had been present at their last meeting, which had taken place under difficult circumstances all around.

"It's not 'sergeant' anymore," Murphy said, relaxing now as he realized that the streets were filled with people going home from work and that maybe Frost wasn't so crazy anymore, although Murphy doubted that. When they were that crazy, they tended to stay that way. "I got to be lieutenant and then I got a law degree and went to work for a living."

"Oh, I know you're a lawyer. I seen you this morning in city hall. You got a leather briefcase and everything, man. Very impressive. You're doing okay, I see."

"Fair. What were you doing in City Hall?"

"I had me some business there."

"Parole officer?"

28

Frost said nothing.

"How long have you been out, now?" Murphy asked him.

Frost paused before he answered, which made Murphy nervous. What also made him nervous was the look on Rhino Frost's face and the memory of what he had done to get sent to prison in the first place.

"Not long enough," Frost said finally. "Not near long enough."

Murphy nodded. "You must have ended up doing what—ten, eleven years?"

Frost shook his shaggy head slowly. Then he said, "Thirteen years, eight months, and seventeen days."

"Roughly," Murphy said jokingly.

Rhino Frost did not laugh. "Hard time, too—some of it, anyway. Until I learned my way around, that is. I learned me a lot in prison. I just lifted them weights every day and took care of my body and learned me everything there was to know."

At that precise moment, Murphy really wished he'd brought his pistol. It was not a mistake he'd make again, leaving it in his desk drawer at home. Especially now, with Rhino Frost out of the slammer. He'd had about enough of this conversation.

"Well," Murphy said, continuing on his way, "it's been huge, Rhino. See you around."

Frost watched him go. "Count on it," he said quietly.

Murphy felt the giant's eyes boring into his back as he walked down South Broad Street. At the corner of South Broad and Locust, Murphy crossed over. He looked back across the street, and Frost was nowhere to be seen. Then Murphy walked up the other side of Broad Street and went into the Bellevue Stratford. He found a phone booth and dialed a number.

"Major crimes," said the voice at the other end. "Patrolman Sanislo."

"Is Lieutenant Wilder still around?"

"Yes, sir. Who should I say is calling?"

"Tell him it's Stan Laurel."

Jim Wilder came on in a moment. "Well, Stanley," he said, "and what fine mess have you gotten us into this time?"

"What time are you leaving tonight?"

"Soon. Why?"

"Can you stop by my place?"

Wilder's tone grew more serious. "Problem?"

"I think so."

"Do you have any beer at your place?"

"Some."

"In that case I'll be there in an hour or so."

CHAPTER THREE

Even though this section of town was virtually all white, Jim Wilder liked Murphy's neighborhood anyway.

Wilder's own integrated, middle-class neighborhood in Germantown—well north of Center City but still very much a part of Philadelphia—was composed of neat brick row houses built back in the twenties. There was always plenty of parking, which emphatically was not an attribute of Center City, but the buildings and streets of Wilder's Germantown lacked the elegant grandeur and grace of the territory Murphy had staked out for himself when he'd left his wife a few years back. Murphy's block of Schuylkill Avenue was typical of the city's eighth ward—impressive four- and five-story brownstones chopped into apartments with spacious rooms, tall trees shading the buildings' carved stone steps, trendy shops on the bottom floors of the buildings on each corner.

Wilder liked the shops, especially the food shops. In this neighborhood, you could buy freshly baked croissants at the bakery on one corner and curried chicken and walnut salad at the deli on the next. You could walk out your door, take fifty steps, and come back with coffee cake still warm from the oven and almost obscenely fragrant with cinnamon and powdered brown sugar.

Wilder and his wife Annabelle sometimes talked about leaving Germantown and moving into Center City so they'd be closer to the good restaurants and theaters which they, as a childless working couple, had plenty of money and time to enjoy. The problem was that they'd lived in the Germantown row house for nearly fifteen years. Wilder had lovingly altered and redecorated it, planting rosebushes in the front and lilacs in the back. Over the years, his hands had touched every inch of the place, inside and out, and that made it a part of him just as much as he had become a part of the house. Besides, after fifteen years in a good-sized three-bedroom row house with its own little yard in back Wilder wasn't sure he could adjust to life in a four-room Center City apartment, food shops or no food shops. True, he'd grown up with his grandmother in a two-room flat in North Philadelphia where the toilets didn't always flush and where heat in the winter was only a rumor. But by now, in his early forties, he'd grown accustomed to more space and comfort.

Besides, parking down here really was a bitch, he thought as he circled Murphy's block for the fourth time looking for a spot. That wasn't a problem for Murphy, he knew, since Murphy had given up his city car when he'd taken his retirement from the department. Now Murphy kept only an aged and rusting Oldsmobile Toronado, which he moved from its parking spot in front of his apartment house on only the rarest of occasions. In this neighborhood, Murphy could easily live his daily life on his feet, without a car. He was only a few blocks from his office and the courts in city hall, and he could take the subway to Veteran's Stadium to watch the Phillies more conveniently than Wilder could drive there from Germantown. Wilder figured that if he actually did move to Center City, practicality would dictate that he'd probably have to give up his own city-owned Dodge, and he'd worked long and hard for a perk like this.

It hadn't been until he'd made detective lieutenant and became second in command of the department's major crimes unit that Wilder had rated an unmarked Dodge for his personal use, he'd be damned if he'd give it up if he didn't have to. Not for a while, anyway.

Wilder had made lieutenant only seven months before, and only after his role in the capture of a homicidal maniac had put him in the hospital for ten days with a shattered spleen. During the collar, the psycho had kicked Wilder in the gut, inflicting serious damage. The lieutenant's bars—and the car that accompanied them—had been awarded to Wilder in his hospital bed, and they had done more to ease the pain than Demerol.

Ah, a spot. A freaky white kid with a dyed green streak through his hair was pulling away from the curb in a battered Mazda. Wilder stomped the gas pedal and pulled next to the vacancy along the curb. Expertly, he backed in and slid into position. A lot of years on piloting a prowl car in an urban environment had made him a master driver. Wilder had begun driving prowl cars when they had still been painted red. Then, in the early seventies, Frank Rizzo had become mayor. Rizzo, who had been police commissioner before his election, had taken two immediate actions upon assuming office. One, he had named his brother fire commissioner. Two, he had ordered the red police cars painted a pale blue. The joke in the police department—and the fire department, too—had been that Rizzo had ordered the new paint jobs so his brother could tell the cop cars from the fire engines.

Wilder locked the car and walked up the street to Murphy's building. He was a smallish, trim, balding man, whip-lean and wiry, with a small mustache and skin the color of polished mahogany. He wore a tan, summer-weight suit and wingtips shined to a mirror image. Jim Wilder had never lost the rigid military bearing he'd gained from his years in the Marine Corps. He never really walked anywhere. Instead, Wilder marched.

He pushed the button inside the vestibule of Murphy's building.

"Who is it?" Murphy said through the intercom.

"Hey, Pancho," Wilder said, "thees ees Ceesco."

Murphy hit the buzzer, and in a few seconds Wilder was up the stairs and inside Murphy's second-floor apartment. Like most of the apartments in the neighborhood, the place consisted of four rooms—a kitchen, a combination living room and dining area, and two bedrooms. There was also a bath off the hallway to the rear. Unlike most of the apartments in the neighborhood, which tended to be occupied by young professionals and neatly kept, Murphy's place was a perpetual pigsty. Murphy never washed a dish until mold grew on it in the sink and threatened to envelop

34

the whole place. He never threw out a newspaper or magazine until the ragged piles of paper threatened to force him out the door. Murphy felt that putting away clothing was a useless waste of energy; he'd only have to take it out again sometime. He could see no point in emptying ashtrays that would only fill up again.

The only neat spot in the place was Murphy's rolltop desk along the wall of the living room. That was where Murphy worked, and he was as meticulous in his work habits as he was slovenly in his personal habits. The two men had lived together in a prowl car for more than eleven years. Cops seldom grew as close to their wives as they grew to their partners. Murphy hadn't, certainly.

"About that beer," Wilder said.

Murphy, in his suit pants and white shirt but sans jacket and tie, went into the little kitchen. Wilder heard him open the door.

"Miller okay?" he called out.

"Bullshit," Wilder told him. "Heineken."

Murphy came out grumbling with the Heineken in his right hand and an empty glass filled with ice cubes in the other. "Thanks a lot, asshole. I've got plenty of Miller, but that's my last Heineken."

Wilder took the beer and drank deeply from the bottle. "Good stuff, too," he said, smiling.

He saw Murphy, holding the ice-filled glass, go over to a cabinet.

"What're you having?" Wilder asked.

"Bourbon," Murphy said, pouring from a bottle of Old Grandad he took from the cabinet. He poured liberally.

Wilder frowned. "Bad day?"

35

"The worst," Murphy said, collapsing on a heap of newspapers on the sofa and ignoring the rustling they made as he put his stockinged feet on a pile of *Sports Illustrated*s on the coffee table. "Guess who I saw today?"

"Who?"

"Rhino Frost, remember him?"

"Shit, yes," Wilder said.

"And he seemed a little pissed off, too," Murphy added.

Wilder's brow knit. "That's one dude who was born pissed off."

Murphy lit a Camel. He offered one to Wilder, who reluctantly shook his head. Wilder was down to five cigarettes a day now. The problem was that he tended to hit his quota no later than one in the afternoon, then he had to twitch for the rest of the day.

"He was waiting for me outside my building," Murphy went on.

"Outside here?"

"No, my office building. I came out after work and there he was, big as life and six or eight times as ugly. I had some things on my mind, and he caught me completely by surprise. I don't carry my piece much anymore, but I will from now on, believe me."

"What did he say to you?" Wilder said, trying surreptitiously to suck in some of the smoke cloud Murphy was exhaling. Since he'd gone to his cigarette quota, Wilder had become a great fan of passive smoking.

"Nothing you can do anything about. No threats, none of that. Nothing overt."

"He didn't cause any trouble?"

Murphy shook his head. "I thought he might, but he didn't. He will, though. You can bet on it."

Wilder nodded grimly. "Yeah, I know."

Murphy downed a slug of bourbon and looked at his friend. "Well," he said, "I'm a civilian now. I'm just one of the great unwashed. So what can you do for me, Lieutenant?"

Wilder sipped his beer. "I'll take care of Rhino's ass," he promised. "I'll get back to you on it."

"Good," Murphy said. "Anything you can do."

They talked for another half hour about other matters, mainly department gossip. Even now, off the force for months, Murphy had an avid interest in departmental politics. After all, he'd lived with it for twenty-two years. The talk finally roused Winston Churchill, Murphy's big and aging bulldog, from his sleep in a heap of soiled clothing in the bedroom. Winston had come waddling around the corner, his stub of a tail going like the blade of a mixmaster, to greet Wilder. Wilder petted the dog and played with him and then watched as Winston retired to the side of the room to perform some canine hygiene. Wilder watched the dog lick at his privates and said, "Jesus, I wish I could do that to myself."

Murphy guffawed out loud, his first good laugh all day. Finally Wilder looked at his watch.

"Annabelle will be looking for me," he said, standing. "Thanks for the beer."

Murphy walked him to the door. "Give Annabelle my best."

"I'll do it. Say hello to Nancy for me."

Murphy frowned. "No need."

Wilder looked at his friend. "Oh?" he said.

Murphy shrugged. "She's gone on to greener pastures. She moved out three weeks ago."

Wilder looked around the littered apartment. "Well, man," he said, "you're going to have to find some other fox to come in here and clean up after you or you're just going to sink and disappear in all this shit you got built up. How're you doing? You okay?"

"Hey," Murphy said, smiling, "I'm cool. Frankly, I sort of like the peace and quiet."

The affair with Nancy Elliott had been Murphy's first since he'd moved out of his house and into Center City—his first in more years than he liked to think about. He'd met Nancy on a case during his last weeks as the DA's chief investigator. Nancy had been a witness and very nearly a victim in a murder spree by a young, rich, and completely deranged Center City banker. Murphy had taken her into his apartment one night for protection, and she'd just never left, which had been fine with him.

Whatever his other flaws as a husband, Murphy had always been scrupulously faithful to Mary Ellen during all the years they'd lived together. Coming to the realization that his marriage was over had been horribly painful for him, and moving out had turned out to be a nightmare for a while. Aside from the guilt he'd felt in leaving, he'd spent months adjusting to the loneliness of living alone with just the dog, which Mary Ellen had insisted he take along. Mary Ellen and Winston had never hit it off. For those reasons, Murphy had at first welcomed a totally unexpected romantic relationship with a woman nearly fifteen years younger—especially one who said she liked the dog. What he hadn't counted on had been their total incompatability in virtually every other aspect of human existence.

Murphy was a slob of epic proportions. Nancy's slovenliness had turned out to be within normal bounds, and this difference was a constant source of friction. Nancy felt compelled to pick up, to at least create clear paths through the apartment from one room to another. One result of this was that Murphy could never find anything.

"Have you seen my sheepskin coat?" he would ask her.

"In the closet. I hung it up."

"Why, for Christ's sake?"

"So you could find it, Frank."

"I could find it before."

"It was under a heap of crap in the corner," she would argue.

"I know. That's where I put it. I keep it there."

"The coat was getting all wrinkled," she said in exasperation.

"Bullshit," Murphy told her. "The sheep used to sleep in the goddamn thing without getting it wrinkled."

She also could never stand his chain-smoking. Murphy habitually went through two packs of Camels a day—more if he was nervous, which had been his usual state since leaving the security of the force for the uncertainty of private law practice.

"Why do you smoke those things?" she would demand. "You're going to kill yourself."

"If I stopped smoking, it would make me nervous. If I got nervous I couldn't keep my mind on what I was doing. If I couldn't keep my mind on what I was doing, I'd probably step off the curb without looking both ways and get hit by a bus. Smoking is good for my health, Nancy."

"I'm serious. You're hooked. You're addicted. You're just like a junkie, Frank. Doesn't that bother you?"

"Not so I notice."

"Frank, do you want to die? Is that it?"

"If I stop smoking, am I going to live forever? Is that your point?"

"Of course not. Don't be ridiculous."

"Look," he told her, "someday you're going to find yourself on your deathbed. You're going to lie there, feeling your heart slowing down, knowing that the end is coming, and you're going to say to yourself, 'This can't be happening to me. I've never smoked.' Think how surprised you're going to be when that happens."

"Frank . . ."

"Or," he said, raising one finger skyward to accentuate a new argument which had just occurred to him and which he liked very much, "it'll turn out that you're right, that not smoking will help you live longer. And you'll end up ninety-three in a nursing home wearing a diaper and thinking you're a tea kettle. How's that sound?"

"There's no talking to you on this topic, is there?"

"I certainly hope not," he said.

Nancy's complaints were endless. She found Murphy's drinking habits incredible.

"Do you realize that you have a drink of that bourbon every day," she told him. "Every goddamned day. Sometimes you have two."

"Yeah?" he said, wondering what her point might be, and knowing that her estimate of his intake was conspicuously low.

"Why in God's name do you drink so much?"

"It keeps me calm," he explained, belching lightly and lighting a Camel.

They had other differences as well.

Murphy's separation from Mary Ellen might have unnerved him, but it had proved a boon to some of his friends. The fact that Murphy now had an apartment of his own meant that the irregularly scheduled poker games he was in the habit of staging with Paul Toddman, Jim Wilder, and several other men involved in various ways in the city's criminal justice system had at last found a permanent home—Murphy's place.

And just in time.

While Mary Ellen had permitted Murphy to hold one or two games in the basement rec room of their house in Mount Airy before ruling the rowdy gatherings off-limits in her house, Muriel Toddman had refused to tolerate them at all. Moreover, Annabelle Wilder had just about run out of patience with the clouds of cigar and cigarette smoke, the raucous laughter and tough language and horribly tasteless jokes that made these gatherings so much fun for the men.

All this meant that Nancy became the new hostess. She sat there through the first game trying to watch *Cheers* before she realized it was a lost cause and went to bed, wrapping the pillow over her head to ward off the bellows, the grunts, the belches and breaking of wind, not to mention the "call you, asshole" and "take that, motherfucker" repartee that accompanied

41

the games.

The next time Murphy's friends showed up at the apartment she had so meticulously cleaned for them, she fled out the door to a movie, but the game was still going strong when she got back, and she had to get up and go to work in the morning at her job as a department store buyer. The games typically went on until nearly 2 A.M. and she finally told Murphy she just couldn't handle it anymore.

"Can you imagine what it's like trying to sleep while a bunch of drunks in the next room holler and scream and make endless remarks about the joys of oral sex until the sun comes up?" she demanded angrily.

Murphy couldn't fathom what all the fuss was about. "It's just a couple of friends getting together to play some cards. What's the big deal?"

"Would you let them talk like that if Patricia was staying over? Would *you* talk like that if Patricia was in the apartment?"

"But she wasn't," Murphy protested.

"That's right," Nancy fumed. "It's just me."

"That's right," Murphy said, "and you're a big girl. This is just a bunch of guys getting together."

"I'm not that big," she told him. "No more poker games in the apartment."

"Nancy . . ."

"None! I mean it."

So the games moved out of Murphy's place and continued to search for a real home. Eventually they'd have to rent a hotel room, the men knew, but nobody relished the idea of spending the money, and Murphy took a lot of good-natured abuse over Nancy's dominion over him. Which pleased him not at all.

42

"Admit it, Frank," Toddman prodded. "You're pussy-whipped."

Murphy sputtered in rage. "And you're not? Why don't you go tell Muriel to screw off and we'll hold the games at your house?"

Toddman shook his head and said, "I just said you're pussy-whipped, Frank. I didn't say that being pussy-whipped was a bad thing."

So, in short, there were a good many Murphy personality traits that Nancy found difficult, at best. On the other hand, she had a few characteristics of her own that drove Murphy right up the wall. Not the least of which was her taste in music.

To the extent that he cared about music at all—and he cared a bit more now that he owned a car with a tape deck—Murphy was a Sinatra fan. To him, Mel Tormé was a little far out. When Murphy listened to the radio or the record player—which wasn't often—he favored music that settled his nerves. Some quiet jazz, maybe. Sometimes, when he felt lively, he'd even listen to the music of his teenage years—the Everly Brothers singing "Kathy's Clown," the Big Bopper doing "Chantilly Lace," Bobby Rydell doing "Volare." The records were nearly thirty years old.

Nancy listened to Motley Crue and Quiet Riot. She listened to U2 and the Thompson Twins. She listened to that crap constantly, day and night. It made Murphy's skin crawl. Often Murphy would retire to the bedroom and turn on talk radio just to kill the sound of whatever was blasting out of the stereo in the living room. The music maddened him, and for more than one reason.

It was, he knew, a concrete manifestation of the

43

difference in their ages. Murphy had just finished up military service and entered the police academy when John F. Kennedy was killed. At the time, Nancy had been in third grade. The difference in their musical tastes reminded them both of that, and the reminder was sometimes startlingly difficult for either of them to accept.

Moreover, Nancy seemed bent on making Murphy over in her image. It wasn't just the drinking and the smoking and the music and her objections to Murphy's friends. Their differences extended even to Murphy's business wardrobe. Murphy dressed carefully, conservatively, and relatively expensively. He spent money on his clothes and always had, even though he didn't like to hang them up. Murphy wore quiet suits and button-down collars and rep stripe or club ties with small, innocuous patterns. Once in a while, when he felt sporty, he'd even wear a bow tie with a blazer or tweed jacket. He favored wingtips and Italian loafers. He always saw to it that his socks matched his trousers. That sort of thing was important to him.

Nancy was always trying to get him to wear something a touch more contemporary and with a bit more flair—argyle sox, baggy pants with pleats, shapeless sport jackets, shirts with little tiny collars. Once, as they were going out for dinner, she tried to talk him into wearing his jogging shoes (in which he made it a point not to jog) with a sport jacket and slacks. Murphy looked at her as though she had gone insane.

When she wasn't fussing about his clothing, she was fussing about something else—anything else, it seemed.

Nancy was a consummate fusser. She fussed over

44

everything, over matters large and small, matters of import and those of no consequence.

"Do you think it's going to rain today?" she asked one Saturday morning in April as she looked out the window at the leaden skies.

Murphy, barely awake and in his underwear at the kitchen table, said, "Only if it rains."

"If it rains I won't be able to go to that antique show out at the art museum."

"There'll be other antique shows."

"What's the newspaper say about the weather?"

"Here," he said, handing her the *Inquirer*.

"It says it might rain. Do you think it will?"

"I think it might."

"Ooooooh. I don't want it to rain."

Nancy did a good forty-five minutes on the possibility of rain. She could do an hour or more on summer heat, more than that on how bad her hair looked, and up to two hours or more if she put on a pound or two.

The essential problem, Murphy knew, was that the woman was hopelessly neurotic. And she was the moodiest person he'd ever encountered. Murphy admitted that he had his moods. Mornings during the week were generally bad for him, especially if he'd been up late the night before. While he would, if left to his own devices, tend to wake up early anyway, he liked the time of his arising to be one of his body's own choosing. The buzz of the alarm clock, however necessary, always unnerved him. The alarm clock pulled him out of sleep resentful and unwilling, and it took him hours to pull himself together. After that, though, he was generally good-humored, failing some incident of some

45

seriousness that made him pensive and thoughtful.

Nancy, on the other hand, was subject to enormous mood swings for reasons that neither she nor Murphy could fathom. Murphy finally wrote it off to the ravages of her menstrual cycle. He commented to her once that she didn't have periods; she had exclamation points. Nancy was not amused.

Matters came to a head after Nancy went home three weekends straight to visit her family in Latrobe, a town near Pittsburgh where her father ran a furniture store and served as a colonel in the local National Guard unit. Murphy had visited there once in Nancy's company, and had returned to Philadelphia badly shaken when he had realized that her father was only eight years older than he was.

Despite all this, Murphy had been nothing less than stunned when Nancy, after her third trip home in five weeks, suddenly told Murphy she was moving back to Latrobe.

"I don't much like my job," she said, "and I need to get somewhere everything is more familiar. I just want to get out of Philadelphia."

Further conversation revealed that Nancy had also, during the first of the three weekends, bumped into an old high school boyfriend who was in the throes of a nasty divorce and needed her attentions more than she perceived Murphy to need them. The parting was more or less amicable, all factors considered. Murphy even drove her to the airport and put her on the plane.

"I'll never forget you, Frank," Nancy said, hugging him. "We were good for each other for a while, there."

He nodded. "You were there when I needed you. If there's anything I can do, ever, you just holler."

Then she left and Murphy went back home. He sat in the living room and drank bourbon until he lurched when he tried to walk. Then he crawled into bed and Winston jumped up on the bed with him. Murphy put a weary arm around the bulldog, pulled him close, and kissed the animal's bristled and wrinkled forehead.

"You and me, Winst," he mumbled. "Just the two of us."

Winston Churchill panted and slobbered in sympathy, and they went to sleep together.

CHAPTER FOUR

In the dim light of early dawn, the alarm sounded. The time: five forty-five. Murphy stirred fretfully beneath the sheet, coming weakly to life with a curse and a groan. A shaky hand ventured forth from the bed. Blunt fingers played limply with the clock until they found a button and pushed it in.

The alarm stilled. Murphy sighed.

The hand retreated slowly back beneath the sheet. For a moment, all was silent except for Murphy's semiregular breathing. Then, at the foot of the bed, Winston snorted. The bulldog stood, slowly stretched his stubby body, then stomped casually up Murphy's legs, over his stomach and chest, as though he were climbing a hill. The dog thrust a bristly snout into his master's face. Winston snorted again and dragged his sopping tongue over Murphy's nose.

"Uuuuuuhhhh . . . shit," Murphy mumbled, pushing the bulldog away weakly.

Early mornings after late nights were not Murphy's best times. He tended to sleep deeply and to awaken resentfully and generally hostile. Murphy disliked and distrusted household machinery and appliances of all

48

description because he neither understood nor fully trusted them. But he reserved a special hatred for alarm clocks, which he was convinced had a perverse consciousness of their own. Murphy's alarm clock liked waking him up. He knew it. It sat there on the night table while he slept, its face alight with anticipation. Then: BZZZZZZZZZZZZZZZZZZZ. . . .

The goddamned thing got a real kick out of it. Nobody was going to tell Murphy it didn't.

This morning he dragged himself from his resting place in a deeper haze than usual, because he had arisen far earlier than usual. In his Calvin Klein briefs, his gray hair thrusting from his head in strange directions, he lumbered awkwardly into the bathroom and pulled his cordless electric razor from its charger in the outlet next to the mirror. He flipped it on and shaved haphazardly as he staggered toward the kitchen through piles of newspapers, magazines, and discarded clothing.

Tap water splashed into a mug adorned with the legend "It's all so much easier since I gave up all hope," a present from the departed Nancy. The mug sat in the microwave for two minutes while Murphy leaned against the wall, eyes bleary and the razor humming as he pushed it around his face. The mug was pulled out of the microwave with its handle hot and the water steaming. Numb fingers found the instant coffee, the sugar, the jar of powdered, plastic cream. During all this, the razor blithely chewed stubble. Murphy found his Camels and Bic lighter on the kitchen table. Nicotine and caffeine entered his system almost simultaneously.

That's better, Murphy's heart said gratefully, beginning to thump with some enthusiasm.

Good morning, Murphy's brain said. How's it going?

Now that that's out of the way, Murphy's bladder instructed, let's pay some attention to me.

Murphy dragged himself into the bathroom, flipped on the shower, put the razor back into its charging cradle, downed the dregs of his coffee, dropped his briefs, and climbed under the water, the cigarette still clenched in his mouth. He managed to get several more puffs from the Camel before the water got to it. Murphy tossed the sodden butt over the shower curtain into the open toilet. It was part of his standard morning routine. He never missed the blind shot over the shower curtain. When it came to that shot, Murphy was Julius Erving.

He stayed in the shower five minutes, remembering that he had forgotten to tend to his bladder and taking care of that, too, as the water washed over him. He could see no sense in leaving the shower to pee. He was pretty sure that it all went down the same drain anyway. Then he toweled himself, blew-dried his hair, brushed his teeth, and lit another cigarette to kill the taste of Pepsodent. He dressed with the radio blaring and the bulldog giving him plaintive looks.

"All right, all right," Murphy snarled at the animal.

He finished dressing then walked Winston for fifteen minutes. He put the dog back inside the apartment with fresh food and water and proceeded to his Olds Toronado on the street outside. He had bought the car secondhand from Harold Warren. Thirdhand, actually. Harold had bought a new Mercedes and given the aging Toronado to his mother, who was ready to take

50

the Mercedes now that Harold was preparing to buy himself a new one. The Toronado's odometer displayed more than ninety thousand miles, but Harold had maintained it well and the car was loaded with every option imaginable except a sauna. Aside from which, Harold had given Murphy a good deal on the car. Murphy liked it, even if it did have a little body rot around the rear panels.

The Toronado, which Murphy used only once a week or so—when he ventured outside his usual stomping grounds—coughed and wheezed into life. Murphy put on a Steve Lawrence tape and drove the car several blocks over to South Broad Street, where he parked it outside the Harvey House. This early in the morning— it was not yet seven—parking was manageable on South Broad. In another two hours, it would be impossible. Murphy bought an *Inquirer,* went inside, and sat at the counter. He ordered more coffee, some pineapple juice, and a heap of corned beef hash adorned with two eggs, sunny side up. He ate and drank coffee and read the newspaper. It was Murphy's habit to spend twenty minutes to a half hour with the *Inquirer* in the morning, giving particular emphasis to Clark DeLeon's items column in the local section.

Then, fortified with breakfast—the one meal Murphy simply couldn't do without—he climbed back in the Toronado and headed for Roosevelt Boulevard. He could get there by two paths. One would be to go up Broad Street to Spring Garden and cut over to the Schuylkill Expressway—known to Philadelphians as the Sure-Kill Crawlway—and cut back to the boulevard farther north. Or he could cruise up Broad all the way. With rush hour starting, Murphy picked the

51

Broad Street route. He couldn't go as fast, and there was a light at every corner, but the flow of traffic would be to the south, toward Center City, and he would be moving against it. He flipped on a Tony Bennett tape and headed up Broad, making his way through the confluence of Broad and Market Streets via the raceway that encircled City Hall, up past the white *Inquirer* and *Daily News* tower at North Broad and Callowhill into the North Philadelphia ghetto. He kept his windows up, the doors locked, and the air conditioner blowing as he rolled through the intersection with Girard Avenue, where the junkies, pimps, and hookers were just calling it a night, and past the sprawl of Temple University a few blocks north, where Murphy had gotten his B.A. and his law degree a few credits at a time over a fifteen-year-period. It took him nearly forty minutes to reach Roosevelt Boulevard. There he hung a right and headed for Northeast Philadelphia, where everybody was white and worried perpetually as they sat in their neat row houses that the blacks might move in one of these days. An increasing percentage of the residents of Northeast Philadelphia dealt with this fear by voting Republican.

Past Cottman Avenue, the boulevard traffic thinned out, and Murphy stepped on the gas. The Toronado responded with a mild sigh of protest and a startling increase in its appetite for fuel. The motel where Hank Kirby was staying was at the extreme northeastern end of the city, hard on the Bucks County border, and it took Murphy another half hour to get there. It was near Liberty Bell Raceway, where Murphy had a lot of money on deposit. The track was holding it for him, was the way he preferred to think about it. One good horse, properly doped and driven, could get it all back.

He pulled into the motel parking lot at eight thirty-two. The motel was a small place with white stucco walls and red trim. The paint was conspicuously faded and chipped and due for another application.

Two prowl cars, Wilder's Dodge, and a meat wagon were parked in front of the door to Hank Kirby's room.

"Uh-oh," Murphy said aloud, and got out of the Toronado.

The entrance to the room was blocked off with a white rope bearing a red "Crime Scene" flag. A uniformed officer stood outside. Murphy approached him.

"Is Lieutenant Wilder in there?" Murphy asked.

"Yes, sir," the officer said. He turned and leaned into the room. As he did, Murphy leaned after him, to see what he could see. What he saw was a mob of cops milling around inside and the flash of a photographer's camera.

"Lieutenant," the uniform said, "somebody out here to see you, sir."

Wilder came to the door. "What are you doing here?" he asked Murphy.

"Everybody's got to be somewhere," Murphy responded. "Can I come in?"

Wilder's eyes narrowed. "Does this involve a client?"

"I don't know yet."

Wilder frowned. "Let him in," he told the uniform. "And don't touch anything, Frank."

"You know you don't have to tell me that," Murphy said, thrusting his hands firmly into his pockets and entering the room as the uniform moved aside the rope.

The motel room was a housekeeping unit with a

53

kitchen along one wall. The floor was covered wtih cheap indoor-outdoor carpeting and off-white vinyl tile. The walls were covered with gray paneling so thin Murphy could almost see through it. On the floor in front of one of the twin beds was a dead man. He appeared to be of medium height and build with sandy hair. He was dressed in jeans and a T-shirt touting the virtues of Miller beer. He wore no shoes. He had no face. His killer had robbed him of that by beating the face with something until it was no more than a mass of ruined flesh and blood. Murphy grimaced at the sight.

A police photographer hovered over the corpse, shooting it from a variety of angles. A fingerprint team was already at work, dusting everything in sight. A uniformed officer moved around the room, collecting items and depositing them in clear plastic bags. The room was large enough for them to avoid bumping into one another, but just barely. The corpse, outlined in white chalk on the carpeting, took up considerable floor space. To stay out of the way, Murphy stepped back against a wall, his hands still in his pockets.

"What do you have?" he asked Wilder.

Wilder eyed him suspiciously. "The victim's name is Henry Raymond Kirby, age thirty-three, Caucasian. When he signed the register a couple of days ago he gave an address in Brooklyn, but his driver's license says he lives in Atlantic City. Also, he has an old Thunderbird out in the parking lot with Jersey plates and a dead battery. He had a visitor last night, according to the guy who owns the motel, but the guy didn't get a look at a car or the visitor."

"About what time?"

"About three, the guy says. He lives in the unit off the office and he heard the car come in."

54

"Light sleeper?"

"Insomniac, he says. Now, what's your connection? Is Kirby a client?"

Murphy shook his head. "No. I never met the guy in my life. I guess I won't get the chance, either. You got a weapon?"

"No," Wilder said shortly. "Listen, Frank, what the fuck are you doing here, if you don't mind my asking?"

"I called your office, and they told me you were out at a motel in on the boulevard on a case. I just came cruising out, casing the motels until I found you. I want to know what you're going to do about Rhino."

Wilder stared at Murphy in total amazement. "You don't really expect me to believe that shit, do you?"

"Well," Murphy said huffily, "if you're going to be that way about it . . ."

He turned to go, and Wilder grabbed his arm. "You will be in your office today, won't you, Counselor?"

"Jim," Murphy told him, "you know where I live. You know where I work. You can talk to me anytime you want. As long as you're willing to drink something other than Heineken's, that is."

Wilder shook his head. "Let this asshole out," he told the uniform at the door, "and don't let him back in. I'll see you later, Frank."

"What about Rhino?"

"I ought to let him chew your balls off, but I'll see him later, too. I've got his address from probation. How would you like to get your ass out of here now? This is police business, and you're just a citizen now."

"Who's entitled to police protection," Murphy pointed out.

*   *   *

He called his office from a gas station pay phone less than a mile away.

"I'm on my way in, Esmeralda. Any calls for me?"

"Yes. A Mrs. Highland called you just after eight-thirty. She said it was important and left a number."

Murphy took down the number and dialed it.

"Hello?"

"Mrs. Highland, this is Frank Murphy."

"Mr. Murphy, thank you for getting back to me so quickly. I have to see you, right away. Can I come down to your office?"

"I'm not in my office right now," Murphy told her, "but I'll meet you there at . . ." he checked his watch ". . . ten or so. Can you make it that quickly?"

"Yes, I can."

"I have some news for you, anyway," Murphy said. "I was going to call you."

"I have news for you, too," she said. "I saw Hank last night. He called me and I went to his motel room."

Murphy was silent for a moment.

"Are you still there, Mr. Murphy?"

"Oh, yeah. I'm here. Tell me, how was Hank when you saw him?"

"He was a son of a bitch. I wanted to just kill him. I'll tell you about it when I see you."

"I think you'd better," Murphy said wearily. Then he thought about Wilder's mood and the fingerprint team back in the motel room. "Maybe it would make more sense for me to come see you," he said.

"Whatever you like," Carol Highland told her lawyer.

CHAPTER FIVE

Carol Highland lived in Paoli, near the western end of the Schuylkill Expressway. It was a pleasant little village with a train station for people who commuted into the city, a few small industrial parks, and some big money. You didn't have to be rich to live in Paoli, but you'd feel a lot more comfortable about living there if you were.

The Highland house wasn't exactly in the village. It was on the outskirts, and Murphy had trouble finding it. This was not familiar territory for him. Murphy had been raised in Fishtown, a smallish row-house neighborhood near the Delaware River where a family with the good fortune to live over a grocery store was considered rather well off. Fishtown had been then— and still was, to a large degree—a neighborhood of lunchboxes and trolleycars and corner taprooms. For recreation on Friday nights, Fishtown's men sat around on the front stoop in their strap undershirts and wondered why God, in his wisdom, had seen fit to make the Phillies grounds crews better athletes than the team's ballplayers. Nobody in Fishtown knew much about polo, which was very big out here on the

Main Line, or about Julys in the East End of Long Island or summers at Saratoga. For somebody raised in Fishtown, Paoli might as well be Mars, and Murphy felt very much like ET must have felt as he rolled around the streets of this alien environment in his thirdhand Toronado.

The Highland house was set back from the road on a treed and heavily landscaped lot that shrouded the backyard and garden from its neighbors. The house was constructed of Pennsylvania fieldstone, and a separate three-car garage sat at the end of the driveway, its doors open. Two bays were empty. In the third sat a silver Audi 5000. Murphy parked the Toronado behind the Audi and knocked on the front door. Carol Highland opened it. Her face was ashen.

"I just heard about Hank," she told Murphy. "It's on the radio."

"Then you know you've got a problem."

"A problem?" She seemed confused and shaken. "Yes, I suppose I do. I hadn't thought of that. Please, come in."

Murphy did. As he did, he looked around, soaking up detail. It was a cop's habit. Murphy was professionally trained to note minutia. The first thing he noticed was that interior decor seemed to be the same in each room of Carol Highland's house—large. The front door opened came into a vestibule larger than the living room of Murphy's apartment. They moved through it into the parlor. The furnishings and decorations were heavy and old. Over the mantel, Murphy noted, was what appeared to be an original Renoir in a gilt frame. He shuddered at the cost of the painting—probably more than the house and grounds and five or ten times the price of Murphy's house in Mount Airy, an address he no longer occupied but did send checks to.

Carol Highland was, despite her obvious distress, a reflexively scrupulous hostess. "Would you like some coffee, Mr. Murphy?"

"Please," Murphy said, glancing around the room—in vain, he was sure—for an ashtray. "Don't go to any trouble. Instant will be fine."

"I already have a pot on. Cream?"

Murphy nodded. "And light sugar."

She disappeared into the hallway. Carol Highland was wearing white shorts and a yellow knit top. Her hair was straight today, and so, Murphy noted, were her legs. She was a pretty woman even without makeup. She would have made a hell of a homecoming queen. If people like this had homecoming queens, he thought, looking around the big house and soaking in the musty but undeniably appealing aroma of old money. And then he remembered that Carol Highland was not one of these people—that's how Murphy thought of them, as "these people"—by birth, but only by marriage. A marriage that was very, very important to her.

Jesus, what a terrific motive.

She returned with two china cups on saucers resting on a tray of blond wood and milky Formica. She set it down on the coffee table between them.

"Are we alone in the house?" Murphy asked her.

"Yes. My mother-in-law is out shopping and my husband is fishing over at Penn Pond. He does that just about every nice morning in the summer. Ev loves to fish."

59

"You have to tell me everything that happened last night," Murphy told her, taking out a notebook and pen. "Every detail."

Carol Highland's expression was strained, but her voice was strong and level. "Hank called me last night. He said he wanted to see me."

"What time did he call?"

"Around eleven. A little after. The news on television had just come on."

"Did anybody else answer the phone?"

"No. I was in the kitchen and I got it."

"Where was everybody else?"

"Ev was in the den watching television. My mother-in-law was in her room. She goes to bed early."

"Are there extensions in those rooms?"

"Yes, there are?"

"Did you hear anybody pick up either of them."

"I don't know. I don't think so."

"Are you positive?"

"No."

"Go on. So what did Kirby say to you?"

"He was calling from a bar of some kind. I could hear music in the background."

"What kind of music?"

"Loud music."

"Did you recognize the song?"

She thought for a moment. "'Proud Mary.'"

"What?"

"It's a rock song. Ike and Tina Turner did it. I heard that, I think."

Murphy scribbled. "What did he say to you?"

"He said he wanted to see me at his motel at two and that I should bring some money."

"How much."

"He said a thousand. I told him I didn't have that much cash. I said I might be able to get as much as five hundred from those automatic banking machines, but I'd have to go to four or five of them. You can't get that much money from a machine in one shot. He said to get as much as I could and to meet him at his motel at two. I told him I couldn't get out at that time of night, but he said I'd better. Then he hung up."

"Then what did you do."

"Then I went back into the den with Ev. He asked me who had been on the phone, and I told him it was a wrong number. Then we watched television for a while and went to bed."

"How did you get out?"

"I just waited until Ev was asleep, and I sneaked out around twelve-thirty."

"You're sure he was asleep?"

"I think so. He was snoring."

"And he didn't stir when you got out of bed?"

"We sleep in separate beds, Mr. Murphy. Twin beds. Ev has a bad back. He had an operation for it a few years ago, and he sleeps on a bed that's too hard for me. There's a big piece of plywood under his mattress."

"Then what?"

"Then I drove to the Seven-Eleven store and got as much cash as I could. I drove to another store a town over and got some more. I used the bank machine at the train station and took out what I could there."

"Did you get the five hundred?"

"Finally."

"Did you make a lot of noise starting the car and getting out of the driveway?"

"As little as possible. The noisiest thing about it was opening the garage door. I thought about taking Ev's car because he'd left the door to his bay open, but I didn't. I wish I had."

"Why?"

"Because something went wrong with my car on the way back from meeting Hank. It started shooting steam from under the hood and the temperature gauge went way up. I was afraid I wouldn't make it home. That would have been all I needed."

"What did you do?"

"I pulled into a service area off the turnpike and—"

"Which one?"

"The one near Ambler, I think. There was a boy there, and he was very nice. He said I'd had a hose come loose, and he fixed it for no charge."

"What did the boy look like?"

She sat back. "I don't know. He was a teenager. He had long hair. That's all I remember."

"Was he tall? Short? Fat? Thin? What color was his hair? What color were his eyes?"

"I don't remember. He was about my height, I guess. His hair was sort of . . . I can't remember."

"Did he have a beard? A mustache?"

"He had a little mustache, I think. I can't be sure. He was the only one on duty at the time. He had glasses, though. I remember that."

"What time did you get to Kirby's place?"

"About two. I remember I was worried that if I was late he might call the house, so I made it a point to get there on time. I might even have been a little early."

"Were you listening to the radio in the car?" Murphy asked her.

"Yes."

"What station?"

"WCAU, I think."

"What was playing when you pulled in to the motel?"

She looked at him in puzzlement. "I don't know. Just music."

"Was the news on when you pulled into the motel parking lot?"

"No. The news had been over for a while."

"You're sure."

"I'm sure. Why is this important?"

Murphy shrugged. "It might not be. What happened with Kirby?"

"I knocked on the door of the room he'd given me, and he let me in."

"How was he dressed?"

"I don't know. Jeans, I think."

"What kind of shirt?"

"He had on a T-shirt."

"What kind of T-shirt?"

"I don't know. Mr. Murphy, why are you asking me questions like this?"

He put down his notebook for a moment. "Mrs. Highland, somebody murdered Hank Kirby last night, and they probably did it very shortly after you were there. I know how the victim was dressed, and so do the police. So does the murderer. There's an excellent chance that you're going to end up a prime suspect in this case, and just what you saw and heard and what you remember—even on details that seem insignificant—can be crucially important later on. Just trust me on this. I've been through a few of these things. Now, what kind of T-shirt was he wearing?"

By the time Murphy had finished his little speech, Carol Highland's face was the color of oatmeal. "How will anybody know I was there?"

"Well, I certainly won't tell them. But don't be surprised if the cops show up at your door one day soon. And if they do, don't talk to them without me present. I mean it. Don't say a goddamn word. Just phone me and keep absolutely silent until I get there."

She sat back in her chair, clearly shaken. "If the police come, Ev will find out about my marriage to Hank, won't he?"

Murphy nodded solemnly. "I'm afraid so. The minute Hank Kirby was killed, you pretty much lost any chance of keeping that quiet."

She was silent for a moment, thinking. Then she said, "What's your advice? Should I tell Ev?"

"I'd tell him about the marriage. I'd keep quiet for a while about your most recent contacts with Kirby."

"I shouldn't tell him that Hank didn't really die?"

"But he did, didn't he? He just died several years later than you'd originally thought."

"I think under the circumstances I ought to tell Ev everything. He might hear about Hank on the news."

"Maybe, maybe not. This won't be the world's biggest story. Hank Kirby was nobody special, as far as I can determine. Your husband might miss it completely. The point is this, Mrs. Highland: any way you cut it, Everett Highland is not your legal husband. That means that he has no legal protection to avoid testifying against you. I don't know what he knows or doesn't know about your outing last night. But if he doesn't know about it, I think it would be prudent to keep him in the dark until this blows over—assuming it does blow over. My advice is to tell him about your marriage to Kirby, which you'd have had to do in any event, even if Kirby hadn't been murdered last night. But, for now, I'd keep quiet about my whereabouts last night. Whatever you tell him can be used against you in court, if it comes to that."

"In court? Do you think I could be charged with anything?"

"Who knows?" Murphy said. "Now, let's get back to last night. What kind of T-shirt was Kirby wearing?"

"I don't know. It was a white undershirt, I think."

Murphy scribbled in the notebook. "Tell me now what happened when you went inside the room."

"Hank was acting strange. His eyes were very large, and he was jumpy and nervous. He asked me if anybody had followed me, and I told him no. He asked for the money, and I gave it to him."

"Then what?"

She reddened slightly. "Then I asked if I could use his bathroom. I . . . I sometimes have to use the bathroom when I'm nervous."

"Go on."

"When I came out, he was sitting on the bed. I asked him when he was going to leave me alone. He said he wanted twenty thousand dollars. If I gave him that, he'd go away and leave me alone."

"Did you believe him?"

"No, of course not. But he wanted something else, too."

"Which was?"

She eyed him levelly. "I think you can figure that out. I had to fight him off. I just ran out of the room."

"Did you hit him or scratch him?"

65

"I just pushed him away. I was furious, but I wasn't frightened. Frankly, Hank wasn't trying too hard. All he wanted to do was humiliate me, and he accomplished that rather nicely. He'd always been good at it. It was just about his only talent."

"And then what?"

"I got in my car and drove home."

"And had car trouble along the way?"

"Yes. But I finally made it."

"Any idea what time you got back here?"

"I'd say between three-thirty and four. I lost about a half hour at the service station."

"Was your husband asleep when you got in?"

"Yes."

"How did you come in the house?"

"When I put my car in the garage I closed the overhead door as quietly as I could. Then I left the garage by the side door and came in the house through the back."

Murphy looked up. "You left by the side door of the garage?"

She nodded.

"You're sure?"

Carol Highland thought. "Yes. I remember fumbling for the knob in the dark. I didn't want to turn on the garage light."

"All right," Murphy said. "Now, I'm going to need some more information from you."

"Go ahead."

"I'm going to need to talk to your principal, Mr. Waterson. How do I reach him?"

"Why do you need to talk to Bob?"

66

"Only because if the police decide to talk to him I want to have spoken to him first."

Carol Highland was truly horrified now. "If the police drag Bob into this . . . Oh, my God!"

Murphy shook his head. "This has the potential to turn into a very nasty situation, Mrs. Highland."

Carol was about to speak when the back door of the house opened and closed. She clamped her mouth tightly shut as a tall, imposing woman entered the room. Carol Highland's smile was totally fraudulent, but effectively fraudulent, Murphy noted.

"Hello, Mother," Carol Highland said pleasantly. "This is Mr. Murphy. He's handling a legal matter for me. Mr. Murphy, this is my mother-in-law."

Murphy stood. "How do you do, Mrs. Highland?" he said with as much pleasantry as he could muster.

The woman was about sixty. She was fully as tall as Murphy and, he guessed, didn't weigh much less. Her hair was iron gray, and her expression was the same color.

"How do you do?" she said. Then, turning to Carol, she said, "Shouldn't Everett be back by now?"

"He said he'd be in sometime this afternoon. I thought we'd all go out for dinner tonight. Wouldn't that be nice?"

"We'll see," the older woman said summarily. "There's a Billy Graham Crusade special on television tonight."

"We can tape it, Mother," Carol Highland said.

"We'll see," the woman said again. "Nice to meet you, Mr. Murphy."

Murphy and Carol Highland stood silently as they

67

heard the old woman's feet on the stairs.

"That's her," Carol said quietly. "My husband's mother."

"A real sweetheart," Murphy noted.

"You can't imagine," Carol Highland said. "Not in your wildest dreams."

CHAPTER SIX

Wilder's office was a battered, glass-enclosed cubicle along an inside wall on the second floor of the Police Administration building at Eighth and Race Streets. The building was called the Roundhouse, because it was round, and Wilder's windowless lair was in a portion of the building devoted to the major crimes unit.

The unit was as ill assorted a group as had ever been gathered together under one municipal roof. Wilder's charges consisted of twenty-eight uniformed and plainclothes officers. Among their numbers were two overt lesbians and at least one guy nobody was completely sure about. Wilder also had one man dying slowly from pancreatic cancer, another who had suffered two heart attacks, a sergeant with an ulcer and an insatiable taste for grapefruit juice, a detective who was the toughest guy on the force until he got above the second story of any building and his vertigo set in, and a diabetic who lunched regularly on Milky Way bars.

He also had eight alcoholics in various stages of disintegration or recovery, a reformed junkie, and only one officer who wasn't a confirmed caffeine addict. His vice was buttermilk—a quart or two of the stuff every day. The group consisted of four devout Catholics, two Methodists, a Lutheran, a Jew, thirteen acknowledged atheists or agnostics—depending on their mood—three born-agains, a Muslim, a Mormon, a Christian Scientist, and one guy who said he was a warlock and professed to worship something called the Great Spider, about which nobody asked too many questions.

They ranged in age from twenty-two to fifty-five. They ranged in education from a seventh-grade dropout who had just barely gotten an equivalency diploma in the Navy to a Ph.D. from Penn who could speak four languages. There were two Korean War veterans, five Vietnam veterans, and a half-dozen or so who, like Wilder, had grown up in North Philadelphia, and could tell gang war stories that made the real thing pale by comparison.

When not in uniform or in street disguise, their clothing styles ranged from expensive Ivy League to South Philly hippy-dippy to punk. Four men had tattoos. So did one woman, although in a place so private that only four of the men in the unit had ever managed a look at it, and that had come amid wild giggling in a cop bar only after some enthusiastic off-duty drinking.

Of the twenty-eight, eight were more or less happily married, with patient spouses and—in all those cases—kids who stayed out of trouble. The unit had one widower and two widows. Five were single and unattached. Twelve were either divorced or in the process of becoming such. Of those twelve, three where shedding the second spouse, one the third, and one was leaving her fifth marriage. She was known to her colleagues as Zsa Zsa, and her most recent lawyer was

70

Frank Murphy.

At whom Wilder was seriously pissed this afternoon.

Wilder and Murphy went back a long way. As partners in their patrol days, they had grown so close that they had learned to communicate more or less by grunts. Locked together in a prowl car night after night, year after year, they had told each other just about everything there was to tell. They had shared intensely personal confidences in sober and drunken conversations. They had shared their philosophies and dreams. They had developed an appreciation for each other's personal rhythms, the ups and downs, the mood swings. They made each other laugh instinctively. They shared a conventional, conservative view of life. They had gone deep-sea fishing together. They had gone bowling together. They had gone to Phillies games together. They had each lost a week's pay when George Foreman knocked out Joe Frazier the first time. They respected each other.

Because of Murphy's insults and urgings, Wilder had gone to LaSalle in his off hours and obtained a degree in English literature while Murphy slogged through Temple and law school. They had served as ushers at each other's weddings. They had shared the satisfaction and pleasure of doing a job well as a team. They had faced danger together. When they were in uniform, Wilder had even saved Murphy's life once, and Murphy had returned the favor this past winter when an encounter with a psychotic killer had put them both in the hospital. They had gotten the bastard, though, and Wilder had gotten his lieutenant's bars out of it. Wilder, the tough little black street kid from North Philly, felt deep affection for Murphy, the tough big white street kid from Fishtown.

But that didn't mean Wilder was going to let Murphy screw up a murder investigation. It didn't mean anything like that.

Wilder sat at his desk going over the preliminary paperwork from the Kirby murder. This didn't look as though it was going to be all that tough. Kirby's background had come through from Trenton. When Wilder had seen that Kirby had traded in a Pennsylvania driver's license to get one from New Jersey, he had hopped onto the Department of Motor Vehicles computer link to Harrisburg to pull up Pennsylvania records on the guy. He had checked the FBI computer as well, and now he had a folder on Hank Kirby that told him just about everything he wanted to know about the man, even his allergies and birthmarks. That had been in his military records. Wilder also had the preliminary autopsy report and the stuff from his own lab guys, which showed fingerprints all over the motel room. No, this didn't look like it was going to be complicated.

Except for Murphy's involvement, that was.

Over the years, Wilder had developed a startling appreciation for the intricate workings of the Murphy mind. Murphy had an exceptional mind, Wilder knew. The guy had gotten through college and law school with top-rate grades while he was working fifty hours a week as a cop. Wilder had seen Murphy's mind at work on countless occasions, watched its gears whir and spin. The man had a disturbing capacity to figure out things. He had a fetish for detail and a conceptual skill for fitting that detail unfailingly into a larger picture. Murphy had been a fearsome detective, instinctively zeroing in on the right theory of a crime, diligently digging out the facts to fit his theory, honing in on one name in a field of dozens of suspects until the perpetrator was out there alone, in the spotlight, waiting to be plucked. Now, Wilder knew, Murphy was on the other side. He was no longer a cop. He was a lawyer, one of a truly despised breed, and he had a client who was somehow tied up in this. There was no other explanation for him showing up at that motel this morning. And even if there had been, Murphy's smartass manner had given him away.

What it boiled down to was that Wilder had what looked like an easy case on his desk—another quick step up the ladder toward his captain's bars—and there was Murphy waiting to screw up everything. Wilder brooded. He didn't need this shit. He didn't need any of it.

"We've got your boy downstairs, Lieutenant."

Wilder looked up. In the doorway was one of his detectives, a florid Irishman in his late twenties named O'Connell whose liver, Wilder was sure, was taking on the configuration of the isle of Crete.

"Where'd you find him?" Wilder demanded.

"In his apartment, right where probation said he'd be. He was watching *Days of Our Lives,* can you believe that? We tossed the place, but we didn't find anything."

This deeply disappointed Wilder. He had never gone out to toss the apartment of a known scumbag like Rhino Frost without finding something—some grass, at least—even if Wilder had been forced to plant it himself. These young cops would learn, but it was abundantly and unfortunately clear that they'd learn at

Wilder's expense.

"One thing we found," O'Connell added. "He had about six hundred bucks in his wallet. And he had a bankbook in his bedroom dresser, a savings account passbook, with about forty grand in it."

"Hmm," Wilder said. "Forty grand? Isn't that interesting?"

Wilder and O'Connell took the stairs down two stories to the basement, where the interrogation rooms were located. Every interrogation room was a small, forbidding, windowless cave, dank and badly lit. Each room was also soundproofed. There had been a time not too many years before when interrogation sessions in these rooms had been a source of great personal satisfaction to Wilder—and Murphy, too, for that matter—because a good many confessions had been produced here without the sound of police persuasion disturbing the top brass on the floor above. The soundproofing had kept the deputy inspectors insulated from the cheery thump of telephone books smashing into suspects' ribs.

The civil libertarians had put an end to all that, however—the civil libertarians and the Philadelphia *Inquirer,* which had won a Pulitzer Prize for its exposés on police brutality. Now the city's crime rate was up three percentage points and you were about even money to get your throat cut any time after sundown waiting for a bus on West Market Street. Wilder hoped they were all happy with what they had wrought. He opened the door to the room and stepped in. Frost was seated behind a table, his enormous bulk filling up one entire wall, his hair and beard wild, his torso straining against his T-shirt. Wilder hadn't seen the man in more than a decade. It hadn't been long enough.

"Remember me?" Wilder asked him quietly.

Frost sat motionless, like a malevolent statue, and eyed the smallish black man in silence. "Yeah."

Wilder nodded almost imperceptibly. He closed the door behind him, turned a chair around, and sat down on the other side of the table. O'Connell stood by the door. Leaning against the wall next to him was his partner, Rosario the diabetic, who had been watching Frost. Rosario was munching absently on a Snickers bar. All three men carried their service revolvers. Wilder felt secure here, despite Frost's eyes boring into him from across the table. Frost was all hair and muscle and a lot of it. More of it, actually, than Wilder had remembered—and harder, too. In the old days, Frost had sported quite a beer gut. Now it was all muscle, no more fat. It was that weight room in the slammer, Wilder knew. Just what Rhino had needed, weight training. Whose idea had that been? Frost sat there, a mountain of sinew and bone. He was easily the most intimidating man Wilder had ever encountered, and that took in some territory. There was something about Frost's eyes. Wilder couldn't articulate it. Something . . .

And with what he had done, with what Wilder knew him to be capable of . . .

. . . Wilder just felt better about everything with two armed officers just behind him and his own Smith & Wesson .38 snubnose on his belt.

"How'd you like it?" Wilder asked the giant.

Frost smiled. It was sort of a smile, at any rate. A smile crossed with a sneer. "Had a great time. Just like summer camp. Why did you assholes drag me

75

down here?"

Wilder shrugged. "Just a little visit. Don't you like to visit your old friends, Rhino?"

Frost said nothing.

"You remember this place, don't you, Rhino?"

Frost looked around, his eyes slits beneath his shock of gray-flecked hair. He nodded slowly. "I remember it." The man's voice was a low mumble, like distant thunder.

"We had some good times here, didn't we?" Wilder asked.

Frost nodded, his expression grim behind his beard. "Some of us did, yeah."

Wilder looked around the little room. "Yeah," he said warmly, "this sure is a fun place. I always liked it down here, where nobody could hear nothing just outside the door. Shit, man, a dude could get kicked in the nuts with service shoes five, six times—real hard, like—and nobody could hear him howl, you know? Nobody could hear him if he had a megaphone to scream into. I'm telling you, Jack, a dude could get his nuts jammed right up to his throat—until he sounded like Michael Jackson with his goodies caught in a car door—and nobody would have even a goddamn hint. Yeah, you could set off a bomb in one of these rooms down here and nobody would hear a thing. Great construction—especially for a city building."

Frost said nothing. Wilder leaned across the table.

"Stay away from Frank Murphy," Wilder said quietly and with as much menace as he could muster, and hoping it would be enough. "You just forgive and forget, understand? You've been away a long time, Rhino, and if you go away again you're going to be an

76

old, old man when they let you out. It'll be wheelchair city before they let you out again, Jack. That's if you get that far, that is. Lots of bad shit—I mean tons of it—can come down on a dude like you if he's stupid. Guys still get killed resisting arrest, you know. It happens all the time. I mean, it's fucking commonplace, man. You dig?"

Frost grinned then. His teeth were thick and horselike, like roughened pieces of white marble. "Are you threatening me, man? Is that what you're doing?"

Wilder's face took on a pained expression. "Rhino," he said in a wounded tone, "we're just talking. I'm just telling you how the world works. I mean, you been out of it a long time now, right? I'm just trying to help you readjust to the larger society again."

"Tell it to my lawyer when he gets here," Frost replied.

Wilder smiled. "What lawyer is that, dipshit?"

Frost motioned to O'Connell and said to Wilder, "The one he let me call before you came in here, dipshit."

Wilder's eyebrows flew together like a thunderclap. He whirled and glared at O'Connell, who blanched. Wilder motioned to the man, and they went out into the hall and closed the door.

"You let him call a lawyer?" Wilder demanded.

"He's entitled to a call, Lieutenant."

"Not unless I say so, you shithead," Wilder fumed. "He's only here for a talk. I wasn't going to book him for anything."

O'Connell gestured hopelessly. "You just told us to bring him in. You didn't say nothing about not booking him. I didn't know we weren't going to book

77

him. You didn't tell me that."

"I didn't know about the forty grand, asshole. Jesus Christ! Now that I do know about it, it might be nice to talk to him for a little while and see if we can't get a little something on him. Only he ain't going to say jack-shit because his lawyer is coming. Nice going, O'Connell."

"Sorry, Lieutenant," O'Connell said lamely. "If I'd known . . ."

Wilder snarled at the man, a wordless sound. Then he went back into the interrogation room. Frost was still sitting there, expressionless. Wilder sat down in front of him.

"The boys tell me you're doing pretty well for yourself, Rhino," he said pleasantly. "They tell me you got yourself a nice nest egg."

"Oh?" Frost said.

He's smug, Wilder thought. This mother is so smug. Wilder didn't like it. He was furious. He kept on smiling.

"Forty grand," Wilder said. "I never had me forty grand in one pop. Where'd you get forty grand, Rhino?"

Frost said nothing.

"Land yourself a nice nose candy sale, maybe?" Wilder asked him. "You used to like skag pretty good, too, as I recall. Maybe found yourself some stuff to sell? That it?"

Frost said, "I don't talk about nothing without my lawyer."

Wilder stood up and turned around, nodding slightly to Rosario the diabetic. Rosario stretched and began to walk around the little room. Wilder scratched his balding head and turned back to Frost. Wilder stayed on his feet this time. He wanted his eyes higher than Frost's. And he didn't want to be too close to the man.

"Where'd the money come from, Rhino?" Wilder asked softly.

Rhino Frost smiled his sneering smile. "From yo' mama, nigger."

Rosario the diabetic was a big man. Not too tall, actually, but wide. He was built along the lines of an oversized fireplug with arms. He was standing next to Frost now, and his forearm caught the huge man squarely on the forehead. Just about any other man Rosario the diabetic hit that way would have fallen over backward in the chair. In Rhino Frost's case, the blow snapped his head back, and he gave out a little grunt of surprise before he leaped to his feet—

—to find three Smith & Wesson .38 snubnoses only inches from his face.

Rhino Frost froze. He was half up, his enormous torso leaning across the table. His eyes blazed, but he sat back down slowly, his hands wide open and well away from his sides. There was silence in the room for a moment as the three police officers stood like statues, their pistols pointing at Frost with barrels that looked like open sewers.

Wilder lowered his pistol first. The others followed suit. Wilder returned his pistol to its holster, and so did Rosario. O'Connell did not. He held his loosely in his right hand as he leaned back against the door.

Wilder walked around the table. He stood directly in front of Frost. No blood. No bruises. That was important, especially with a lawyer on the way. Wilder knew how to do this.

"Where'd you get the forty grand?" he asked, his

voice barely above a whisper.

"I came in first on the Twenty Thousand Dollar Pyramid," Frost said. "Twice. Dick Clark just about shit himself."

Wilder's hand moved in a blur. Four slaps, two on each cheek. In the confines of the little room, they sounded like a bullwhip. Frost started up, cheeks burning, and Rosario caught him in the crotch with the top of his right shoe. Frost sank back in the chair, clutching his groin. His face was the color of old wine, and his eyes bulged.

"Shit!" he got out. Then he moaned in a low voice and his face sank down to the tabletop. His breath came in short gasps.

Wilder grabbed a handful of Rhino Frost's hair and lifted up his head. Their faces were only an inch apart.

"One more time . . ." Wilder began.

And then came the knock at the door.

"Who is it?" O'Connell demanded.

"Richard Silver," came a voice. "I'm told my client is in there. Open the door, please."

The three officers exchanged glances. Wilder knew Richard Silver. Quick Silver, he was called. Like all the city's big criminal lawyers, he was a former assistant DA. You came out of law school shaving maybe three days a week, you got your ass kicked in court by the defense bar sharks for a couple of years until you learned their tricks, then you went out and joined one of their firms and did it to somebody else. Quick Silver. Shit, he was expensive. Wilder looked at Frost. It was an indulgence, Wilder knew, but he couldn't resist it. He slammed Frost's face into the tabletop, hard. Then he called out, "Who's your client?"

"Wendell Frost. I know he's in there. I insist you open the door."

Wilder looked down at Frost, whose nose was bleeding from its impact with the table.

"Which Wendell Frost?" Wilder called out. "We got a whole headquarters full of Wendell Frosts. Is this Wendell Frost the mugger or Wendell Frost the dope dealer or are you looking for Wendell Frost the all-around scumbag?"

"Open this door," Richard Silver said. It was not a request.

Wilder shrugged. O'Connell opened the door. Richard Silver was not quite forty, a man of medium height with wire-rimmed glasses, graying hair, and a suit that would have cost Wilder a week's gross pay. He came in cautiously.

"What do you schmucks think you're doing here?" he demanded. "Are you all right, Wendell?"

Frost wiped his bleeding nose on a naked forearm the size of a four by four. "I'm cool. Just get me out of here."

Richard Silver glared at Wilder. "I know you. You're Lieutenant Wilder, aren't you?"

"No," Wilder said. "Actually, I'm Richard Pryor. Let's step outside."

In the hallway, Silver said, "What the hell are you guys doing? You know better than this."

Wilder reached for a cigarette, remembered he'd quit, and swore to himself. "Your guy has forty grand in a passbook account. Where'd he get it?"

"His mother died while he was in prison and left him the family house. It was sold and went to closing several months ago. I can produce the paperwork if necessary."

Wilder shook his head. "He's been hanging around Frank Murphy, and you probably know why. I think you might have been in the DA's office when Rhino went through. If you were, I think you'd remember."

"I remember," Richard Silver said. "What do you mean he's been hanging around Murphy?"

"I mean he's been hanging around. Murphy's seen him."

"Where?"

"On the street, outside his office."

"How many times?"

"Once," Wilder said lamely.

Richard Silver sighed in exasperation. "That's hanging around? For that you bring him in and work him over?"

Wilder stepped back and held up his hands in protest. "Hey, that dude tripped. We tried to catch him so he wouldn't hurt himself on city property."

Silver shook his head. "Charge him with something or I'm taking him with me. Now."

"Tell him to stay away from Murphy," Wilder warned.

Richard Silver gave Wilder an incredulous look. "I'm going to tell him? You already told him, I would presume. And rather forcefully, it would appear. What makes you think I'd have any more influence with him than you did?"

Wilder shook his head. "All right, take him. Get his ass out of here."

Silver turned for the door. Then he turned back to Wilder. "Lieutenant, you know this is the last time for this. You guys touch him again—if you even go near him again—I'll file against you so fast that your heads will spin. That's a promise."

"Just get him the fuck out of here," Wilder told the lawyer.

"Murphy."

"Frank? Jim."

"Feeling better? You're not good in the morning, Jimmy. You are not a morning person. Did anybody ever tell you that?"

"I had Rhino brought in."

"And?"

"Nothing. We had a heart-to-heart with him, only his lawyer showed up."

"Who's that?"

"Quick Silver."

"Oh, shit."

"We're out of luck, Frank. I can't do it again."

"Do you think it did any good?"

"I wouldn't bet the ranch on it."

"I don't have a ranch. But if I had one, I wouldn't bet it, either."

"What are you going to do?"

"Pack my piece. I forgot it this morning, but I won't forget it again. Not now."

CHAPTER SEVEN

Morning in Paoli.

Not much like morning in North Philly, Wilder thought. Here, when the sun came out, so did the songbirds. In North Philly when the sun came out, it meant only that the junkies were going in. And the only birds around North Philly were pigeons, which were sort of like junkies, in a way, except that the junkies were cleaner. Wilder rang the bell.

Everett Highland answered it. He looked a little like Dick Van Dyke looked when he was playing that television comedy writer on TV so many years ago. At least, Wilder thought so. Highland was tall and lanky, and he wore his hair in the same 1960's Ivy League style and he had the same confused expression.

There the resemblance ended.

Wilder flashed his shield and Everett Highland spoke. His voice and speech patterns were more like George Plimpton's. He had that nasal, Eastern-establishment, prep school lockjaw that sounded vaguely British, but not quite.

"I'm afraid my wife is out, Lieutenant," Highland

said as he stood in the doorway of the big house in Paoli. "I'm not sure when she'll return."

It came out: "I'm nut shooah when she'll re-tawn." Wilder hated people who talked like that.

"I wonder if I could take a few minutes of your time, Mr. Highland," Wilder said.

"Certainly," Highland said. It came out "Soo-ten-ly." Everett Highland added, "Won't you come in?"

Wilder did. And he looked around the house as he came through the vestibule and into the living room. That was professional training, but it was also personal curiosity. At forty-three, Wilder had seen a lot and been a good many places, but he'd never before been inside a big house on the Main Line. Whoever had built this place had enjoyed serious wealth when Wilder's grandparents were chopping cotton in Georgia. Not bad, he thought as he cased the joint. Not too bad at all. There were definite virtues in being rich. Of course, then you'd have to live with rich people, and Wilder had never met one of them he had liked.

"Might I ask you," Everett Highland inquired in his annoyingly pleasant manner, "why a Philadelphia policeman is interested in talking to my wife?"

"I'm here about a man named Henry Kirby," Wilder told him. "Is that name familiar to you?"

Highland looked slightly startled. Then he said, "Yes, it is. The name Hank Kirby is, at any rate. What about Mr. Kirby, Lieutenant?"

"You know that Hank Kirby is dead, I assume."

Everett Highland's face took on a strange expression. "No, I didn't know that. How long has he been dead?"

Wilder glanced at his watch. "Roughly thirty-two hours. He was murdered in his motel room not far

85

from here."

Highland's legs failed him then. He sank into an overstuffed chair and looked up at Wilder, his eyes wide. "Murdered?"

"Bludgeoned," Wilder told him evenly. "With just what, we're not sure. But whatever it was, it did a nice job."

"Where?"

"At a motel out on Roosevelt Boulevard."

Highland shook his head as if to clear it after a heavy night's sleep. "And you want to talk to Carol about it?"

"She was his wife, Mr. Highland. I presume you know that as well."

"Yes," he said slowly. "I haven't known it long, but I know it now. How do you know it, may I ask?"

"Computer check. We took all the computer information on Mr. Kirby and cross-referenced it. We can do that sort of thing these days. It's amazing what you can find out when you have a man's social security number and birthdate. Everything is filed under one number or the other."

Highland smiled ruefully. "Then it's true, then. We're all just numbers in a computer. It's come to that, has it?"

"I'm afraid so. Has your wife talked to you about Hank Kirby?"

"Yes. Last night. It was the first time I heard of the man. Carol told me all about him. And now you show up at my door to tell me he's been murdered. That's amazing. Truly, it is."

"Not so amazing," Wilder said. "People get murdered all the time. I'll tell you what's interesting about it, though, Mr. Highland. First, however, I'd like you to tell me where you were the night before last."

Highland shrugged. "I was right here, at home. I spent the evening here with my mother and Carol and then I went to sleep."

"And you slept all night, right in this house? You never woke up or left?"

Highland nodded. "I sleep well and deeply, Lieutenant."

"And your wife?"

"She was here all evening, too."

"And all night as well?"

Highland gave Wilder a quizzical expression. "Yes."

Wilder nodded. "Okay, then, let me tell you what's interesting about the Kirby murder. Do you know what a police lab is, Mr. Highland?"

"I think so."

Wilder smiled grimly. "Do you know how good our police lab is in this city?"

"I have no yardstick by which to judge something like that."

"Well, let me tell you, that this is one of the best police laboratories in the nation. In the world, actually. They just don't come much better than our guys. And do you know what they found in Hank Kirby's motel room?"

"I have no idea."

"They found your wife's fingerprints."

Wilder watched Everett Highland blanch. The color faded from the man's face, leaving it the hue of milk, and not fresh milk at that.

"How did it happen that you had her fingerprints on file?" Highland asked.

Wilder said, "She got a job at an A&P in high school

87

as a cash-register operator. She was under eighteen, so they took her prints. The store sells beer, you see, so they print all the under-age register operators. The local cops took the prints, and they sent them to the FBI. It's routine. If anybody has ever been printed for any reason, the prints are on file. That's the American way."

Wilder watched Highland nod almost imperceptibly. Then Wilder said, "In any event, our lab guys found your wife's fingerprints in the main room. They found them in the bathroom. They found them on a bathroom glass, on the bathroom doorknob—both sides—on the towels, on the arm of a chair. They found them on a torn T-shirt in Kirby's dresser. You know, they even found a partial fingerprint of your wife's on Kirby's right eyeball."

"His eyeball?" Highland asked incredulously.

"Oh, yeah. The lab guys can do that sort of thing. You can't take fingerprints from skin. Body oils screw that up. But you can find latent prints on eyeballs, on fingernails, even on hair, depending on the particular characteristics of the victim's hair. They use laser beam machines to do that. Damndest thing you ever saw. A guy with curly hair—like mine, for instance, what's left of it—they'd have a hell of a time. But a guy with long, straight hair like Kirby, they can get prints off something like that, sometimes. Let me tell you what else they can do. They can tell a person's blood type from his or her saliva. And they found a touch of saliva on Kirby's jeans. It was from a person with type O blood. And do you know what your wife's blood type is, Mr. Highland? It's type O. I know that from her driver's license. Kirby's blood type was AB. Now, let me ask you again, where was your wife the night before last?"

Highland stared at Wilder in clear and deep shock. He said nothing.

Wilder waited a moment, then he said, "And, if you will, let me remind you of something. Due to the particular circumstance surrounding your marriage— by that, I mean the fact that your wife already had a husband when she married you—you have no immunity against testifying. In fact, you don't really have any choice about it, unless you want to face a charge of obstructing justice. I forget the penalty for that, but it's impressive. You get nailed on a charge like that, it's not the sort of penalty you're likely to forget."

By the time Wilder was finished, Everett Highland's face was the color of new-fallen snow. When he spoke, his voice was thin and strained.

"I'm afraid I can't help you, Lieutenant," Highland managed to get out.

Wilder frowned. "This is a serious matter, Mr. Highland. We're talking about a murder here. I need to know anything you can remember. Did you wife get up during the night? Did she go out?"

Highland stood up. "I can't tell you anything. I'm afraid now that I must ask you to leave."

"How would you like it," Wilder said slowly, "if I insisted you come with me down to headquarters to answer some questions?"

Everett Highland's jaw tightened. "I'm afraid I'd have to consult my attorney first."

At the word "attorney," Wilder's teeth began to grind. "All right, Mr. Highland, have it your way. But please have your wife call me the minute she comes in.

Here's my card. And if she doesn't call me, I'll be back. Make it a point to tell her that, if you will."

Highland took the card and stuffed it into the pocket of his Izod shirt. "Permit me to show you out, Lieutenant," he said coldly.

"I can find my way," Wilder said, and did.

Outside, in his city Dodge, Wilder scribbled down notes from the conversation. Highland was home that night, stayed all night in bed, sleeps soundly, wouldn't say shit about his wife. None of which Wilder believed. Not a word of it.

Then he started his city car and drove back to the Roundhouse.

CHAPTER EIGHT

"Department of Psychiatry."

"Doctor Weiner, please."

"And may I say who's calling?"

"Frank Murphy. He knows me."

"Are you a patient?"

"Any day now, but not quite yet."

"One moment, please."

There was a pause, then: "Frank? You've got an interesting one here. I'm just going through it."

"You got it, then?"

"Yeah, came in this morning. I couldn't get to it until after lunch. I'm about halfway through. I should have it finished by bedtime. How'd you get all this, by the way? You've got all the presentencing examination reports, all the stuff from the prison shrinks. This had to come from either the DA's office or state corrections or both."

"I imposed on friends."

"I guess you did. This is all confidential, and you're a private citizen now. It's against the law for you to even see this stuff, much less have copies of the files."

"My legal specialty is circumvention of the law,

Barry. It's on my shingle. Look, if you're not going to finish it up until late, what do you say about breakfast tomorrow?"

"Oh shit, Frank. Tomorrow's Saturday. Why don't you come over to my place, and I'll have Ella whip us up something? I don't feel like getting cleaned up and going out on a Saturday morning."

"About nine?"

"Ten, for Christ's sake. You know, there are some people who don't like to set their alarms on Saturday mornings."

"Fine. Barry, I—"

The intercom buzzer sounded.

"Barry, can I put you on hold for a minute?"

"Don't worry about it. See you in the morning."

"Right," Murphy said, hitting the intercom buzzer. "Yes, Esmeralda?"

"Mrs. Highland is on two. She says she has to talk to you right away."

Murphy hit the button. "Hello, Mrs. Highland."

"The police were here this morning."

"Did you say anything to them?"

"I wasn't here. They talked to Ev."

"Did he say anything to them?"

"No. That is, he talked to them, but he didn't say much. He told them I was home all night the night Hank was killed, and he told them he was home, too. But the officer told him something, too. He said they found my fingerprints all over the room."

"You knew they would."

"I didn't even think about it."

"I did. I should have mentioned it to you. The police will have no problem placing you in that room and

92

placing you there at about the time of Kirby's murder. They can do that from lab work alone. Now listen, and pay attention. They'll be back. Tonight or tomorrow, they'll be back. You have my numbers. When they show up, you refuse to speak to them without me present. Just tell them you can't answer any questions without your lawyer present and call me immediately. Don't wait for them to take you into custody before you call, either."

"Custody?" Carol Highland sounded horrified. "Do you think they might do that?"

"It depends. If they have any evidence that points to somebody else as well as you, maybe not. But if you're the only lead, there's an excellent chance they'll take you into custody. They may or may not charge you, however, depending on what you say to them, so don't say anything. Understand?"

"I understand. I can't believe this. I can't believe any of it."

"Don't worry about a thing," Murphy told her. "You're in good hands."

Ten minutes later, Murphy was in the Toronado with Nat King Cole on the tape deck heading over the Ben Franklin Bridge into Jersey. There was little doubt in his mind that if Carol Highland was not a prime candidate for arrest in the murder of Hank Kirby—and she would have been had Murphy been heading up the investigation—her personal life would, at the very least, be subjected to intense scrutiny by Jim Wilder and company. And the part of her life most vulnerable to that scrutiny was her affair with the principal at her school, Bob Waterson. Murphy had called Waterson that morning at his house in Haddon Heights, introduced himself, and asked for a meeting.

"Feel free to come on out here," Waterson had suggested. "My wife and kids are visiting her folks in Harrisburg for the week, and I'm just doing some work around the house."

Waterson's house turned out to be a pleasant Cape Cod on a quiet street just off the White Horse Pike. Murphy looked at the place and figured it had gone up in the thirties, maybe the twenties. The house and neighborhood reminded Murphy of his own house and neighborhood, the one occupied by his wife and daughter and which he saw only when a pipe began to leak or something else needed fixing. On those occasions, Mary Ellen would offer Murphy a choice of hiring somebody to do the work or coming out and doing it himself. With money as tight as it was, Murphy invariably tried to fix things himself before calling on professional help. He also invariably screwed things up so badly that the repairs ended up costing more than they would have if he'd never attempted the job in the first place. Murphy was not handy. Electricity was a mystery to him. Plumbing baffled him. Carpentry work left him wounded—thumbs battered by hammers, splinters in his fingers. His only worthwhile skill in home repairs seemed to be limited to writing checks to pay for them.

He found Waterson in the one-car garage behind the house, his sneakered feet sticking out from under a 1967 Pontiac GTO convertible that was only slightly rusted.

"Mr. Waterson," Murphy said to the feet, "I'm

Frank Murphy."

"Hi," the feet said. "Be right with you."

Murphy heard the clink and clunk of tools from beneath the car. He inspected the vehicle. It was in nice shape.

"Some car," Murphy said.

"Isn't it, though?" Waterson said, crawling out from beneath it. Bob Waterson turned out to be a burly, dark-haired man of about forty with ready smile and a beer belly that rivaled Murphy's. He wore jeans and a well-faded Rutgers T-shirt.

"I picked it up a few months back. My wife drives the new car, and I'd been driving an old Honda when a guy in my bowling league got rid of this. It goes like a son of a bitch when it's running right."

"Sounds like you've been having problems with it."

"It needs a couple of rebuilt carburetors," Waterson told Murphy. "The damn thing floods if you look at it wrong. I've got to get that fixed before cold weather comes along. The new car goes in the garage here, and this one sits out on the street. Goddamn thing'll never start in the winter if I don't get those carburetors replaced. Listen, I've got to run out and get a muffler put on this thing. I just put a can over the hole in the one that's on it now. Want to take a quick run with me? I hope you don't mind. We can talk at the muffler shop."

"Sure," Murphy said.

It had been a long time since Murphy had been in a convertible. The wind blew his gray hair all around as Waterson piloted the GTO down the White Horse Pike, but Murphy like the feel of the big engine throbbing through the seat beneath him. You couldn't buy a car with an engine like this anymore. The wood on the dash looked real, too.

"This is fun," he told Waterson.

"Yep. That's why I got it. I always loved GTOs when they were out, but I could never afford one new. When I was in college, I'd have killed for a car like this."

Interesting choice of words, Murphy thought.

The muffler shop was down the highway in Magnolia. They dropped off the car and walked a few blocks to a bar named the Grinch. It was a neighborhood joint, and they went through a couple of beers while they talked. Murphy liked Bob Waterson. He could see why Carol Highland liked him, too. They talked for half an hour about the Kirby murder, Murphy telling Waterson what he knew and Waterson asking good questions. They then talked about Waterson's affair with Carol Highland.

"Look," Waterson said, "you know how these things start. Carol's marriage is boring and mine . . . well, we've had our troubles. When you work with somebody every day, when a man and a woman work so closely, relationships develop. You grow close to each other. That's how it happened with Carol and me. I've been married fourteen years, and I have two kids and this is the first time I've been involved with another woman. I'm not going to leave my kids. I just won't do that, and Carol doesn't want me to, anyway. Carol and I agreed early on that we wouldn't let things get out of hand, and they haven't—not until lately, that is, with all this crap. Are they really going to try to pin this on her?"

"There's a good chance of it. If they don't have any other suspects and the physical evidence fits even remotely, they'll at least go for an indictment. They'll

96

hope to get her to plead to manslaughter one or two, maybe. But if they have even a hint that she did it, they'll go after her, balls out."

"Shit," Waterson said, his expression grim. "What can I do to help Carol?"

"Probably nothing to help, but you can do plenty to hurt. There's a chance that the police are going to be coming to see you. I'm not saying they will, but if they get Carol in the grand jury and start asking her about her personal life—about affairs, for instance—your name is going to come up. I'm not going to let her perjure herself. So if the cops come to see you, tell them what you've told me. Be honest about everything. If you start telling lies, you're not going to do her any good."

"If I tell the truth, I'm not going to do myself any good. If my wife finds out about this, I'm dead meat."

"I wouldn't worry too much about that. I was a cop for a good many years, and you'd be surprised at how often you come across this sort of thing in investigating a crime. The police will be discreet about it—unless they figure you're lying to them. That's another reason to answer their questions honestly."

Waterson shook his head. "This is a real pile of shit, isn't it?"

"Let me tell you one of the questions they're going to ask you."

"What?"

"They're going to ask you where you were in the early hours on Wednesday morning, when Kirby got killed."

"Home, in bed."

"Any witnesses?"

Waterson shook his head. "Nope. Connie and the kids are in Harrisburg until the day after tomorrow. I've been here alone all week, like I said. Ordinarily, I'd have seen Carol a fair amount this week, but when Kirby called her we both agreed that we'd better cool it for a while. I haven't even spoken to her since Wednesday when she called me to tell me what had happened to Kirby."

"Had you known about Kirby beforehand?"

"Yes. She'd told me."

"She told you and she didn't tell Everett Highland?"

Waterson shrugged and sipped his Pabst. "I tell her things I don't tell Connie. Also, I tend to be a more understanding sort than Ev Highland. And a hell of a lot more understanding than that wacky mother of his."

"Did you ever meet them?"

"I've met Ev—at faculty parties, and things like that."

"Do you like him?"

"Not too much. Cold fish. I've heard enough about his mother from Carol to form my judgments on her." He glanced at his watch. "The car ought to be done by now."

"I'll pay," Murphy said, reaching slowly for the bar bill and hoping Waterson would wrestle him for it. He didn't.

Back at the muffler shop, Waterson drove the GTO out onto the White Horse Pike. "It's quieter," Murphy said.

"You didn't hear it before I got that Hawaiian Punch can around the hole in the old muffler. It sounded like a B-fifty-two coming down the street. Oh, Christ, what

98

the hell is this?"

The car bucked and sputtered and the engine died. Waterson swore bitterly and guided it as it glided into the parking lot of a Seven-Eleven store.

Waterson got out and threw up the hood. He tinkered for a moment, and then Murphy got out. "What's the matter?"

"The fucker is flooded again," Waterson said heatedly. "It's those goddamn carbs. Goddamn!" He slammed down the hood. "Well, we're just going to have to wait it out. It usually takes twenty minutes or so to clear."

"I've got to make a phone call," Murphy said.

"Well, go ahead. I'm sure as shit not going to go anywhere for a while."

Waterson settled into the car while Murphy went into the Seven-Eleven and found a pay phone. He pumped in quarters and dialed the number while he glanced at the covers of magazines on the rack along the wall. Strange, he thought. All the men's magazines have pictures of women on the covers and so do all the women's magazines—the same sort of women in different poses, wearing different expressions. What did that signify, Murphy reflected? That men are interested primarily in women and that women are interested primarily in themselves? He'd have to ask Weiner about that at breakfast. Then he thought he'd better not. Weiner could do a good, solid hour on a topic like that, and Murphy didn't have the time.

"Hello."

"Hi, Mary Ellen. Patricia there?"

"Nope. She's gone down to your place already."

"Do me a favor. Give her a call at my place and tell

her I'm going to be a little late. I'm over in Jersey with some car trouble. I'd call her myself, but I'm running low on quarters."

"And besides," Mary Ellen said, "if I call you save fifty cents."

"Every little bit helps, sweetheart," Murphy said, and hung up.

He went back out to the car to find Waterson sitting in the front seat, frowning. It was hot as hell with the sun bouncing off the parking lot blacktop. Murphy took off his suit coat and tossed it in the backseat. Waterson looked at him quizzically.

"You always carry that thing?" he asked.

Murphy looked down. His service pistol was in its belt holster on his right side.

"Lately, yeah," he said as he got into the car. "Don't worry. I have a license and a permit. No luck with this yet?"

"Ah, I suppose it's time to give it another try."

Waterson turned the key. The GTO cranked enthusiastically. Waterson tried again, and this time the engine caught with a roar, spewing out a cloud of black smoke.

"All right!" Waterson said, putting the car in gear.

They pulled into Waterson's driveway ten minutes later, just as the blue Ford was pulling into the driveway next door. A heavyset man in his fifties got out of the Ford and stood next to it, looking over, until Waterson killed the engine on the GTO.

"How's it going, Bob?" the neighbor called out.

Waterson waved. "Fine. How're you?"

"I see you got the new muffler on her. Or, rather, I can hear that you got it fixed."

"Yep. Just now. It's a lot quieter."

"Well, that's good," the older man called out and went inside.

"Who's that?" Murphy inquired.

"Bill Boynton. He does something for RCA. Pretty good guy."

Murphy stuck out his hand. "Nice to meet you, Bob."

"Good to meet you, too. Look, I'll do what you told me. I hope they don't come around, but if they do I'll be straight with them. I just want to do anything I can to help Carol. And if there's anything you need . . ."

"I appreciate it," Murphy said.

It was late rush hour by now, and the flow of traffic into the city was light compared to what was coming out. Murphy got back to his own place in forty minutes. No Patricia. No Winston, either. Murphy felt a thrill of alarm. He called Mary Ellen.

"I spoke to her no more than twenty minutes ago, Frank," Mary Ellen said. "She probably just took the dog for a walk."

"Why the hell would she do that?"

"Probably because the dog had to pee, Frank. If she's not back in half an hour, call me back and we can panic together. If I don't hear from you, I'll figure everything's all right."

Patricia came in a few minutes later, with Winston on his leash. Patricia kissed her father. Winston slobbered on him affectionately and scratched at Murphy's legs with blunt claws.

"I was worried about you," Murphy told her. "Your

mother told me you'd be here."

"Well, here I am. Where are we going for dinner?"

"Wherever you want," Murphy told her, and he meant it. He didn't have much cash, but Patricia came to visit only about one weekend in three, and their Friday night ritual on such occasions—which Murphy valued above all else in his life—included dinner out. When she went away to college in a few weeks, these outings would largely cease. The prospect of that made Murphy miserable.

"Italian," she said with a gleeful smile.

"We can do that, or we can have a steak at Frankie Bradley's."

Patricia made a face. She wasn't much for red meat, and she was always bugging Murphy because he loved great red dripping slabs of beef. Murphy couldn't imagine a diet without tons of cholesterol to make food palatable.

"Chinese, then," Patricia said.

"Chinatown it is. Just let me run the razor over my face." Murphy started toward the bathroom, then he turned. "Patricia?"

"Yes, Daddy."

"Do me a favor. While you're here, don't go wandering off like you did today, okay?"

She looked at him, puzzled. "Why not?"

"This is a city. You wander around by yourself it could be dangerous."

"I'll have Winston with me."

"Yeah," Murphy said, looking over at the ugly dog flopped like a sack of flour on the sofa, snoring already. "He'd be a big help, all right."

*   *   *

They took a cab to Chinatown. Murphy knew better than to try to find a parking spot there on a Friday night. The cab driver had a "Thank Your for Not Smoking" sticker on the clear plastic barrier that separated him from the passenger seat, and he roared through Center City traffic like a lunatic. Murphy, no slouch himself in city traffic, was somewhat unnerved. The cabbie got up to fifty-five as he whipped around city hall, weaving in between cars and missing buses by fractions of an inch. When they got out, Murphy—still pale—gave him a fifty-cent tip.

"Thanks a lot, Mac," the cabbie snarled.

"I always tip big when I ride with a guy who's so concerned about his health," Murphy told him.

Inside the China Palace, they ate won ton soup, egg rolls, moo goo gai pan, fried dumplings, sweet and sour shrimp and beef with pine nuts. Murphy drank a pot of tea all by himself. He would take caffeine where he could find it. They talked about everything. Patricia was bubbling and alluring and the image of Murphy's mother as a young woman. Murphy's fortune said: "Love is best found in familiar places."

"What does yours say?" he asked his daughter.

"You look at it."

Patricia passed over the fortune. It said: "A warm heart protects against a killing frost."

"That's a weird one," Patricia said. "I like yours better."

"Me, too," Murphy said quietly.

CHAPTER NINE

Murphy awakened at seven. Even without the alarm, he awakened early all the time now. He suspected it was a sign of age.

As a teenager and a young man, when his body was growing and needed rest while new cells grew, he had routinely slept long into the daylight hours in a more or less comatose state. A nuclear attack would have failed to rouse him. He remembered his old man coming into his bedroom when he was seventeen and unceremoniously yanking him out of the covers at noon, annoyed for no reason he could articulate that his son slept while the rest of the world was active outside the windows of the family's row house in Fishtown. The old man had awakened early every day that Murphy had known him. Murphy had written if off as some sort of medical disorder.

But in his late thirties Murphy had found himself awakening relatively early, even on his days off and regardless of how late he'd been up the night before. Now, at nearly forty-five, it was his habit—like so many other habits his father had exhibited that Murphy had thought were simply the old man's personal quirks. It was a rare day when Murphy could stay in bed past eight. In a sense, he was grateful. He was aware that time was passing quickly, another sign of age. As he logged more days into his memory cells, each new day was somehow shorter than its predecessor in his growing frame of reference. If he ever made it to seventy, Murphy reflected, he was sure a day would pass in the blinking of an eye. He had spent four years in high school, which had seemed interminable. His nearly four years in the DA's office had taken about two weeks by comparison.

Patricia still slept soundly on the living-room sofa, Winston curled at her feet. The bulldog routinely abandoned Murphy's bed when Patricia slept over. Winston had come into the house over Mary Ellen's spirited objections when Patricia was ten, the first pet the family had ever had, unless you counted guppies, which Murphy didn't. She had loved the ugly dog, and when Mary Ellen had thrown Murphy out and insisted that he take his "goddamn Alpo-burner" with him, Patricia hadn't been sure which she would miss most, her father or Winston. When she visited, she fussed over the bulldog, walking him every hour, scratching incessantly behind his bent ears, kissing him squarely on his shiny black lips, which even Murphy wouldn't do. There was a bond between the girl and the dog, and Winston was always mopey for a few days after Patricia left.

Murphy stood in the doorway to the living room for a moment, studying Patricia as she slept in the dim light through the drapes. Yes, she had his mother's face. There was no doubt about it. The same mouth and jaw, the same set to the eyebrows. Patricia had

Mary Ellen's coloring, and there was no doubt that she had inherited her mother's willfulness, but her face was a Murphy face. Or, rather, a Kelly face. Murphy's mother had been a Kelly. God, he loved her. His only child, now clearly cast as a woman, with a woman's body and a woman's thoughts. Whatever evil had been produced by his union with Mary Ellen, all that goodness and beauty lying on the sofa had made it all worthwhile. How bad could they have been together if they had been able to produce such a perfect human being? Murphy thought about Mary Ellen, thought about the way she laughed when she was amused, thought about the way she moved and smelled. The separation had not been his idea. That had been all Mary Ellen. She had wanted him out. Period.

He turned, frowning deeply, and went into the bathroom. He shaved in front of the mirror and showered. Then he pulled on a pair of briefs, worn jeans, and a knit shirt with a pocket to hold his Camels. He put on sweat socks and a pair of docksiders. On his way out of the bedroom, he picked up a light jacket from the heap in the corner, where he usually kept it. In the living room, he considered waking Patricia. But they had stayed up late playing rummy—with Murphy getting waffled, as usual—and he decided to let her sleep. She knew where he'd be anyway. He went over to her quietly and stroked her hair lightly with the back of his hand. Winston stirred, and Murphy knelt beside him. He rubbed the bulldog's wrinkled forehead.

"Take care of Patricia," he whispered. "You screw up and I'll belt you so hard that all your puppies will be born dizzy."

Winston snorted affectionately and licked Murphy's

chin. Murphy patted the dog's head again and was gone.

Barry Weiner lived in Society Hill Towers, a swanky apartment complex near the Delaware River. At this time of day, the city air was cool and the sun gentle. Murphy had time to kill, so he walked it. It took him about a half hour. He passed early-morning joggers and late-night winos. He smoked his first two Camels en route to Weiner's, and he was desperate for coffee when he got there.

Weiner lived in a corner apartment with glass walls on two sides, looking back at the city instead of overlooking the river. Weiner could easily have afforded an apartment overlooking the river—he had inherited a personal fortune from his family in Boston, and Murphy had never met a poor psychiatrist whatever his family history—but Weiner liked looking out over the city lights at night, so he had taken the cheaper apartment. Murphy thought he'd made the right choice.

Ella met Murphy at the door. She was Weiner's roommate, lover, keeper, and, nursemaid. Ella was a bovine blonde in her late twenties whom Murphy had never heard mumble more than a few words, although she smiled a lot and loved Joan Baez records. She would just sit and listen to Weiner ramble, which he did in fascinating fashion. Weiner and Murphy had been friends for years, after working together on a case. Forensic psychiatry was one of Weiner's specialties. Another was drinking, which he did to excess even though he'd had a heart attack a few years before and had been ordered by his cardiologist to cut down.

"Hello, Frank," Ella said at the door. She had a

placid, whispery voice that always made Murphy feel at peace. "Barry's not up yet. You're a little early."

"I'm only two hours early. Actually, I couldn't afford the time to sit around and wait to talk to him. Could you get him up for me, Ella?"

"Sure. You just go into the kitchen and sit down. There's coffee in the Mister Coffee machine."

Murphy went into the kitchen, poured himself a mug of black coffee, and went into the living room. He lit a cigarette and then looked in vain for an ashtray. Ella must have renewed her campaign to get Weiner to stop smoking by hiding all the ashtrays. Murphy went back into the kitchen and got a saucer, which he placed on Weiner's glass coffee table. He leafed through a copy of that morning's *Inquirer* as he heard Ella pull Weiner out of bed. The Phillies were still eighteen games out of first, and here it was August. Murphy guessed there'd be no World Series in Philadelphia this year. Again.

Weiner came into the room in his pajamas and robe, his thinning gray hair sticking out at all directions and his thick, black-rimmed glasses—as usual—smudged with fingerprints. Murphy often thought that Weiner looked like a combination of Woody Allen, Arnold Stang, and a Chinese laundry struck by lightning.

"What time is it?" Weiner moaned as he collapsed on the sofa.

"It's late, Barry. The whole goddamn world is up except you."

Ella came into the room and Weiner motioned weakly for her to get him coffee. She complied wordlessly. Where does a man find a woman like this, Murphy wondered? Not in his house. Not either of them. Weiner made believe he was smoking. Murphy gave him a cigarette, which he lit with Murphy's Bic and inhaled gratefully. Ella came in with more coffee and large glasses of orange juice for both of them.

"How does corned beef hash sound," she asked, "with a fried egg on top and some bacon?"

"Great," Murphy said.

Ella looked at Weiner with profound displeasure. "Thank you, Barry," she said quietly.

Weiner looked at the cigarette as though it had mysteriously appeared in his hand by magic. "Frank made me take it," he explained to Ella. "He insisted. I was just being polite."

Ella put her hands on her hips. "Thank you, Barry," she said again. She might have been speaking to a child of four.

"Just this one?" Weiner pleaded.

"You're going to have all this stuff for breakfast that you shouldn't eat," she told him in the same disappointed tone, "and you're going to smoke, too?"

Weiner smiled weakly. "Just this one. Promise."

Ella left the room with a weary sigh. Weiner leaned over the coffee table and whispered to Murphy, "Give me one more for later."

Murphy slipped him a Camel, and Weiner stuck it furtively in the pocket of his robe. "Thanks. She'll go out later and I'll be able to smoke it on the balcony."

"Did you finish the file?" Murphy asked.

Weiner leaned back and sipped his coffee. "Last night. I stayed up late to read it. God, this coffee is good. I can feel my brain starting to kick in."

"And?"

"And what?"

"What do you think of this guy?"

"Whacko," Weiner replied.

Murphy shook his head. "Could you give me your opinion in less clinical terms, Doctor, so I can be sure I understand?"

"Yes," Weiner said slowly. "Wendell Frost is nuts, crackers, looney, not playing with a full deck, rolling along on three wheels, out to lunch, not hitting on all cylinders, flaky and—what we call in the trade—a standing eight-count. The man is a candidate for a rubber room. How's that, Frank?"

Murphy said nothing. Weiner's expression grew more serious.

"This one's really bothering you, isn't it?"

Murphy nodded silently. He couldn't get that goddamn fortune cookie out of his head.

"All right," Weiner said. "What did he do? What's he being investigated in connection with?"

"Nothing—so far. He's just gotten out of Graterford."

Weiner opened his palms in puzzlement. "So?"

"So I'm the guy who put him away. I think he's carrying a grudge against me. I've seen him around, and he seems agitated. Graterford doesn't seem to have calmed him down. What I want to know is whether you think, based on your examination of his psychiatric history, that he's the kind of guy who'd be likely to take a run at me all these years later."

Weiner pondered the question. "It would depend. Were there special circumstances behind the arrest?"

Murphy sat back and lit another Camel as Ella brought breakfast. She brought in two plates, each buried under a mound of corned beef hash and that topped with a fried egg, sunny side up. She also

110

brought a bowl of cubed summer melon, toast and butter and a jar of Smucker's strawberry preserves.

"I'm going to the store, Barry," she said. "Enjoy your breakfast."

"See you later, sweetie," Weiner said, digging in.

From the front door, Ella called back. "Enjoy your cigarette, too, Barry." Then she gave the door a vicious slam on the way out.

Weiner smiled self-consciously. "Just a little gesture of rebellion against father figures."

"She's going to take a walk on you one of these days, you know."

Weiner shook his head. "Never happen," he said through a mouthful of corned beef and egg. "Ella has a deep-seated psychological need to care for me. It fulfills her need to be needed. She's classic caretaker personality, totally devoted to others."

"And you?" Murphy asked. "How would you characterize your own personality?"

"Who, me? I'm a putz. That's a clinical term. You wouldn't understand. Don't worry. I understand Ella, and she understands me. She knows I smoke and drink and eat fatty foods and refuse to exercise only so she can get pissed off at me and show me how much she loves me. She needs to fret about me, and I need her to fret to confirm my own sense of self-worth. We both know I'm going to die one of these days. You'll die, too, Frank—eventually, anyway. I'll make you a bet on it."

"Are you ever going to marry her?"

"Get married again, at my age? Not unless she walks out on me. That'll be my trump card. Oh . . . uh . . . by the way, don't mention that to her, okay?"

"Back to our friend Frost. You asked about the circumstances surrounding his arrest."

"Shoot."

Murphy explained what Rhino Frost had done. He explained it in detail. Weiner listened carefully. He had a strong stomach. No one who works in forensic medicine can survive without one. But, after a while, he stopped eating.

"Why isn't this in the record?" Weiner asked.

"Because we couldn't get him for it. The girl committed suicide, and she was the only witness. What we could get him for was possession with intent to sell, as you can see. And, given his record, it was enough to get him sent away for a long time. The problem is, Barry—and I'll deny ever saying this—I planted the stuff on him."

Weiner nodded. "Well, I can see where that might annoy him even after all these years. Yeah, that might piss him off, all right."

"There's more."

"More?" Weiner said. "Do go on."

"This isn't funny."

"Yes, it is. I'm not shocked, Frank. I've worked with the police too long for that. And, to be honest, I think you did the right thing."

"I just had to get this guy off the streets, Barry. That's all. If you'd seen her . . . Jesus. Anyway, I was a detective second then. We knew who we were looking for. I was playing the Easter bunny at a PBA Easter party for the orphans at St. Anne's. I got a call that they'd picked him up, and I ran out and jumped in my car—Easter bunny suit and all. I drove down to the Roundhouse and went down to the interrogation room. Jimmy Wilder and a few other guys were there, using their best powers of persuasion to get Rhino to confess and not having any luck. So I came in and worked him over good."

"Wait a minute," Weiner said. "You mean this guy is down there getting pounded and suddenly the Easter bunny walks in and starts kicking the shit out of him?"

"Yep."

Weiner collapsed with laughter on the sofa. "That's hilarious."

Murphy's face was grim. "Nothing about Rhino Frost strikes me as funny. Not a thing. Look, you know that suspects used to get bounced around a bit. But I lost it with this guy. I broke his nose and a couple of his ribs, and he had to go to Philadelphia General to have a testicle removed. I got carried away. I admit it. But if anybody ever had it coming, he was it. I've never worked a guy over that badly before or since. And before the ambulance came, since I hadn't gotten anything out of him despite all that, I planted half a kilo of smack on him."

"Half a kilo?" Weiner asked in amazement.

Murphy shrugged. "It was in the building. It hadn't been checked in officially. In those days, we used to keep stuff around for special occasions like that. I'd never used it before, but I used it that time. I wanted him gone and gone good. And he went."

"How did you explain the beating?"

"Resisting arrest, what else? We actually talked about killing him. We should have, now that I think about it. I'll tell you this: I wish I had it to do over again. I really do."

"And then what?"

113

"And then he went away. That was the last I heard of him until I saw him on the street the other day. Wilder tried to help, but this guy's got a good lawyer. Jimmy has to keep hands off until he does something. Do you think he's going to do something?"

"Well, based on what's in the file and on what you've now told me, I'd say the odds are that he'll probably try. You see, this man has an unusual personality. He's almost a classic sociopath. He's totally self-oriented. He has no empathy whatever for other living creatures. Did you see the stuff in the file about the first contacts the police had with him when he was a juvenile, the setting fire to cats and things like that?"

"Yeah?"

"That's a classic sign of sadistic personality. It was with him early. In that context, what you told me he did fits in very well with that pattern."

"But why?" Murphy demanded. "What makes people behave like that? How can people do things like that?"

Weiner lit another one of Murphy's Camels. It was not the first time Murphy had asked such a question. One of the things Weiner admired about Murphy was his intense curiosity about human motivation combined with his outrage at human behavior. Ordinarily, the two traits did not go hand in hand. Most police officers tended simply to write off criminals as scum and let it go at that. Murphy wanted to know why they were scum, what forces had made them scum. He was still judgmental. He believed in punishment and retribution. He judged the behavior of others by his own standards. But when someone committed a horrible crime, inflicted great hurt—especially against a stranger—

Murphy wanted to know why. So did Weiner. He had devoted his professional life to just such questions, and he liked Murphy because such questions were also a challenge to him. The information Weiner was able to provide over the years had, of course, been used primarily to catch criminals. Murphy had used it that way, too. But the information had also seemed to fulfill another need in Frank Murphy. It quenched, if only temporarily, his fire to know and understand what went on inside the minds of the other men.

"Look," Weiner said slowly, "this guy apparently came from a good home. It says in the file that his father was a welder at the Navy yard, a good solid sort. He died when Frost was an infant. His mother was a good woman. She belonged to church groups, worked hard to raise him, all that shit. All the information indicates that he was raised in a perfectly calm, rational home—no boozing, no doping, no particular family tension. But adults represent authority, and it's natural at a certain age that a kid should rebel against authority. It's part of the biological process. It's Darwinian. Unless they come to hate their parents and rebel against their values—at least for a while—they won't ever leave home."

"Well, Rhino certainly rebelled. But against what? That's the question."

"Anything," Weiner said, "anything at all. Maybe he got pissed off when his mother made him eat his peas. Maybe his mother caught him masturbating and successfully filled him with so much shame over the whole process that he had repressed sexual feelings that manifest themselves in sadism and violence. Maybe his mother was overprotective, teaching him to hate

115

strangers. Maybe he seethed for years with hatred because she sent him to bed at a specific time every night. Maybe the people he picked as role models had a bit of a mean streak, and he carried that to an extreme degree. Maybe the mother, raising him alone, was so strict with him that he got the idea that everybody looked down on him and decided to get even with the world. Maybe he just got worked up over the way adults related to kids, the way adults always excuse their own errors in front of kids—in an effort to appear all-knowing."

"Shit, Barry, we all do that sort of thing to our kids. It's part of civilizing them."

"To be sure. But some kids are harder to civilize than others. Some kids react to ordinary parental guidance in extraordinary ways. For example, when adults get sick, we just get sick. But when kids get sick, we always tell them it's their own fault. It's always because they didn't go to bed early enough, or they ran around with their coats open. Adult illness is the result of working so hard to make the kid happy, we tell them. But when the kid gets sick, it's the kid's fault, because he didn't work hard enough at keeping the adults happy. You think kids don't pick up on that? They do."

"I don't get your point," Murphy said. This was a problem he frequently had in these talks with Weiner.

"All right," Weiner said. "What it boils down to is this: What we all do with our kids—I did it with mine, for Christ's sake, and what my kids do with my grandchildren—is teach them that they're unworthy, which they indisputably are. They become worthy by conforming to our standards of behavior, by getting civilized. Knowingly and unknowingly, we teach kids

116

that if something bad happens to them, it's their own fault."

"Yeah. So?"

"Well, in some kids, that works to deprive them of any sense of conscience whatever. They mug somebody and they say, 'Hey, it wasn't my fault. That old lady shouldn't have been out there wandering around the neighborhood with that big purse.' A rapist, he says every time, 'She was asking for it. It was her fault, not mine.' Some kids, with the best of upbringings, grow up with that kind of thinking. It's a twisted interpretation of what conscientious parents tried to instill in them. And if you throw in there direct rebellion and rejection of the parental standards they were raised with, you can get some pretty fucked-up people."

"And you think that fits Rhino."

"Well, look at the file. The prison psychiatrist says he complained endlessly about the rigid rules in his household as a child. He made a fetish out of disobedience at every stage of his life. The use of force subdued him only temporarily as a little boy, and he seethed in resentment over it. When he got bigger, there was no man around to enforce the rules. He could effectively do what he wanted to do, whatever that might be. And what he apparently felt like doing was engaging in juvenile sadism—the cats he set fire to when he was ten or so, the neighbor's dog he disemboweled with a kitchen knife. Did you see what he said? He said the animals should have been smart enough to run away from him. You see, he wasn't to blame. That's what he was saying. And the biting. He's always been a chomper, Frank. It's all right out of the textbook—especially with what you told me about him. I would have loved to have gotten a run at him when he was in prison in those early years. Not that I could have changed him, mind you, but I could have dug down deep inside those brain cells. That would have been fascinating."

Murphy was silent for a long moment, drawing on a cigarette and thinking. Then he said, "Barry, I've never asked you this. Do you believe in evil."

The question surprised Weiner. "Evil?"

"Yeah," Murphy said. "Evil. You remember evil. Do you believe in it?"

Weiner sat back on the sofa. He thought for a moment. "I don't know."

"What do you mean you don't know?" Murphy demanded.

"I mean I don't know. Evil isn't a clinical term. It doesn't have anything to do with what I do."

"Forget all that shit," Murphy said. "I'm not talking business here. I'm talking philosophy. Do you believe in the existence of evil? Do you believe that people can be evil?"

Weiner pondered the question for a moment. "Yes. I suppose I do. Yes, I believe in evil. It's a value judgment. It's not a scientific term. But, yes, I believe that some things—some people, maybe—could be classified as evil. Hitler was evil. Yes, I believe in it. So, what's your point?"

"I don't know that I have a point," Murphy said. "I just know that I think that somebody like Rhino Frost is evil. He thinks evil thoughts. He does evil things. He had all the reasonable advantages, and none of that can explain why he does the things he does. To me, that's evil. Do you buy that?"

Weiner thought for a moment. Then he said, "Clinically, no. Sick? Yes. Evil? That's not part of a psychiatrist's vocabulary. We're trained not to think in those terms. We're trained not to be judgmental. You want me to call this man evil? I can't do it."

"Even knowing what you know about him?"

"Even then. No, I won't say evil."

Murphy frowned. "Look, maybe what I'm saying is this. Maybe there are people who are born with a missing synapse in the brain or something—"

"That's the old XY chromosome theory," Weiner broke in. "That's been pretty much discredited. That was a clinical attempt to isolate the factors of evil, if you want to put it that way. It didn't work. Evil isn't a scientific concern in that sense. If it exists at all, it can't be weighed and measured and quantified."

Murphy looked at Weiner and shook his head. "If it exists at all, eh? Barry, you know you guys have really helped to fuck up society. You know that, don't you? Thanks to shrinks, there's just no concept of evil anymore. Everybody is sick. They're maladjusted. They're misunderstood. But they're not evil. You guys are to blame for that, Barry."

"You're a moralist, Frank," Weiner said, smiling.

"I plead guilty to that," Murphy told him. "And somebody has to be a moralist. Somebody has to say this is right, this is wrong."

"The question is, who appointed you?" Weiner demanded.

"I don't know," Murphy said slowly. "I do know this, though: there are absolutes in this world. There is a right, and there is a wrong. Lines exist. And you know it, too. You just won't admit it, because it makes

119

all this complicated bullshit to which you've devoted your life fundamentally worthless. You guys exist to provide excuses. And for some things—for the kinds of things Rhino Frost does—there's no excuse."

"That's Catholic education talking," Weiner said.

Murphy nodded. "I suppose it is. I remember being in the fourth grade, and we had this nun, Sister Benedict. She was about a hundred and four years old, and we used to call her Sugar Ray because she could stun you with a punch from any direction. She used to carry this thimble on her finger, and when you got out of line she'd come over and nail you with it, right in the middle of the forehead. Your eyeballs would roll right back in your head when she did that. Until I was about twelve or so, I used to have this little grid mark right in the middle of my forehead. It looked like an Indian caste mark. Let me tell you, Sister Benedict understood evil. She had no difficulty in grasping the concept, and her weapon against evil was that goddamned thimble."

"The joys of growing up Irish," Weiner observed.

"So, you think he'll come for me? You're sure of it?"

Weiner shook his head. "Sure of it? No, I'm not sure. You see, with most criminals violent crime is a youthful phenomenon. In all but the rarest of cases, you can take the worst asshole you ever saw and keep him in prison until he's thirty or thirty-five and when he comes out he won't harm a soul. The sap runs thinner, or something. If Frost were ten years younger, I'd have no hesitation about predicting that he'd go for you. At his current age, it's hard to be definitive. But, as I said, it seems to be a reasonable possibility. I'd be careful."

Murphy stood up. "Well, that's what I wanted to know. Barry, thanks for the hospitality. I've got to get back home. My daughter's with me for the weekend."

Weiner walked him to the door, puffing hurriedly on another of Murphy's cigarettes before Ella returned. "Let me know how all this turns out."

"I'm just going to have to figure out a way to get him back in the can. I'm going to ask Wilder to keep an eye on him, lawyer or no lawyer. He'll do it for me. He owes me a couple."

"Frank," Weiner said, "if this guy does end up in custody again, I'd be grateful for a few hours with him, at the very least. Actually, I'd take as long with him as I could get. The other psychiatrists didn't know what you told me. It wasn't in the file. Armed with that kind of information, if I could get him talking about it, there might be a paper in it for me."

Murphy looked at Barry Weiner. "Oh, well, shit, Barry. A paper? I'd do just about anything I could help you out on that one."

"I'm serious."

"I know. To you, all the scumbags are just white rats to study."

"Aren't you glad that somebody studies them?"

"Actually," Murphy said solemnly, "I am."

Graterford Correctional Facility, 1974

Frost had been a guest of the city several times in the past.

In the beginning, it had been foster care—six months in a group home for errant juveniles, courtesy of Orphans Court, for a rather serious assault rap when he was thirteen. Later, he had done time as an adult in Holmesburg Prison, Philadelphia's Castle Dracula-like municipal jail that loomed up starkly, a forbidding mountain of sandy-colored stone, next to the Delaware Expressway. He had done ten months in Holmesburg on a misdemeanor drug possession charge at seventeen. He had done four and a half for an assault and battery the following year. At age twenty, he had copped a plea on a burglary charge and done twenty-seven weeks on a breaking-and-entering beef.

In terms of sheer meanness, Frost knew from experience that Holmesburg was in the same league with any state prison, so the prospect of going to Graterford hadn't bothered him. It was the prospect of staying there for all those years—year after year after year after year. That's what bothered Frost.

In Holmesburg, first awaiting trial and then awaiting transfer into the state system, he heard stories about Graterford. He had heard them before, but now they captured his interest.

"The place is all gangs, man," said a muscular West Philly pimp named Pinky, who had done a two-spot at Graterford and would probably be going back when his current trial for manslaughter ended in its inevitable guilty verdict. "That's what's different from here. And you got badder dudes in them gangs than you find here, too. There's a gang for white dudes like you that's got some bikers in it. There's two or three black gangs. There's a Muslim gang. There's a lifers gang, and most of them dudes got dual membership in some other gang. It's just like the street, man, except ain't nobody in there taking his bitch downtown on a Friday night to catch a movie, you dig? There's a gang for everybody, because if you ain't in no gang then you might as well hang it up. I don't care how tough you think you are, man, you ain't in a gang some dudes gonna come along and kill your ass. The Man don't run Graterford. He know it, too. The Man just keep the doors locked. Inside, the population be in control, don't you know."

"What gang are you going to join when you go back?" Frost asked Pinky.

Pinky pondered the question. "Well," he said finally, "that's going to depend. Whoever be the baddest, I suppose. Don't want to be with no pussy gang in Graterford, man. If it be the Black Prisoners Unity Movement that's kicking ass, then that's who I'll try to get with. If it be the Muslims, then I gonna become Muhammed Somebody or other and stay away from pork and smack while I do my time. Them Muslims, they be strict and not the most fun you ever saw, but nobody mess with them most of the time. How about you?"

Frost shrugged, remembering how one of his brothers in the Demons had ratted on him. His brothers' bullshit, he thought. "I've had it with gangs. I might try it on my own."

"You a fool, man," Pinky told him solemnly. "You figure you're one mean dude, and maybe you are. But you ain't in a gang in Graterford, then you got to be a bitch. You got to be some jocker's bitch, you dig?"

"I'm not going in for none of that faggot stuff," Frost assured him.

Pinky just smiled and shook his head. "You'll see, man. You want to keep from having fifteen dudes do you in the shower like you're some bitch, you better make yourself some friends. Can't do it alone 'less you

123

willing to kill somebody to protect yourself, and you do that the Man ain't never gonna let you out. You'll see."

Recollections of that conversation were in Frost's mind as he was processed in at Graterford. He had arrived by bus, wearing chains and linked to thirty-five other men. Frost was one of a minority of whites on the bus, just as he knew whites would be a minority at Graterford—less than thirty percent, to be precise. But he was also one of the biggest men on the bus, just as he would be one of the biggest in the prison. His size and his readiness to fight had made him a man to be respected, if not feared, at Holmesburg. He had no reason to expect this would not be the case in the state system. He might be a greenhorn at Graterford, but he could handle himself as well in a prison of two thousand as he could in a jail of five hundred.

They made him take some aptitude tests at the processing center, then a bored guard asked him questions from a form.

"Do you ever hear anybody talking to you inside your head? Do you hear voices?"

"Nah."

"Do you ever think about sex with other men?"

"Do you?"

The guard looked up. "Do you sometimes wish you were a girl?"

Frost blew the guard a kiss.

The guard smiled at him. It was not a nice smile. "You're going to like it here, smart guy. In fact, you're going to fucking love it, I promise."

From the processing center, Frost and the other prisoners were led through the gates. From high on the walls, Frost could see other inmates looking down on the new arrivals, studying them. Pinky had told him why they did that.

"Your worst enemy come to the house," Pinky had said, "you want to know he's there before he knows you're there."

Frost and the others were issued their gear by a bored guard with a bad complexion. He looked like a bumpkin, a country boy. So did all the guards. That's because they were. The prison primarily housed inner city criminals. Their keepers were blue-collar men from rural backgrounds. The result was culture clash. In the overall picture, it didn't count for much. But it counted for something. Everything counted for something.

Frost was issued two pairs of jeans, two denim work shirts with his number emblazoned on them, a laundry bag bearing the same number, three sets of underwear, sheets, a pillow and a pillowcase, three pairs of white sweat socks, a pair of work shoes, a pair of high-topped canvas sneakers, and a brown paper bag containing a toothbrush, toothpaste, soap, a razor, shaving cream, and two worn towels.

A guard led him and several others onto a cellblock four stories high. It was different from Holmesburg, which had been a one-story prison, with cell blocks sticking out from the central dining hall like the spokes of a wheel. Graterford was twenty sprawling acres of stone walls, concrete gun turrets, steel bars, and social misfits. Despite himself, Frost was slightly awed. The noise alone was astonishing. The four-story-high cellblock to which he was led was a giant room containing hundreds of households, and the accumulated din of male voices, soul music, blaring television sets, and slamming steel doors was deafening. Fourteen years of this noise ahead of him.

As he walked in line, Frost rubbed at his remaining testicle, still swollen after all these months from Murphy's foot and the surgery that had removed its twin. He stared up at the vast area of the cellblock— listened to the racket and smelled the stink of men living closely together, like rats in a hole. He thought of the detective sergeant who had put him here with lies and planted evidence. Frost closed his eyes and called up Murphy's features. He fixed them in his mind. Rhino Frost planned to think about Frank Murphy a lot in the coming years. He planned to dream of Murphy every night.

What he did not plan to do was forget.

CHAPTER TEN

Patricia came awake, felt the weight on her ankles and said, "Hey, Winst. Move your buns, okay?"

Winston looked up at her. His wrinkled pink and black muzzle parted in a pointed-tooth smile. The smile made his eyes disappear into thick folds of bulldog face. His stub of a tail twitched sleepily. Patricia's heart melted. She held out her arms.

"Baby, baby," she said. "Give me a kiss."

Winston crawled up next to her on the sofa, grunting happily. He wheezed in greeting, and Patricia enveloped his big head in her arms, kissing him squarely between the eyes.

"Uuhhh . . ." Winston said in delight.

"Sweet baby," Patricia told him.

She scratched his belly. Winston rolled over against her, his rear legs waving awkwardly. Patricia grinned and scratched with genuine abandon. Winston's right leg began to kick the air as her fingers danced over some deeply buried nerve in his torso.

"Like that, do you?" Patricia asked.

"Uuhhh," Winston replied. "Uuuugggghhh!"

"Want to go for a walk?"

Winston sat up instantly. His ears raised. He shook his entire body. All this meant yes. He snorted and slobbered for further emphasis.

Five minutes later, the girl and the bulldog walked along Schuylkill Avenue, the warming morning air swirling around them, the sun a phlegmy haze among the tall trees that lined the street. Patricia was a tall girl, nearly five ten, another legacy from her grandmother. She moved with the easy grace of an athlete, which she was, a four-forty runner on her high school track team. This had helped her get into college, although she had not been good enough to win an athletic scholarship to any place where she wanted to go. Her hair was a dark blond or a light brown—depending on the time of year and its exposure to sunlight—and hung straight to her shoulders. Her eyes were a brown the color of beef gravy that tended toward amber, then toward green around the pupil. Her features were regular, but not startlingly pretty. The attractiveness of her face stemmed from a subtlety and animation of expression, a vibrance that wasn't there when she slept. Her mind was first rate. She had scored nearly twelve hundred on her college boards. She liked her own way and fought for it constantly. She laughed easily. Only some of this was apparent on the street as she walked briskly behind Winston on the leash.

From nearly a block back, the big man watching her could have told you only a portion of all that, and only the knowledge that this was Murphy's daughter would have been of interest to him. He surveyed Patricia carefully from the aged and battered Ford van that contained a sleeping bag and pillow and some other personal possessions. The rest of his stuff, including his

128

bike, he kept at his apartment in Olney, which he had been avoiding ever since the cops had picked him up there. He would go back, but only after he'd accomplished something. He'd gotten worked over for absolutely nothing this last time, and he would not go back to the apartment until he got in a shot of his own.

Rhino Frost had seen Patricia late last night as she and Murphy had entered the building after dinner. He had awakened from his sleeping bag several times during the night to relieve himself out the van's rear door into the street and to assure himself that his prey was still in its hiding place. And Murphy was prey, as far as Frost was concerned—prey to be stalked and studied and, eventually, taken. Frost would be patient about it. He understood patience now as he had not understood it in his youth. He understood its virtue as a tool and recognized its value as an enhancer of the pleasure of the climax. He watched carefully, but he was in no rush. No rush at all. Waiting was part of his nature by now. It fed his hatred.

Each time he had looked out the van during the night, he had watched for Murphy to leave the apartment, which he had not done until early morning, when the daylight and the early-morning joggers and dog walkers had made action on his part too risky. Then the big man had waited for the girl, whom he presumed was a pickup, since he had watched Murphy enough during the past month to determine that the ex-cop lived alone, except for his bulldog. Frost had watched Murphy for a long time before permitting himself to be seen the other day on the street.

Finally, the girl had come out shortly before eleven, and the big man had been waiting. He turned the key, and the old van coughed into life as Patricia rounded the corner. The van rolled slowly down the street. Frost wished he had some fruit juice. He wished he had been able to brush his teeth. He wished, too, that Murphy had come out of the apartment before sunrise. That, he wished most of all. But for now he would follow the girl. At least she wasn't carrying a pistol, and he had determined by the bulge under Murphy's jacket that he had been.

As the van turned the corner, Frost rubbed at his crotch. It was an old habit by now, scratching through denim at his one remaining testicle, which worked fine, thank you. He had found that out in prison, and the realization had come to him in a gasp of relief he would never forget. Two were better than one, but one would do. There had been one brief moment of utter terror back in the Roundhouse when Rosario the diabetic had kicked him there, but it had turned out all right. That last nut must be a tough one to crack, because it had been through a lot through the years. It had survived Murphy, who had smashed its partner so many years ago. It had survived Graterford, too.

Frost moved the van along at a slightly faster pace now because the girl had broken into a jog, and the bulldog was running beside her, its short legs pumping, its pink tongue hanging over its pink and black lips. He maintained nearly a block's gap, permitting cars to pass him as he crawled along near the row of parked vehicles. The girl jogged nearly a dozen blocks, up and down streets, doing it easily, as he followed. Then she halted at Rittenhouse Square and released the dog. Frost passed the square and saw her sitting on a bench as the dog wandered the little park. He began to look for a parking space. It being Saturday morning, he found one a block and a half away. It was illegal, which deterred him not at all. Frost shut off the van and walked, bent over, into the back of the vehicle. He dug through his possessions until he found something. He stuck it in his belt. It felt cold against the bare skin of his thickly muscled middle.

Then Rhino Frost got out of the van, locked it, and walked slowly back toward Rittenhouse Square.

Patricia breathed deeply after her run, but with no real strain. She was perspiring only lightly. It would take a longer distance and more speed to make her actually sweat. Her resting pulse was fifty-two beats a minute, and her blood pressure, taken at the last track team physical, was one-ten over seventy. The run had only loosened her up, which had been its purpose. Her father had told her disapprovingly that running like that, with her breasts bouncing, would eventually leave her with boobs like the ears of a beagle, but she was reasonably sure that he couldn't jog a dozen blocks without gasping for an hour afterward. He could probably pick up the front of a car, she supposed, because he was strong enough, but the muscle was layered now with flab, and running had never been Murphy's strong suit. Ever since he had left the uniformed ranks, he had used his body primarily as a means of locomotion for his brain, which mattered much more to him.

She looked around the square and made sure she could see Winston, who was wandering. She knew from long experience that he wouldn't leave the square.

He had done it only once, the summer before. Patricia had caught him and slapped his crumpled nose and shouted at him, and the bulldog had whimpered like a puppy. He was on the other side of the square, free of his leash in blatant violation of the city's leash law, but his stubby tail was whirling like the blade of a mixmaster, and she would give him a few more minutes of freedom. She watched Winston sniff trees and park benches and chase pigeons and frolic. He had been much happier at home in Mount Airy, with his own lawn. Here in Center City the animal found grass only here in the square or, on those rare occasions when Murphy had time to drive him there, in Fairmount Park or on the grassy spaces that lined the Schuylkill. Patricia would make her father take her on a picnic in the park today, and they would take Winston. Who would see that the dog got his recreation when she was away at school? The thought saddened her.

Rittenhouse Square takes up a full block in Center City Philadelphia. It is a patch of greenery surrounded by co-op and condo apartments. An apartment in one of those buildings bestows upon its inhabitant a prestige address in exchange for stunningly high rents. Murphy couldn't afford to live on Rittenhouse Square and wouldn't have if he could have, since he loathed high-rises. But he lived close enough to permit his daughter to bring his dog here. The square was studded with oaks, elms, and sturdy benches along its walks. Patricia leaned back on one of those benches and stared up at the city sky. The clouds rolled in like the waves of smoke she had seen billow across the stages at an Air Supply concert she had attended the previous week at the Spectrum. Patricia stretched and thought about leaving home. It was about all she thought about these days.

Frost sat down on a bench on the far side of the square. From here he could see the girl. But so could a lot of people. It was late morning now, and people were coming out of the apartment houses around the square. Cars went by on each of the four streets surrounding it. There were perhaps a dozen people in the square—an old woman feeding pigeons from a paper bag; a couple necking on the grass, his hand on her breast and neither of them much caring who was watching; an old man with a cane, wandering; a junkie, some gays off in a corner.

Too many people.

The girl would make noise. She would shout for help before he could finish, and if she did that people would look at them and they could identify him later. Besides, there were cops around here. It was a rich neighborhood, and there were always cops in a rich neighborhood. That's what cops were for, to protect the rich people. The poor people were on their own. That's what Bobbi had always said. Whatever her other failings, Bobbi had been nobody's dummy. Frost would give her that. She might have been seriously screwed up in the head, but Bobbi had thought about things in terms that had seemed like revelations to Frost.

He looked away from the girl and turned his gaze toward the dog, who was much closer than the girl. The dog was scampering around the square. He wagged his tail at the old man, who nudged him away with the cane. The dog went over to the couple on the grass, sniffing them. The man turned and told the bulldog to get lost, which he did. It wandered back to the walkway, sniffing the ground, sniffing aimlessly.

Frost stood up. The girl was on the other side of the square. Frost's eyes narrowed.

"Here, boy," he said quietly to the bulldog.

The dog looked his way. Frost smiled at it. He snapped his fingers a few times.

"Here, boy. Come on over here."

Winston wagged his stub cautiously.

"Come on, fella."

Winston came.

Frost scratched behind the dog's ears. Dumb dog, he thought. Stupid dog. Shouldn't have come to a stranger. It's the dog's own fault if he's dumb enough to come to a stranger.

Patricia thought about school. She would be leaving in a few weeks for Skidmore College in Saratoga Springs, New York. She had been there only once before, in the early spring, when Murphy had taken her around to several colleges in the Northeastern U.S. that had accepted her. Skidmore was the one she had settled upon. The campus was lovely. The little city it occupied was elegant and graceful. It was close enough to Albany to provide entertainment. And it was close enough to the Adirondacks and Vermont for skiing weekends. It was also about six hours away from Philadelphia by car, if you drove slowly and stopped twice along the way. Six hours away from her mother.

Close enough for Patricia to get home in a hurry. Far enough away to give her privacy. Heaven. She couldn't wait.

Patricia worried about leaving her father. True, she saw him only every few weeks now, but she talked to him frequently by phone. He was only a half hour or so away if she really wanted to see him. She knew he was struggling in his law practice and was still floundering after her mother had thrown him out. There had been Nancy, whom Patricia had barely been able to tolerate, and, thankfully, was now gone. Nancy had been fifteen years younger than Patricia's father and ages younger emotionally. Emotionally, she had been younger than Patricia, and by a fair margin. That was what her father was spending time with, wifty women with boobs like zeppelins and the brains of parakeets? He deserved better than that, Patricia thought—some small measure of happiness, at least. All he had were worries and money problems and a deeply felt loneliness he would never admit. Patricia worried about him. He wasn't getting any younger. And he smoked and drank too much, despite her best efforts at straightening him out. On that, she agreed with her mother. That was about the only thing, though.

"Good boy," Rhino Frost said.

He was squatting, bent over the dog, scratching his broad chest. Winston snorted pleasantly. He wheezed in satisfaction. He slobbered on Frost's arm. Frost reached inside his belt, thick fingers grasping what he sought. He scratched harder at the dog's chest. The bulldog loved it.

"Uuuuhhhhhhh," Winston said.

Frost looked around. He was near a stately oak, blocking anyone's view of him on one side. On the other, the couple in the grass groped at each other, oblivious to all else. Rhino Frost leaned over the bulldog. He had done this before. It would be better this time.

This was Murphy's dog.

Patricia looked around.

"Winston?"

She stood up and swept the square with her eyes . . .

"Winston!"

Where the hell was he? If he'd taken off again . . .

. . . then gazed down the walkway toward the big oak in the middle of the square, and she saw Winston. She also saw a very big man moving away at a dead run and crossing the street and going off to her left. But that didn't register, it didn't sink in, because all she could see at that particular moment was Winston and he filled up her eyes and made her heart sputter.

"Winston!" she shrieked, and ran to him.

CHAPTER ELEVEN

"Eighteen," Mary Ellen Murphy gasped, "nnnnnine-uh!-teen . . . TWENTY!"

She collapsed back on the floor, her abdominal muscles gasping right along with her.

Leg-lifts. Those goddamn leg-lifts. She hated the leg-lifts. She did them ever day, though. They helped keep her a size ten, which she had been since age sixteen, which was so long ago that she refused to think about it. The leg-lifts and the sit-ups and the stretching exercises and the walking and the cottage cheese with chunks of pineapple to disguise its disgusting taste—they all helped. Mary Ellen despised all of it.

Except being a size ten, that is. That, she liked.

She got up off the living-room floor and wiped her brow with her sweatshirt. She wore the sweatshirt despite the summer heat because she wanted to sweat. Somebody had said that was good for you. Richard Simmons or somebody else on TV. It probably wasn't true, but Mary Ellen wasn't taking any chances. She walked her two miles every morning, faithfully, even when it rained. She did her exercises daily. She watched what she ate. And she sweated, just to be sure.

She was thirty-nine years old, separated, the mother of a semihostile teenage girl who was going off to college in a few weeks to leave her in an empty house and she would have given ten years of her life at that particular moment for a piece of chocolate cake with a cherry on top of the sour cream icing. Instead, she was going to dine on Lean Cuisine. Frank's inelegant description of the human condition flashed into her head. Life was a shit sandwich without the bread. Crude, but indisputably accurate. Mary Ellen Murphy was not in a good mood today.

She had the fillet of fish florentine in the microwave when she heard the car pull into the driveway. Doors opened and closed. She went into the hallway and was heading for the front door when it burst open. It was Patricia, in tears.

"What's going on?" Mary Ellen asked, baffled.

Patricia made no response. Instead, she tore up the stairs, sobbing horribly. Mary Ellen walked to the bottom of the stairs and saw her disappear into her room.

Then Frank was in the doorway, his expression as dark as she had ever seen it. Mary Ellen turned to him in silent bafflement.

"Frank . . ." she said.

"Come on in the kitchen," he told her. "We've got to talk."

"What is this? What happened?"

He closed the door behind him and took her by the arm. "In the kitchen," he said brusquely.

Mary Ellen went with him. But once in the kitchen—her kitchen, goddamn it—she whirled on him. "Will you please tell me what the hell is going on? What's

138

wrong with Patricia?"

"It's Winston," Murphy told her, lighting a Camel. "He's seriously injured, and he's less than even money to make it through the night."

Mary Ellen sighed in relief. "God, I thought it was some disaster. You two scared the daylights out of me."

Murphy frowned, his face clouding up. Mary Ellen had never liked that expression. It was one of many things about Frank she had never liked.

"Is there a beer in this house?" he demanded.

"In the refrigerator. Help yourself."

Help yourself, Murphy thought. Goddamn right I'll help myself. He found a Schmidt's Tiger Head Ale in the rear of the lower shelf. He was convinced it had been there since he had moved out eighteen months before. Mary Ellen never drank beer, and she never threw anything out, either. Their basement had always looked like a Salvation Army thrift store. He popped the top off the bottle and drank deeply.

"What happened to Winston?" Mary Ellen asked.

"Sit down," Murphy told her.

She sat. She knew that tone. He was troubled. He loved that foolish bulldog, even though the dog had always insisted on crapping in the living room, right where Mary Ellen did her exercises.

"Do you remember Rhino Frost?" he asked her.

"No."

He shook his head in exasperation. "I told you about him. I remember. He was the biker. The drug peddler. Think back. It was not long after Patricia was born. After a year after I made detective second."

"I think I do. I'm not sure. You were always talking about such marvelous people all the time. I had

139

problems keeping track even then, much less now."

"All right, forget that. He's a bad guy—a real bad guy—and he tried to kill Winston this morning. Patricia had taken him to Rittenhouse Square, and Rhino apparently followed them from my place. She let Winston go, and Rhino stabbed him. He cut a huge hole in his gut. The vet operated, but he says Winston might not make it. Probably won't make it, is what he said."

Mary Ellen's eyes widened. "Is Patricia all right? Did she get hurt?"

Murphy shook his head. "No, she's fine. Frost didn't want her. Or he didn't think it was safe to go after her in Rittenhouse Square in broad daylight, which is probably more accurate. But she's just about beside herself. Winston apparently took a nice bite out of the guy and put up a hell of a fight, and Frost took off when he couldn't get it done quickly. Patricia got a glimpse of him running down the street. She blames herself for the whole thing, and she's scared, too. And she ought to be. This is a bad, bad guy—about the worst guy you can possibly imagine. And he was sending me a message with this. That has her worried, too."

Mary Ellen sat back in the kitchen chair. "You're sure she's all right?"

"I'm all right," Patricia said from the doorway. She came in red-eyed and sat at the table with her mother while Murphy leaned against the sink in his knit shirt, a cigarette in one hand and the beer in the other.

"He cut a big hole in Winston's stomach," Patricia said in a wavering voice. "Winston was lying there on the sidewalk bleeding and with his intestines hanging out, right there on the pavement. They looked like

140

sausages. He was howling and crying. I never heard him make noises like that before."

"There was a prowl car in the neighborhood," Murphy went on. "They took Patricia and Winston out to the Penn veterinary school, and some veterinary student worked on him. That's where he is now. It's touch and go."

"Oh, Mama," Patricia said, and fell into her mother's arms, weeping vigorously.

"He'll be fine," Mary Ellen said as the microwave went off. She ignored it. She couldn't stand fillet of fish florentine anyway.

Murphy sat down at the table across from her. "We've got to talk. We have a bad situation here, all of us. This guy is bad news, and he's after me. There isn't any question about it now."

"Why don't you have him arrested?" Mary Ellen demanded.

"For what? For stabbing a dog? I could have him arrested, but he'd be out on the street in fifteen minutes. He's got a good lawyer, and the streets are full of people who are stabbing other people. That's a big summer sport in some parts of this city, Mary Ellen—bigger than baseball, even. I couldn't keep him inside for more than an eyeblink on this."

"Can't you do anything?"

Murphy sighed. "I don't know. I called Wilder from the vet's, to see if he could get him on a probation violation. Jim was out, but somebody else checked for me. It turns out that Frost finished his probation last week, just before he showed himself to me on the street outside my building. He's free as a bird now. Wilder brought him in the other day, to scare him, but his

141

lawyer sprung him. Jimmy's guys are supposed to stay away from him, but I'm going to ask Jim to try to keep an eye on him anyway, after this. We might get something on him, and then we can do something, but I don't know how much. The reality is that he's out there, and he's after me and I'm pretty much on my own until he goes for me. Or—more to the point—until and unless he goes for one of you. And he might. That's what has me really worried."

When Murphy said that, Patricia paled. And visibly. Mary Ellen's face grew suddenly calm. That was typical, Murphy thought. She handled crisis well. She always had. He recalled how she had helped him through the death of his parents, one after the other, so many years before. He had disintegrated, fallen apart totally. Mary Ellen had been there for him, a rock of stability, an anchor. He had loved her then. He loved her now. He watched her wrap her arms around their daughter. Why did I ever let her force me out of here? he thought.

"You said you told me about this man," Mary Ellen said coolly. "Tell me again. I don't remember, Frank. I'm sorry."

Murphy got up from the table. He walked to the sink, extinguished the stub of his Camel under the tap, and lit another. He leaned back against the sink. They were both watching him. Yes, he would have to tell them. He would have to tell them as much as he could. They were entitled to that, he supposed.

"His name is Wendell Frost," Murphy said. "He's the only child of a couple who lived in Olney. His father died when he was a kid, and his mother died later, after he went to prison."

"He was in prison for drugs?" Mary Ellen asked.

Murphy nodded. "In a way. Let me tell this chronologically. It's easier for me that way."

"Go ahead," Mary Ellen said.

"He was always a big kid, a bruiser. Early on, the other kids in the neighborhood started calling him Rhino. If you ever saw him, you'd know how well the name fits."

"He's really huge, Mom," Patricia said. "I saw him."

Murphy frowned, and Patricia noticed it. He'd always detested being interrupted. It was an unavoidable fate as the only man in a house with two females, but he still didn't like it.

"May I?" he asked Patricia.

"Sorry."

"He started getting into trouble early. He had a juvenile record a mile long, mostly assaults against anybody who got in his way and a lot of people who were just minding their own business. He also liked to kill animals—dogs, cats. He'd strangle them, set fire to them, cut them open. He was a sweetheart. The precinct cops got to know him real well. By the time he was fifteen or so he had a well-earned reputation as a notorious NFG."

"What's that?" Patricia asked.

Her father looked at her, "Well, the 'N' stands for 'no' and the 'G' stands for 'good.' It's a term you hear cops use."

"Why would anybody slaughter house pets?" Mary Ellen asked, shaking her head.

"I asked Barry Weiner about that this morning. Remember him?"

"Yes. One of your poker buddies."

"That's him. He's a shrink. He said it's a classic sign of a sadism complex. They all start that way."

"Why?" she asked again.

Murphy shook his head. "Barry has no idea. He can pretty much predict how a nut will react to a given situation, but he can give you only some broad guesses as to why without a detailed examination. Rhino Frost's psyche would be a playground for Barry."

"Didn't they get any help for him?" Patricia asked.

"He was referred to school psychologists, but when he was sentenced, the only school records were sketchy. This guy isn't all that much younger than I am, and they didn't do much of that sort of thing then. What they did was pitch your butt out of school if you got out of line, and that's what happened to Rhino. He was expelled from Olney High School at sixteen as an incorrigible. By then he was already a member of the Demons. That's a motorcycle gang that was head-quartered up in Olney back then. It's all broken up now. All the members are dead, in jail, or have joined other gangs or have said good-bye to the whole life-style. But back then they were a bunch of real hard-asses, and Rhino got in with them when he was a sophomore in high school, largely because he was as tough and as mean as any of them even then. He ended up as their warlord."

"What's that?" Mary Ellen asked.

"When the gang went to war, Rhino was in charge. And they went to war a lot in those days. They took on the Warlocks, who are still around, and they did okay, even though they were outnumbered by a fair margin. They took on a black motorcycle gang—that's something you ought to see if you want to see something scary, a black motorcycle gang—and they held their own. The Demons are rough, bad guys. And Rhino at sixteen, was one of the roughest. And he was far and away the craziest."

"How did you get involved with him, Daddy?"

"Well, he'd been with the Demons for a number of years. He worked in construction for a while—when he worked at anything—and he was notorious for his weapon. He carried a twelve-inch chain saw on his belt. I guess that when Rhino decided to take apart a bar, he really took apart a bar. If you think about it, a small chain saw like that is a hell of a weapon. I was a detective second just out of uniform and looking to make good. I was assigned to work on a rape case up in Olney. What had happened was that a high school girl who had been hanging around with a member of the Demons had been found on the street by a prowl car. Her name was Theresa Hawthorn. I remember her very well. She was in bad shape—I mean, real bad shape—and she wouldn't tell the uniformed guys anything. She refused to cooperate at all. I got sent up there to see what I could find out. I saw the girl in Northeast Hospital. It was the worst thing I ever saw. I mean the absolute worst. My skin crawls just to think about it."

Murphy visibly shivered as he spoke. Mary Ellen, who had heard stories like this before, suspected that even this ugly tale was being sugar-coated.

"I think, under the circumstances," she said quietly, "that you ought to tell us about it in some detail, Frank."

His eyes met hers. She nodded silently. Murphy looked over at Patricia, listening with eyes wide.

"Okay," he said in a clipped tone. "The girl had been

145

raped, all right. That was clear enough. We got some partial prints off her clothing. We typed the blood of her attacker by his saliva. Other things had been done to her, too. Rhino is a chomper. Do you know what that is?"

Both women shook their heads.

"It means he bites. You get people like that once in a while. They like to bite other people. He'd bitten this girl. He . . ." Murphy paused. Shit, he had to tell them. "He'd bitten off both her nipples."

He could watch his wife and daughter pale visibly. Involuntarily, Patricia's arms went across her chest. The gesture made Murphy self-conscious. He looked down at the vinyl floor.

"Good God!" Mary Ellen whispered.

"The girl was totally traumatized," Murphy went on softly. "The lab got impressions of his teeth from her . . . from her flesh. We had good enough evidence that we thought maybe we could identify him with from the lab guys. One by one, we dragged all the members of the Demons in and questioned them. We had problems taking blood samples, privacy problems. So we got some blood out of them other ways. We had the same problem with teeth impressions. Nobody knew a thing. Then one of the Demons, I forget which one, gave us a hint that it had been Frost who'd done it. Just a hint. Nobody was going to testify or anything. Anyway, the uniformed guys managed to find Rhino. He was at his mother's house, and she swore he'd been with her all day long on the day we knew the attack had taken place. She volunteered the information without being asked. I was at a PBA Easter Party for orphans, and the uniformed guys called me and told me we had the guy. So I went down to the Roundhouse."

"Did he admit it?" Patricia asked.

Murphy shook his head. "He wasn't going to admit a goddamn thing. We didn't scare him even a little bit. He'd been around too many cops before. We did manage to take a tooth impression—after some heavy persuasion—and the lab said it might be a match. Just, 'It might.' That was as good as it was going to get. What they had from Theresa Hawthorn was good, but it wasn't perfect. When you're dealing with flesh instead of wax, you're dealing with a hard impression as compared to a ragged one. The flesh gets shredded when it's ripped away like . . . Well, you get the idea. Anyway, it was an okay match, but not as complete as it might have been. The same thing was true with the partial prints. Rhino had a whorl pattern in his prints, and so did the rapist, but it wasn't ironclad—not with the mother's story. His lawyer could find experts to refute our experts in court. All we really had for sure was the blood type. It was type O. Half the world's population is type O."

"Couldn't the girl have identified him?" Mary Ellen asked.

"She could have if she'd wanted to. But she'd been afraid to cooperate at first, and then it was too late. She was dead. Theresa Hawthorn went home from the hospital into her parents' care. She went to take a bath, which was perfectly natural. And while she was in the tub, she took her father's razor blades from the medicine chest and very carefully cut her wrists. The girl wasn't all that stable for starters, or she wouldn't have been hanging out with those creeps. Maybe she had planned it all along. Maybe she'd just looked down at herself in the tub, and decided to do it on the spot. You know, the disfigurement. It was pretty bad, Mary Ellen. Actually, it was real bad. He'd taken away a good piece of each . . ."

Murphy shut up. They had the idea. He wished they didn't, but they had the idea all right. Actually, Frost had gnawed one adolescent breast almost down to the pectoral muscle.

"Anyway," he went on lamely, "by the time we found Rhino, she was no help to us. That left us with no confession, no witness, no totally irrefutable evidence. It was at least even money that he'd have walked."

"How did you finally get him into prison?" Patricia asked.

Murphy shrugged. "Luckily, he had some heroin in his possession at the time of his arrest. Given his record and the extenuating circumstances—which were explained to the judge in chambers—he got the most the state could give him. He went away for a long time. Now he's out again, and he's apparently after me for sending him up. I was the detective in charge of the investigation. He remembers me real well, believe me."

Murphy finished his beer and lit another Camel. He had no more to say. There was silence in the kitchen for nearly a minute.

Then Mary Ellen said, "What can you do about it?"

Murphy came over to the table and sat down. "Legally, not much. Like I said, I can get him for what he did to Winston, but Patricia already told me she didn't see his face. Even if we could convince a judge that he did it, we're only talking about a dog here. He won't do a day of jail time. And if by some miracle he did, he'd be back out and after me so fast it wouldn't make any difference. What I can do is have him watched, and Wilder's guys are already doing that, no matter what his lawyer says. There might be one or two other things I can do, too."

"Like what?" Patricia asked.

Murphy looked at her levelly. "I'd rather not go into it. I can take care of myself, honey. Don't worry about that."

"I do."

"So do I," Mary Ellen told him.

Murphy looked at her and smiled. "Well," he said, "that's something, anyway."

Mary Ellen reddened and turned her face away.

Murphy stood up. "Look, I'm heading back home. You two make sure you lock all the doors tonight, and don't take any chances. I'm pretty sure that he's after me and only me, but I don't know what's going through his head. I can only guess. This is a bad, bad guy. You don't know what he might do."

Mary Ellen looked at the tabletop. She didn't speak for a moment. Then she said, "Frank, under the circumstances, I think both of us would feel better if you stayed here tonight instead of going all the way back down to Center City."

Patricia's eyes lit up. "Will you?"

He glanced over at his wife, frowned and shook his head. "I better go back to my place."

Mary Ellen looked up at him. "I mean it, Frank. It's not for you; it's for us. We'd both feel safer if you were here."

Murphy cocked his head in surprise. "Well, where would I sleep?"

"The guest room," Mary Ellen told him.

"Terrific," he said without enthusiasm, but Patricia was enthusiastic enough for both of them. She jumped up and grabbed his arm.

"Will you?" she demanded. "Please?"

Murphy patted his daughter's hand and sighed softly. Then he looked over at Mary Ellen.

"Well, how could I turn down a moving invitation like this?" he said.

CHAPTER TWELVE

Frost had leaned over the bulldog and positioned the knife beneath the animal's gut. Then he had scratched behind its ears and, without warning, thrust quickly upward. He had felt the survival knife punch through the bulldog's thickly muscled torso, had felt its edge slice through the gristle, had felt a gush of warm thick blood wash over his arm.

After this was over, Frost had planned to go back to his place in Feltonville, in Philadelphia's Olney section, and get on the bike and ride, to feel the Harley's power under his groin and between his legs, to feel the city wind in his face, to listen to the music of the bike's throaty roar. The thought had been in his mind as he drove in the knife, feeling its point shoot through the muscle and into something soft and vital inside.

Frost had expected Murphy's bulldog to react the way other dogs had reacted over the years to stab wounds he had inflicted upon them. He had expected the bulldog to jump wildly away, to roll up in a tight ball, trying instinctively to keep its insides from falling out onto the pavement. He had expected it to yelp in terror and pain.

Only, instead, the fucking dog had bitten him.

As the knife went in, the bulldog struck back, without warning and in utter silence, with not even the hint of a growl. Frost had taken the bite in his meaty right bicep. The teeth had dug in easily and deep—like spikes going into a thick steak. The bulldog had massive, frighteningly powerful jaws. And the teeth had held. The bulldog didn't slash with them. Instead, he merely clamped onto Frost's arm and squeezed ever tighter, the teeth driving in up to the gums and the pressure on Frost's huge bicep immense and unbearable in less than a second. His arm was in a vise. The vise bled silently.

Frost leaped frantically to his feet, a fifty-pound weight fastened by four fangs dangling from the upper portion of his right arm. Frost struck viciously at the dog with his left hand, his hamlike fist slamming into the animal like a sledgehammer, again and again. The bulldog merely followed his instinct, which told him to hold his grip. The grip was the thing, only the grip. As he was battered and swirled about, a roll of Winston's intestine slipped out of the bloody rent in his middle. The dog closed his eyes and freely allowed himself to be swung awkwardly against a nearby tree. His instinct permitted this, even encouraged it. He made a strange sound as Frost tried to shake him free, an almost blissful sound. He was being a good dog.

Winston's kind had been bred for the grip—bred seven hundred years before to latch onto the noses of bulls as they charged, and then to keep the grip and keep the grip and keep the grip as the bull thrashed about trying to free itself. A big bulldog's weight was only a tiny fraction of a fighting bull's. Sometimes the bull would free itself and trample the dog into shreds. Sometimes, though, the bulldog would manage to get its grip on the bull's throat instead of its nose, and the bull would bleed to death. Or be throttled by the tightening vise on its windpipe. Winston's forebears had—like him—been only moderately bright, but they had lived or died by the strength of their grip, and in a fight a bulldog's blood demanded that he keep his grip at all costs.

This was Rhino Frost's unforeseen problem in Rittenhouse Square.

The battle had been fought in silence and had gone on less than thirty seconds when Frost became aware that people were beginning to notice. The groping couple in the grass was looking, wide-eyed. Frost felt a rush of panic to accompany his pain. Blood from his arm wound mixed with the bulldog's on the ground beneath them. He scratched at the dog's eyes with his fingernails. The dog's eyelids bled. His grip was unaffected.

The couple in the grass began to rise now, eyes wide, expressions of shock on their faces. Frost switched the knife he still held in his now numb right hand to his left and jabbed it into the bulldog's heavily muscled right shoulder. He felt the tip strike bone. Blood flowed. It smelled like copper, like freshly minted pennies.

The grip weakened slightly.

Frost stabbed again. Again and again and a fourth time. But then he lost the knife. It stuck in the dog as he tried to pull it out, and then it slipped from his gore-soaked fingers and clattered as it hit the walkway. Frost tried to pry the bulldog's jaws apart. The effort was futile. The fingers of Frost's left hand were covered with bulldog spittle and blood as they pulled against the animal's slippery gums, dug nails into them.

Then, to his delighted surprise, the bulldog went suddenly limp. The grip held, but it was weak now. The force was gone.

Winston's ancestors had enjoyed an advantage in combat. Bulls didn't carry knives, inflicted different wounds. No amount of battering would have induced Winston to free the man, but the reduced flow of blood to his brain—both from his position and horrible wounds—forced him into a blackout. Still the jaws held, but now Frost managed to force them apart. The bulldog thumped to the walkway, his pink, shiny intestine protruding like a sausage roll nearly a full foot from Winston's torso wound. Frost staggered away from the dog and grabbed his knife. He stood erect as the couple from the grass approached at a run.

"Hey, Mac," the man called out, "that dog got you good. Let me—"

Frost clutched his wounded bicep with his left hand as he brandished the bloody knife with the right.

"Don't piss me off," he warned.

The lovers stopped in their tracks. They froze. The man reached behind him for the woman's hand, and—saucerlike eyes on Frost's huge and crimson form—began to back away slowly. Frost turned away from them and took in the scene in the rest of the square with a quick glance. The people nearest him were gazing at him in undisguised horror. At the far end of the walkway, nearly a full block away, Murphy's girl was standing up, her eyes searching the square but not yet falling on Frost and the bulldog. She'd see in just a

154

second or so . . .

Rhino Frost turned and ran.

His apartment was forty minutes from Center City when traffic wasn't nightmarish, which it was not late on a Saturday morning. Frost had three rooms over a garage, where he kept the Harley and the van. At a red light on Fifteenth Street, he tied a rag over the dog bite. The bicep was swollen and bruised, but the only wounds that produced blood were four punctures in the muscle, two on one side and two on the other. In between each set of punctures were smaller wounds where smaller teeth had dug into his skin. The bleeding wasn't bad after he tied on the rag, but the mother hurt like a son of a bitch.

He'd suffered worse, though. In Graterford, he'd suffered worse. He could handle this.

He pulled into his garage around eleven. He locked the doors behind him and climbed the stairs to his place. It had come furnished—cheap chairs, cheap curtains, cheap silverware and dishes. Frost didn't care. He had grown up in a modest but neat house and despised elegant surroundings. All he cared about was a clean kitchen. Rhino Frost didn't want to catch germs. Bobbi was a health freak, and she had taught him to be careful about germs.

He went into his bathroom, found some Bactine, and ripped off the bloody rag. He poured the stuff into the puncture wounds. The bleeding had pretty much stopped. The swelling and bruising was not good, though. He went into the kitchen and got some ice

155

cubes and put them into a dish towel. Then he went into the living room, flipped on the TV set and the VCR and flopped on the sofa. He held the ice pack over his ravaged arm and flipped around the dial. Saturday morning TV. He went from He-Man to Alvin and the Chipmunks to the Three Stooges to French Chef to Laramie on CBN to Soul Train. Shit. All of it shit. Frost had just missed the wrestling. That came on Channel Forty-eight at ten. Frost liked wrestling. He should have set the VCR when he left yesterday, only he wasn't sure yet how to really work it, except for watching rented tapes. There had been no VCRs when he had been sent away, and if there had been the old lady would never have bought one anyway because she'd been too cheap.

Frost settled on the Bugs Bunny and Tweetie Show. He watched for a while, unmoving, feeling it come on him again. The torpor, the malaise. It had come on him ever since he could remember when he had nothing to do. He wanted to ride the bike, but the arm hurt too much right now. He was in too much pain and too keyed up to sleep. There was aspirin in the medicine chest, but he didn't like to take too much of that. He took half an aspirin in the morning, along with a multivitamin pill, but that was all. He didn't like to take chemicals into his body anymore. He'd done that for too long. Bobbi had taught him not to do that. Bobbi said you didn't need drugs, that drugs made you weak. Bobbi had been full of shit about a lot of things—and totally untrustworthy on top of it—but she had been right on that.

Frost sat for more than an hour, unmoving. He sat through all of Bugs Bunny and Tweetie and then

156

through all of the All-New Ewoks and then through part of Laser Tag Academy before switching to a black-and-white Tarzan movie made in the thirties and starring some swimmer turned actor. He moved only slightly, his eyes glazed over. He was thinking.

He was thinking about the bulldog. He thought about the knife going in, the feel of it. He thought about the blood, its color and smell. He smiled slightly once or twice as he gazed off into space. Buster Crabbe fought a lion. Rhino Frost sat as if in a trance.

After a while, he got up and got a tape from a shelf along the wall. He found Marilyn Chambers in *Insatiable*. He put it on the VCR and watched what she did, what the men did to her. He fast-forwarded through the parts where they talked. They had to do that, he knew, but he wished they wouldn't. At the end, when John Holmes did Marilyn Chambers with his Twelve Inches of Dangling Death, Frost felt a stirring. He reached down and rubbed himself through his jeans. He heard Marilyn Chambers cry out in pain as John Holmes entered her, drove into her. Frost watched intently. Her face was contorted in agony. Only, was it agony? It could be acting. She was an actress. No, Frost decided for the hundredth time, it was real. Holmes's thing was huge. He would have been somebody's pride and joy at Graterford, some punk's prize jocker.

Frost watched John Holmes finish with Marilyn. She moaned.

"More," she said. "More."

Holmes leaned forward and placed his mouth over Marilyn's breast.

Rhino Frost felt his horselike teeth grind in delight.

CHAPTER THIRTEEN

Murphy awakened about seven to a familiar symphony.

He became aware first of the morning cicadas in the vegetable garden out back. The cicadas on this lot spoke in a unique voice, one he heard only from this house, and it had been a long time since he had listened to their song. He lay in one of the narrow twin beds in the guest room and listened to them for nearly fifteen minutes. Could these be the same cicadas that had been here when he lived here? Cicadas lived only about twenty minutes, didn't they? Still, they sounded the same. A concert for the prodigal lord of the manor.

Then he got up and stretched. The house was silent. He was the first to escape sleep. He felt like showering, only he didn't have a robe here anymore and he'd have to get back into these same clothes anyway. Any old clothes he might still have in the closet in the master bedroom wouldn't fit anyway. Murphy was thirty pounds heavier than he had been when the split occurred. Instead, he put on his jeans and knit shirt and went into the bathroom. His electric razor was back at his apartment in Center City, but he dug through the medicine chest and found his old Gillette and some Foamy he had apparently left here when he stomped out two winters before. He shaved with a new blade, the first time he had used one in several days. He left the bathroom with bits of toilet paper stuck to his cuts. His face had grown soft, especially since he'd started using the electric razor.

Murphy descended the stairs and prowled the house in solitude. He had always liked the way light entered this house on Sunday mornings, in filmy rays through the summer curtains. He put on a pot of coffee and considered calling the vet about Winston. He decided it was too early.

The Sunday *Inquirer* was on the front porch, all ten pounds of it. Murphy sat down in the sunlight on one of the front porch chairs and dug through the paper until he found the sports section. He lit his first Camel of the day as he read. The Phillies had gone down again. Damn. They should never have let Carlton go, even if he was old. They should have turned him into a reliever. And they had lost to the Mets, too. Murphy hated the Mets more than any collection of humanity he could imagine.

He turned to Clark DeLeon's column, his second favorite features in the newspaper after sports. DeLeon was picking on Jimmy Tayoun, a South Philadelphia politician Murphy knew slightly. He was also picking on cats, one of his treasured targets. DeLeon had a good news, bad news item; the bad news was that Siamese cats have nasty dispositions but the good news is that they go well with Ritz crackers, if they are sliced thinly enough. That would make him a lot of friends, Murphy was sure.

He read the paper for a good twenty minutes, skimming every page, stopping only when something caught his eye. He listened through the open door for the coffeemaker to finish its work, and he listened, too, to the birds. This was not a new neighborhood. The trees were tall and mature and home to robins, English sparrows, cardinals, bluebirds, and other feathered creatures of all description. The Murphy house sported a birdbath and a bird feeder in the side yard. As the birds sang, Murphy's attention to the newspaper flagged. He would read it more carefully later in the day, when he got back to his apartment. Newspaper reading was an ingrained habit in Murphy. He read both the *Inquirer* and *Daily News* faithfully during the week, and he picked up *The New York Times* at the City Hall newsstand every time he went to court. He had almost wept when the *Evening Bulletin* had gone under a few years before. The *Bulletin* had been the paper his family had received at home during his childhood, the newspaper of the row-house neighborhoods, gray and sedate and ultimately so boring that it had to quit publishing. Then he found out that his favorite *Bulletin* sports columnist, Ray Didinger, had been picked up by the *Daily News,* and the pain had been eased.

It was a nice summer morning, not too hot yet, and slightly breezy. Murphy leaned back in the old rocking chair on the porch and was infused with an unfamiliar sense of well-being. He liked this house. It was a sturdy brick colonial, not too big but with a bay window in front and a nice backyard. He and Mary Ellen had moved in here eighteen years before, just before Patricia's birth. At the time, the house had been far too expensive for them, but they had bought it anyway. As time went by, the mortgage payments had become more manageable. Today, only seven years from the mortgage payoff, payments were laughably low by current standards, and Murphy knew that he and Mary Ellen had some nice equity built up in this property.

The house had an attached one-car garage, a living room, kitchen, dining room, and half bath on the first floor. On the second were three bedrooms and a full bathroom. The basement had been converted into a storage area and a nice TV room on one side and, on the other, two small dens—one for Mary Ellen and the other for Murphy. Each of them needed the space to work at home. When Murphy had moved out, the only piece of furniture he had taken with him had been his desk, an immense rolltop number with bird's-eye maple drawers he had bought used at a Germantown antique shop ten years before. He had brought it home in a rented truck. He wondered absently what Mary Ellen had in that room now. She surely had taken over his file cabinet. Mary Ellen never had enough space to house all her school papers.

Along one side of the yard, Murphy had erected an arbor vitae hedge some years ago to shut out a particularly obnoxious neighbor, who had then promptly moved. Now the hedge was nearly ten feet high, and it ensured privacy to such a degree that Murphy had no idea who now lived to the right. There could be a tribe of Shoshone Indians in there for all he knew. Along the other side of the yard, he had planted fruit trees—several apple trees, an apricot tree, some peach trees, and one pear. They provided fresh fruit each summer, and he could see that they all were lush with fruit now. He got up and went over to pick an elberta peach. The juice exploded into his mouth when he bit into the fruit. It was a touch overripe. He would pick some fruit to take with him when he went back home. He had planted the trees, after all. If anybody was entitled . . .

Home.

It was strange to think of his Center City apartment as home. Until eighteen months ago, it had never occurred to Murphy that he would think of any place but this house as his home. He had grown up in a neighborhood where couples settled in early in their marriages, stayed in the same house until their kids were grown, and then just stayed, leaving the houses to the kids when they died. When he and Mary Ellen had bought this place so many years before, he had the same thought about this house. This would be home. They would raise their kids here—as it had worked out, they had had only the one—then they would stay here until Murphy got fed up and took his retirement from the police department. At that point, they would go down to Florida where Mary Ellen would play tennis all day while Murphy would do deep-sea fishing, drink rum, and complain about having nothing to do.

They were not going to be like those suburban couples, always looking for a new house, always looking for a chance to "move up" in housing. Murphy instinctively rejected the trappings of the suburban life-style. He would not own a vegetable steamer, a pasta machine, a Vidal Sassoon blow dryer, a jogging suit, racquetball equipment, roller skates, a ten-speed bicycle, or a Sony Walkman. In his refrigerator there would be no Perrier or tasteless cheese from France.

He believed in simple pleasures, and he believed in simple accommodations. Mary Ellen had shared those values.

This was to have been the family home for as long as the family existed—the place Patricia would always think of when, as an adult, she looked back on her childhood. It was a good place in a good location—only a few blocks from Temple Stadium, where they had taken Patricia on Saturdays as a child to watch the Temple Owls get waffled by teams like the University of Delaware and Bucknell. Now Temple played in Division One, against Penn State. They got waffled by a better class of opponent, and they mostly did it downtown, in Veterans Stadium.

Still, the house was the same—close to Mary Ellen's teaching job in suburban Cheltenham, far enough away from bad neighborhoods to be secure. The house was still home to Murphy, even though he didn't live here anymore. And at this moment, he wished he did. He truly wished he did.

The starkness of this realization depressed him, and he went inside to pour some coffee. He also called the vet's, early or not, and to his surprise the vet himself answered.

"You're in early," Murphy said, "especially for a Sunday. This is Frank Murphy. I'm calling about my dog."

"He's hanging on, Mr. Murphy. I've dressed all his wounds, and the abdominal wound wasn't as bad as it looked. I just shoved everything back in there and sewed him up. The big fears now are shock and infection. We're pumping him full of antibiotics, and we're keeping our fingers crossed."

"How long before you have an idea?"

"We should have some idea by Wednesday or Thursday. He's going to be here with us for a while under the best of circumstances, I'm afraid."

"Thank you, Doctor. I'll stay in touch."

Mary Ellen entered the kitchen as Murphy hung up the phone.

"Winston?" she asked.

"He's still hanging in there. There's some coffee on."

Mary Ellen, in a robe but with her hair nicely arranged, poured a cup of coffee as Murphy sat down at the kitchen table with the *Inquirer*. She sat down across from him.

"I feel sorry about Winston, Frank," she said. "I know how much you love that dog."

"Well, he's pretty tough. He might make it."

"Patricia is badly shaken up over all this. I heard her crying in bed last night, after we went up."

"I did, too. The kid never learned to cry quietly. She always has had a howl like an air raid siren."

Mary Ellen smiled. Even without makeup and closing in on forty, she was an extraordinarily pretty woman. She could pass without hardship for a woman ten years younger, Murphy realized.

"I haven't seen you smile at anything I've said in a long time," he said to her.

"Somehow, you haven't been amusing for a while. You used to be. You used to be able to make me laugh all the time."

"Maybe you just lost your sense of humor."

"Possibly," she conceded. "And maybe your sense of humor changed, got more of an edge to it."

"That could be, too. We just had too much going on,

with Patricia and your work and my work and going to school all the time, both of us. How far are you from your doctorate now?"

"Another nine credits and my thesis."

"Doctor Murphy," he said. "The first doctor in the family."

"You have a doctorate. You have a J.D."

"Yeah, but that's not really a doctorate. All it is is a trade certificate, really."

"You're having a really tough time in this practice, aren't you?"

"Not that bad. I'm paying my bills, at least. I find myself doing an awful lot of civil work for cops—divorces and wills and real estate closings. I've had one or two decent criminal cases. Nothing big yet, although I have something going now that looks like it might be big. I'd like to get something in product liability or personal injury. That's where the real big money is unless you're politically connected, and I'm not. I know a lot of people, but I've never done any work for the party, and I'm not anxious to, either. The business is coming in, slowly but surely. In a few years, I should have a decent enough practice for one guy. It beats the DA's office, believe me. It beats the Major Crimes unit, and it beats working for Fletcher Lake by a country mile."

"Tell me about this case you have that might be big," she said.

When they had lived together, Murphy had often talked about his work to Mary Ellen. He hadn't told her every detail, of course—the details of detective work in a big city usually were not the sort of thing that made for pleasant pillow talk—but he'd always enjoyed discussing with her the investigative aspects of his job, the running down of leads, the reading of personalities, the deductive thought processes that led to the solving of crimes. And Mary Ellen had often been helpful in that process. She possessed a shrewd intuition, and she could often predict a suspect's response to a given situation just from Murphy's description. He wished he had been able to talk over with her the case of the stomper murders around last Christmas. Maybe he wouldn't have ended up with a broken collarbone and a couple of cracked ribs making the collar. It seemed strange to him to hold such a discussion now, when he had grown so accustomed to keeping his own counsel.

"I have a client, a woman named Carol Highland. She lives with her husband out on the Main Line. He's a college professor, and his mother lives with them."

"That sounds like trouble already," Mary Ellen said.

"It is," Murphy told her, then he went into the details of the case—Carol's affair with her principal, Hank Kirby's murder, Wilder's involvement. Mary Ellen listened attentively, asking only a few terse questions.

"Do you think Jim is going to charge her?" she asked finally.

"I'd be surprised if he didn't. He has enough to get an indictment. First he'll have to go through a preliminary hearing to see if a judge will let the DA's office present the case to a grand jury, but that shouldn't be any problem for them. My problem is that I'm way behind on all this. I should be out investigating the case to see what they have and what they might have missed, and I haven't had time with all this business with Rhino Frost."

"Do you think she did it?" Mary Ellen asked.

He shrugged. "I don't know. Frankly, I don't think so. That's only instinct, though. I've got to find out a lot more before I can make a definitive judgment. And then I'd have to have enough so I could convince a jury. They're going to come to me with a plea bargain after they get their indictment, and unless I have another theory of the crime with evidence to back it up, I'm going to be hard pressed to refuse to offer it to her."

"Even though you don't really think she did it?"

He looked at his wife. "You really don't understand. Once a case like this is opened, Wilder and Toddman and everybody else is under severe pressure to clear it, to get it off the books—especially when Fletcher Lake is the DA. Fletcher isn't interested in justice; he wants convictions. He figures that kind of record will get him into the governor's mansion or maybe into the Senate. Toddman and Wilder don't know if she did it, either, but they want to think she did because it gives them a target. The most frustrating thing in the world is to have an open case and no target. What they do—what I did when I was on that side—is they look at the evidence and say, who's the likeliest suspect? Are there any other logical explanations? And if they get a no to that second question, they go after somebody, balls out. Most of the time they're right, too. That reminds me, I've got to call my answering machine. I left Carol my numbers, but I didn't leave her this number because I didn't expect to be here."

Murphy reached for the wall phone next to the kitchen table and dialed his home phone. He heard his own voice come on the line. "Hello. This is Frank Murphy. I can't come to the phone right now, but I'll get right back to you if you'll leave your name and number after the beep." Then came the beep. Murphy hit his own pocket beeper, the one that made his messages play back to him when he sounded it into the phone. Then came this:

"Mr. Murphy, this is Carol Highland. The police were just here. I did what you said. I refused to talk to them without you present. They're taking me—"

The message ran out.

"Oh, shit," Murphy said.

"What's the matter?" Mary Ellen asked him.

"Hold on," he said, dialing again.

"Hello."

"Mr. Highland? Frank Murphy."

"We've been trying to reach you since late last night, Mr. Murphy. The police were here."

"I'm sorry. I've been out of pocket. I just called my answering machine. Where's Carol?"

"She's in police custody downtown. They took her down after she said she wouldn't talk to them. They let her call you, but you weren't there. I've been here trying to reach you ever since. I must have gotten your answering machine a dozen times. I've been going out of my mind, Mr. Murphy."

"I'll go right down there and get her out," Murphy said.

"Please do," Everett Highland said coldly.

Murphy hung up. "Wilder's got Carol."

"Well, you'd better go, then."

"Give my love to Patricia," he told her, heading for the door.

"Frank," Mary Ellen called to him.

"What?" Murphy's tone was harsh. He was kicking

himself mentally.

"What about this Frost character?"

"Keep the doors and windows locked, and be careful. I'm going to have somebody watching him by tonight if I have to hire somebody to do it. I'd rather have Wilder do it, though. I'll take care of Rhino one way or the other."

"Be careful yourself," Mary Ellen said.

Murphy looked at her and sighed. He wanted to kiss her good-bye. He knew better, though.

"Don't worry too much about me," he said as he left.

And he wasn't sure she would, either.

Murphy found Carol Highland in an interrogation room in the basement of the Roundhouse and got her into an office down the hall. Then he went back to the interrogation room to see how much damage had been done. Wilder had left just before Murphy's arrival, taking off for the morning and planning to come back in the afternoon, if Murphy didn't show up to spring the suspect. Since Wilder's departure, questioning had been handled by O'Connell, playing the bad guy, and Zsa Zsa, playing the understanding, sisterly sort. Carol Highland's face was badly drawn, and there were dark circles under her eyes. She'd been in interrogation for many hours now. Murphy was livid.

"I hope you Mirandaed her," he steamed at Zsa Zsa.

Zsa Zsa was a hard-nosed little woman in her early thirties with big, brown eyes that men wanted to do swan dives into. She had a dark skullcap of hair and favored hoop earrings. She was one of the best detective firsts on the force, and she was deadly in interrogation, Murphy knew. Zsa Zsa could charm a statue, and she turned it on Murphy now, who was largely immune to it.

"She's okay, Frank," Zsa Zsa said soothingly. "All we've done is talk a bit, that's all. We wanted to find out what she knew."

"You were hoping she'd spill her guts," Murphy said. "And you know, I'm sure, that nothing you got out of her is worth shit because I wasn't here."

"Well, we didn't get diddley-squat, anyway," O'Connell said. "And we did Miranda her, by the way. We Miranda everybody."

Murphy shook his finger at Zsa Zsa. "I'm telling you now—and you can tell Wilder—that you're not even to ask her her fucking name unless I'm on hand. You know the rules."

Zsa Zsa smiled. Her teeth were white and even. "I know what I was taught," she said smoothly. "And I know who taught me."

"Well," Murphy said lamely, "that was then, and this is now."

"When do we take depositions on my divorce?" Zsa Zsa asked him, switching topics after having made her point.

"I was going to do it this week," Murphy said, "but I don't know now. This case is going to take priority, Zsa Zsa."

She frowned. "I may have to find myself a new lawyer, then."

Murphy was pissed, and it showed. "Get yourself any lawyer you want then, goddamn it. Just tell me who to send the paperwork to. I don't need this shit, Zsa Zsa. This isn't some West Philly social note. This woman is a solid citizen, and you don't treat people like this. Has Wilder lost his mind, for Christ's sake?"

"Why don't you call him yourself?" O'Connell suggested. "He ought to be home by now. We're just following orders, Frank. You don't have to jump all over us."

"I'll use the phone in the office where I've put Carol."

"You can leave your quarter on the desk," Zsa Zsa told him. "It's a city phone."

Murphy glared at her. "I can see why you can't stay married."

"Like you can?" she said with an evil grin. "When are we going to have the depositions, seriously?"

"I don't know. Call me Monday. It depends on how complicated this gets. And it's going to get pretty complicated if you guys keep on pulling this kind of shit on me."

Murphy went down the hall to Carol. She was sitting in a metal chair covered in green vinyl, standard city issue. "Are you all right? Did you say anything to them? Anything at all?"

She shook her head. "All I did was keep on telling them that I wouldn't say anything without my lawyer present. And I told them to charge me or let me go. They didn't do either. That lieutenant, the black guy, he's absolutely vicious. And so is that other guy in there. The woman, she's all right, though."

"She's a viper," Murphy said. "Did you say anything to her?"

Carol looked at the floor. "Well, when we were alone for a while, she started talking about her first husband, about what a louse he was. He beat her up, you know. So I told her a little about Hank, then."

171

"Told her what?"

"How he used to knock me around when he was high. I told her things like that."

"Things like that?" Murphy muttered. "They call that sort of thing motive, Carol. I knew her first husband. He was the one who used to get knocked around. She's a second-degree black belt in karate. Zsa Zsa could kick the shit out of me and six other guys my size without working up a sweat. You just sit there and relax. I've got a call to make."

He went into the next office and dialed Wilder's number. Annabelle came on the phone.

"It's Frank, Annabelle. Is he in yet?"

"Just came in. I'll get him for you. How's it going, Frank?"

"Just ducky," he told her.

Wilder came on the phone. "Hello."

"Hello, scumbag."

"Frank. Great to hear from you."

"Guess where I am right now."

"I'd rather know where you've been. Your client was trying to reach you for hours. Pick up on some debutante and show her your stuff, did you? Murphy, you dog, you."

"I'm taking my client out of here right now. And I'm serving official notice on the department. You can't talk to her. She'd under no obligation to speak to you, and she's not going to."

"Not unless she's charged. That's right."

"Are you going to charge her?"

"That's up to Toddman. I'll let you know tomorrow. Just tell your client to stay close to home. And to keep her toothbrush packed."

172

"I'll do that. I want you to do me a favor, too."

"Anything for an old buddy, Frank."

"Frost. Take care of him for me. Plant something on him. Do what you have to do. I'd do it myself, only I'm off the force now."

"Shit," Wilder said. "I've already got Quick Silver on my ass. I can't do it, Frank. We could never make it stick a second time, not after we already bumped into Silver on this. It just wouldn't fly."

"He got Winston."

"Got Winston? What are you talking about?"

"Yesterday morning, in Rittenhouse Square. Patricia took him for a walk, and Frost went after him with a knife. Winston is in bad shape, Jim. I'm just lucky it wasn't Patricia. That's the message I get."

"I can't," Wilder said. "Have you thought about Catrelli? He could use the business."

"I thought about him. I guess it'll have to be him if you really can't do it."

"He might be more useful to you, if you know what I mean."

"It might come to that, then."

"Keep me posted," Wilder said.

"I will. And remember what I said about the Highland woman."

"You'll hear from me on that."

"I'm sure," Murphy said, and hung up.

He stood up to go next door and pick up Carol. As he left, he frowned, dug into his pocket, and tossed a quarter on the desk next to the phone.

CHAPTER FOURTEEN

Driving a weeping Carol Highland out the Schuylkill Expressway in his Toronado, Murphy encountered a man in a Honda Civic hogging the far left hand lane and driving fifty-five. The Honda was like cholesterol in the vein of a major highway, slowing progress.

Murphy would never have owned a Honda Civic, not even as a joke—unless he could rig it up some way to function as a riding lawn mower. What he liked best about the Toronado was that it seemed to terrify the drivers of Honda Civics and other cars of their ilk. The Toronado roared up behind them and sat there on their tails, like some kind of enormous creature from Detroit that feasted daily on Honda Civics and spit out their grilles.

"Get over, schmuck," Murphy muttered.

"What?" Carol Highland said.

"Nothing," Murphy told her, and pulled the Toronado up until it sat virtually on the rear bumper of the Honda Civic, only inches away. Murphy grinned an evil grin. This had been a rough day so far. Now it was time for a little fun.

Murphy leaned on the horn. The Honda Civic driver

glanced in his mirror and gave Murphy the finger. Murphy frowned. The Civic driver was doing precisely fifty-five—no more, no less. Murphy's car had power windows, power seats, a tape deck, air-conditioning, and cruise control. It had a long list of options that were essentially useless in the sorts of traffic situations he encountered every time he got behind the wheel.

What Murphy wished he had was a series of buttons on the dashboard. Button one would flash a sign to people who, like him, were tailgating. The sign would say, "Hey, Asshole, You're Too Close." Button two he would push if the driver ignored the sign. Button two would be his oil slick. The oil slick would drop out behind his car on the pavement, and the asshole who was tailing him would hit it and lose control and slide into the median divider, which would teach him to mess with Frank Murphy.

Button three would be Murphy's favorite. That would be the button that would launch Murphy's heat-seeking missile. This missile would roar out from under the engine of Murphy's Toronado and turn a car like the Honda Civic in front of him into a flower of oily flame. Then Murphy would casually pull to the right and pass the smoking hulk and punch on his Tony Bennett tape, so he could hear Bennett sing "When Joanna Loved Me." Now, there was an option he could use.

Only he didn't have it now, and he was stuck behind this stupid bastard in the Honda Civic who thought the speed limit was really fifty-five. Murphy didn't know what the speed limit was. Nobody did. This was a secret known only to traffic cops. Maybe it was fifty-five in the slow lane. Maybe it was fifty-five in Nebraska or somewhere. But the speed limit in the far left-hand lane of the Schuylkill Expressway was not fifty-five. It was sixty-five—maybe seventy, depending on the mood of the cops on a particular day. But fifty-five it wasn't. Not ever. Murphy wouldn't expect a dumb bastard in a Honda Civic to know that. He wished he had his heat-seeking missile. As it was, he was forced to move into the middle lane and roar by the asshole in the Honda Civic and give him the finger back.

Once past the Honda, Murphy began to settle down. There was something about the act of driving that drove every vestige of civilization out of him. Driving was a private thing, usually done when no one else was around, and it occurred to him that once behind the wheel—in the anonymity of his car—he lost all the civility he had accumulated in nearly forty-five years of life. He thought violent thoughts that would never have occurred to him in another setting, and he knew it happened to everybody. It was a wonder more people didn't die on the road, he thought. The lengths to which we all go to get from one place to the other in two or three fewer minutes. Darwin's law had never taken the automobile into account. If it had, his book would never have been published, because twentieth-century man invariably reverted to Neanderthal man with only the flick of a key.

Carol Highland was utterly silent as they drove, and Murphy had little to say as well. He was furious at himself, furious at Wilder, furious at Zsa Zsa, furious at life in general. As they pulled into the driveway of the big house in Paoli, Carol Highland said, "What's going to happen to me?"

Murphy killed the engine and said, "I think they're probably going to charge you with Hank Kirby's

176

murder. Your prints are there. They apparently have nowhere else to go."

Her eyes filled. She opened the car door silently and ran into the house. Murphy got out and followed, acutely conscious that he was wearing yesterday's clothes and had missed his morning shower. Wouldn't he make a hit, though?

Everett Highland and his mother were in the vestibule.

"Mrs. Highland," Murphy nodded. Then he stuck his hand out to Carol's husband. "I'm Frank Murphy."

Highland shook the outstretched hand absentmindedly, then he said, "Excuse me. Carol went upstairs. I have to go up after her. Is she all right?"

"Just fine," Murphy said. "They only wanted to ask her a few questions."

"I think I'll go up anyway. Pardon me, Mr. Murphy."

Highland climbed the stairs and disappeared. Murphy found himself in the vestibule of the big house with Highland's mother. They eyed each other awkwardly, suspiciously. This was, Murphy supposed, as good a time as any.

"Could I talk to you for a few minutes, Mrs. Highland?" he asked.

She fixed him with a level gaze. "If you insist. Won't you come into the kitchen, Mr. Murphy? I was just fixing some coffee."

"I could use some."

The kitchen of the Highland home was as large as the living room of Murphy's former home in Mount Airy, all copper-bottomed pans and white Formica cabinets with blond wood trim. It was well appointed and neatly kept. Coffee bubbled from a Mister Coffee machine on the counter. It was, Murphy noted, a more expensive model than his. That figured.

"How do you take your coffee, Mr. Murphy?"

"Cream and sugar. Sweet 'N Low, if you've got it. Every little bit helps. A moment on the lips, a lifetime on the hips. That's what they say."

Everett Highland's mother did not laugh. "Cream and sugar are on the table, Mr. Murphy."

"Call me Frank, please," Murphy said. "What's your first name, Mrs. Highland?"

She looked at him quizzically. Murphy said nothing. It was important for him to have this woman's first name. She was so superior in her manner, and he was going to question her now. It would be useful if they were on a first-name basis. Even if she didn't want to call him by his first name, he would use hers. It would give him an advantage, an edge. The use of her first name would make her somewhat ill at ease, and that's what Murphy was after. The use of his first name, on the other hand, would give him an intimacy neither of them could avoid. It was an old cop trick, and it worked unfailingly.

"Margaret," she said.

Murphy sipped his coffee. "Good coffee, Margaret. Very good."

She sat down across from him. "Thank you."

"Tell me about the other night," Murphy told her.

"Which night was that?"

"The night of the Kirby murder, Margaret. You know which night, I think."

She looked down at the tabletop. "Yes, I know which night that was."

"Tell me," Murphy said, "what you all were doing."

178

Margaret Highland said. "I was asleep. I tend to go to bed early. It's been my habit since my husband's death. I read a little, then I go to sleep."

"It sounds like a peaceful routine."

"Yes, it is. I'm past sixty, Mr. Murphy. I've had a difficult life. Peace is what I'm after. Live long enough and it'll happen to you, too."

He laughed. "It already has. You seem to have found it, though."

"Jesus has helped me in that."

"Do you mind if I smoke?"

"Go ahead. They're your lungs, aren't they?"

"Thank you," Murphy said, lighting a Camel. "You used to smoke, didn't you?"

"Yes. How did you know that?"

"Just a guess. Ex-smokers seem less neurotic on the topic. Either that or more neurotic. If you weren't an ex-smoker, you'd probably have said no. If you were one of the neurotic ex-smokers, you'd have been horrified at the question. There's seldom an in-between. Your daughter-in-law, for instance, she's one of the neurotic ex-smokers."

"You're quite right. Carol used to smoke Marlboros. She stopped right after she married Everett."

Murphy studied the older woman. "You don't like her much, do you?"

Margaret Highland stiffened. "That's a presumptuous question, Mr. Murphy."

He nodded. "I know it is. Ordinarily, I wouldn't bring it up, but the cops will probably be here in the morning to place her under arrest for Kirby's murder. It seems to me that under circumstances like that certain niceties call out to be set aside, Margaret. Since

179

I'm going to have to defend her, I'd sort of like to know for sure where everybody stands. I'm sure you understand the need for that."

"Should I expect to be called upon to testify?"

"It's possible. Now, you don't like her much, do you?"

Margaret Highland took a sip of her coffee. "We're not close, if that's what you mean. But I love Carol, Mr. Murphy. I love her despite her sins, despite her failings. It's my Christian duty."

"Did you hear anybody leave this house the other night?"

"I did not."

"Did you hear a car door open or close?"

"No."

"Did you hear a loud sound of any sort?"

"I was asleep."

"You heard nothing in the early hours of the morning?"

"No."

"A car backfire? Anything?"

"I might have heard a car backfire."

"What time?"

"I can't say."

"Is there an ashtray around here?"

"Let me get you one."

She went to a kitchen cabinet and brought out a small, ceramic ashtray. She put it in front of Murphy and sat down again.

"What's your objection to Carol?" Murphy demanded.

"She's not the sort of woman I'd hoped Everett would marry. I've always known it. When I found out the other night that she'd been married before and somehow neglected to mention it to my son my suspicions were confirmed. She's not a woman of particularly good character, Mr. Murphy, and that troubles me because I love my son very much. Since his father's death, Everett is all I have."

"Tell me about your husband, Margaret."

She leaned forward and smiled slightly. "My husband was a very fine man. He came from a good family that had lost much of its money. He worked his way through Yale and he made most of the money back in residential real estate. He was a good salesman, Mr. Murphy, a man with push and drive."

"Does Everett have push and drive, would you say?"

"Not like his father, no. But he has a good many qualities his father never had. He's gentle. Arthur never was. Everett is sensitive and warm. Arthur was rather gruff in his later years—except with me. Even after we found Jesus together, Arthur was never a warm man, Mr. Murphy."

"Everett, I take it, hasn't found Jesus yet."

"No, not in just that fashion. But Everett lives a gentle life, and Jesus valued gentility."

"What kind of car do you drive, Margaret?"

"I drive a Cadillac."

"What color?"

"It's brown. Tan, actually."

"Would you rather your son had married someone else?"

"Yes."

"Were you angry that he married Carol?"

She thought about the question. "Not angry, exactly. Jesus teaches us that anger is a temptation."

Murphy leaned back in his chair. "You're too good to be true, Margaret."

She smiled at him slightly. "You don't think much of my faith, do you, Mr. Murphy."

"Frank, please. No, I think everybody is entitled to believe what he or she finds most comfortable."

"What do you believe in, Frank?"

Murphy pondered the question. Then he said, "I was brought up Catholic. You may or may not know what that means, given your own background. I suspect you don't. Let me tell you what I was taught. I was taught that if you forgot what day it was and ate meat on Friday, that was a venial sin. If you knew what day it was and ate meat anyway, that was a mortal sin. You got into deep, deep trouble for that. We were talking purgatory at the very least, and that was only if you got to confession. If you got hit by a truck on the way to confession before you got to bare your soul, that was tough luck. We are talking Hell there. Then, one day, somebody decided that it wasn't a sin to eat meat on Friday—not a venial sin, not a mortal sin. And I was left to wonder what happened to all those poor bastards who got hit by the truck. I still haven't figured it out. Are they still in Hell? You could argue it either way. I could be defense counsel or prosecutor on that one."

"That sounds very cynical."

Murphy shook his head. "Not cynical. Just confused. You see, I never even knew who to pray to for sure. You could pray to God, but which God? Father or son? And did you really need to pray to God if you could pray to his mother to make your case for you? Who was he more likely to listen to, you or her? And if you weren't sure where you stood with her, you could pray to this saint or that saint. Saint Jude was a good catchall. He's the patron saint of the hopeless. He's always a good saint if you're feeling particularly down. You see how confusing it all is, Margaret?"

She frowned slightly. "You're a humanist, Mr. Murphy—"

"—Frank.'

"—Frank, then. You're a humanist just the same."

"But I'm not," Murphy assured her. "I believe in a supreme being. I'm just not sure what I believe about him. Or her. That's always a possibility, too."

Margaret Highland pursed her lips. "You must look upon people with my faith as slightly ridiculous."

"Not at all," Murphy said. "One thing about fundamentalists—and I presume you don't mind being lumped into that category—it's not your kids who are out taking drugs and knocking over Seven-Elevens. It's not your kids out smoking crack or mainlining smack. That's not the objection people have to the Christian movement."

"And what is the objection? Your objection, that is."

He held his hands open wide in protest. "My objection? Wrong. I have no objection. I am tolerance personified, Margaret, believe me. But some people will say that the problem with born-agains is that they insist on hitting everybody over the head with their beliefs. They insist on everybody believing what they believe."

"I don't insist on that," Margaret Highland said.

"No? Isn't that one of your objections to Carol, that she doesn't share your beliefs?"

She thought about her response. "Yes. That's one of

them. All I want her to understand is the beauty of Christ's love. If she'd just give it a chance . . ."

"You want to share it with her."

"Yes. That's it exactly."

"And if she's not interested?"

"Well, she doesn't seem to be."

"So she's a sinner?"

"Aren't we all?" Margaret Highland asked.

"Some of us are bigger sinners than others."

She looked across the table at Murphy. "You regard me as a suspect, don't you, Frank?"

Murphy drew on his Camel. "Margaret, the only thing I know for sure is that I didn't kill the guy. With anybody else, I can't be sure."

CHAPTER FIFTEEN

When Murphy got home from the Highland house, there was a message on his answering machine. It was from the vet. Murphy called.

"I'm sorry," the vet told him. "Your dog died late this afternoon."

Murphy said nothing for a moment. He merely took a slow, deep breath. Then he said, "I wonder if you'd be kind enough to make arrangements for burial? There's a pet cemetery on Route 73 over in Jersey . . ."

"I know the place. Petlawn, it's called."

"You can have him buried there. It's not far from the mall in Moorestown where I bought him as a pup. I'll call the Petlawn people later about a stone."

"I'm sorry, Mr. Murphy. We did all we could. He was badly injured."

"I know. I know. I appreciate it, Doctor. Send me a bill, please, and include whatever expenses are incurred in the burial. You've got the address. And thank you."

Murphy hung up. Then he dug out his address book and dialed a number.

"Yeah?"

"Cantrelli?"

"Yeah. Who's this?"

"Frank Murphy. How are you doing?"

"Frank? How you doing, my man?"

"I've been better. I've got some business for you. Could you be at my office tomorrow morning, about nine? I'm in the Fidelity Bank Building."

"Gee, that's pretty early . . . Hey, shut up in there. I'm talking. Sorry, I didn't mean you, Frank. Nine, you said?"

"If you could. It's important."

"Well, gee, it's early and all. But what the hell? I'll be there."

"Good, Dom," Murphy said. "See you then."

Murphy hung up the phone and rubbed his eyes with the heels of his hands. He felt weary and worn. He went into the kitchen, dropped ice cubes into a tumbler, and filled the spaces around them with bourbon, all the way to the rim. He sat on the living-room sofa and turned on the TV set with his remote control. It was Sunday night, and there wasn't much on. He considered calling Mary Ellen and Patricia and giving them the news. Then he chickened out. Tomorrow would be soon enough for that.

Shane was on one of the cable stations. Murphy had seen it a dozen times. He had tuned in just as Jack Palance was gunning down Elisha Cook, Jr., in the mud outside the saloon and the Scandinavian guy was getting ready to drag the body away to his wagon. Jack Palance looked down at the corpse in the mud and laughed his devilish laugh. Murphy watched that for a while and sipped his bourbon and tried to light a cigarette. He couldn't manage it.

186

Alone and very quietly, Frank Murphy wept for Winston Churchill.

Graterford Correctional Facility, 1974

Graterford's warden felt strongly that violence within the institution could be reduced if as many inmates as possible could be housed with members of their own race. He had arrived at this conviction after several incidents in which white inmates housed with black ones, or the reverse, had been beaten or raped—usually both—within hours of their arrival in their new home.

Rhino Frost's new home consisted of a windowless twelve-by-fifteen-foot room on the third tier. He shared it with a smallish, skinny-armed robber from Pittsburgh and a fat biker from suburban Philadelphia who had beaten his half brother to death in a dispute over a woman. Few men in prison were referred to by more than a single name, usually their surname, and those who were not addressed by their last name were generally known by a nickname. This was especially true of bikers, virtually all of whom had been identified only by nicknames on the street. So it was that Robert James Poulson, armed robber and recovering alcoholic, was known simply as Poulson. William George Stopinski Jr., who would have been a murderer had not a soft-hearted Delaware County DA agreed to a plea bargain for manslaughter, was known as Bear. And Wendell Charles Frost was known as Rhino, his old street name.

Poulson was a quiet, flint-eyed youth of twenty who went faithfully every other night to a meeting of the prison chapter of Alcoholics Anonymous. He was nine months into an eighteen-month sentence—less, if he behaved—and he spent virtually ever moment sleeping, working in the kitchen, writing letters to his wife, and watching television. He never laughed, seldom spoke, and avoided all possible human contact in prison. Despite his small, slight frame, no one messed with him. Poulson was spared from molestation because of an incident that had convinced all who knew him that he was crazy.

During his first two weeks in Graterford, a lifer who also worked in the kitchen had reached out one day and rubbed his upper leg.

"I'm hip to your fine ass, bitch," the lifer had said.

Poulson had gone after the man with a butcher knife. He had been pulled away—literally foaming at the mouth—before doing serious damage, but the word had gone out quickly that Poulson was a whacko.

"You got three kinds of people in here," Poulson told Frost during his first night in the cell. "You got the oppressors. They rob guys and push them around and do what they want with them. You got the victims— guys who decide they need a protector and let him do what he wants if he keeps other guys away from him. And you got those motherfuckers so crazy that nobody will mess with them. I don't want to be either of the first two kinds. And if I've got to kill somebody to prove that I'm one of the last kind, then I'll do it. I'd rather stay in here until they put me in a coffin than have some jocker sticking it up my ass every night while I'm here. I ain't big, but I'll die to keep my manhood. And people know it."

Poulson had told the story for a reason, Frost realized, and he had wasted his breath. Frost had no interest in him. His sentence was a long one, but Frost would not have sex with another man. He was no faggot, and he wouldn't let Graterford turn him into one.

After Poulson said his piece, he turned his back to Frost and ignored him, as he did everyone else. Bear was another matter entirely. He was a gregarious man, and he recognized Frost for what he was, another biker, another outlaw. On the outside, Bear had been a Warlock and Frost had been a Demon, members of warring gangs. In Graterford, the two men felt a kinship.

"You ought to join the club," Bear had urged Frost as the two men lay on Bear's bunk, smoking dope beneath pinups of naked, spread-eagled women and Harley-Davidson posters. "Join the club and nobody's going to mess with you."

"I don't need a club," Frost said. "Anybody who messes with me is going to go to the infirmary."

"You were in a club on the outside," Bear pointed out.

"Not toward the end. The Demons turned into a bunch of pussies. I quit the club. And I'm not joining it here, neither."

"Have it your way, man," Bear said, dragging deeply.

Bear was slightly older than Frost. He had been in prison since his early twenties and planned to get out in his mid-thirties, barring mishap. He was a shade under

189

six feet and weighed nearly three hundred pounds. He ate prodigiously, and he smoked marijuana constantly, which he willingly shared with Frost. Poulson refused to smoke weed, and he refused in particular to drink the wine that was distilled on a regular basis by the other kitchen workers, using fruits and jams and jellies and baker's yeast.

"Where do you get all this weed?" Frost asked Bear during his third night in the cell.

"My old lady brings it in when she visits me."

"You got an old lady?" Frost asked in surprise. "You still got an old lady on the outside after all these years?"

Bear took a toke. "This is a new old lady. The other one split a long time ago. This new old lady—her name's Shirley—she started writing to me after I put an ad in the classified section of the newspaper asking for somebody to write. She started visiting me after that. She digs me, man. Shirley digs inmates. I'm her third old man in here."

"What's she like?"

"Old. She's about forty-five. She's a librarian, and she ain't too pretty. But she brings me weed and keeps me company, and we get off once in a while in the visiting room."

"How?" Frost demanded.

"How what?"

"How both of them? First, how does she bring in the weed?"

Bear grinned, displaying yellowed teeth and gaps teeth had once occupied. "She brings it in with her in her snatch, in a balloon. Then she goes to the john and takes it out and puts it in her mouth. Then I kiss her, and I take the balloon in my mouth, and I go

190

to the john. I take the balloon and stick it up my butt, man. After visiting hours, the guards make some dudes strip down and they look up their asses, but they can't do that with everybody, and they don't want to, neither. That's how most of the dope gets in here. All the old ladies do that. Hell, there's all kinds of shit in here. The Man knows it, too. Take away the dope and The Man's got a riot on his hands, so The Man don't try so hard to keep it out. Shit, guys get dope in canned goods. They get it in Christmas presents. It comes in all the time, man. There's more shit in here than there is out on the street."

Frost smiled slightly. "How do I get me an old lady like that?"

Bear shrugged. "You got to be a lady-killer, like me. All the chicks dig old Bear."

It quickly dawned on Frost that neither Bear nor Poulson would be his real companions in prison. His only constant companion would be boredom. His prison counselor assigned him to work in the carpentry shop, making furniture for state offices. But the reality was that there were too few jobs and too many convicts. Frost spent most of his time sleeping in his cell, watching television in the dayroom or sitting around the prison exercise yard. After a week, when he had learned all there was to know about Graterford, the boredom rested on him like a weight. He took to showering several times daily. The ritual of washing his huge body, rubbing it dry, and changing from one set of prison clothes to the other gave him something to do.

"A dude can get himself too clean," Bear told him one night as he toweled himself off in the cell. "A little stink is good for a man."

Frost looked at him quizzically. "What are you talking about?"

"You wash too much. Washing that much is a nasty habit."

Frost shook his head at the fat man. "You're nuts."

Bear went back to his pornographic magazine. Such reading matter was common in Graterford. It was brought in by visitors, mailed in, even carried on the racks of the prison store. The prison administration felt it was harmless enough, even a release for men without women, although publications that catered to violent tastes—military magazines, for example, with their back-page ads for guns and edged weapons of all description—were strictly banned. And, unlike the ban on drugs, this one was more or less enforced.

Within a few weeks, Frost had developed regular habits in the showers. He would strip in his cell, wrap a towel around his ample middle, and wander down to the shower. He would stand under the stream of warm water and pretend he was somewhere else, anywhere else. His stomach full, his muscles relaxing from the massage of water, he could almost believe it. He would lose himself in his reverie, thinking about the joy of riding his pan-head Harley—the one he knew his mother had already sold while he had been in Holmesburg. He would lose himself, remember, dream.

So when the attack came, it caught him totally by surprise.

He had been in the shower after a heavy dinner of chili and salad, almost asleep under the stream of water, when he felt the hands on him. His eyes had opened, and he had begun to turn, but then a blow had caught him near his remaining testicle, and he had hit the floor, hands over his scrotum to protect himself. Then he felt them on him, perhaps a dozen men. He could hear their voices, thought he recognized some of them. They knelt on his back, on his legs, on his shoulders, on his neck. As big and powerful as he was, Rhino Frost was immobilized by the sheer weight of them, by their numbers. They had taken him totally unprepared, and he hadn't had time to mount the sort of defense of which he was capable.

"What the fu—" he started to say, but they shoved his face in the water, and he had to struggle to keep from drowning. The shower sprayed down on all of them. He tried to shake free, but he felt a hard blow to his ribs, and his breath left him. He lay there in the water, gasping for air, pinned down by hard knees and elbows and tightly gripped hands.

"You just hold still, man," he heard a voice say.

Then he felt a warm body pressing on his buttocks. And he felt something pressing hard between his cheeks.

"No!" Rhino Frost got out.

And than a fist slammed his face against the concrete floor of the shower. Hands tightened on him. How many of them were there? Jesus, there must be twenty of them. He couldn't budge.

He felt the rapist enter him. The rapist entered Frost wtih great force, jamming into him. Frost let loose a pained shriek. He felt he would be torn apart. He couldn't move a muscle. He struggled against the intrusion, tightened as much as he could.

"Ah," the voice said, "I dig that, man. Do that some more."

Then the rapist began to move. He drove in hard. Frost, immobile and helpless, felt him finish quickly, then be replaced by another. Frost tried to fight, but there were too many of them. Too many, just too many.

Eventually, Rhino Frost began to weep as they raped him, his tears mixing with the shower water. He counted them as they came out and entered. All in all, there were twenty-two. One of them he recognized from his voice, from his grunts of pleasure and triumph.

It was Bear.

When they were finished, they left him there on the shower floor. Frost made no attempt to rise and fight them. He was beaten. It was a new experience for him. Later he came back to the cell. Poulson slept on his bunk, his back turned to his cellmates. Bear lay hairy and naked on his bunk, leafing through *Hustler*. Frost put on his shorts and climbed into his bunk. He lay unmoving and silent for a long time.

Then Bear said, "You really ought to join the club, man. I tried to tell you that. You ought to trust old Bear. Old Bear wouldn't steer you wrong."

"All right," Frost said quietly. "I'll join."

Bear's bearded face split into a broad grin. "That's my man," he said.

That was the end of talk for that night. Lights out came soon after, and the barred door to the cell slammed shut automatically, controlled by remote hands at the end of the cellblock. The sound of all those doors slamming at once awakened Poulson, who rolled over with a muttered, "Shit."

Soon Poulson went back to sleep. After a while,

Rhino Frost could hear Bear's snoring. Frost did not sleep that night until very near morning. He lay awake in his bunk, his mind working. He thought of what had happened in the shower. He thought about the life that faced him there.

He thought, too, about Frank Murphy.

CHAPTER SIXTEEN

Dominic Catrelli, absently stroking his bushy mustache, sat at the counter sipping coffee and watching the waitress. The waitress wore a name tag that said "Linda." Catrelli wore a T-shirt that said "Mustache Rides, $1."

Catrelli fondled his mustache. He also fondled his Charter Arms Bulldog .44-caliber pistol, which rested in a holster under his windbreaker. The windbreaker made the gun reasonably unobtrusive but no less useful in a pinch. In his wallet, Catrelli had a permit to carry the pistol. The permit was nestled right next to his private detective's license. He would rather be carrying the gold shield he had carried until four years before, but the P.I.'s license was good enough. And working as a private detective was more lucrative than the gold shield had ever been, even when Catrelli had been attached to the Center City precinct and there had been an abundance of pimps and B-girls to shake down.

Frank Murphy was paying him a bargain rate—two hundred a day plus expenses—to shadow the biker at the other end of the counter. Catrelli had canceled other, more profitable business for a divorce lawyer to take the job. He and Murphy had worked together, and he figured he owed the guy this one. Murphy had saved his ass on a couple of occasions.

Murphy would have saved his ass with the black guy in the gold Lincoln, too, if he'd been able to manage it. The black guy in the gold Lincoln had given Catrelli some lip during a routine license and registration check and had gone to the hospital for his trouble. The only problem had been that when Catrelli and his partner had dragged the guy, bleeding and semiconscious, into the emergency room at Philadelphia General, a nurse had looked at him and said, "Dr. Walker!" and Catrelli had realized instantly that his ass was grass. When the guy got out of the hospital he had filed a four-million-dollar suit against the city. Catrelli's resignation from the force had been part of the settlement.

Catrelli missed it. He had been a cop for fourteen years. Now, here he was—a little skinny guy pushing forty and peeping through motel windows with his camera, clicking shots of errant husbands. Still, it was a living, and every once in a while he got to kick some ass, which was his great pleasure in life. Dominic Catrelli was small and almost emaciated, but he was rock-hard and as fast as light. And mean. Don't forget the mean. That had always counted for a lot.

He stroked his mustache and sipped his coffee and watched. This would be the night he got something on the biker, he was pretty sure. He'd followed the guy for two nights now, and nothing much. Tonight the biker had come out on his new Harley 1200, a restless expression on his face, and Catrelli had sensed that this would be the night. A quick phone call to Wilder if this guy got out of line and Catrelli would have done his

197

duty, earned his money.

He saw the biker eye the waitress. He saw her eye him back. Yeah, this might be the night, all right. It sure might. The biker had ranged far out of his regular territory, way down here in South Philly where Catrelli had been raised and knew every manhole cover. That had to mean something. An itch, maybe. He might have the itch tonight.

The waitress looked out the window of the diner. She saw the big Harley parked on the sidewalk, looked over at the guy who'd rode in on it, and heard the voice again.

This is a mistake, the voice inside Linda's head told her. She had heard that voice before. It had spoken to her once or twice a month since she turned thirteen. Mostly, she ignored it. That was one of the reasons the old man had tossed her out at seventeen, nine years and two marriages before. Which had been fine with Linda. She hadn't liked the way the old man had been looking at her ever since she'd figured out why men look like that at women.

This is a mistake, the voice told her again. Linda ignored it. Other voices routinely spoke to her as well, and they came from other parts of her body. They spoke with louder voices than the one inside her head.

"Nice bike," she said.

Not really surprised, the long-haired man looked up from his *Daily News* and his chef's salad. His eyes traveled in a flash all over the waitress. He seemed to like what he saw, but he wasn't too obvious about it. Linda could read his mind as she watched him. He was thinking: A little hard around the edges, maybe, but there's enough to make it interesting. Take the glasses off her and get her into some jeans and tank top and she'd be fine. That's what he was thinking, she figured.

And he was right, too.

The contacts were rough on her eyes, though. She couldn't wear them at the end of a long day. And she knew she looked good in jeans and a tank top.

Then he smiled slightly through his beard. His voice was low-pitched when he spoke. "I'll take you for a ride if you want. There's room on the back."

Linda Miller shook her head. "I'd probably fall off the back and kill myself."

"Nah," he told her. "You could hold on to me. I wouldn't let you fall off."

She shook her head. "I don't think I'd like it," she lied.

He shrugged and went back to his salad.

"Besides," Linda told him, "I have another forty minutes before I'm off."

He shrugged again. "I can wait."

Now it was Linda Miller's turn to smile. "Okay. You can give me a lift home if it's on your way. Otherwise I can take the subway and walk it."

"Where do you live?"

"Twelfth and Passyunk."

"How are Mommy and Daddy going to like it when you come home at midnight on a hog?" he asked her.

Linda understood the question perfectly. "Mommy and Daddy can stuff it, for all I care. I don't live with anybody who tells me what to do."

He laughed, a hearty sound. "Aren't you the big girl, though?"

"Big enough," Linda told him.

The voice inside her head was hollering bloody murder after she said that. Silently, as she waited on

199

other customers at the counter, Linda Miller told the voice to stuff it, too.

He ate while he waited. He ate a lot. He ate a second chef's salad and then a bowl of fruit cocktail and then a tuna surprise. She offered to get him some french fries, no charge, but he said no, he didn't eat fried foods.

"Bad for your insides," he told her.

They weren't bad for her insides, but Linda didn't argue. She loved french fries. French fries were her favorite food. She could eat them by the ton and never gain an ounce. Sometimes she ate dinners that consisted of double orders of french fries and can after can of cherry Coke. And she never gained an ounce, not one. She was one-oh-seven every morning when she woke up. But this guy was clearly fussy about what he ate, which made sense when you looked at him. For the next forty minutes, Linda looked at him every chance she got. He looked at her, too, over the top of his biker book. The voice in her head was a high-pitched howl by this time. Linda shut it out.

The diner was on the east side of Broad Street in Philadelphia, fifteen blocks south of City Hall. It was incongruous in an urban setting, an old-style aluminum can closed in on both sides by stores with apartments on the second, third, and fourth floors. At each table, and at several spots along the counter, there were jukeboxes hooked up to a sound system with speakers in each corner. The jukebox had music of all kinds—from Robert Goulet to David Bowie. This guy popped in quarters while he waited, Linda noticed, and played The Stones. He really dug The Stones.

The diner went back a ways—a lot farther back than Linda. By this time, she had worked here eight months,

200

after she got sick of running a sewing machine in a clothing factory fourteen blocks away. Besides, they'd laid her off, and the union had been no help. All the work was going to Taiwan, they told her.

The hours at the diner were rotten—four to midnight—but the tips were good, and she had most of the day free. She'd get home from work in time to catch most of Letterman and the late, late show after that. During the day she got up in time most mornings to watch Donahue and Sally Jessy Raphael and the Love Connection and, later, the soaps. Sometimes, from September to June, she took the subway up to Center City and walked alone around the stores. She hadn't been able to do any of that when she had worked at the clothing factory, so it wasn't too bad. She couldn't do it now, in the summer—at least not by herself—but that was okay, too. Things could be worse, Linda knew. She knew because they had been worse—twice—and she had the divorce papers to prove it.

When her shift ended, he was waiting outside for her, leaning against the huge bike. It was black and candy apple red and spotless. Awesome, as Lenny might say. Rad. He might say that, too.

"Ready?" he asked her.

"What the hell," Linda laughed.

He got on and kicked the bike into roaring, smoke-belching life. Linda got on the back and wrapped her arms around him. He looked over his shoulder at her.

"Go for it," she told him.

Linda had done a lot of things over the years, gone through a good many adventures, but she had never gotten around to riding a motorcycle. She had been unprepared for the sudden thrust of the thing, the sensation that it was going to race out from under her. She had been unprepared, too, for the sheer speed, for the force of the wind as he roared out onto South Broad Street. She clutched him tightly and buried her face against his back to keep her glasses from flying off onto the pavement.

"Don't sweat it," he yelled to her as the bike's engine whined. "Just hang on."

He gave the bike more gas. Linda felt as though they'd just been launched into space. She had no idea how fast they might be going, only that they were going like hell. She knew they were darting in and out of traffic, her legs coming perilously close to bumpers as he directed the Harley in and out of one lane and then the other. She felt his long hair flying back over his shoulders and over her own head. She clutched at his heavy leather jacket and wished she had one, too. She felt the power of the Harley surge and whine between her thighs and Linda Miller thought: God, this is something.

"Left here?" he called back.

She looked up and over his shoulder to get her bearings. "Yeah."

He sailed through the red light and cut in front of two lanes of oncoming traffic. For a moment Linda thought they had had it, and she closed her eyes. The squeal of brakes and angry shouts surrounded them. Then, just into the turn, he gave it the gas and they shot onto Passyunk Avenue unscathed. Linda heard him laugh, felt it as she clutched him around the middle.

"You're crazy," she called out in a delighted tone.

The words came back to her on the wind. "Fuck the red lights."

Linda clutched her arms around him. Yeah, fuck the red lights. The red lights could stuff it.

Linda's place was on the bottom floor of a row house on Twelfth Street just south of Passyunk. When they got there, her hair was a twisted tangle. She looked like a witch. He pulled onto the sidewalk, cut the motor, and kicked down the stand. She climbed off awkwardly, clutching her purse and straightening her glasses. He swung one long leg over the seat and stood in front of her.

"Well, Little Mama," he asked, "how did you like your ride?"

She was flushed and smiling, still trying to catch her breath. "It was great. God, it was just super."

He looked down at her, his teeth flashing in a grin behind his flowing beard. He ran a hand through his shoulder length hair. "What's your name?" he asked her.

"Linda. What's yours?"

"Rhino."

"What?"

"My friends call me Rhino—at least they used to. You know, like in that animal with the horn on its nose."

"Rhino," she laughed. "I can see how you got that name. Want to come inside for a while?"

Rhino did. That had been the whole point, hadn't it? "Sure."

The place was small and dingy but surprisingly well kept. Linda kept the place clean and picked up, and sometimes that was a real chore. When she had been younger, she'd never cared much about things like that, but that had changed. Some things changed.

She flipped on the lamp near her worn sofa and said. "We can't make too much noise. Want a beer?"

He shook his head. "I don't touch beer no more. Not in years."

"Some grass, maybe?"

"Nah." He reached out and touched her snarled hair. It was, considering the size of his hand, a surprisingly gentle touch. "Just you," he said.

She came into his arms. "We have to be quiet, though."

Outside, Catrelli was sitting in his Chevy.

It wasn't a new Chevy, but it had the big four-fifty-four engine with the dual Holley carbs you couldn't get anymore, and it went like greased hell. A good thing, too, because he'd have had a tough time keeping up with Frost's bike in any other car. Catrelli had already staked out a pay phone less than a block away. He had Wilder's number handy. This might not amount to anything that would be worth a phone call, but Catrelli knew Rhino Frost's background. He had been in on the arrest and the questioning, even if Frost hadn't recognized him in the diner.

Catrelli knew what kind of guy Rhino Frost was, and he suspected that this might well turn into something worthwhile. All he needed was one small sign—a noise from inside that indicated that Rhino was up to his old tricks—and he would make his call. Catrelli waited.

He was good at waiting.

They were well into it on the sofa when Linda

realized that this was beginning to get rough. His huge hands, which had been caressing, began to squeeze and squeeze hard.

"Easy," she whispered. "You're hurting them."

He made no sound, but his hands tightened on her breasts. Inside her head, the voice piped up. I told you, it said.

"Ow," Linda said, and tried to push him away.

Which was when he bit her. She saw the blood come from her nipple, and she realized that he had bitten her and that he was—Jesus, he was gnawing on her, like he was a dog. He was making sounds deep down in his throat. They were sounds that frightened her almost as much as the blood and the pain.

Linda screamed then.

It was a scream of shock more than anything else as she lay naked under this huge, hairy man on the sofa and he bit at her and chewed at her and grunted and growled like an animal. He was inside her and had her pinned to the sofa and she screamed again. He kept her pinned there, but he pulled his torso up and drove a hard punch into her face. Linda felt it crash into her right cheek. She heard bones crunch, and blood gushed from her nose. She tried to scream again, but he put one hand over her mouth. Her eyes rolled in terror.

"What are you doing to my mother?" Lenny called out.

Rhino stayed inside her, but he turned his head. The little boy, no more than seven, stood in the doorway to the back room. He wore only his He-Man underpants and a terrified expression. Rhino looked down at Linda. "Get rid of him, bitch," he hissed at her hoarsely.

Linda choked it out. "Go back to bed, Lenny."

"You yelled," the child argued. He couldn't see the blood, only his mother and this giant on top of her in the shadows, and he heard the scream and deep inside his little heart he was more terrified than he had ever been in his life.

"I'm okay," she told him. "I'll be in in a little while. Go to bed."

Lenny went. Rhino began moving again. He looked down at Linda in the dim light and drove silently into her, again and again. Linda lay there, her face broken, bleeding from her nose and her right breast, where his teeth had found her. She no longer moved; she made no sound.

When he finished with her—finished with a deep-throated grunting sound that seemed only vaguely human—he stood up and put on his clothes. Linda still lay unmoving as she watched him. He was gigantic, with a tattoo on his chest she hadn't noticed before. She could see it now in the dim light, but she couldn't make it out. She watched him as he zipped his fly and stuck his feet into his boots. Then he came over and and sat next to her on the sofa. Linda's nose had bled freely all over her torso and down her sides and onto the fabric. She could see her blood on his beard. She didn't dare move a muscle.

"That was real good," he told her. "That's how I like it."

He stood up and looked down at her. He loomed over her in the shadows like a colossus.

"Too bad you got a kid here," he told her. "Otherwise we could have had us a good old time."

Then, thank God, he left. And the voice inside

Linda's head said: A close one, honey. Real close this time.

Frost stepped outside into the arms of two uniformed cops and a little skinny guy wearing a big mustache and a bigger smile. Their guns were drawn. Frost raised his hands slowly.

"What's this?" he demanded.

"Soo-prize, soo-prize!" Catrelli said, just like Gomer Pyle.

CHAPTER SEVENTEEN

"Hello."

"It's Jim."

"Anything new?"

"We got Rhino."

"That's great. What did you get him on?"

"Not so fast. We've got to let him go."

"What happened?"

"He picked up this honey at a diner on South Broad and went home with her. Catrelli was on him, and he called me when he heard a scream from inside. I sent some uniforms there, and they got him coming out."

"What did he do with the girl?"

"Broken cheekbone, some bite marks."

"Where were the bite marks?"

"You know where."

"Bad?"

"Not as bad as the girl in Olney. Only this girl won't press charges. She's scared shitless."

"No way to talk her into it?"

"She's got a little kid. She's afraid for the kid. She

wants to forget it. I've got to let him go, Frank."

"Tell Catrelli to stay with him."

"It'll be tough. Rhino's made Catrelli now."

"Have him do what he can."

"I'll tell him. Sorry, Frank. We all did our best."

"Hey," Murphy said, "that's show biz."

CHAPTER EIGHTEEN

Donahue was worked up. He stretched out his arms as he talked, the way he always did when he was worked up, waving the microphone.

"A lot of people say this country is in big, big trouble just because of that kind of narrow-minded, reactionary thinking, Senator," he told Jesse Helms. "A lot of people think the right wing—which you represent, like it or not—is starting to take over, and that makes them nervous. What do you have to say about that? How do you answer those people, Senator?"

Jesse Helms shook his head, "Mr. Donahue," he began, "just whose fears are those supposed . . ."

Then the bell on the front desk sounded.

"Goddamn," Joe Dolan said aloud. "Goddamn it all. Son of a bitch."

Joe Dolan hit the remote control, and the television set died quietly. Dolan would have liked to have heard what Jesse Helms was about to say to Phil Donahue. Joe Dolan watched Donahue five days a week, when he wasn't asleep at nine in the morning, and he would have liked to have heard what Helms told that left-wing, liberal, Commie-pinko bastard Donahue. Helms would have fixed Donahue's ass good. And now Joe Dolan would miss it because somebody was at the front desk looking for a room.

The bell sounded again, and Dolan got up reluctantly. He was a pot-bellied man of thirty-eight with a limp left him by a Bouncing Betty in Vietnam and a motel he had bought five years before with the proceeds of a lucky State Lottery ticket. Life as his own boss had rescued him from mind-numbing labor in the produce department of the Bustleton Avenue Shoprite and given him time to indulge his primary passions, which were not having to get up in the morning unless he felt like it and watching television. The only problem with the motel was that he had to be here all the time and that dumb bastards routinely came in to rent rooms when he was watching something good. Business had been hopping lately. Joe Dolan hadn't watched a day-time program all the way through in nearly a week.

"Can I help you?" he asked as he passed through the curtain which separated his small apartment from what laughingly passed as the motel's lobby.

The chunky, gray-haired guy in the too-tight suit flashed his business card. Dolan grunted. A lawyer. Involuntarily, he put his hand on his back pocket, where he kept his wallet.

"I need to ask you a few questions, if you don't mind," Murphy said.

"About what?" Dolan demanded, and not pleasantly, either. If this was some kind of lawsuit, he'd have this big guy's ass out of here so fast he could still catch Donahue sputtering after Helms jumped on his face.

"I need to have some information about the murder that took place here," Murphy said. "It involves a legal

211

matter for a client I'm representing."

"And who's your client?" Dolan asked suspiciously.

Murphy smiled. He hoped it was disarming. Sometimes it was. "Actually, my client is the widow of the murder victim. This is about the insurance."

"I told the cops everything I know," Dolan said. "You can get what you want from them."

He turned to walk back inside his little apartment, but Murphy said the magic words. "There's some money at stake here, and my client would be willing, I think, to pay for the information she's after."

Dolan turned in mid-step and came back to the counter. That changed things. Joe Dolan never turned away an easy buck. It was part of his religious faith. He thought of himself as a devout miser. "How much?"

Murphy shrugged. "Depends on what I hear. You got a minute?"

Dolan came around from behind the counter and directed Murphy to two orange vinyl chairs and a cheap, plastic-covered coffee table near the wall. The two men sat. Dolan studied the lawyer. Murphy was a bit older, a bit bigger and wore a suit that looked like he might have a buck to two, even if he couldn't button the jacket. Dolan hoped so, anyway.

"What's your name again?" he asked.

"Frank Murphy. And yours is?"

"Joe Dolan. Joseph R. Dolan. Tell me, Mr. Murphy, you ever in the Army?"

"Navy."

"Officer?"

"Afraid not. I guess I wasn't the type. Why do you ask?"

"I didn't like officers much," Dolan told him. "Never

met one I liked. This is my place here, and if you'd been an officer, I'd have thrown your ass out of here."

Murphy laughed. "Well, you can relax. I did my time and I got out. And I never liked officers much, either."

Dolan eyed him suspiciously. "How come you weren't an officer? You went to college and all."

"Not when I was in the service. That was later. I went on the GI bill."

Dolan nodded. He was satisfied. He would never have missed the rest of Donahue for an ex-officer, not even for money. "What do you want to know?"

Murphy produced a small notebook from inside his suit coat. "Did you hear anything that night?"

Dolan shook his head. "Not a thing. Not a blessed thing."

"The police told me you heard a car."

"Oh, yeah," Dolan said. "I heard a car come in. But that's all. I didn't hear nothing after that."

Murphy stifled a frown. Clearly, this was not going to be easy.

"What time was this?"

"Around three, I'd say."

"How do you know that?"

"I don't. I'm guessing."

"Were you awake?"

"Sure. How would I have heard the car if I wasn't awake?"

"What were you doing when you heard the car?"

"Watching TV."

"What you were watching?"

"I was watching a movie."

"What movie?"

Dolan looked up at the ceiling and rubbed his chin.

213

"*Rocky*. I was watching *Rocky*. You know, that one with Stallone? I never got to see that movie before."

"Which Rocky was that?"

"The first one, the one where he wins the heavyweight title."

"That was the second *Rocky*," Murphy said.

"Well," Dolan said slowly as he thought, "this was the one where he was a loan shark's enforcer and fights the colored guy for the title. I thought he won that one."

Murphy took notes. "What was going on in the movie when you heard the car?"

Dolan cocked his head. "That's a weird question."

"Do you remember?"

Dolan thought about it. "Yeah. Rocky had just knocked down the colored guy. The first time, that is. Then the colored guy started to beat the shit out of him. But that was after, though."

"After what?"

"After Rocky knocked him down the first time. The colored guy was pissed. You should have seen him. Man, he was pissed. I don't know how Rocky ever beat him. That was one mean spade, let me tell you."

Murphy scribbled. "What station were you watching?"

"HBO."

"You're sure?"

"Hey, no commercials? That's HBO."

"When you heard the car come in, what did you do?"

"I watched the movie. What would you do?"

"You didn't get up to look out the window? It was pretty late, wasn't it?"

"So? This is a motel. I got fourteen units here. People

214

come and go early and late. Besides, I was watching that fight. I wanted to see what the colored guy was going to do after Stallone knocked him down."

"What did the car sound like?"

"It sounded like a car."

"Could you tell where it parked in the lot outside?"

"Near the middle of the row of units."

"That's where the victim's room was, wasn't it?"

"Yep."

"Did the car sound American or foreign?"

"Who knows?"

"Did you have your windows open that night?"

"Sure. That's how come I heard the car."

"Was the car radio playing when it pulled in?"

Dolan pondered the question. "Yeah, now that you mention it. I heard music. It died when the engine was cut off."

"What kind of music?" Murphy asked him.

"Violins. Trumpets."

"Violins?"

"Yeah."

"Any voices? Any singing? Any song you recognized?"

Dolan shook his head. "No. Just violins and stuff, like an orchestra. Oh, and like cannons going off."

"Cannons going off?"

"Yeah, like with the violins playing at the same time."

"Did you tell this to the police?" Murphy demanded.

Dolan shook his head. "They didn't ask me about no music. They just asked me what I heard and saw, stuff like that. And I told them I heard the car, but I didn't look out the window or nothing. So they asked me a few more questions and that was that. And I told them I heard the car, but I didn't look out the window or nothing. So they asked me a few more questions and that was it."

"What did they ask you?" Murphy asked.

"They asked me stuff like when this Kirby guy had checked in, if he'd been alone at the time, if he'd said anything to me, if he'd had any visitors. Stuff like that."

"What did you tell them?"

Dolan said, "I told them when he checked in. I told them I didn't see nobody else go into his room, and I told them he didn't have no visitors that I noticed."

Murphy scribbled and then stared at his notes. His handwriting got worse by the day. He thought about some departed nuns who had beaten the Palmer Method into him and how disappointed they would be in his current hen scratches. "Can I call you later, Mr. Dolan, if anything else occurs to me? Would you mind?"

"How much?" Dolan asked.

Murphy dug into his wallet and produced a twenty. He handed it to Dolan, who stuffed it in the pocket of his khaki trousers.

"Yeah," Dolan said. "Give me a call if you want to. I got nothing to hide from nobody. I told that to the cops. I'll tell it to you."

Murphy rose and stuck out his hand. "I might be in touch, Mr. Dolan."

Dolan stood and took the hand. "Any time."

As Murphy turned to leave, Dolan said, "You're sure Rocky didn't win that fight?"

Murphy nodded. "Yeah, I'm sure."

Dolan shook his head. "Shit," he said, "I must have

fallen asleep at the end, there. Goddamn. I thought sure Stallone was going to win, even though the colored guy looked real tough. Did you see the one where Rocky takes on the wrestler?"

"Missed that one," Murphy said.

"That was *Rocky III,* I think. You ought to see that one when it comes on TV. That was a real good one. You can rent it on tape, you know, if you got a VCR."

"I'm going to have to get one of those things," Murphy said. "Everybody keeps telling me I ought to."

Every time Murphy visited the two floors of Philadelphia General Hospital that housed the city medical examiner's offices and morgue, the smell of the place struck him. It smelled of ether, of disinfectant, of deodorizer, and of something else—something he couldn't quite put his finger on. It wasn't quite the sickly sweet smell of death, of putrefaction. It was more subtle than that. It was, instead, the combined aroma of other substances designed to mask the odor of death and decomposition. Murphy had always caught that odor in hospitals, but on the floors with living patients it was combined with the essence of steamed food and clean linen and hints of body fluids. Here, those odors were largely absent. Sweat and urine and vomit were smells of the living. And in the medical examiner's complex the living generated too few of those odors to compete with the smells of the dead and the substances used to overpower them.

The place always gave Murphy the creeps, and he had spent more of his life here than he cared to think about.

"Moriarty did it," Murphy said as he stuck his head into the private office of the city's medical examiner, Dr. Marvin Weinberg.

Weinberg's snow-capped head snapped up from the leather-bound volume of *The Hounds of the Baskervilles* he was perusing. The old man frowned. It was something he did exceedingly well.

"No, he didn't, you ill-read oaf," Marvin Weinberg snapped, closing the book and setting it to one side on his desk. "Not in this one, anyway. You probably never even read this, did you, Murphy? Your reading is limited, I'd imagine, more or less exclusively to the box scores, the Racing Form, and the dirty letters in *Penthouse*. And maybe a smutty novel now and then. Admit it."

Murphy came in and sat down. "This is the one where Holmes figures out that the guy wasn't tiptoeing around the moors, the way his footprints made it seem, but was running away from something, right?"

Weinberg scratched absently at the liver spots on the backs of his gnarled hands. "This is the one, that's right. You must have seen the movie."

"No," Murphy said, "I read it years ago. I think I was in high school. I don't remember now who the killer was, but I do remember that that was the big hole in the story. I remember thinking that any moron could figure out that the victim had been running instead of sneaking around on tiptoe by the distance between the footprints. Somehow, that never seemed to occur to your idol—what was his name, Arthur something—and that's when I stopped reading Sherlock Holmes novels."

"Arthur Conan Doyle," Weinberg said quietly.

"And that was when you switched to the dirty letters in *Penthouse?*"

"About that time, I'd say. I'd probably have done that anyway, though. Sex always interested me more than murder."

"Not me," Weinberg said honestly.

Probably true, Murphy reflected. Weinberg was nearly seventy, one of the world's great forensic pathologists and equally highly ranked as an ogre. He had been widowed for nearly twenty years, which had brought a welcome end to his joyless and childless marriage, and he now devoted his time to running his city office, to flying around the country to testify as a highly paid expert witness in criminal cases and to his passion for Sherlock Holmes. Murphy sometimes wondered if Weinberg had murdered his wife. If anybody would know how to do it and get away with it . . .

"How come you're reading that crap when you're on city time?" Murphy demanded.

"Screw the city," Weinberg said pleasantly. "No mayor in thirty years has had the guts to try to fire me. Not Dilworth, not Tate, not Rizzo, not Green, not Goode—not one of them. And do you know why? Because nobody else with any talent would take this shitty low-paying job. That's why."

Murphy was too polite to point out that the medical examiner was paid more than the mayor, even before he went out collecting outrageous fees for expert witness testimony. He was also too polite to point out that the last two mayors had simply figured that firing Weinberg was more trouble than it was worth because the old man was statistically dead already. He'd had two bouts with cancer, wore a pacemaker, and smoked twenty or thirty bowls of pipe tobacco daily. But the mayors came and went and Weinberg kept on breathing. He did this, Murphy was sure, out of sheer contrariness. Annoying powerful people was another one of Weinberg's hobbies. It kept him young.

One of the great mysteries of Murphy's life was why Weinberg, who so detested all but a tiny portion of humanity, seemed fond of Murphy. That affection, whatever its source, had been helpful to Murphy over the years, and he knew he maintained it primarily by his willingness to insult the old man as freely as Weinberg insulted everyone else.

"Why should they fire you when you're so god-damned insignificant to begin with?" Murphy said. "Who cares about a surly old fart who cuts up stiffs for a living? You flatter yourself, Doc."

Weinberg grinned, tobacco-yellowed teeth showing beneath his white mustache. "So why are you taking up my time? You aren't even cluttering up the city payroll anymore. I guess somebody finally got woke up and pulled that tit out of your mouth. Don't you have some ambulances to chase or something, Murphy?"

"Who did the cutting on a guy named Kirby?" Murphy asked. "He was brought in last week."

Weinberg shook his head. "Kirby? Kirby? I don't remember any Kirby."

"Beating death. White guy? No face?"

Weinberg nodded. "Oh, I remember him. I gave it to one of the new guys. Small-time stuff."

"I don't suppose the autopsy report is around anywhere? Or are you so senile that you can't find it?"

Weinberg's grin grew wider. "Sit tight."

He got up and went out to his outer office, where he berated his secretary until she found the file. Weinberg came back in and sat down behind his battered wooden desk, which had been well-worn city issue, Murphy guessed, when Ronald Reagan was still being toilet trained. Weinberg scanned the file quickly while he lit his pipe.

"Sort of sloppy," he said at last. "You can't get good help these days. Everybody decent wants to be a neurosurgeon. I get the guys who went to medical school in some banana republic and didn't put on shoes until they got off the plane here. Half these new guys wear turbans, for Christ's sake."

"Could I see it?"

"Not a chance," Weinberg told him. "You're not authorized."

"So what?"

"So I'm just a struggling public servant. You expect me to put my job in jeopardy to help some quack lawyer?"

"You're the quack," Murphy corrected. "I'm the shyster. Look, if you won't let me see the file, just tell me what's in it."

Weinberg shrugged and puffed. "Just ask me questions. See if I give you any answers you can use."

"Cause of death?"

"Massive wounds to the frontal lobe inflicted with a blunt instrument."

"What kind of blunt instrument?"

"A small baseball bat, maybe. Very small, actually. The area of impact was under ten centimeters in each case. There were wood slivers extracted from the broken portion of the skull. They put them under the

221

microscope and determined they were white oak that had been varnished with liquid plastic. Maybe it was a Louisville Slugger made for a midget."

"How many blows?"

"Twenty-two."

"That's a lot."

Weinberg nodded. "Whoever did it was apparently pissed off about something."

"Could your guy determine the height of the attacker?"

"The estimate here is between five eight and six two."

"That's a big help."

"And that may be off. Let's assume that the victim saw the first swing coming and bent over slightly trying to avoid the blow. That would make the first blow strike him higher on the head, and it would affect the estimate of height. Let's assume, too, that the victim went down with the first blow, and the attacker belted him twenty-one more times while leaning over him. It's possible. The pathologist took those possibilities into account, and this is the height range he came up with. You can't be more precise than that. The first blow is the key, though. That was hard enough to disable your friend Kirby, as near as I can determine from all this. If you assume that it caught Kirby standing straight up, the attacker would be over six feet. If he bent slightly, the killer would be slightly under. If he bent down more as it came down, the killer could be at the low end of the range. When the blows come from the front like this, you can't be too specific."

"Is the killer right-handed or left-handed?"

"Left-handed. At least the blows were delivered with the left hand."

Murphy nodded. That was something. "I understand there was a partial print on the cornea and on the hair. Anything else like that?"

Weinberg studied the file and shook his head. "No. If the victim was touched, it was on flesh."

"Time of death?"

"Anywhere from two-twenty to three-ten."

"You're sure?"

"The room was air-conditioned, and the air conditioner was set for seventy-three. That means a steady temperature. You do the math, figuring how many degrees would be lost from the body every hour after death in a constant seventy-three-degree environment, and you figure the body temperature taken when the lab guys arrived, and you end up with that time range. You also have surface lividity to work from—how quickly blood will pool in the lowest portion of the corpse after death. If the thermostat was accurate, this seems to be a good time range, Frank. I'm doing the math in my head right now, and it seems to be holding together."

"So he could have been killed after three?"

"Or before two-thirty. Or any time in between."

Murphy sat back and lit a Camel while Weinberg puffed placidly on his pipe.

"What's your guess?" Murphy asked finally.

"On what?"

"Time of death."

"You have the range."

"I don't want the range. Not a range that big, anyway."

"I didn't do the cutting."

"I know that."

"All I have to go by is the report."

"Okay. Be brave. You're not on the stand now."

Weinberg frowned. "But I might be at some point."

"It could happen."

"You're representing the prime suspect, aren't you?"

Murphy nodded.

"The time range fits, doesn't it?"

"Just barely. Look, could it be earlier or later, and by how much?"

"Not earlier, I wouldn't think," Weinberg said. "These air conditioners in cheap motels, they're not always set right. The guys who operate places like that, they usually want to cut down on energy costs. They have the air conditioners set a few degrees higher than they register. If this one was set lower than the actual temperature, the time of death could have been a little later. But that's only an if."

Murphy jumped up. "I've got to go. Thanks, Doc."

Weinberg rose slowly. "Remember, you didn't hear that here."

"Hear what?" Murphy asked on his way out the door.

Dolan slept. He had dropped off during *Another World,* and he was snoring deeply when the bell in the lobby sounded.

"Uuuuhhh . . ." Dolan said.

The bell rang again. He stirred weakly.

"Mr. Dolan?" Murphy called out.

Dolan stirred.

"Mr. Dolan? Frank Murphy again. Are you there?"

Dolan rose and staggered through the curtain. It was

the lawyer.

"Yeah?" he grunted.

Murphy slapped another twenty on the counter. "Let me into the room."

"Which room?"

"Where the murder took place."

Dolan was coming awake now. What was this shit? "It's rented."

"They're out. I knocked. Nobody home. Let me in for five minutes. You can watch me."

Dolan looked at Murphy, looked at the twenty. "Let me get the passkey."

Murphy followed him back into the tiny apartment off the lobby. He wasn't letting this guy get away. Murphy came through the curtain into a small living room with a sofa, a coffee table, and a TV set, still blaring. On the coffee table was a pile of Sunday *Inquirer* TV books. He dug through them as Dolan got the passkey.

"You got last week's book in here?"

"I don't know," Dolan said, mystified.

"Here it is. Can I have this?"

"Five bucks."

"For last week's book?" Murphy said, outraged.

Dolan shrugged. "Do you want it or not?"

Murphy slapped the five down on the coffee table and stuck the book into his inside pocket. "Just get me into the room."

The two of them went outside and down the row of doorways to the room. Dolan knocked on the door. When he was satisfied it was empty, he inserted the key and opened the door. Murphy slipped past him into the room. Dolan followed.

"How long you going to be?"

"Not five minutes. You can watch."

Murphy produced from his breast pocket a photographic thermometer he had bought in a photo supply store on his way out Roosevelt Boulevard. He went to the air conditioner, which was blasting air into the empty room. The dial read seventy-two. He turned it to seventy-three. Then he set the thermometer on the floor in roughly the spot where Kirby's body had been found. He stood up and looked down at it.

"Now what?" Dolan demanded.

"Now," Murphy said, "you close the door and I go back to your place while I use the phone. Don't worry, I'll give you a quarter for the call."

The two men trooped back to the lobby and Murphy phoned his office.

"Any messages, Esmeralda?" Murphy asked.

"A man named Catrelli called you. He says he's waiting in a phone booth."

"Give me the number."

Murphy took it down in his notebook, hung up, and dialed Catrelli.

"Zip," Catrelli told him. "I'm in a candy store down the street from Frost's place, and he ain't been out since he went in last night after Wilder let him go. This is starting to run into money, Frank. You're into me for six hundred so far. I thought I ought to let you know the meter's still running, but there's no action anymore."

"He'll probably lay low for a while."

"I don't know," Catrelli said. "All I know is he ain't gone nowhere so far today, and I got other work waiting at regular prices."

Murphy sighed mightily. "All right. Call it quits and

send me a bill. But I might want you again on short notice. Can you handle that?"

"I'll try, but I got a business to run."

"Dom, I appreciate it."

"Hang loose," Catrelli said, "and watch your ass with this dude."

Murphy hung up the phone. "Shit," he muttered to himself.

"That's two calls," Dolan told him.

Murphy frowned and handed the motel operator two quarters. "Let's go back now."

Dolan led him back to the room, and Murphy went inside to retrieve his thermometer. He held it up and looked at it carefully. He chuckled to himself.

"Bingo," Murphy said. Then he smiled broadly at Dolan. "This calls for a drink, I think. Tell me, is there a bar in the neighborhood?"

It was late, and Murphy was dragging. After leaving a bar on the boulevard, where he'd had just a touch too much to drink, he'd gone to a store and rented a complicated piece of equipment. He'd spent the evening at his apartment trying to figure out how to use it, and Murphy's mechanical abilities were virtually nil. He'd finally managed to get it to do what he wanted it to do, but it had been a bitter struggle, and it had left him exhausted.

He'd never even bothered to buy a microwave over for the apartment, even though he knew how handy the damn things were, because he knew he could never figure out how to operate the damn thing properly. He could boil water for coffee with the one in the kitchen of the Mount Airy house, but anything more complicated than that baffled him completely. In the technological revolution, Murphy was a noncombatant.

Now, out later than he wanted to be and struggling to stay awake at the wheel, he slowed the Toronado and turned it onto the exit off the turnpike into the service station at Ambler. He yawned as he pulled in front of the pumps. Then he cut the engine and sat there for a moment, waiting for service.

Nothing.

Murphy glanced over at the station. Parked on the side of the building was an aged Mustang with mag wheels and dual exhausts sticking out from under the rear bumper. The car's ass-end was jacked up about a foot. Murphy hit the horn.

The kid who responded was about medium height with a shock of long hair and a wispy mustache. He looked something like Doug Henning, the magician, Murphy realized. The kid removed the Toronado's gas cap and grabbed a pump handle.

"How much?" he said.

"Fill it up," Murphy told him, getting out of the car.

The kid inserted the nozzle and squeezed. The odor of gasoline wafted into the air as it flowed into the Toronado's twenty-two-gallon tank. The monster car would probably soak up five gallons just getting back to Center City.

Murphy yawned. "You work here every night?"

The kid looked up at him. "Yeah."

"A woman came in here the other night with a popped hose. Remember her?"

The kid's forehead furrowed. He was thinking, and he was clearly unaccustomed to the process. "I don't

228

know," he said finally.

"She was in a silver Audi," Murphy persisted. "Good-looking woman about thirty."

The kid nodded slowly. "Yeah. I remember her."

Murphy smiled at the kid. Sometimes he absolutely loved this line of work.

"You know what," he said, "she remembers you, too."

Graterford Correctional Facility, 1976

The queen moved down the walkway and into the exercise yard. She wasn't walking; she was sashaying. No other word would do. She was twitching her hips and rolling them around and trying to look good— trying to look *fine*—because she knew she was going to be here for some time. It was important that she be noticed early, and by the right kind of people, too. So she sashayed, strutting it for all she was worth. And it worked.

"Hey, bitch," Bear called out to her, "you lookin' fine."

The queen laughed. Her name was Robert Earl Hammond, and she was a whore from West Philadelphia. She was new in the place. She had stuck a gravity knife into her pimp four months before when she got sick of being beaten up every time he got high. Then she had let him bleed to death in a row-house bathroom while she laughed. Holmesburg had not been all that bad for her, but Graterford was another matter entirely. Here she wasn't sure what to expect.

"You're nothing but a big pig," she told Bear, but she kept her smile as she said it. He really was a pig, but you never knew.

"And you love it, don't you?" Bear said, chuckling.

The queen just twitched her hips under her new prison-issue jeans and walked away. She had never bothered with the sex-change operation, figuring she was what she was, however bizarre some might find it. She was perfectly comfortable with her dual sexual identity—male organs and a female psyche—which might come in handy here. She wore foundation makeup, rouge, lipstick, and false eyelashes. She knew she needed to find a jocker, someone to care for her and protect her. Even though it was clear that Bear possessed awesome powers of protection—she could tell that just by looking at him—and that he had his eye on her, she would hold out as long as she could for the best deal she could find. She knew that life for her without protection would be unimaginably horrible in Graterford, even if she tried to hide who and what she was. So she decided instead to flaunt it. If you're ever going to flaunt it, she told herself, this is the time and place to do it. Bear watched her go by and grunted and chuckled in appreciation.

"Good stuff, eh?" Bear asked Rhino.

Frost's eyes narrowed as he watched her. He hadn't realized it until this moment, but this was what he had been waiting for. He had been uncharacteristically pensive and subdued lately. He had been a long time without a good many comforts, and he now realized that his moods had a specific cause. As he studied the queen, he became aware of what it was, and he knew it was time to do something about it—past time, actually.

He knew there was no stigma. Not here, there wasn't. What happened here had no connection with what happened on the outside. All the rules were different, all the standards of individual worth had been altered to fit the circumstances. Men who lived together in close quarters with other men for year after year with no women found other mechanisms to deal with natural drives. That's what he hadn't understood before. He understood it now. He understood it viscerally, down deep in his guts. It had been long enough for Rhino Frost. The other queens were all taken. This one was new. This one was up for grabs.

"She'll do," he said finally. "She's all mine, Bear. Spread the word. This one belongs to Rhino."

Bear laughed raucously as he leaned against the high stone wall of the yard. "You got her, baby. You got her if you can hold her."

Frost eyed his friend, his brother in the club. "I'll hold her. If it means I stay here forever, I'll hold her. Spread the word."

"You got it, man," Bear said.

Bear would spread the word, too, Frost knew. Under it all, Bear was a romantic. He might even help Frost hold the queen, if it came to that. Probably not, though. Bear's respect for personal property was not overdeveloped.

Rhino found the queen in the prison store. She was buying chocolates with "white money," real cash from outside. She was small and soft-featured with a tight, curly skullcap of hair. She was shaped more or less like a woman, except for the tits. She had no tits to speak of, although she'd been toying for some time with the idea of taking hormones to see if she could grow them.

231

She was just sort of little and rounded here and there and you could pretend she was a woman without working too hard at it. She pretended. After two years here, so could Frost.

"You're going to need some help," Rhino told her.

She looked at him, sizing him up. "And what kind of help do I need, sir?"

"You'll need a friend," Frost told her. "Believe me, that's what you're going to need."

She put her hands on her hips and sort of thrust them at Frost. He felt himself shiver a little bit as she did that. "And you want to be that friend? Is that what you're saying?"

Frost nodded. "It's me or somebody else. You know that just like I do. How long you been in here?"

"I came in yesterday," she said.

"You ever been here before?"

"First time, sweetie. It's all such an adventure, you know?"

Frost nodded. "You need a friend, all right. How much time are you doing?"

She bit into a chocolate, a raspberry-filled number from the Whitman's Sampler box she had just bought. The raspberry filling flowed over her full lips. She licked at it greedily. Frost noted that. It did not escape his notice.

"Nine, anyway," she said. "Maybe twelve. Depends on how I behave, honey."

"You behave for me, and I'll keep you cool."

She eyed the big man. He was rugged from the weight room, where he spent most of his days now, fighting the boredom and the horrible tediousness of it all. She had always liked muscles. In this place, she liked them more than ever.

"How long are you here for, honey?" she asked.

"Years, yet. I'll be able to take care of you for a long time."

The queen studied the big man. She looked at him long and hard. "You'll treat me right?" she asked. "Promise?"

Frost nodded.

"There'll be plenty of others," the queen warned him. "If you don't treat me right, I can find somebody else."

"I can take care of you," Frost promised her.

She smiled at him over her chocolate. She batted her false eyelashes at him.

"Well," she told him, "we'll see about that, won't we?"

CHAPTER NINETEEN

Murphy was moving slowly. He tried to move more quickly, but it was as though he were in water, with pressure working against his arms and legs. All was cloudy and smoky and filmy. He could hardly see, and he was frightened.

Where was Frost? Frost was here somewhere, Murphy knew. Murphy reached for his pistol, found it, brought it out, held it with barrel pointed up, the way he had been schooled. He moved with agonizing slowness through the mist. Behind him he heard a buzzing—faint at first, growing louder. He turned his head, heard the chain saw near him, saw the enormous shadow of Frost behind him. Murphy turned, slowly, slowly. He was caught in the mist. It held him, impeding his movements. He saw the saw blade now, the chair whirring, making a buzzing sound, then turning to a ringing, like a bell. Murphy struggled to move, the blade moving ever closer, toward his face. He tried to point his gun toward it, but the gun was caught. Murphy struggled, terror all over him. He could taste it, acid in his mouth. The chain saw came closer. It rang. It rang and rang . . .

. . . and Murphy came awake.

He found himself tangled in his sheet, the linen covering his face. He had rolled himself up in the sheet like a rug, and he fought to free himself while he became aware that the phone was ringing. He fought an arm free, clutched at the phone, found it, brought the receiver to his ear.

"Hello," he managed.

"It's Carol. They've arrested me."

It took only a fraction of a second for this to sink in on Murphy. He struggled to free himself from the sheet and fell without warning out of bed, striking the worn hardwood floor of his bedroom with an "oof!" and a curse.

"Hello?" Carol Highland said. "Are you there, Mr. Murphy?"

Murphy sat up, still clutching the phone. "I think, under the circumstances, you better call me Frank."

"I'm in custody, at the police administration building. This is my phone call. You've got to help me."

"I will," Murphy said, wondering who was going to help him out of his tangled bedding. "Is Wilder there?"

He heard Carol hold the phone away. "He wants to talk to you, Lieutenant."

"Morning, Frank."

"Have you charged her?"

"Just about to book her. You can come over and watch, if you like."

"Big mistake, Jim. She couldn't have done it, and I can prove it. You book her and you're going to end up looking like a raving asshole. Believe me on this."

Wilder paused before answering. "You're on the other side now, Frank. You've got zero credibility

235

when a client of yours is involved."

Murphy ripped the sheets away and sat up on his bedroom floor. He was fuming.

"Zero credibility? All right, goddamn it. You go ahead and book her, you dumb prick. You fingerprint her and take her picture and go through the whole routine. Meanwhile, I'm calling Toddman, and I want a bail hearing this afternoon."

"That's between you and the DA's office," Wilder said calmly.

"Put her back on," Murphy snapped.

"Hello," Carol Highland said weakly.

"They're going to book you," Murphy told her. "Just don't say a word to them, not one goddamn word. And don't let this process get to you."

"What's going to happen?"

Murphy sighed. There was no way to sugarcoat any of it. "First they're going to fingerprint you and take your picture. Then they're going to take away from you all jewelry, any belts, any sharp objects—even high heels. If you're wearing a bra, they'll take that away, too. They've had suicides hang themselves with bras. Then a matron will ask you to undress, and they'll conduct a body search. That means they'll look . . . inside you, to make sure you're not hiding a weapon or some contraband. After that you'll go into a holding cell."

"Oh, Jesus," Carol Highland said. She began to weep.

"I know it's all a terrible indignity," Murphy told her, "but I'll have you out in a few hours. Don't resist them. Do what they tell you. But don't say a word to them. Not one word. Understand?"

"I understand."

"Good. I'll be right over."

Murphy hung up, fought his way free from the torn bedding, and walked in his underwear into the bathroom. He urinated, then lit a Camel. Then he went into the living room, pushed a stack of newspapers off the sofa onto the floor, and picked up the other extension of the phone. He dialed quickly.

"Toddman."

"This is Murphy. Do you know about the arrest of the Highland woman?"

"Sure, I know about it. I okayed it."

"And you couldn't have given me the courtesy of a phone call? You couldn't have let me bring her in and try to straighten this out?"

"Frank," Toddman said patiently, "a murder charge isn't the sort of thing you try to 'straighten out.' You know that. You and your client haven't exactly bent over backward to cooperate in this investigation. I saw no reason to extend either of you special privileges."

Murphy drew on his cigarette. "Fletcher got on your ass, didn't he?"

"I beg your pardon?" Toddman said.

"Fletcher got on your ass. Admit it. It's a Main Line murder, and Fletcher is a Main Liner, and I'm sure talk of this is all over his little circle of prep school friends. Maybe they talked about it over white wine at the weekend polo matches or something. And then he got on your ass and you caved in. You made a bust when you didn't have everything locked up, right? Come on, Paul, don't bullshit me."

He could hear Toddman's manner harden. "I'm not in the habit of discussing the inner workings of this

237

office with members of the defense bar, Counselor."

"You don't have to say peep one," Murphy said. "I just want you to know that you made one big, fat, fucking mistake, Paul. I'm applying to Joe Luce for a bail hearing. If I were you, I'd keep close to the phone, because you'll hear about it soon. And you might want to show up yourself, because it might be instructive to you to see how foolish I'm going to make you look, you dumb bastard."

"Murphy, you go into private practice for a few months, you get one lousy case of any significance, and all of a sudden you think you're Melvin Belli. I remember how hard you had to bust your ass earlier this year just to pass the goddamn bar. Let me tell you something, you've got a client with motive, opportunity, and who left fingerprints all over the scene. I'm going to personally hand you your ass on this one. How's that grab you?"

"See you in court, Paul," Murphy said, and hung up.

He called Judge Luce and arranged a bail hearing for just after lunch. Luce was a good judge, an old friend and a man with funny ideas about bail. He thought that bail ought to conform to the United States Constitution. The purpose of bail was to ensure that the defendant showed up for trial. It was not to keep supposedly dangerous people off the streets until they could be convicted and put away legally. Luce believed that a defendant was innocent until conviction and entitled to liberty in exchange for reasonable bail, and he insisted on bail hearings being held promptly. There had been a time—and not long ago—when that point of view had irritated Murphy, but now it delighted him. Wilder was right. He was on the other side now, and he was playing all the angles. Judge-shopping was one of the angles. Murphy did it shamelessly. He thought sometimes that they should teach courses in it in law school.

Murphy showered, shaved, drank coffee, and thought about what Carol Highland was going through about now. He called her house and got her mother-in-law.

"The police arrived about seven, Mr. Murphy," she said. "They told Carol she was under arrest, put handcuffs on her, and took her away. Ev followed her in his own car. As far as I know, he's still with her at police headquarters."

"I'm sorry about all this, Mrs. Highland," Murphy said. "I'll have her home this afternoon."

"What you said the other night," Margaret Highland said, "about you knowing that you didn't do it but not being sure about anyone else. Do you think it's possible that Carol actually committed a murder? This is just you and me, Mr. Murphy. I need to know, because I'm worried about my son. I ask you to be candid with me."

"She didn't do it," Murphy said. "I wasn't positive the other night, but I am now."

"Then who did it?" Margaret Highland demanded.

"Well," Murphy said, "it could have been you, you know."

There was a moment's silence on the other end of the phone. Then: "I knew you were thinking that."

"I know you knew it."

"Good-bye, Mr. Murphy."

"Please," Murphy said, "call me Frank."

It was not necessary that Carol Highland be present

at her own bail hearing, and Murphy saw to it that she wasn't. Having her there would have meant having her husband there, and Murphy didn't want either of them on hand. He had things to say, and if either of them heard what he had to say, life in the Highland household would be strained, to say the least, once he sprang her.

The hearing was held in Joe Luce's chambers on the third floor of City Hall. It was informal, the only person not directly involved in the proceeding being a court reporter. She was a plump black woman with an electric haircut like Don King, who took a transcript. Luce was a smallish, gray-haired man in his early fifties with wide eyes behind horn-rimmed glasses. He had gone to the YMCA to run laps during his lunch hour, and now he was studying the case file carefully and chewing at a ham and cheese on seeded rye while Toddman presented his case. Wilder and Murphy sat in chairs on either side of Toddman while the first assistant district attorney quickly detailed the state's evidence—Carol Highland's secret first marriage, her legally invalid marriage to Everett Highland, Zsa Zsa's notes from her interrogation of Carol Highland in which Carol had admitted both her marriage to Kirby and her animosity toward him. Toddman also offered Wilder's typed notes of his interview with Everett Highland in which Highland had said that he hadn't known of Hank Kirby until shortly before Wilder's visit. Toddman stressed in particular Carol's refusal to speak to police and her resulting lack of a stated alibi.

"Finally, the defendant's fingerprints were found at the scene, Your Honor," Toddman said. "The lab report is in the file, along with the autopsy report. I

240

think you'll agree that this is a strong case, and the state is concerned that this defendant won't show up for trial. Moreover, these are wealthy people, Your Honor, and a high bail wouldn't deter Mrs. Highland from skipping out."

Joe Luce—eating, reading, and listening all at the same time—looked up at Toddman. "So you're recommending what, then, Paul? No bail?"

Toddman nodded. "That would be the state's preference, Your Honor—at least until after the grand jury hears the evidence and makes a formal present-ment. This woman did it, and now that we're so hot on her tail she's more than even money to skip, in my judgment."

"Horseshit," Murphy muttered.

Joe Luce looked up. "This hearing is informal, Frank, but it isn't that informal." Luce turned to the court reporter. "Did you get the horseshit remark?"

"Yes, Your Honor."

"Well, strike it, please. Try to remain calm, Frank, if you will."

"Sorry, Judge. I'd like the opportunity to rebut, however."

"Just a minute," Joe Luce said through a mouthful of bread, meat, and cheese. "Just let me go over the rest of this stuff."

Luce skimmed the multi-page file in only a few moments, finishing the rest of his lunch as he went. Then he reached into the small refrigerator beneath the credenza behind his desk, pulled out a Diet Pepsi, opened it, and took a swallow. He folded his hands and looked at Murphy.

"Proceed, counselor," he said.

241

Murphy stood up and began to pace. He wanted to be higher than the judge and the others, and he wanted to move freely while he laid out his thoughts.

"First of all," he said, "the evidence that my client won't show up for trial and should therefore be denied bail isn't just weak, it's simply nonexistent. One, this woman has no prior record. Two, she's a solid citizen with roots in the community, a good job, a husband—"

"—not a legal husband," Toddman pointed out.

"So what?" Murphy demanded.

"Just thought it was worth mentioning," Toddman said casually.

Murphy turned to Luce. "Joe, would you tell him to let me finish."

"Yes," Luce said with irritation. "And don't call me Joe. This is a goddamn bail hearing." He turned to the reporter. "Strike that, too, please."

"Which should I strike, Judge?"

"Strike the 'goddamn.' Strike everything up to when I told Mr. Murphy here to make his case."

The court reporter studied the sheets her machine had produced. "You didn't tell him to make his case, Judge. You said, 'Proceed, Counselor.'"

"Well, pick it up from there, then." He turned to the lawyers and shook an angry finger at them. "Now, no more of this shit, you two. Strike that, too. Look, let's just get on with it."

Murphy glared at Toddman, who was smirking. "The point is just this," Murphy went on, "she's not going to go anywhere. And you can't deny her bail because Toddman thinks, on the basis of no evidence except his intuition, that she might. In addition—and this shouldn't be a factor in all this at this stage, but I'm going to mention it anyway—she didn't do it, and these guys would know that if they'd done their homework."

"Do tell," Wilder said. "And I left my boots home, too."

"Strike that," Joe Luce ordered. He glared at the three of them. "Would you gentlemen like me to put on my robes and we can all move out into the courtroom? It can be arranged, you know."

"Sorry, Judge," Wilder said.

"Your Honor," Toddman said, "I'd like very much to see Mr. Murphy prove his contention that this investigation is focusing on the wrong subject. If he can convince me that we're going down the wrong road, the DA's office will not only agree to release the suspect in her own recognizance, we'll even consider dropping all charges against Mrs. Highland."

"Well," Murphy said, hands on his hips, "then we'll even consider not filing a false arrest suit against you and District Attorney Lake and Lieutenant Wilder—if my client hasn't been so severely humiliated that she's suffered irreparable emotional damage, that is."

"Enough with the threats," Luce said.

Murphy motioned to the court reporter. "I'd just as soon this be off the record for now."

Luce looked at the reporter. She shrugged at the judge.

"All right," Luce said, "I'll adjourn this hearing and we've now retired to chambers. Now let's get this rolling. I've got an armed robbery trial to run out there."

"Here's the way I've put it together," Murphy said. "My client got a call from Kirby the night of the murder, and he told her to meet him at his room at two in the morning. He was calling from a bar, she thought. She heard music playing. She waited until everybody in the house was asleep, then she left at around twelve-thirty, which left her with plenty of time to drive from Paoli out to the motel where Kirby was staying. But she got there a little late. It was several minutes after two."

"Why?" Toddman asked. "And how do you know when she got there, aside from her telling you?"

"Two reasons. One, she had to pull some cash out of some bank machines. I checked on that. She gave me a letter authorizing me to look at her bank records, and the computer verifies that she took out the cash in two chunks at precise times. She had to scramble around to get all the money Kirby demanded she bring along—"

"—he was blackmailing her, then," Toddman said.

Murphy hesitated. More motive, he knew.

"He wanted money from her," Murphy said. "That's all I'll say about that now. In any event, I can prove by bank computer records where she was between twelve-thirty and one-fifteen. Then she drove out to the motel. She couldn't have gotten there before two-ten. I know that because I drove the same route at the same time last night. Even if you speed —which I did—you can't make it from the last place where she picked up cash to the motel in under fifty minutes. Too many lights, too much traffic from around the racetrack. Aside from that, she was listening to WCAU on the radio. She said the news had ended some minutes before she arrived at the motel. I checked WCAU's logs—I know a guy on the news staff there—and their local news comes on at five of the hour and goes off at the hour."

"So, big deal," Wilder said. "She got there at two-ten or so. The autopsy report sets the time of death at two-

244

twenty to three-ten. That all fits."

"That's right," Murphy said. "But it's nice to know what you're talking about, right? What I'm getting at is that the level of investigative work on this case isn't the highest I've ever come across."

"You've had a little advantage there, Frank," Toddman pointed out, "since she's talked to you. You haven't permitted her to talk to us."

"And for a good reason. Those fingerprints—and the motive—has you guys convinced she did it. Nothing she was going to say was going to change your mind."

"And nothing you've said so far has, either," Wilder told him.

"Okay," Murphy said, lighting a cigarette. "Then listen up, Jimmy. The guy at the motel says that the only car he heard come in came in around three. If my client was there at two-ten or thereabouts, then he couldn't have heard her car. He must have heard somebody else's."

"Or he has the time wrong," Wilder said. "That guy, Dolan, isn't the brightest guy I've ever come across. He doesn't even wear a watch, in case you didn't notice. And there's not a clock in the living room of his apartment there. He was just watching TV and he was guessing at the time."

"Yes, he was," Murphy said. "But he did know what movie he was watching at the time, and he knew what scene he was watching when the car rolled in. He was watching the fight scene in *Rocky*. Stallone had just knocked down Apollo Creed the first time when Dolan heard the car. I checked the TV book, and Rocky started on HBO that night at two. I rented a tape of the

245

movie last night and I rented a VCR to go along with it. It took me until almost dawn to get the goddamn thing working, and I timed at what point in the movie the knockdown took place. It was fifty-eight minutes from the opening credits. So that means that Dolan actually did hear the car around three, guess or no. It was goddamn close to three, in fact."

"Maybe it wasn't Carol Highland's car, then," Wilder said.

"Exactly my point," Murphy told him.

"So somebody drove into the parking lot after the Highland woman left. That doesn't mean that she hadn't already been there, killed the guy, and taken off. None of this shit proves anything, Frank."

Murphy held up a cautioning hand. "Stay with me. You're right. The car Dolan heard must have been another car. He obviously didn't hear Carol drive in or leave, for whatever reason. In fact, I know for a fact that by the time he heard that other car, Carol was long gone. I know it because I have a witness who can place her at another location at just about three. Her car broke down on the way home, and a kid who works in a gas station fixed it for her. He can identify her."

Wilder's eyes narrowed. "Who is this witness?"

Murphy smiled. "No way, Jim. I told you that I drove the route last night. I drove it both ways. I found the service-station attendant, and if you guys insist on going to trial he'll make a terrific defense witness. You can check every service station along the boulevard to the expressway if you want to, though. It'll be good exercise for you."

Murphy had mentioned the expressway and the

boulevard on purpose. He knew that Carol had taken the turnpike home, but he would just as soon not have Wilder know that at this point.

Toddman was frowning. "So we have just your word on this for now."

Murphy nodded. "Until and unless we go to trial, yes. This witness will kill you anyway, whether you find him or not."

Wilder grunted. It was not a sound of pleasure.

"There's more. Carol told me that when Kirby called her, he was calling from a bar, and she could hear a song called 'Proud Mary' playing in the background. I just took a chance yesterday and checked the bars around the motel. There are several of them within walking distance. I wanted to see if Kirby visited any of them."

"How do you know he called her from a bar within walking distance of the motel?" Joe Luce asked, interested in all this.

"Kirby's car had a dead battery that night," Murphy told the judge. "He couldn't have gone far. Carol also said the guy seemed sort of stoned when she saw him that night, and I figured that a guy with habits like that might like bars he could walk to. I could have been wrong, but it turns out that I wasn't. There's a bar across the boulevard and up a ways from the motel where they had 'Proud Mary' on the jukebox. It turns out that Kirby—or somebody who looked and dressed a lot like him—had been hanging around there a lot that week. He was in there that night, and the bartender remembered his asking to use the phone that night."

Wilder had his notebook out. "That one we can find

pretty easily," he said.

"Now that it's been pointed out to you," Murphy said.

"Okay," Toddman said, "so he called her from this particular bar earlier in the evening. So?"

Murphy stubbed out his Camel and immediately lit another one. "Well, Kirby and Carol had some words. In fact, he made a run at her, and she had to fight him off. That's when she ran out the door and took off. She told me that when she'd seen him, he'd been wearing a white T-shirt, an undershirt. But when I saw the body—and you were there, Jim—Kirby was wearing a T-shirt with a beer label on it. I think it was dark blue."

"So she lied."

Murphy shook his head. "Nope. The white T-shirt was found in one of his drawers, according to the inventory. Also, I asked the bartender. He said that Kirby had been wearing a plain white T-shirt the last time he saw him. And he said that he'd seen him last sometime after two-thirty when he came in, bought some cigarettes out of the machine, and had a quick beer."

Wilder sat bolt upright. "He was in the place twice that night?"

Murphy nodded. "He was in there earlier in the evening to make the call, and he went in there after Carol left him. When he got back to his room, he changed his T-shirt—maybe he spilled beer on it, or something—and that's how he was dressed when the killer showed up and offed him."

"Oh, shit," Wilder said, sinking back in his chair.

Toddman lit one of his enormous cigars. Joe Luce

248

made a face. Murphy's cigarette was bad enough. But he said nothing. This was almost over, anyway, he could tell.

"Jim," Toddman said, "check that bar right away. Make sure Frank is right on his times."

"Oh, I'm right," Murphy said. "The bartender alone ought to be enough to get her off the hook."

"Maybe," Toddman said.

"One more thing," Murphy told him. "The time of death in the autopsy report is wrong. It's a bit too early."

He explained how he had checked the difference between the temperature recorded on the air conditioner in Kirby's room and the actual temperature. "There's a four-degree difference," Murphy said. "That could push the time of death back as much as an hour. My guess is that it probably wasn't that late, but Kirby was clearly alive at three, when my witness can place Carol at the service station."

"How did you know about the time of death before you just heard it here?" Toddman demanded, but he already knew the answer. Murphy did not respond. He only looked at the first assistant DA and smiled pleasantly.

"Well, gentlemen," Joe Luce said, "I'm prepared to go back on the record to release the defendant on her own recognizance. Paul, you can either recommend that she be bound over for grand jury action, or you can take other action—like dropping the charges. My suggestion would be to consider that, at any rate. Now, what shall we do?"

Toddman held out his hands in helplessness. "We'll

consider dropping the charges. I'll have to discuss this with Fletcher first. Meanwhile, we'll agree to release her without bail."

"Thank you," Murphy said. "You know, none of this had to happen to begin with."

Wilder stood up, his hands in his pockets as he looked at the floor and chewed on his lower lip in frustration. "Shit, Frank. We had the prints. We had the motive. It was logical."

"Yeah," Murphy said, "and that's the problem. If I'd still been on your side, I'd probably have done the same thing. Let her prove she didn't do it. The only problem is that it's the whole power of the state up against somebody like her—high-powered hotshots like you two. She had no way to prove it wasn't her."

"She did pretty good," Toddman said with a rueful smile.

"Luck," Murphy said, knowing it wasn't. "I just went out nosing around and bumped into some things. The gas station attendant and the motel operator, I'll take credit for that. But the bartender was sort of a shot in the dark. I'll give you his name. I'm going to keep my gas station guy until you formally drop charges, though."

"Good instincts, Frank," Joe Luce said.

Wilder was furious at himself. He was better than this, damn it. Murphy was right. He just hadn't tried hard enough.

"So," Wilder said to Murphy, "if she didn't do it, who did?"

"How the hell would I know?" Murphy asked. "You're the cop, not me."

Janet Frost had obtained permission to visit her son by requesting and then returning a notarized form to the prison administration. Wendell was entitled to a total of ten authorized visitors. So far as she could determine, he had never had even one. Certainly not her. Janet Frost had not visited him. She was doing so now only because of special circumstances.

Janet Frost was a big woman. She was large-boned and nearly six feet tall. All her family had always been big people. One of the reasons she had been attracted to her late husband, Raymond Frost, had been because at six five he had been one of the few men she had ever known who made her feel tiny. She had always wanted to feel tiny. She had always wanted a great many things, and she had gotten very little of what she had dreamed of and prayed for. Of that, she was acutely aware.

Janet Frost was sitting in a reception area of the prison. It was eleven in the morning on a warm Wednesday. She was surrounded by perhaps fifty other people, mostly women and children, who were here for the same purpose—to visit a loved one who now lived inside this terrible place. She had been sitting there now for more than a half hour, and to fight the boredom she read and reread the small printed form she had been sent that set forth the rules governing visitors.

"The following items are prohibited in the visiting area," the rules said. "No hats, wigs, or scarves. No folding money, cigarettes, cigarette lighters, candy, food, gum, or drinks. No purses, billfolds, combs, brushes, lipsticks, or nail files. No tank tops, tube tops, extremely low-cut, transparent or midriff blouses. Absolutely no medication."

"Janet Frost?"

Janet looked up. A female guard, a worn-looking woman of perhaps thirty, was standing up at her desk, scanning the room. Janet stood and walked over to her.

"I'm Janet Frost."

"Come with me, please."

The two women entered a tiny room behind the information desk. Janet towered over the guard, the difference in their sizes accentuated by the closeness of their quarters.

"I need to search you," the guard said.

Janet said nothing in response, only nodding slightly.

The guard asked Janet to extend her arms, which she did. Then the guard ran her hands over Janet—under the arms, over the torso, around her buttocks, and down her legs. Janet stood unmoving, eyes closed. The guard could, she knew from the literature the prison had sent her, ask her to disrobe and conduct a skin search. Janet hoped it wouldn't come to that. The guard's hands paused on her breasts.

"What do you have in there?" the guard asked suspiciously.

"A prosthesis," Janet told her. "Two of them, actually."

"I'll have to check."

Janet Frost undid her blouse and bent over. The guard looked inside her bra. Where Janet's once beautiful breasts had been—the breasts Raymond had loved so dearly so many years before, the breasts that

252

had nursed Wendell—there were now only plastic cups that filled her bra so she wouldn't look strange and ugly on the street. Janet could sense the guard shuddering as she saw what she saw. Janet stood erect and arranged her clothing.

"You can go in now," the guard said.

Janet followed the guard's directions to the visiting area on the second floor of the administration building. It was a large room, the size of a small hotel lobby, and it was decidedly unprisonlike. The floor was carpeted and the walls were clean and freshly painted. Prints of pastoral scenes decorated the room. There were perhaps two dozen seating areas composed of inexpensive but solid furniture. There were also groupings of folding chairs scattered about. Already men were here with their women and children. Children flitted about the large room, playing tag and laughing. A television set played in one corner, ignored by everyone. Janet looked for her son. She saw him near the far door, standing in a group of several men. They were all bikers, Janet realized. Even in prison clothing she could tell that. It was the way they wore their hair, their tattoos. Bikers loved their tattoos.

For the ten thousandth time she cursed herself for letting Wendell buy that third-hand motorbike when he was twelve. Perhaps if she hadn't given in on that . . .

He saw her and came over to her. Janet looked up into her son's bearded face—a beard showing decidedly vivid flecks of gray, she realized with a start. She wondered where that had come from. Raymond had died young, too young to go gray. But she, at fifty-four, still could brag that she had not even a touch of gray.

Wasn't that strange?

"Hi, Ma," Frost said. "You look good."

They did not touch. There was no hug or kiss.

"So do you," Janet told him. "You've slimmed down some."

"Weights," he said. "I work out with weights every day. You want to sit down?"

"Yes, let's do that."

They sought out two chairs in a corner beneath a sign that read: "Let's Keep Our Visiting Area Clean." It was signed, in smaller print, by the Inmate Advisory Council. There was a moment of awkward silence between them.

Then Janet said, "It's been a long time, hasn't it?"

Wendell nodded. "A long time."

"I couldn't come here, Wendell. I just couldn't. I hope you understand. This place . . ." she gestured with her hand ". . . I just couldn't come here."

"So why are you here now?"

"To see you. It's been a long time."

"You said that before."

"How are you getting on here?"

He shrugged his huge shoulders. It was a gesture that reminded Janet of Raymond. "Okay. I got me some friends here. I got this real good friend, Bob. We get along real good."

"What do you do with your time here?"

"Work out, mostly. I got a job in the laundry a couple of hours a day. I watch TV a lot. That kind of stuff."

"Why haven't you written me? I know they give you three stamps a week."

"I'm not much for writing. You know that."

"What do you do with the stamps?"

"Sell them."

"And what do you use the money for? I know you can get drugs in here, Wendell. I hope you're not still doing drugs—not after where it got you."

Frost grinned widely. "Nah, I'm not taking no drugs. My friend got me off drugs. "Bobbi—my friend, Bob—is down on drugs. Bob is into health stuff. No smoking, no drinking, no drugs. That's what got me into lifting, and now I don't do no drugs. Bob would throw a fit if I came into the cell stoned."

"That's very good. I'm proud of you, Wendell."

"Ah," Wendell said, dismissing his mother's pride with a gesture of his huge hand.

Janet Frost studied her enormous son. Wendell gazed absently around the room. It was getting crowded now, and Janet realized with a start that some of the couples were actually making love here in the visiting room, in front of everybody. Several guards lounged at a corner table, seemingly oblivious to it all. Not ten feet away Janet could see one couple using the woman's long summer gown more or less as a privacy tent. The inmate was sitting on the floor. His wife or girlfriend sat on his lap, facing in the same direction. Her flowing shirt hid the naked mechanics of what they were doing, but just barely. The woman—no, Janet couldn't call her that; the girl was no more than eighteen—sat buttocks to crotch on the man's lap, the folds of dress obscuring their bodies below the waist. Her eyes were open, staring off into space. The man's eyes were blissfully closed, and his mouth was slightly open as he panted more or less quietly. Janet could see them move under the folds of skirt.

God, she thought, what kind of place is this? But she knew, of course. It was a maximum security prison. It was filled with the worst humanity had to offer in a large state. And yet, women came here to give themselves to these men, to give themselves shamelessly and publicly, as this girl was doing. These men—the small minority who had regular visitors—were loved despite it all. They were loved in spite of what they had done, in spite of what they were. It had not saved them. It certainly hadn't saved Wendell, who had been loved—was loved at this very moment—by his mother.

Perhaps if Raymond hadn't somehow developed that bubble on a blood vessel in his brain then maybe it would have turned out all right. By the time Wendell had reached ten years of age, he had been beyond Janet's control. He had been beyond all control except maybe that of a strong man, who would have beaten him and terrorized him and instilled in him some fear of authority. As it was, Wendell despised all authority, refused to recognize it, spat in its face and worse. He felt no sympathy for the weak, no guilt for his sins against them. Janet knew all this. She knew she had borne a man unfit and unable to live in the company of others who were not precisely like him in emotional outlook.

Janet Frost watched the man on the floor as he climaxed, his jaw tightening and relaxing as he finished. She looked over at Wendell. She hoped they would never let her son out of this place.

"How's the food here?" Janet asked him, not knowing what else to say.

"Okay," he said in a bored tone.

"Not like home, eh?" Janet said, trying to make him smile.

Wendell turned to her. His eyes narrowed. Janet felt a tingle of warning. She had seen that expression before. It had always marked the rage bubbling up for no reason that made any sense, the inexplicable grudge taking tangible form.

"No," he said slowly, "not like home. I'm glad, too. You want to know what food was like home? I'll tell you. I remember being a little kid and having you put food in front of me. It was boiled vegetables and slabs of meat with fat on the edges, potatoes with lumps in them. And you said I had to eat it. I'd say no. Then you'd say 'Not all of it.' That's what you used to tell me. 'Just eat a little, that's all.' It was like barfing a little. It's just as bad as barfing a lot. And you made me eat that shit, day after day."

Janet felt her heart begin to race slightly. He wouldn't lose control here. He wouldn't do that. She knew that much.

"Wendell . . ." she began.

"Remember that?" he asked her, his face reddening beneath his beard. "Remember that shit you always made me eat?"

"I just wanted you to get good nourishment," Janet said, her voice almost a plea. "I wanted you to eat food that was good for you. I wanted you to get enough sleep so—"

"Sleep," Frost said. He made the word an accusation. "As far as you were concerned, nothing was more important than sleep. Having a good time, that wasn't important. You were always telling me to calm down, to take it easy, not to get excited. You were always saying to me that I couldn't have fun just because there were more important things to do. Remember? Cleaning the house, that was more important than having a laugh or two. I could never leave a jacket on a chair or a magazine on a table. No, no. We never had nothing on a table unless it was that shitty food you used to cram down my throat. Clean, clean, clean. The house always had to be perfect. That way people would know we weren't niggers, right? Isn't that what you said? What would the neighbors say if they could see this mess, you used to say. Fuck the neighbors. You hear that, Ma? Fuck the goddamn neighbors."

A guard stood up at the table in the corner. Wendell glanced at the man and tried to settle himself down. He felt anger churning inside him. He had told all this to Bobbi and some of it to that fat prison shrink. It hadn't made him feel any better, though, so he had stopped talking about it. Why had she come here, anyway? He was doing fine without her. If he was screwed up, then it was her fault, not his.

The guard walked over. He was a short stocky black man. He looked like Gladys Knight in drag. "You better settle down, fella," he said.

Rhino Frost nodded. "I'm cool."

The guard went back to the table and resumed his place, eyeing the Frosts. Janet was shaken, but she was grateful the guard had been there. She felt tears well in her eyes.

"Wendell," she said quietly, "I tried to do what was right for you. I tried to raise you as a decent boy. That's all I wanted for you. That's all I ever wanted."

"Bullshit," Frost said quietly. "You wanted me to be like you. Don't drink, don't take dope. Work hard in school. Don't fight with people who go around just begging to get beat up. That's what you said. You think that worked for you, don't you? You've spent your whole life trying to do the right thing, right? And what have you got? You got a little house with a mortgage that holds you like a slave chain. You spend every second in that insurance office, typing letters and answering the phone and grubbing around for every nickel. And you wanted me to live like that?"

"And how are you living now?" Janet Frost asked her son, tears streaming down her face.

He looked at her, and he said nothing. Then he looked down at the floor. Janet was glad he had turned away. In his face she had seen only the anger, always the anger. It burned like a beacon in him. To Wendell the world had always been full of enemies. And somehow he had gotten the idea that enemies served only one purpose—to be subjugated and taken advantage of and, if they resisted, destroyed. They weren't him. And if they weren't him, they didn't count. Janet knew how his mind worked. What she didn't know, couldn't understand, was what she had done or had failed to do to make his mind work that way. If she'd known what he would become, she would have strangled him in his cradle.

"I'm going now," she said.

"So go," he said, still staring at the floor. "Why'd you come in the first place? It took you long enough."

She sighed. Then she said slowly, "I came because I'm dying, Wendell. I had a double mastectomy last December. They thought they got it all, but now they know they didn't. I have another tumor, down on my lower spine. They can't operate on it. I came to see you

259

one last time. I'm going to leave you the house and some insurance. It'll be in trust for you until you get out. I'll send you a letter with all the details. I just wanted to see you one more time and to tell you that."

Wendell Frost looked at his mother, his face expressionless. If this news shocked or saddened him, he didn't show it. Janet hadn't expected him to be moved in any way. After all, it was only happening to someone else. It wasn't him.

"You probably got it from those cigarettes you used to smoke," Wendell said to her.

"I stopped smoking years ago, Wendell."

"Yeah," he said. "I remember. But you didn't stop soon enough, did you? You got cancer, it's your own fault. That's what you always told me when I got sick, that it was my own fault. Remember that?"

Janet Frost stood up. She was calm now. Actually, she had been calm for some weeks now, ever since she had gotten used to the news of her impending death. At this point, she almost welcomed it—especially right now, sitting here in this awful place. Her legacy to the world, she knew, would be this horrible man to whom she had given birth. How could the marvelous love she and Raymond shared have been perverted into what Wendell had become? Janet would have to ask God about that. She'd be in a position to do that soon enough.

"Good-bye, Wendell," she said. "I hope you use the money to build some kind of life for yourself. However else I might have failed you, maybe this will help."

"Hey," Rhino Frost told his mother, smiling slightly, "money never hurts."

CHAPTER TWENTY

Mary Ellen knew her weaknesses.

Chocolate was one. When she was around chocolate, she had to fight against going into a feeding frenzy, like a shark. When she was around the television set on a weekday afternoon, she had to struggle against becoming involved in the soaps, against sitting there like a zombie for two hours, and losing the time to more worthwhile pursuits. And in a shopping center, she had to guard against her consumer impulse. If she let her urges run unchecked, Mary Ellen could buy out an entire department store and still have enough buying lust left over for the catalogue shops. Once, when a purse snatcher had grabbed her pocketbook in Center City, Murphy had tried to cheer her up by pointing out that the thief, using her credit cards, would probably do less damage to the family finances than she did herself. She had not laughed. Shopping mania was not a humorous topic to Mary Ellen.

So it was that when it came time for Patricia to go to the mall to shop for college clothes, Mary Ellen had refused to go inside with her.

"I'll meet you here at four," Mary Ellen had said in

the car. "You be right out front here in front of Wanamaker's."

Armed with her mother's MasterCard, Patricia prowled the mall. So far she had bought some jeans, a good wool skirt, two tops, a new pair of Docksiders, some dress pumps, three pairs of panty hose, and a brown leather jacket. It hardly seemed like enough to supplement what she already had, but the bills were high enough to give her pause. Patricia glanced at her watch. She still had twenty-five minutes before her mother would be there to pick her up. She sighed with boredom and dropped into a B. Dalton bookstore to browse. She glanced through the latest Stephen King paperback, then she paid three-ninety-five plus tax for a soft-cover version of an historical novel called *Yellow,* which was a good read, the clerk assured her.

Patricia was heading for the mall entrance when she saw Frost.

He was near the door, and he was unmoving, like a statue. Along with a bemused expression, he wore his headband, his worn jeans, and, despite the oppressive heat outside, his biker jacket. He towered near the glass doors leading outside, looming up there like a monolith.

He was looking straight at her.

Patricia felt her heart sputter and begin to thump like it was being played by Rod Stewart's drummer. All the blood left her mid-section, flowing to her arms and legs. She trembled as it did, clutching her packages. She looked around. The mall was filled with people, even on a weekday. He wouldn't dare try to hurt her.

But Rittenhouse Square had been filled with people, too.

Frost was a good hundred feet away. His eyes fully on Patricia, he began to move toward her. Patricia did the only thing that seemed sensible, under the circumstances. She ran like hell.

She turned and cut to her right. She couldn't tell if he was after her, but she made the assumption he was, crowd or no crowd. Patricia bobbed and weaved through the throng of shoppers, cutting right and left like Walter Payton, zigging and zagging. Her target was the other end of the mall where there was another door. There were no cops here on private property. There ought to be some security guards, but she couldn't be sure, and if they were here she had no idea where they might be. Patricia ran and dodged and ran some more. She moved quickly and well. She was out the other door in less than a minute. Out and up to the curb that bordered the parking lot.

And Frost was there. She almost bumped into him.

Patricia's eyes widened. She had emerged from the other end of the mall, at the Strawbridge & Clothier end. And there he was, not twenty feet away, sitting on his bike, waiting for her. Instantly she knew that he hadn't followed her. He'd simply gone outside the door where she'd seen him, hopped on his bike, and ridden down to this end of the mall to await her appearance. He'd guessed what she would do when she began running, and he'd guessed right. Patricia stood, frozen and Frost merely looked at her as the crowd moved around her. Neither of them moved. Neither spoke. Then, very slowly, Patricia began to move backward, back into the mall. Frost only watched. Patricia bumped into someone. She turned her head at the impact, then turned back to Frost, her eyes locked on him. She pushed her way back into the crowd.

Rhino Frost, on his huge Harley, only watched as she faded away. He made no sound. His silence was message enough.

Patricia made the run back to the Wanamaker end of the mall in only slightly less time than she had made the first trip. She went out the door cautiously. Her mother's car was waiting. She looked both ways, seeing nothing. Then she sprinted for the Datsun. She leaped inside and locked her door. She leaned over across a startled Mary Ellen and locked hers, too. Then Patricia hung over the back of the front seat and slammed down the button on each back door.

"What's going on?" Mary Ellen demanded.

"Let's get out of here," Patricia gasped, eyes as huge as pizzas.

"What is it?" Mary Ellen said again, irritated now.

"He was in the mall. He was watching me."

Mary Ellen put the car in gear and got the hell out of there.

Buzz.

"Yes," Murphy said. He'd just gotten in after driving Carol Highland all the way home to Paoli. Carol had been understandably hysterical, and not even Murphy's protestations that she was probably off the hook completely had calmed her—not after she'd had two matrons poking around her private parts. His nerves were frazzled, too, after all that. Murphy had slept all of about two hours last night.

"It's your wife," Esmeralda told him.

Murphy sighed. He knew he was paid up for the

month. He hit the button. "Hi."

"Frank, that man Frost was at the mall. He followed Patricia."

"What?"

"Don't worry, she's all right. We're both at the house. I've got all the doors and windows locked."

"I'll be right there."

Murphy slammed down the phone and grabbed his suitcoat. He barreled out of the place. Esmeralda looked up as he came roaring through. She shook her head and went back to her typing.

Lawyers, she thought.

Murphy hit rush-hour traffic on his way out to Mount Airy. He leaned on his horn and shook his fist. He wished for the thousandth time that he had his heat-seeking missile. It took him an hour to get to the house. He parked in the driveway behind Mary Ellen's Datsun and pounded on the door. Mary Ellen opened it without even peeking out first.

"I know that slam," she explained.

"Where's Patricia?" he demanded, rushing inside.

He found her at the kitchen table. Patricia was calm now, and she told about the encounter in a level voice.

"He didn't touch you?" Murphy said. "He didn't get near you?"

She shook her head.

Murphy looked at Mary Ellen. His face was red. She couldn't remember seeing him so angry. She didn't like it, either. She knew that Murphy was slow to truly anger, but he had difficulty regaining control when it happened. He was having that difficulty now.

"I'm going to kill the son of a bitch," Murphy said.

"Just calm down, Frank," Mary Ellen told him. "Nobody got hurt."

"Somebody's about to get hurt. Rhino Frost is about to get hurt. He might even get dead."

Mary Ellen didn't like it. He was pacing the kitchen. Only with Frank, she knew, the pacing wouldn't release tension; it would only exacerbate it.

"Why don't you call Jimmy?" she suggested.

"He can't do anything."

"Can't he keep him away from us?"

Murphy glared at his wife. "He wasn't bothering you. He was in a public place. He didn't do anything wrong. Jimmy can't touch him. I'm going to have to handle this myself. There's no other choice."

Mary Ellen said, "Stay here for a while and calm down. There's some bourbon in the cabinet."

He shook his head. "No. I'm going to go see him. I know where he lives. Catrelli told me that."

Patricia was on her feet. "Don't do that, Daddy."

"I have to do that. Don't worry," he said, patting his pistol on his hip beneath his suit coat, "I can handle myself."

Which was what Mary Ellen was afraid of. "If you go to see him, Frank," she said quietly, "leave that here."

"Are you crazy?" he demanded.

Mary Ellen spoke quietly. "You know I'm right."

Murphy quivered with fury.

"If you go there with that," Mary Ellen said, "you know what'll happen, and so do I."

Murphy took deep breaths. Then he pulled the holster off his belt and laid the pistol on the table.

"Don't lose it," he said.

"Daddy," Patricia wailed.

Murphy said nothing. He merely stomped out of the house and slammed the front door behind him. They heard the Toronado start up and pull out of the driveway. Mary Ellen's face was impassive. She was icy calm. Patricia turned on her mother, her eyes flashing.

"Why did you make him do that?"

"Because your father would kill that man if he had that gun."

"And what'll happen to him now?"

"Now," Mary Ellen said, "he'll calm down on the way, and he'll change his mind about going to see him."

That was what she hoped, anyway.

She was wrong. Murphy was still trembling with rage when he pulled up outside Rhino Frost's garage in Olney. The garage and the apartment over it were in an alley lined with the backs of row houses on each side. Murphy got out of the car. Dusk was falling. Light was scarce now. He wished he'd brought the pistol. He thought about leaving. He went around to the Toronado's trunk and found his lug wrench. He brought it up and laid it on the front seat, next to his seat belt. Then he kicked at Frost's garage door. It was a hard kick. It made noise. He did it again.

"Frost," he called out. "Come on out here."

Murphy went back to his car and leaned on the horn. He blasted the horn once, twice, three times. Then he went back and kicked the garage door again, almost breaking his foot in the process.

Nothing.

He sighed, feeling the rage finally begin to bubble

267

down. Then he sighed and got back into the car. He turned the key. He was putting the car in gear when Rhino Frost came out through the garage door on the driver's side of Murphy's car. Murphy saw him and grabbed the lug wrench. Frost bent over and gazed in through the window on the passenger's side. He smiled broadly in at Murphy.

Murphy shut off the engine and opened his door. He stood up, one foot still inside the car and the lug wrench clutched tightly in his right hand. Frost began to move around to the front of the car.

"Stop right there," Murphy ordered.

Frost stopped. It was an authoritative voice, a cop's voice, and Frost had been conditioned by years in prison to stop when he heard such a voice. It had been painful conditioning. He remembered it.

They stood unmoving for a moment, Murphy in his car with his weapon, Frost looming over the hood of the old car. Frost said nothing, and his grin was maddening.

"How much?" Murphy asked him.

Frost cocked his head. "How much?"

"You heard me. How much will it take for you to leave me and my family alone?"

Frost shook his head. "I'm not bothering nobody. I got a few guys, they've been bothering me. They've been putting cuffs on me and kicking me in the balls—I should say, ball—but not me. I ain't been bothering a soul."

Murphy's face was impassive. "How much?"

Rhino Frost's face clouded over. The grin vanished. His eyebrows rose in a thick arch. His lips parted slightly, just enough for him to draw a deep breath. His chin lowered. His huge shoulders straightened, and he seemed to expand, to grow, to blow himself like a blowfish. Murphy tightened his grip on the lug wrench. He knew in that moment that Mary Ellen had been right. If Murphy had had the gun with him, he might have emptied it at that moment into the enormous shape at the end of his hood. It was possible, anyway. He didn't think he'd do it, but he might have. It was just as well that the pistol was back in Mount Airy. Murphy watched Frost. The big man said nothing.

"Be reasonable," Murphy told him. "It's over. Take some profit from it. I'll pay you what you want."

When Frost finally spoke, Murphy had to struggle to hear the voice. "Thirteen years, eight months, seventeen days. You ever been inside Graterford, Sergeant?"

Murphy nodded. "I've been there."

"You know then."

"Know what?"

"You know that you ain't got enough. If you've been there, then you know. Nobody's got enough."

Then Frost turned and walked back into the garage. He cast Murphy one blood-chilling glance before he closed the door, the sort of look Murphy imagined an alligator gave off as it approached a waterbird from beneath, its jaws flexing. Then Murphy was alone in the alley, his hand still clutching the lug wrench. He let his breath go slowly and got back into the car. Murphy turned the ignition and drove back to Mount Airy.

"What happened?" Mary Ellen asked as he came into the kitchen.

Murphy's face was no longer dark with rage. It was

pale and grim. He had been thinking on the way home. He had stopped at a neighborhood taproom and pondered the situation over an old-fashioned.

"Where's Patricia?" he asked.

"Upstairs, asleep."

"Where's that bourbon?" he asked, going into the kitchen.

"The cabinet over the sink."

Murphy took down the bottle of Old Grandad and found a glass. He poured himself a stiff jolt, sipped at it, decided it wasn't enough and poured more. He returned the bottle to its resting place and sat down at the kitchen table. How many serious discussions had taken place right here, he thought?

"What happened?" Mary Ellen said again.

Murphy looked up at her. "He won't let it go. I offered him money."

Mary Ellen smiled. "It's a good thing he said no. You don't have any money."

"That I would have worried about later. It doesn't make any difference, anyway."

She sat down across the table from him. "What are we going to do, Frank?"

"I think you and Patricia ought to get out of town for a while."

She looked at him in surprise. "And go where? And for how long?"

"For a week or so. I'm very close to wrapping up this Highland case. It's my first big case, and if I can get her off completely it'll get the practice going right. Only it's going to take every second for a few days."

"Where would we go?" Mary Ellen said again. "I've got to go back to work pretty soon. Patricia has to go

270

off to school."

He sat back in the kitchen chair and lit a cigarette. "Harold Warren has a client who owns a new development of cabins up in the Poconos. The guy tried to hawk me one a few weeks back when he was in the office. Just what I needed—a vacation house in the mountains. But I remembered it tonight. I called Harold. He called his client. You could go up and stay in one of the new cabins for a while. It's all worked out—if you're willing to do it. It makes sense to me."

Mary Ellen made a face. "It would have been nice if you'd talked to me about it first. What if I don't want to go?"

Murphy sipped his bourbon. He gazed over the rim of the glass at her. "Knowing what you know about this guy, don't you want to go?"

Mary Ellen thought about it. "I suppose I do. But what happens when we get back?"

"I'll have him taken care of by then."

"How?" she asked.

"Trust me," her husband told her.

"Hello."

"Dom? Frank."

"Hiya. What's up?"

"Want to make some money?"

"Frost again?"

"Yep. Only this time I don't want you to count on Jim to help. He can't help with what has to be done now."

"You're not talking about the whole route, are you, Frank?"

271

"Not the whole route, no."

Catrelli thought about it. "I'll have to take on some help for this."

"Give me a price."

"A grand."

"Come on."

"Seven-fifty. Good help don't come cheap these days, Frank."

"All right," Murphy said. "Good enough."

Catrelli chuckled into the phone. "I could use the exercise, anyway."

CHAPTER TWENTY-ONE

"Shrimp cocktail," Everett Highland said. "And a piece of scrod. You can go light on the butter."

"Very good, sir," the waiter said, taking his menu. He turned to Murphy. "And you, sir?"

"Same for me on the shrimp," Murphy said, "only I'll take lobster newburg for the main course. And a Lowenbrau dark with the meal."

"Thank you, sir," the waiter said, taking Murphy's menu and walking away toward the kitchen.

Everett Highland looked casually around the Presidents' Room of Old Original Bookbinder's. It was smaller than the cavernous main dining room, and what Murphy liked best about the Presidents' Room was that the bar was located along one wall, within easy reach. They made terrific bloody marys here, and Murphy was finishing his second one, which he had loaded up with horseradish from the jar on the table. Murphy seldom drank vodka, and when he did he always made it a point to drink it here, where he could punch up the bloody marys to a properly fiery potency.

"You know," Highland said, "I've lived in and around this city all my life, and I've never been in

Bookbinder's before. I always thought of it as sort of a tourist trap."

"Well, it is that," Murphy conceded, "but the food is great, anyway. When I was in the DA's office, I used to come here for lunch every Friday and have a shrimp cocktail, a bowl of bouillabaisse, and a piece of strawberry shortcake for dessert. There was a whole group of us who used to come here every Friday for just that meal. We had a reserved table right in this room, and we'd take two-and-a-half-hour lunches and make it up by working later during the week. This is a good joint. I have real affection for the place."

Everett Highland smiled. It amused him that food could be so important to anyone. To him, it was a topic of monumental indifference, which went a long way toward explaining his trim frame.

"Well," he said finally, "I'm grateful for the opportunity to see the place. Now, what's on your mind. Mr. Murphy?"

Murphy sipped his drink and lit a Camel with a Bic plastic lighter. "You might as well call me Frank. For some reason, I can't seem to get either of the women in your family to use my first name, but considering how involved we've all become it seems the logical thing to do."

Highland smiled slightly. "All right. I'll call you Frank, and you call me Ev. You know, it's strange. In America, people signify intimacy or familiarity by using first names. In Britain, familiarity between friends is signified by the use of the surname. If we were in Britain, I'd call you Murphy and you'd call me Highland. Here, the use of surnames has, at best, an impersonal quality to it, and in some circumstances an

274

insulting one."

Murphy said, "I never understood the British to begin with. Here they are, our closest political ally, and while we make such a fetish of democracy, they insist on clinging to the monarchy. I just can't imagine a more useless institution than the British monarchy."

"Oh?" Highland said. "Do you really think so?"

"Well, just look at who these people are," Murphy said. "There's the Queen Mum, I think they call her. She seems like a nice enough old lady, everything considered. She smiles and waves a lot, and I've read that she likes to take a nip now and then. That makes her more or less okay in my book. Then there's Prince Philip. He seems like a nice enough guy, only he's got nothing in life to do. Queen Elizabeth is sort of a grim dowager with a smile made out of solid plastic. The only thing I ever heard about her that even remotely impressed me was how cool she was when that psycho broke into her bedroom in Buckingham Palace a few years back and she had to keep him entertained until the guards showed up. She split her pack of cigarettes with him, according to the *Inquirer*. Nice touch, I thought."

"I think I remember that," Highland said.

"I remember it vividly. I kept thinking what would have happened if the nut had wandered into Princess Margaret's bedroom. He'd probably have run out screaming to protect his virtue. From what I've read about her, she spends all her spare time on some warm-weather island entertaining rock groups. And Princess Anne is supposed to be a nasty-mouthed sort who lives only for her horses. She has this husband—Mark Phillips, I think his name is—and he's supposed to be a horse nut, too. Only from what I've read in the newspapers, he must feel uncomfortable around their superior intellects."

Highland laughed aloud. "That's quite funny," he said.

"Not if you're a British subject and you're got to pay to support all these people in such sumptuous style. I mean, look at Prince Charles. He gets paid a ton of money every year just to cut ribbons and stuff like that. And Lady Di's job seems to consist of having kids—when she's not having her hair done. And who's the younger brother, the one who got married a while back?"

"Prince Andrew."

"Yeah, Andrew. Nice kid. He was running around with that porno actress before he finally married this honey with the red hair. Not that I blame him. But the kid's twenty-five or twenty-six, I think. Isn't it time he got a goddamn job? At twenty-five, I was rolling around in a patrol car with drug dealers shooting at me every Friday night. I mean, who are we kidding with all this? And, for some reason I can't quite fathom, the British seem perfectly willing to pay whatever it takes to keep these useless people living high on the hog. So when you tell me that they take it as a sign of endearment to call people by their last names, that doesn't surprise me. That's a weird country. The queen proves that."

Highland shook his head, amused. "I've never heard it put quite like that. I presume that with views like that and an Irish name, you support the IRA."

Murphy shook his head vigorously. "They're a bunch of Commie bombers. This IRA doesn't have much to do with the IRA people think of back in the early part of the century when Britain ruled all of Ireland. I don't support political bombings. I don't care what the cause is. I've got some cousins who are all for that kind of crap, but not me."

The waiter brought their shrimp cocktails. Murphy watched Highland eat.

"Left-handed, eh?" Murphy said.

"Yes," Highland told him. "So is Carol. What are the odds of a husband and wife both being left-handed, I wonder?"

Murphy frowned. "I don't know," he said sourly.

"Mother is left-handed, too," Highland said. "That's who I got it from, I suppose. My father was right-handed. We left-handers are supposed to be more creative, you know."

"Really," Murphy said. His frown was deeper now. He swallowed a shrimp almost whole, hardly tasting it.

"This is very good," Highland told him. "Now, Mr. Murphy—Frank, I mean—you asked me here for a reason. May I inquire as to what it might be?"

"All right," Murphy said crisply. "You know that Carol is not quite off the hook, but almost. You're aware of that?"

Highland put down his fork. "I'd been under the impression that the dropping of charges against Carol was more or less of a formality at this point. There seems to be conclusive proof that she couldn't have done it."

"Maybe," Murphy said, "and maybe not. Do you know the district attorney, Fletcher Lake?"

"We've met."

"I imagine you have. You'd move in more or less the same social circles. What do you think of him?"

Highland shrugged. "He seems ambitious."

"Ambitious?" Murphy said. "Listen, you look up the word ambitious in the dictionary, they have Fletcher's picture next to it. He's elevated ambition to an art form. He's made it a science. A rational man would drop the charges against your wife in a second. But Fletcher wants to be governor, and he'd love a society conviction and all the publicity it would bring. He might still drop charges against her, but he won't do it until he has another suspect. And until he drops them, Carol is still in danger."

"That seems hard to believe. Lake has always struck me as a responsible man. He's a public servant and—"

"—he's a flaming asshole," Murphy broke in. "I know the guy. I worked for him for a few years. Believe me, I know."

"But surely there are others who would be involved in the decision as to prosecute."

Murphy nodded. "There are. And, for the most part, they're good people trying to do a good job. But you've got to realize something here. This is the state you're up against. This is the same state you go to to get your license plates, and you know how screwed up Motor Vehicles is. It's the same state you bump into when you're looking for the refund on your state income tax. There are good, talented, conscientious people in government, but they're all part of a vast, cumbersome system that doesn't work very well even under the best of circumstances. On top of that, a lot of them stumble under the weight of all that government. They report to politicians—people like Lake—and they have to be responsive to people who win elections or their careers go right down the drain. If Lake decides to go on this, nobody in the bureaucracy can stop him. You can't go to his boss. He doesn't have one. For four years, he's a goddamn emperor. The only power that can restrain him is the courts. And for the courts to stop him from sending Carol to prison to further his career and to make some headlines, Carol would have to stand trial. There's always a risk in that."

"Is it really like that?" Highland asked, somewhat shocked.

"That's the way it works," Murphy assured him. "That's why the law makes it so difficult for the state to convict and jail any individual. The system takes a long time to work, and it's loaded with protections that usually are taken advantage of only by scumbags. But every once in a while, an innocent person—somebody like Carol—becomes the target of the state. When I was on the other side, I used to find those protections a huge pain in the ass. But now, doing what I do, I'm glad they're in place. However difficult they make it to put away people who deserve to be put away, they also protect innocent people from the weight of the bureaucracy and from the occasional jerk like Fletcher Lake who manages to convince a sleeping electorate that he's something other than what he really is."

Highland thought about what Murphy had said. "What can we do, then?"

"What seems clear to me is that the only way we can ensure Carol's safety is to come up with a new suspect for Fletcher Lake. That's why I asked you here today. I need to ask you some questions. I need to point the DA's office in another direction."

Highland nodded. "What direction do you have in mind?"

"That's the problem. I don't have a direction in mind. I have no idea in the world where to look. Jimmy Wilder—he's the police lieutenant who arrested Carol—he's finally on board. He doesn't think she did it, either. And neither does Lake's key deputy, Paul Toddman. They're checking all of Hank Kirby's past acquaintances, trying to come up with something. If they do, fine. But if they don't, then the only suspect is Carol, and Lake will continue to hold charges against her until and unless he has somewhere else to go. With all the press this case has already received, he can't afford to leave it unsolved."

"So Carol is definitely still in danger?"

Murphy nodded. "Lake may take a run at her even without having a sure thing. He can't let this one go unsolved. If he got lucky—if he got a dopey jury, for example, and that's happened before—he might even manage to convict her. Even if she were to get off, he'd do his best afterward to make it seem that the judge and jury had screwed up. That's how he'd get off the hook in this. And Carol would always be a killer in the eyes of the public, even though the jury had exonerated her and all the people involved in the investigation would know that she was clean. It's her reputation you have to worry about now. And a person's reputation has some value."

Highland nodded solemnly. "Yes, it certainly does. So what do you propose?"

"I propose to find the real murderer. I can't think of any other way out. Maybe the cops will do it before I can, but I have a suspicion—based on nothing I can put my finger on—that the murderer isn't one of Kirby's old acquaintances. I think it's somebody involved in some way in his relationship with your wife. That's pure gut instinct talking, but I've learned over the years to count on it."

"What can I do to help?" Everett Highland asked as the main courses came.

Murphy dug into his lobster newburg. "Tell me everything you told the cops. And tell me the things you didn't tell them, too."

Murphy ate while Highland talked over his cooling piece of scrod. He recounted what he had told Wilder, and he finished up by saying, "That's what I told the police, and I'm afraid I can't tell you any more than I told them. I just don't know any more."

"All right," Murphy said. "Let me ask you some questions. You're sure you didn't hear her go out?"

Highland shook his head. "I didn't hear a thing. I slept soundly until morning."

"What time did you get up the next morning?"

"Seven, I'd say. Maybe earlier."

"And what did you do when you woke up? Did you awaken Carol?"

"No, I went fishing. In the summer, when I'm not teaching at the university, I spend just about every morning fishing on Penn Pond. It takes me about forty-five minutes to get there, and I stay there in a rented rowboat until lunchtime or so. Then I come back home and spend the rest of the day with Carol. She tends to rise late. It's her habit."

"You fish alone?"

Highland nodded. "It's sort of a time of meditation for me, Frank. I enjoy it. I take along a book and lie in the rowboat and read. Sometimes I catch a bass or two, but I usually throw them back. They're fun to catch but not very good eating. The only ones I keep are the pike. They're bony but tasty. Mother makes a fine fish stew from pike."

"I know what a bass is like," Murphy said. "My old man used to take me fishing in the Delaware, back when it was still mostly water. There were bass in there, all along the shore. I never caught a pike, though. They're those big, skinny fish with the bills like ducks, aren't they?"

Highland smiled slightly. "That sounds like a pike. They're rather mean. And they have teeth. They're sort of like a little fresh-water barracuda. With a bass, you can put your hand right in their mouths and pull out the lure. They don't have any teeth, and they can't hurt you, unless you're small enough for one of them to swallow you whole. But you put your hand in a pike's mouth and you can lose a finger or two. They're positively vicious. I've had pike come right up the line for my hand when I pulled them out."

"Sounds like a fun fish to have in the boat with you. How do you get the lure out of their mouths?"

"Oh," Highland said, "you have to knock them silly first. You hit them with a fishing club."

"Oh?" Murphy said. "You have a fishing club?"

"Yes. You need one if you're going to catch pike. It's either that or lose your lure."

"How big is a fishing club?" Murphy asked casually.

Highland held his hands about eighteen inches apart. "About like this."

"What's a fishing club made of?"

Highland cocked his head and studied Murphy before answering. "Wood."

"Like a little baseball bat?"

"Yes, exactly."

"And where's yours now?"

"I don't know," Highland told him. "Usually it's in my car, but I haven't been able to find it for a few days now. I haven't been to the pond since all this started. Well, that's not quite right. I went out the morning after the murder, but I didn't know then that there had been a murder."

"Was the club in your car that day?"

Highland shook his head. "No, that's when I realized it was missing. I . . . I didn't attach any importance to it. I thought I'd left it out at Penn Pond."

Murphy said nothing.

"This could be important, couldn't it?" Everett Highland asked.

"It might be. Where did you buy the fishing club?"

"I bought it at a sport shop in the village last summer. I'd broken my old one on a particularly mean fish I'd caught. What is this about? I'm curious."

"I'll tell you when it's firmer in my mind," Murphy told him. "Eat. You haven't touched your scrod."

Highland took a forkful of his fish. He chewed slowly. "I'd love to know what you're thinking," he said to Murphy.

"So would I," Murphy assured him.

The two men passed a pleasant meal. Afterward, Murphy picked up the check—he would get back the money when he collected his fee—and he asked Highland to drive him to his office. They rode in silence in Highland's blue Cadillac, the radio playing on the city's best classical music station. Highland let Murphy out on South Broad Street in front of the Fidelity Bank Building.

"I hope I've helped you," he said.

"I'll let you know," Murphy told him.

"I've very worried about this," Everett Highland told Murphy.

"Well," Murphy said, climbing out of the Cadillac amid the strains of Bach, "I don't blame you a bit."

CHAPTER TWENTY-TWO

Catrelli sucked on his mustache.

It was a nervous habit, and when he realized he was doing it, he made a conscious effort to stop. That made him want to do it all the more. He chewed on his lower lip instead. And he slapped the blackjack lightly against his leg. That was all right, he supposed. That would get him more in the mood, at least.

"Hey," Guarino said after listening a while to the slap-slap of the blackjack. "You want to quit that shit up there? You're making me nervous."

Catrelli looked over his shoulder into the backseat. He could hardly see Guarino, who came across in the darkness as no more than a hulking, dark shape in the rear of the Chevy.

"Jumpy?" Catrelli asked.

"Sick of waiting, that's all," Guarino grumbled back. "When's this guy supposed to get here?"

Catrelli shrugged. "When he gets here, that's when. You're sure you're not jumpy? I can always take you home so you can watch *The Partridge Family* on UHF or something. Then Elmer and me can come back here and handle this ourselves." Catrelli turned to Elmer

Lee, who sat in the passenger seat. "We can do it ourselves, right, Elmer?"

Elmer Lee, black even when sunlight poured down from the heavens, said, "He was supposed to be here already."

"Hey, who said he kept regular hours?" Catrelli demanded. "Did I say that?"

"You said he'd probably be home by midnight," Guarino argued.

"Probably," Catrelli said. "I said 'probably.' Does that sound like a blood oath to you, Elmer?"

Elmer stretched lazily and yawned. "It is getting late, man," he pointed out. "I got me a job to go to in the morning, you know?"

"Me, too," Guarino grumbled, lighting a cigarette. "I can't wait here all night."

"Just be cool," Catrelli told him, and resumed chewing on his lower lip.

Where was the son of a bitch? Catrelli wondered. He'd charted Frost's habits carefully enough. The big bastard was always home by this time of night. He always came down the alley on his hog and unlocked his garage door and rode inside and locked it behind him. Catrelli had watched the man for three days, trying to pick the time when he would be most vulnerable and when there would be the least chance of spectators. And now Frost was running well behind schedule and the hired help was growing restless, Catrelli went back to sucking on his mustache. He couldn't help it.

Catrelli had used Guarino and Elmer Lee before. They were both guys with real jobs during the day. Guarino was a security guard at the Navy yard and

Elmer Lee was a steamfitter who had been a decent light heavyweight in his younger days. They were tough men, bruisers, and they picked up what extra money they could find by working for Catrelli when he called them. They would each get a hundred bucks for their work tonight, tax-free. Catrelli would keep the rest of the seven-fifty for himself. This was business. And, besides, he'd earn it.

If the big bastard ever showed, that was. Where in hell was he? Catrelli sucked on his mustache and slapped the blackjack against his leg and waited in the Chevy, feeling more than a little jumpy himself. He always got this way before something like this. He always had, even when he'd been on the force. He was a little guy, and little guys always needed the edge in situations like this. They needed the nerves, the extra speed the nerves provided—the extra guts and toughness.

But enough was enough. Where was the fucker?

After awhile, Guarino said, "You want to call it quits for tonight? He ain't coming home."

"Be cool," Catrelli said. "Any minute now."

As it turned out, Catrelli had been right, even though he had only been guessing. Frost turned the corner at their rear. He came slowly down the alley on his Harley twelve hundred, the headlight shooting out a single beam of yellowish light. Catrelli heard the noise and looked into the Chevy's mirror.

"This is him," he said, feeling his heart start to pound. That would pass with the first blow. The first blow always discharged the electricity Catrelli built up inside waiting for action.

Guarino stirred in the backseat. "Let's go get his

ass, then."

The three men climbed out of the old Chevy as Frost pulled up in front of his garage. He wasn't immediately aware of them until they had gotten out of the car—Catrelli made it a point to have no bulb in his dome light—and had started across the alley toward him. Frost saw their shapes in the streetlight. His eyes narrowed.

"What do you want?" he demanded.

"A friend sent us," Catrelli said, slapping the blackjack against his open hand. "He says you've been bothering him."

Frost's yellowish teeth showed through his beard. It might have been a smile. "Who's the friend?"

"You figure it out," Catrelli told him.

Catrelli stood directly in front of Frost, just out of easy arm's reach. As he spoke to the big man, Guarino and Elmer Lee fanned out toward Frost's sides. He caught them out of the corner of his eyes. But he kept his gaze fixed on Catrelli. He knew this little guy. He recognized him. And he knew who had sent him. Frost knew, all right.

"No way out of this, right?" Rhino Frost asked quietly.

Catrelli shook his head. He knew Frost didn't really want out. "Not this time, man," Catrelli told him. "But you can keep us from coming back again. And you know how."

Frost, already off his bike and his back against his garage door, flexed his fingers once or twice. He kicked the bikestand in place and stepped away from it, toward Elmer Lee, who didn't move. Frost eyed the black man. Not too big, but probably fast, probably with some muscle. The fat guy on his left would be even stronger but a lot slower. The little guy in front, though. He was going to be the toughest one. Frost didn't like tough little guys. You had to just about kill them to get them to stop fighting. Frost eyed all three men as they stood around him. Then he shrugged his big shoulders.

"Well," he said, "let's get down, then."

And they did.

Ring.

Murphy stirred in his covers.

Ring.

Murphy groped for the phone, found it, pressed it to his ear. "Hello."

"You made a big mistake," the voice told him.

Murphy came instantly awake. "What?"

"You didn't send enough guys."

Murphy, sitting up in bed in the darkness, said nothing.

"You can send more next time," Frost told him. "You try that. Just go ahead. Won't do you no good, though."

Murphy sighed deeply and said, "You won't let this go, will you?"

Rhino Frost, blood streaming from a dozen wounds as he stood in the darkness of his apartment, said, "Not as long as I'm alive."

Murphy flipped on the light next to his bed. He could hear Frost's labored breathing over the phone line.

"I'll have to see what I can do about that," Murphy

said at last.

Then he hung up the phone.

Murphy sat in the bed for a moment, collecting his thoughts. Then he got out from under the covers, went into the living room, and lit a Camel. He dragged deeply into it until he was fully awake. Then he went back into the bedroom and dialed a number. The phone rang several times before Mary Ellen answered.

"Hello," she said.

"I'm coming out to the house tonight," Murphy told her. "Make up the bed in the guest room again."

"Frost?" she said.

"Yeah. I can't leave you alone anymore."

"I'll leave the door open for you, then."

"Why don't you make it a point not to do that?" Murphy said sharply. "Just stay up until I get there."

Mary Ellen did not respond well to harsh words when she had just been awakened. "Then get here in a hurry, Frank. You woke me up, and I'm exhausted. I need to get back to bed."

"You think you're exhausted," he said, and slammed down the phone.

Murphy, cigarette clenched in his lips, dug through the morass of his room looking for clothes to wear.

"One of these days, Mary Ellen," he muttered to himself, "pow! Zoom!"

CHAPTER TWENTY-THREE

All the way out to Mount Airy in the middle of the night, Murphy steamed. Johnny Mathis on the tape deck did nothing to relax him—not even *Johnny's Greatest Hits,* which was just about the greatest makeout album anybody ever made. Patricia had been conceived to it, if the truth be told. And it had been around a long time even then.

The problem was that Murphy was tired—exhausted, actually—and he was hassled and he was also scared. That's what he had hoped Mary Ellen would pick up on without him having to tell her—that he was scared.

Murphy was scared about a lot of things. He was scared that he was going to blow the Highland case. It was his first big case, and he wanted it—needed it—to work out well. It was one thing to blow a big case when you were twenty-five and just out of law school and had time to make up for it later. Murphy was forty-five today—a milestone on which no one had bothered to congratulate him, including his estranged wife—and he was scared of reaching forty-six as a bum. He had always known the security of a city job, of government employment and benefits, of a regular paycheck reassuringly issued by a municipal computer. Now, with Patricia going off to college in a few weeks, he was in a panic about paying the bills. He needed this case. He needed it to give Patricia a chance.

Murphy was no feminist. He had never been able to figure out what all the fuss was about. All the women he had known well—most of them, anyway—had been as firmly in control of their own lives as the men. More in control, most of them. But he had to admit when pressed that there had been those few women he had known who had gotten married early, gotten knocked up early—and not always in that order, either—and ended up locked in loveless marriages to complete and utter bastards they didn't dare leave because they needed a man to support them and their children. He thought about Patricia in a crummy apartment somewhere with a baby crying in the background and some guy maybe knocking her around when she gave him some lip. When he pondered that prospect, he knew he had to get her an education. He had to put her in a position where she would have choices in life. That's what the Highland case was all about to Murphy—a chance for choices for Patricia.

And Murphy was scared he'd screw it up. He'd already screwed up so many things.

He was scared, too, of Frost. Frost was an added complication. He was the ultimate complication. Murphy didn't know what Frost might do, but he knew what the man was capable of. Frost was capable of damned near anything. Winston had proved that, although there had been no need of proof. Murphy remembered the guy. He had needed no further confirmation that Rhino Frost was a living nightmare.

Under normal circumstances, he'd have dropped everything and done whatever might be necessary to take care of Frost. But with the Highland case hanging over his head, he couldn't do that. Frost had him worried. Murphy couldn't watch Frost, and he couldn't control him, either.

He wondered vaguely how badly Catrelli had come out of his confrontation with Frost. Murphy knew that he hadn't come out of it particularly well, because if Catrelli had won, Frost wouldn't have been able to phone Murphy tonight. He'd have been in a hospital somewhere, wondering where his legs had gone. That had been the plan, after all. Catrelli must have taken on Frost head on. There had been a time when Catrelli would have known better than that, but he'd been out of it for a while, taking photographs for divorce cases and running down deadbeats. He'd clearly lost a little of his touch. Otherwise, Rhino Frost would be in traction tonight.

Murphy found his street and pulled the Toronado into the driveway. Mary Ellen opened the door for him.

"That was fast," she said.

"No traffic this time of night," he said, coming in and heading for the kitchen and the bourbon bottle. Mary Ellen, in robe and slippers and hair awry, followed him. She watched him take down the bourbon bottle, pour four fingers, and settle down at the kitchen table, staring at the wall, his thoughts far away as he sipped the Old Grandad. Mary Ellen sat across from him.

"What happened?" she asked him.

Murphy lit a Camel. "I sent some friends out to see Rhino. The idea was that they would encourage him to find some other way to occupy his time. Apparently, it didn't work out. He called me, and he was pissed. I'm going to have to get both of you out of town."

"You sent men out to beat him up?" Mary Ellen asked. Her tone of voice indicated surprise.

"What did you expect?" Murphy demanded. "Nothing else has worked."

"You hired thugs?" was her response.

"And not very good ones, either, it would seem," Murphy told his wife. "Frost sounded very healthy and not even a little bit happy."

She shook her head. "I can't believe you did that."

Murphy sipped his drink and smoked his cigarette. "You live in some kind of dreamland, don't you?" he said finally. "What do you think we're dealing with here? This guy is a brute. He's scum, Mary Ellen. He's a psychotic. If this keeps up, I'm going to have to hire somebody to kill him. Or I'm going to have to kill him myself—which I'll do gladly rather than have him do to you and Patricia what I think he has in mind."

"You don't know for sure what he has in mind," she said. "You put a man in prison, and then you wonder why he comes out angry. And then you talk about having him killed. Jesus, Frank. Maybe you should be in prison, not him."

Murphy choked back his first, furious response. It was not easy for him.

"You know," he said quietly, "sometimes I forget about all that liberal bullshit you carry around inside your head."

Mary Ellen's eyes flashed. "Frank . . ." she began.

"Don't 'Frank' me," Murphy said. "You don't know a goddamn thing about people like Rhino Frost. You've never dealt with people like him."

"I teach school," she shot back. "I see more problem people in a day than you see in a week."

"Seventh-grade English," Murphy said with a sneer. "You get screwed-up kids who've got overactive hormones and think the world hates them—which it probably does—and you think you understand a psychopath like Frost. Listen, Mary Ellen, this man is a hardened, vicious criminal. He's spent his entire adult life not just outside the law but outside any standard of civilized behavior. He's not even like most other criminals. Most guys who go that way do it to make a living. They might as well be mailmen. It's a job for them. That's the way their minds work. Robbing gas stations, pushing dope—that's all in a day's work. But a guy like Frost—these bikers and guys like that— they're nothing more than outlaws. They reject basic societal values. And they despise and look down on people who don't see the world the way they do to such a degree that they figure it's all right to do anything to them. I mean, anything at all. This guy is like a rogue lion looking for prey. And you and Patricia are the prey. Don't you get it yet? He's going to do to you what he did to that girl all those years ago. And he's not going to do it just to get at me. I'm his excuse, that's all. He's going to do it because he likes it. What he did to Winston? He liked it. Do you understand? And you wonder why I'm thinking about having somebody off the son of a bitch? Good Christ."

Mary Ellen sat back in her chair, using her hand to wave away the smoke from Murphy's Camel. She did not look happy. Nor, Murphy noted, did she look particularly convinced.

"You take a man," she said methodically, "usually a

minority group member from a poor family in some wretched slum somewhere who had no chance whatever in life, you put him in prison and you leave him there all those years. He lives under terrible, dehumanizing conditions, the worst conditions imaginable. He's degraded and humiliated—year after year after year. He's in the company of nobody but other men who've had the same experience, and they all end up feeding on one another's anger. Then he comes out and people like you wonder why he's full of rage against the society that put him away to begin with. You constantly astound me, Frank. Why is it such a mystery why people like Rhino Frost behave badly? How would you behave in similar circumstances?"

Murphy had heard all this before. He hadn't liked it then, either.

"Behave badly," he said. "That's sort of a novel description for the way Rhino conducts himself. And what would you suggest we do with scumbags like that? Do you think we should give each of these guys his own television show, maybe?"

"That's ridiculous, Frank, but it hardly addresses the real problem, does it?"

Murphy leaned back. "Well, I don't know, Mary Ellen. I'm not sure I know what the real problem is. And that's frustrating to me, because I've spent most of my adult life trying to figure out what you do with guys like this. You can't let them run around the streets. I've figured out that much. And when you slap their asses in prison, how nice should you make it for them? You make it too pleasant, and what's the point? Nobody learns anything. You make it too bad, and they go nuts on you. You end up with something like the Attica riot

296

back in nineteen seventy-one. Besides which, if you make it too rough, people like you bitch and moan about it. Oh, look at what they're doing to those poor, poor murderers and rapists. How inhumane it all is."

"Somebody has to be concerned about it," she said. "Almost all of them come out again, don't they? They come back and live among us again. And if you had your way, you'd make prison so bad that they'd all come out like our friend Mr. Frost. Whom, incidentally, you're now talking seriously about having murdered. I wonder what the courts would think about that, Frank—an officer of the court conspiring to commit murder. Isn't that a crime punishable by imprisonment? I wonder how you'd come out after the courts gave you ten or fifteen years in a prison."

"Funny about the courts," Murphy told her. "The courts seem to go along with people like you—for reasons nobody in his right mind can figure out. You know something? The courts are making life very nice for these guys, everything considered. Do you know that these guys have TV sets in prison? They have more dope than they know what to do with. Their wives and girlfriends come to visit them and they end up screwing in the visiting rooms, right in front of the guards. And that's in prisons where they don't have conjugal visits. And do you think that keeps the peace? Does that keep them calm? Not quite. In 1986, there were over thirty-three thousand civil rights suits filed in federal and state courts in the whole goddamn country, and nearly half of them came out of the prisons. Nearly half, for Christ's sake. You take away an inmate's teddy bear because he filled it with rocks and beat some guard half to death with it and whammo, you've got yourself a lawsuit. In the old days, he wouldn't have had the goddamn teddy bear for starters. But that was before left-wing dipshits were elected judges. Now it's all different, and I've got an animal like Rhino Frost out running around when he should be stuck somewhere in a cage with people pushing him in his food at the end of a pole. Or, he should be fried like a piece of breaded veal. That would be better yet."

"Frank," Mary Ellen said, "You're still a totally reactionary jerk."

Patricia appeared in the doorway, catching her mother's last remark.

"I thought I felt a disturbance in the force," Patricia said, and turned and went back upstairs.

Despite his weariness and anger, Murphy smiled as he heard her go back up the stairs. "Not bad," he told Mary Ellen.

"No," she said, "she's got a quick wit when she wants to use it. And she's got a mouth on her, too, Frank. You don't have to put up with it, but I do."

"Well," he said, "if she's got a mouth on her, then we know whose kid she is."

"Yes. She's both of ours. She comes by it honestly, I suppose."

Murphy and Mary Ellen sat quietly at the kitchen table for a few moments without exchanging words. Nowhere did Murphy feel more comfortable than here in this house and in the company of this woman, with whom he disagreed about so much in life. How, he wondered, had they ever gotten together to begin with? Had it been all glands? No, he didn't think so. His hormones were running thin these days. He saw a pretty girl on the street, and his first thought was that she was somebody's daughter. The hormones, clearly, were at low ebb. And yet he still felt so much for Mary Ellen, despite their differences. Like it or not, they shared a commonality of experience he was aware of every time he was in her company. He could only guess at her feelings these days. She seemed to get along very well without him. Murphy wondered if he would die alone. He hoped not. He had difficulty enough just sleeping alone.

"I do want you to get out of town," he said at last. "This guy is no joke, and I can't be sure I can protect you."

Mary Ellen looked up at him. "You know I'll have to come back soon."

He nodded. "By then I'll have it taken care of." He saw her expression. "No, I'm not going to have anybody kill him. I'd sure as shit like to, but I won't. If he comes at me, I'll kill him myself, but that's legal. I won't do anything else that's not legal with regard to Rhino Frost. Not if you get out of town like I'm asking you to."

"Promise?" she asked.

"I swear it."

Mary Ellen shrugged and leaned back in her chair. "Then tell me where you want me to go and I'll go there for a while. I could use the vacation, anyway."

Murphy got a notebook and drew a map. "You follow Route 611 up to here, take a right at Stroudsburg, and you'll come to this spot on the highway."

Mary Ellen looked carefully while he wrote directions.

"You go up this little road," Murphy told her, "and

the cottage is supposed to be about three-quarters of a mile in. It's the only one that's completely constructed. It's the model. The key is supposed to be in the mailbox. Can you follow all this?"

Mary Ellen studied the directions and the map for a moment. "Yes, I've got it. Is there a phone there?"

"No. But there's a phone at a general store down the highway. At least, there's supposed to be, anyway."

"When should I leave?"

"I'd like you and Patricia to be out of here tomorrow morning, early. I should have everything wrapped up by this weekend. Then I'll come up and join you. Harold tells me it's nice up there. Lots of woods, the way you like it. There's a small lake right in front of the cottages. You and Patricia should like that."

Mary Ellen studied the directions. It did seem plausible. It was, she knew, precisely the sort of place she and Patricia would like and Murphy would detest. He didn't like the country. They did. Woods made him nervous and he swam so badly he could drown in a bathtub. Mary Ellen and Patricia both liked rural settings, and they both swam like fish. A free week or so in a Pocono cabin didn't sound bad to Mary Ellen.

"One more thing," Murphy told her. "I'm going to try to send Catrelli up to keep an eye on you. You know him. If Frost hasn't put him completely out of commission, I'll feel better if he's around."

"Where are you going to get the money to pay Catrelli, Frank?" Mary Ellen demanded.

"I got a grand up front from the Highland woman," he said. "I also borrowed two grand from Harold, which I'll give him back when I submit my final bill to the Highlands. And Catrelli will let my bill ride for a while if it comes to that. He owes me, and he knows it. You just get out of town early tomorrow. In fact, I'm going to be here to get you both moving."

Mary Ellen yawned. "All right, then. I'm going to go to bed if you're going to get me up early."

"I will. I'll set the alarm in the guest room."

Mary Ellen looked at her husband. "Look," she said, "I don't want you to get the wrong idea, but you can sleep in your own bed if you want to. Now, don't get any ideas, Frank. But you look like hell, and you need a good night's sleep."

Silently, Frank studied her for a moment. Then he said, "And you figure I'll get a good night's sleep in the same bed with you? After a year and a half? Somehow I think that might tend to keep me awake. Thanks anyway, Mary Ellen, but I'm not going to sleep with you tonight or—"

"—in the same bed," she said, correcting him. "Sleep in the same bed with me, not sleep with me."

"Whatever. I'm not going to do that one night and then go back to that apartment and sleep alone the next night. You can forget that."

Mary Ellen stood up. She was somewhat flushed with either embarrassment or anger, or both. Murphy couldn't be sure. "I was just trying to be nice, Frank. I'm sorry you misunderstood. You go ahead and sleep where you want. It was really a rotten idea. I apologize."

Murphy started to respond with something clever and unpleasant, but he was just too tired. He merely shook his head wearily. "Just go to bed. I'll see you in the morning. Early in the morning."

"Fine," Mary Ellen said.

She left the kitchen. He heard her on the stairs, the familiar creaking of old wood under her slippered feet. Then he heard her call his name, softly to avoid waking Patricia.

"What?" he said.

"Happy birthday, Frank," she whispered. "I didn't forget, see?" Then she went into the master bedroom.

Murphy downed the rest of his bourbon and stubbed out his Camel. He frowned deeply. Forty-five today. Forty-five years on this planet, struggling to figure out what the hell was going on and still without a decent clue. Some happy birthday, Murphy thought to himself.

Then he got up wearily, shut off the kitchen light, and slowly climbed the stairs, aching with every step. In the upstairs hallway, he stood silently for a moment. He could hear Mary Ellen settling into bed. He saw the light showing from beneath the closed door die with a click from inside. Murphy thought about it for a long moment. Then he sighed deeply and opened the door to the master bedroom. In the dim light of the streetlight that shone through the window, he could make out Mary Ellen's shape in the bed.

"About the offer . . ." he said.

Mary Ellen's voice came back: "Come on in, Frank. And shut the door behind you."

Murphy did.

And it turned out to be not all that bad a birthday after all.

CHAPTER TWENTY-FOUR

Murphy had known for a long time that he thought best when he was asleep. One of the reasons he so detested missing sleep was that sleep deprivation dropped his waking mind into slow-cycle and gave his resting consciousness less time to do its work—less time to free associate without the distractions of wakefulness. In his own bed for the first time in a long time, with Mary Ellen's head on his shoulder, he slept deeply. The sounds of the house were familiar and not at all distracting.

It was while Murphy was asleep with Mary Ellen in his arms that he settled on the identity of Hank Kirby's killer. When he awakened, surprisingly alert and refreshed at six-thirty, he was more than reasonably sure of the killer's identity. He would have liked to have been positive, but there was no time for that. Murphy would have to wing it.

He roused Mary Ellen and Patricia and made them a big breakfast while they packed. They came downstairs carrying more suitcases than they would be able to fit into the little Datsun wagon.

"You're only going to be gone for a week or two at

303

most," Murphy told them. "Cavalry regiments travel lighter than that."

"You have to take more when you don't have time to pack carefully," Mary Ellen said. "We'll eat while you pile this stuff next to the car. I'll load it in. You'll just complain that it won't fit, but it will if you do it carefully."

"Careful with this one, Daddy," Patricia said, handing him a small bag. "This has my IUD in it."

Murphy looked at her in shock, and Patricia laughed and gave him a kiss and a hug. "I'm just kidding. I guess having you around the house again makes me feel sort of silly."

Murphy studied her, his expression both grim and confused.

"I am kidding," Patricia assured him, "really."

The women ate while Murphy loaded the ton or so of baggage next to the Datsun's tailgate. A lot of it was loose. Each of them, he noticed, was taking two hair dryers, and each of them had a hair curler. A casual passerby would think they were packing to attend a hairdressers' convention. Murphy went back in as they were emptying dishes and loading the dishwasher. He glanced at his watch.

"This is taking too much time."

"We're almost ready," Mary Ellen said.

Then she and Patricia went outside to pack the car while Murphy sat down next to the kitchen phone and dialed a number.

"Hello."

"Well," Murphy said, "you're still alive, anyway."

Catrelli sounded awful. "Just barely. It ended in kind of a draw. I took two other guys, and he fought all three of us to a standstill before he got loose and got inside. He was tougher than I'd thought, Frank. He's banged up a little, but I got a couple of loose teeth and one of my guys, Guarino, we had to take him to the hospital. He's got a broken wrist. How'd you know we hit him last night?"

"He called me."

Catrelli was silent for a moment. Then he said, "He was sort of pissed off, I guess, right?"

"You could say that."

"Shit," Catrelli hissed into the phone. "He don't discourage easy, does he? Well, what now?"

Murphy told him.

"For how long?" Catrelli demanded. "Christ, that's hours from here."

"No more than a few days," Murphy assured him. "Maybe even just tonight and tomorrow. Then I think I'll be able to go up there and take over myself by tomorrow night, at the outside."

"Should I take any help, do you think?"

"That's up to you. You'll have to pay for it out of what I give you, though. I've had to borrow to handle just your fee, let alone anybody else."

"In that case I can handle it myself. Tell me, Frank, do you really expect him to go all the way up there? How the hell is he going to even know they're there?"

"I'm going to leave him a trail even a moron like him could follow."

"How?"

Murphy lit a Camel. Mary Ellen and Patricia were still outside, packing, unable to hear him. Then he said quietly, "After last night, he's not going to wait anymore. He figures the next step is that I have

305

somebody waste him. Tonight, tomorrow night at the latest, he's going to come busting into this house. He's going to find it empty, but he's going to find a set of directions to the Poconos on the kitchen table. It'll look like somebody was sitting at the table looking at them, then left and forgot to take them along. At least, I hope it'll look that way. By the way, not a word of this to my wife and daughter, dig?"

"I never tell women nothing. Only how do you know he'll hit your house? What makes you think he won't go for you in your apartment?"

"He'll come here because I won't be at my apartment. I'm going to move in somewhere else until I have some important legal business worked out."

"How does he even know about the Mount Airy house?" Catrelli demanded.

"I think he's been following my daughter. In fact, I'm sure of it. He let her see him once at a mall near the house. It was like a cat playing with a mouse. I'm pretty sure he knows where this place is, and if he does he's probably cased it pretty good by now. And I'm still listed in the phone book at this address. He knows about this house all right, and he knows who lives here. After last night he's not going to let any grass grow under his feet getting in here, either. My only choice is to sit here with a shotgun night after night waiting for him to hit this joint or to get him out of the city into unfamiliar territory and someplace where we can wait for him to come in on our terms instead of his. I can't let this go on any longer."

"All right," Catrelli said. "Let me get a pencil here, and you give me directions. Christ, the things I do to make a living. The fucking Poconos, yet."

Murphy pulled a set of detailed directions from his trousers. He read them off to Catrelli. When he had finished, he stuffed the directions back in his pocket. He hung up the phone and went outside to see how the packing was going. Mary Ellen had the little wagon's luggage area so tightly jammed that daylight could not break through.

"Snug," Murphy told her.

Mary Ellen wiped one palm against the other. "But everything is in. Now, where are those directions?"

"Here," Murphy said, reaching into his shirt pocket for the directions and map he had produced as they had sat together the night before. The sheet from which he had read to Catrelli was folded in his pants pocket.

The women went back inside for individual trips to the bathroom while Murphy moved the Toronado out into the street to permit Mary Ellen's car an exit out of the single-lane driveway. Mary Ellen and Patricia came out and got into the wagon. Patricia automatically put on the headphones to her Walkman and leaned back in the seat, eyes closed. She always traveled in this fashion on long trips, lost in sound, surrounded by the strains of Twisted Sister or something else Murphy found equally repulsive and incomprehensible. Murphy leaned toward her window and kissed her on the cheek. She smiled and hugged his neck. Then Murphy went around the car and stuck his head in the driver's window.

"It shouldn't take you more than a few hours to get there," he told his wife. "Catrelli will be in sometime today, certainly before dark. I might make it up as early as tomorrow night."

"I wish the place had a phone," Mary Ellen said.

Murphy sighed. "So do I. That's the only thing I don't like about all this."

"Frank," Mary Ellen said, "is Catrelli going to bring a gun with him?"

"I didn't ask him, but I think he's going to bring every gun he owns, and his apartment looks like the FBI museum."

"I don't know," Mary Ellen said, "whether that frightens or reassures me."

"It reassures me. You just do what he says and play it safe until I get there."

"All right," she said, and started the car. "By the way, there's a birthday card for you on my dresser."

"Oh?"

"Yep," Mary Ellen told him, smiling somewhat self-consciously. "I never got around to giving it to you last night."

"Well," Murphy grinned, "something came up, as I recall."

"Yes," Mary Ellen said, "it still does that."

Murphy kissed her cheek. Then she backed out and drove away. Murphy went back into the house, shaking his head. He went up to the bedroom and found the card. It wasn't funny, and it wasn't sloppy. It was sort of an innocuous card, made special only because she had taken the trouble to go out and buy it for him. And she had invited him into the bedroom last night, too. The gesture of the card—and now the thought of last night's invitation—mystified Murphy totally. In the year and a half they had lived apart, their relationship had actually been better than it had been the last few years they had lived together. It had been strained, of course, during his months with Nancy, but ever since Nancy's departure, Mary Ellen had been more or less civil to him—except when he was late with the check. Now this card and what had happened last night. Murphy couldn't figure it out.

Then again, he'd never been able to figure out Mary Ellen, never been able to understand what was really going on inside her head. Those first few years together had been marvelous. Then Patricia had been born, and Murphy had suddenly found himself more or less shut out of Mary Ellen's life. Mary Ellen had seemed to have room for their daughter, for her teaching, but not much room for her husband. Or so it had seemed at the time. Maybe it hadn't been like that and he had only imagined it. In any event, it had seemed real enough to him at the time, so Murphy had started going to college nights, and then there had come law school at eight credits a semester. During all this he had gotten his detective's shield and had moved up in rank in the department and had finally come to realize that he was spending very little time at home and even less time with Mary Ellen.

Then he had taken that political job in the DA's office and had moved out on Mary Ellen after a disastrous New Year's party at which he had gotten viciously drunk and told her what he thought of her—castigated her for her coldness and sharp, wounding tongue—in front of all their friends. After that, he had found Nancy and gone into private practice and that brought them up to date.

In light of all that, he couldn't figure this birthday card. When he had turned forty-four, they hadn't even been speaking, and now this a year later.

He went back downstairs and called Wilder.

309

"You want to make an arrest in the Highland case today?" he asked.

"What's the gag, Frank?" Wilder demanded.

"No gag. I think I've got it figured."

"Who? And how and why and all that shit?"

Murphy outlined his thinking to Wilder, who listened carefully then said, "Could be. What do you want to do?"

"I want to meet you at the Roundhouse at eleven and then let's drive out to Paoli and put this thing on the table."

Wilder thought about it. Murphy was the family's lawyer, and this would be done at his suggestion. Wilder could see no hooks in the plan for either him or the department. "All right. I'll see you at eleven."

"Good. I presume you're going to call Toddman and bring him in on all this."

"Goddamn right."

"Well, you should. It's your job. Listen, one more thing. How would you like a houseguest tonight?"

"Who?"

"Me. Just for this one night, I think."

"It's okay with me. Want to tell me why?"

"I'll tell you on the way out to Paoli."

Murphy hung up and went around the house, locking it up. The sliding-glass door leading out to the screened porch at the rear of the house would be Frost's likeliest path of entry. He made sure he locked that door. He didn't want this to look too obvious. Then he went back into the kitchen and reached into his pants pocket. He pulled out a hand-written set of directions to the place in the Poconos. He placed the sheet of paper faceup on the kitchen table.

310

Come on, Rhino, he thought as he left the house through the front door. You just do your stuff here tonight. Then, the next night, I'll be waiting for you.

Graterford Correctional Facility, 1987

Bobbi Hammond had become a prostitute ·at thirteen. Given her appearance, manner, and proclivities, few other options had been available to her. Besides, in her West Philadelphia neighborhood prostitution was a fact of life. There was some stigma to being a sporting woman, but not all that much—especially if you were the way Bobbi was. There was enough stigma in just being the way Bobbi had been born, a woman's soul inside a man's body. Working as a whore was not likely to greatly diminish her social status.

On the outside, she had run into The Man on a number of occasions before she had exhibited the bad judgment to cut her pimp's throat, let him bleed to death in a filthy bathroom, and get herself shipped to Graterford for her trouble. There had been a nasty scene in a cocktail lounge with a particularly mean jocker. Bobbi had sliced off his ear as neatly as you please with the straight razor she had taken to carrying in her purse for protection. Given the circumstances, The Man had let that one pass. But there had been another time in a hotel room with a conventioneer from Montreal. He had hurt her and laughed about it and Bobbi had left him lying on the floor in just his strap undershirt, clutching his severed carotid artery.

He didn't die, but Bobbi had done nearly a year in Holmesburg that time around.

Despite its hardships, she had found in Holmesburg a life far better than the one she had known outside. In Holmesburg, she had not been a pariah. She had become a sex symbol, not unlike that black lady on *Dynasty* who was so pretty and whom Bobbi resembled so strikingly. She thought sometimes that her experience in Holmesburg—her position as an accepted and admired member of the population—had instilled in her a desire to spend her life in prison society, even though there had been rough moments in Holmesburg because she hadn't been able to find a jocker to protect her for any length of time. She had been passed around from man to man, and she had been determined not to let that happen to her in the state prison system.

Nonetheless, despite the harshness of her time in the Philadelphia jail, she knew she had found a home in inmate society. Perhaps that was why she had hung around while her pimp's lifeblood poured out, waiting for The Man to show up and take her into custody. Holmesburg had taught her that men who would have spat at her on the outside—or done far worse than that—came to see her in a different light inside prison walls. Bobbi was by far the most desired woman in Graterford, and she reveled in the attention and admiration that fact inspired in others. Rhino didn't like it, but Bobbi flaunted it every chance she got.

She made it a point to wear clothes that accentuated her feminine charms—imitation gold hoop earrings, tank tops that drew attention to the small breasts she had grown with smuggled hormone pills, jeans tight enough to hug her hips and yet loose enough to allow

312

comfort for her indisputably male genitalia. She strutted, shook her ass, made eyes at the men, and flirted shamelessly. She made Rhino jealous all the time. Bobbi liked it when Rhino showed he cared for her.

"Bitch," he bellowed one night, slamming her across the cell. "Goddamn whore. I heard about you coming on with Bear down in the laundry this morning. Do you think I'm deaf and blind?"

"We didn't do nothing," Bobbi said innocently, knowing that Rhino couldn't bring himself to really hurt her. Mostly, he just threw her around a little and made a lot of noise.

"That ain't the way I heard it," Rhino said, half in a rage and half in a sulk. "The word is around. You've got to stop that shit, Bobbi. I'm warning you."

Bobbi got up and hugged him. She loved her big man, her Rhino. She'd always wanted a man like Rhino, and here she had him, and she could manipulate him and make a fool out of him whenever the whim struck her. Bobbi liked that enormously. She liked the power.

"Poor Babyman," she said, stroking his cheek. "You jealous of your Bobbi, are you?"

Rhino tore her arms from around him and stomped over to the bars, looking out over the cellblock. He was very angry. She had been seen with Bear, and he probably knew in some detail what she had been doing to him. He knew, too, that she would lie to him about it. Bobbi was a whore. Once a whore, always a whore. Rhino wished he didn't love her. But, love her or not, he told himself, he would not put up with this forever. Especially not with Bear.

"You do it with Bear again and he's dead," Rhino said softly. "And once he's dead, you do it with somebody else and you're dead. You got me. You understand me, Bobbi, you bitch?"

Bobbi watched him. She had heard this before. One of these days, she was sure, he would try to make good on his threats. But not with Bear, she was pretty sure. Bear was his buddy from the club. Bear was his friend. Also, Bear was Bear. He was nobody to fool around with, even if you were Rhino. Bear and Rhino might well be a dead heat. Each of them knew it, and so did Bobbi. But sometimes Rhino said things that indicated that perhaps Bear was not such a good friend, that he distrusted Bear, that he perhaps had a score of some kind to settle with him, something from long ago. There were plenty of such scores to be settled in this place, she knew. Bobbi was only guessing at that, though, because Rhino Frost was a solitary and secretive man—even with her. He hung out with the club because there was no choice here except to be a punk, like her, or to be in a gang or to be a crazy, and they never got out of prison. The crazies killed people who tried to muscle them without regard to what might happen to them, and consequently they were avoided by the general prison population, which was their primary motive to begin with. Rhino wasn't a crazy, she knew. But she also knew he was capable of crazy things if pushed too far.

She came up behind him and put her arms around his waist. Bobbi buried her face in Rhino Frost's strong back and kissed him between his shoulder blades.

"I love you, baby," she said. "Only you."

Frost turned around and looked back at her, his

deep-set eyes glittering. "No more," he said to her hoarsely.

"No more," Bobbi promised him.

She had lied, of course. Lying was part of Bobbi's nature. She liked the men. She liked nearly all the men. And she especially liked Bear, who was big and funny and who could make her laugh while he did with her what he liked to do.

Bobbi was Rhino's punk, and everybody knew it. But, now and then, she would sneak down to the laundry to see Bear. If Bobbi had not been Rhino's punk, she would have been Bear's. When Rhino left, as he would in just a few months, Bobbi would move to Bear's cell down the block. It was an unspoken agreement with them. Rhino had taken Bobbi and held her all these years. But soon Rhino would be gone, and Bobbi and Bear would still be here. Bear had years yet to serve, and Bobbi planned on never leaving. When her time to leave came close, she planned on doing something crazy, and then they would have to keep her here, which was home to her.

Bear had a part-time job in the laundry. Most prison jobs were sort of a joke. The inmates made furniture for state offices, and they stamped out license plates, but they did no real work, and it was difficult to find a job that provided an inmate enough hours to make any real money—which the inmates needed to buy cigarettes and dope. The Pennsylvania Business Council, one of the state's most powerful lobbying groups, saw to that. What did businesses need competing with goods made at slave wages by prison inmates? What outside business could compete with that? So the inmates' work was limited, and the best jobs were in places like the kitchen and the laundry, where you at least got four or five hours of work a day because those places supplied services that were desperately needed and were not competitive with those offered on the outside by private businesses.

The job Bear had was operating a huge speed ironing and folding machine used to finish off sheets and other bedding that came out of the enormous industrial washing machines and dryers. The ironing and folding machine was thirty-feet long, six feet high, and six feet wide. It was fed by a moving canvas belt that sent semidry, wrinkled sheets from the dryers into a vast hole where they went through twenty giant rollers, ten on top and ten on the bottom. The cylinders inside the machine were filled with superheated steam that went up to three hundred and fifty degrees. The rollers exerted nearly a thousand pounds per square inch to erase wrinkles as they smoothed and folded the sheets.

Every morning, Bear fed sheets into the machine. On the huge table at his side sat mounds of sheets from the washers and dryers. They were heavy, but Bear was strong. He would pick up each sheet separately, smooth it onto the canvas belt, and feed it into the machine. It would come out the other end dry, ironed, and folded. Once a week the prison gave each of the two thousand inmates new sheets and collected the old. It took a full week to wash, dry, iron, and fold the dirty sheets.

Bear liked the job. Because there was too little work in the prison, he was often alone in the enormous prison laundry. He liked the privacy. He liked the lifting. He liked playing the radio over the rush of steam in the pipes. And he liked Bobbi coming down to the laundry once or twice a week so they could romp in the wrinkled sheets on the big table next to the speed ironer.

Bear and Bobbi were in the sheets when Rhino caught them. Bobbi was on her stomach, pants around her ankles. Bear, his own pants around his ankles, lay on Bobbi's back, moving and moaning and having a good old time. Rhino hit him with a wrench on the back of the head. Bear never knew what hit him. Bobbi heard the wrench hit and felt Bear go limp, all three hundred pounds settling on her as dead weight. Then she felt Bear pulled from her and she felt strong hands on her. She felt a surge of terror as Rhino pulled her off the table amid the wrinkled sheets and brought her face up to his.

"Bitch," he said, and he hit her.

The blow caught Bobbi on the right side of the jaw. She fell back into the sheets, dazed, her pants still around her ankles and the proof that she wasn't really a woman exposed for anybody to see. She was too groggy and hurt and scared to care, and nobody else was there anyway. "Bitch," Rhino said quietly. "You watch. You watch, and you don't move and you remember what you see. You remember, bitch, because it'll happen to you if you pull anything like this again."

As Bobbi lay dazed and terrified in the pile of sheets, she saw Rhino bend down and lift up Bear, which was no small feat. Bear was unconscious, bleeding from his head wound, and Bobbi would have figured it would take a crane to pick him up. But Rhino managed. Bobbi had convinced him to lift weights, and he was

317

very strong now, which was one of the things she liked about Rhino Frost. Bobbi liked strong men. Usually, that is.

Rhino put Bear on the moving canvas belt, head-first toward the gaping mouth of the machine. Bobbi realized what he was about to do, and she began to struggle to rise, but Rhino, free of Bear's weight, sent her back down with a kick.

"Watch," he ordered.

Bobbi watched.

The belt ran no more than six feet into the open mouth of the speed ironer. It carried Bear inside in a matter of seconds. His head went in first, then his huge torso, then his naked lower half. Bobbi heard Bear come awake as the steam hit him. She heard him scream inside the machine. His voice sounded as if it came from a million miles away. Then she heard the machine begin to press and fold him. She heard a crunching sound from inside the machine. Bear's scream stopped suddenly. She heard the crunching sound continue for a number of seconds as Bear traveled the thirty feet through the speed ironer. Then, from the other end of the machine, she heard Bear come out. He came out in pieces.

Bobbi screamed. She screamed and screamed and screamed. Then Rhino hit her. He slapped her face, hard. She went down in the sheets.

"Shut up," he told her. "Get your pants up. Go on, do it."

She did it. She pulled her jeans back to her hips, zipped them, and climbed to her feet as Rhino looked around the empty laundry suspiciously.

"You go out first," he told her quietly. "Get away

from here. Go into the yard. Go to the cell. Go anywhere. Just get out and get away. And remember, do it again and you're next."

Bobbi ran out of the laundry. She went up the stairs to the yard and through the breezeway and into the cellblock and up the stairs and into her cell, where she collapsed sobbing on her bunk. Rhino showed up a few minutes later. He stood in the doorway, blotting out the light. Bobbi saw him and whimpered.

"You get the picture now?" Rhino said.

Bobbi, eyes wide, nodded in terror.

"Good," Rhino Frost said, a small smile playing about his lips. "That's good, bitch."

CHAPTER TWENTY-FIVE

Murphy drove the Toronado back to Center City, his mind working on two topics—the Kirby murder and the whereabouts of Rhino Frost. It took him nearly forty minutes to find a parking space anywhere near his apartment building—he was forced to settle for one two blocks away—and he hurried in off the street as fast as he could without looking foolish. He didn't know where Frost was, and while he doubted that the man would try to hit him during the day you never knew about these things.

Inside his apartment, Murphy phoned Esmeralda, took his messages, and told her he wouldn't be back before mid-afternoon, at the earliest, and that he might not be in at all. Then he made another call to directory assistance. He got the number he wanted, called it, and found who he was looking for. They talked for fifteen minutes or so. Then Murphy phoned Carol Highland's house.

"It's Frank," he told her. "Something has come up in the Kirby murder. Is there going to be a time today when you and Ev and Margaret will all be home together? I'd rather not discuss it over the phone."

"Yes," she said. "I expect everybody to be home for lunch."

"That would be about what time?"

"Probably about twelve-thirty or one."

"Fine. I'd like to meet with everybody at that time."

"All right. I'll put on an extra plate."

"Put on two, then. I'm bring somebody with me."

Murphy shaved with his battery-powered electric razor while he fixed himself some coffee and a bowl of Cornflakes. Then he breakfasted quickly as he looked over the *Inquirer* that had been dropped at his door. DeLeon was complaining about cats again ("In some parts of the world, they're considered quite a delicacy," he wrote.) while in sports Bill Lyon was complaining about how bad the Eagles looked in preseason practice. Murphy had expected that. Thank God for the point spread. If you beat the point spread in an Eagles game, then even a team loss could be a moral victory.

He showered and dressed carefully. He put on a white oxford cloth shirt with a button-down collar, a dark red tie with a subdued paisley design, a good blue pin-striped suit that looked okay on him unless he tried to button the jacket, and black wingtips. Murphy combed his gray hair carefully, then packed a suitcase with enough clothing and cosmetics to last him several days. Before he left the apartment, he checked his old service pistol, which he had stolen from the city when he left the police department. He made sure the cylinder turned freely and that there were cartridges in five of the six chambers. Murphy always carried a pistol with the hammer resting on an empty chamber, for safety's sake. He put the pistol in its holster and attached the holster to his dress belt. He locked the door as he left and watched carefully as he made his way down the street to his car. Murphy drove to the Roundhouse thinking about what was coming up. He rehearsed it in his mind. He tried to anticipate what would be said in response to what he had to say. That would be the key, to anticipate the responses. If he got the response he suspected, then he would know.

Wilder was waiting out in front of the building as Murphy drove up a few minutes after eleven. He climbed in the car and said, "You got a cigarette?"

Murphy fished for his pack as he pulled away from the curb. "I thought you quit."

"That was before this Kirby murder," Wilder said, lighting up gratefully. "I'll quit once we get this resolved. If we do get it resolved today, that is."

"I think we're going to be all right on this one. It all came to me last night. I did some checking this morning, and it all makes sense. Everything fits. There's just this one thing we have to do out in Paoli to ice it."

"Let's do it, then," Wilder said.

They spoke little on the way out the expressway. Murphy's mind was working, and Wilder knew from long experience that it didn't pay to disturb Murphy's thought processes so close to something big in a case. Wilder was mildly annoyed that, once again, Murphy was going to be the key to breaking a case. Of course, Murphy had enjoyed a distinct advantage in this one. The parties involved had spoken to Murphy freely, and Wilder had been able to question only a few of them—and those under difficult circumstances. He hadn't had the advantage of all Murphy's information. Still, it all pissed him off a little bit. After all, Murphy wasn't even

322

a cop anymore.

They made a brief stop in Paoli and arrived at the Highland house about twelve-fifteen. Carol's Audi was in the garage and so was Margaret Highland's tan Caddy. The bay that normally held Everett Highland's blue Cadillac was empty. Murphy parked the Toronado in front of Margaret's bay and they rang the bell. Carol Highland came to the door, saw Wilder, and paled visibly.

"He's with me today," Murphy told her simply. "May we come in?"

"Yes," Carol said, eyeing Wilder warily. "I'm in the kitchen making lunch. It's not ready yet. I do have some coffee on, though."

It was a warm day, and even though the big house was cool with air-conditioning, Carol Highland wore shorts and a T-shirt that proclaimed itself to be the property of the University of Pennsylvania Athletic Department. They followed her into the kitchen and sat at the table, where she served them coffee and then went back to preparing a bowl of crab and avocado salad.

"What do you have to tell me?" she asked Murphy.

"I'd rather wait until everybody is here."

"Mother is upstairs, and Ev will be here momentarily. He went fishing today. Pretty soon classes will start again, and he won't have the time."

As she spoke, they heard a car enter the driveway. Its engine died, a door opened and closed, and in a moment Everett Highland was entering the kitchen through the back door. He was dressed in a worn sport shirt and old chino pants. He was startled when he saw Murphy and Wilder.

"Hello," Highland said, extending a hand to each man, Murphy first, then—with more trepidation—to Wilder.

"Something new has come up in the murder case," Carol explained.

"What's that?" Everett Highland asked.

"Well," Murphy said, "let's bring your mother down and eat some lunch and I'll go over it."

Everett Highland went to the stairs and called up them. "Mother. Lunch is served."

Margaret Highland came downstairs in a robe as Carol was setting the dining room table with old and expensive china and good stainless steel flatware. She looked at Murphy and Wilder with the same surprised expression.

"You know Lieutenant Wilder, don't you, Margaret?" Murphy said.

"Yes," Margaret Highland said coldly. "I was here when he took Carol away."

"Just doing my job, ma'am," Wilder said softly.

"Yes," she said, "I suppose you were."

"Let's all sit down," Carol suggested.

The group moved into the dining room. The table was set for five. It could have just as easily held twelve. The dining room was far larger than the living room in Murphy's Mount Airy house. Carol Highland had served a nice lunch—the salad, a bowl of rolls, iced tea, and a fruit cup. Murphy ate greedily. The coffee and cereal of a few hours before had done nothing for him. Besides, he was nervous, and when he was nervous he either ate or smoked. Smoking, he knew, was banned in this house.

After a decent interval into the meal, Everett

324

Highland finally said, "What do you have to tell us, Frank? We're all dying to know."

Murphy wiped his lips with an expensive linen napkin. "I think I know who killed Hank Kirby."

"Who?" Carol said instantly.

"Well," Murphy told them, "this might take some explaining. Do you mind if I stand? I think better on my feet."

"Please do," Margaret Highland said.

Murphy got up and began to slowly circle the table. "Well, for starters we all know that Carol didn't do it. We know that when she saw Kirby, it was at least a half hour before his death. The medical examiner will bear that out. We also have a witness who can place Carol at a gas station on the turnpike at about the time of the murder."

"The turnpike?" Wilder said. "You told us it was a gas station on Roosevelt Boulevard."

"No, I didn't," Murphy corrected. "I said that she went to the motel via the expressway and the boulevard. I never mentioned the route she took home. You just assumed it was the same way."

Wilder frowned deeply. "So I've had guys checking every gas station on the boulevard and the expressway for two days for nothing. Thanks, Frank."

"It's a small point anyway," Murphy said. "You already knew about the bartender."

"What bartender?" Everett Highland asked.

"There was a bar near the motel that Kirby hung out in. The bartender told me—and I presume the cops, too, by now—that Kirby had been in there that night at a time that made it impossible for Carol to be the killer. He was seen in the bar after Carol would have had to

325

have left the motel to have been at the gas station at the time she was there. Kirby was also wearing a different shirt than he'd been wearing when Carol saw him. So, any way you cut it, Carol is off the hook."

"You still haven't answered the essential question," Margaret Highland said. "Who did murder Mr. Kirby?"

Murphy turned to her. "You think that I think that you did it, don't you, Margaret?"

Her face was impassive. Margaret Highland was making it a point at that moment to say precisely nothing. A smart old lady, Murphy thought.

"Let me tell you what might have happened that night as I see it," he went on. "Carol got her phone call from Kirby earlier in the evening. She thought nobody else knew about it. But we know that there are extensions throughout the house, so let's imagine for the sake of argument that somebody picked up one of them and listened in on Carol's conversation with Kirby. That person would have known then when Carol was going to leave and where she was going to go.

"Carol came downstairs after you"—Murphy motioned to Everett Highland—"went to sleep. She got into her car, drove around to withdraw some cash from the bank machines, and then drove out to see Kirby. After their meeting, Carol left to come home and had car trouble on the way back, which delayed her.

"Now," Murphy said, "let's suppose that the killer left the house and followed her. Let's suppose that the killer got into his or her car and followed Carol to the motel. Let's suppose that the killer watched her go

326

inside, sat there for a while, and then watched her leave. Then, a little while later, Kirby comes out. He walks to the bar, has a quick beer, and comes back. And all the while the killer is sitting there, watching. When Kirby goes back into his room, the killer takes a weapon that's lying there handy in the car, goes to the door, and knocks on it. When Kirby comes to the door, they talk for a minute or so. Kirby says the wrong thing and—pow! The killer hits him with that weapon and he goes down. Then the killer hits him a few more times, because the killer is angry now, just about out of control."

The room was silent for a moment. Murphy spoke slowly. He wanted to get this just right. "Then the killer drove that car out of there and went like a son of a bitch trying to beat Carol back here. The killer didn't know that Carol would have car trouble and wouldn't get back until later. When the killer got back to this house, the killer put the car in the garage quickly and rather thoughtlessly, as it turns out. That was because the killer was afraid that Carol would be pulling into the driveway any second. The killer did take time, though, to pull down the garage door behind the car. The killer was so rattled that the killer had forgotten that the garage door to that particular bay had been open before when the car was taken out."

Carol Highland's hand went to her mouth in shocked realization. "That's right," she said. "When I came back, the garage doors were closed, but when I'd left the door to Ev's—"

She stopped suddenly, realizing what she had just said. Murphy said nothing for a moment. All eyes were on him now.

"That's right," he told her. "When you came back, the doors were closed, and you were afraid to turn on the light, so you had to stumble through the darkness to the side door. Let me tell you something else, too. The guy who runs that motel heard a car come in later that evening. He didn't look out at it, but he remembered he could hear music coming from it. Somebody was playing the radio. He said he heard violins and guns. So I checked with the classical radio station to see what that piece of music might be."

"That would be the *1812 Overture*," Everett Highland said quietly.

"That's right," Murphy said. "Their log indicates that the *1812 Overture* was played that night right about the time of Kirby's death. You know that station, Ev. It's the one you had your radio tuned to when I rode with you from the restaurant the other day. There's not much question that the killer rode in your car that night. In fact, that seems fairly incontrovertible. I also suspect that the murder weapon was your fishing club, the one you told me was missing. I stopped on the way here and picked up one of those fishing clubs at the sports shop in the village. The medical examiner's office will have no problem identifying a club like that as the murder weapon. So that seems to pretty much remove all doubt as to what car was used and what the weapon was."

"I didn't murder Hank Kirby," Everett Highland said softly.

"No," Margaret Highland said. "I did."

All heads turned to Margaret Highland.

"Mother . . ." Everett Highland said.

She raised a hand. "It's all right, Everett. Let me tell

328

them. You're right, Mr. Murphy. I listened in on the telephone conversation. I realized that Mr. Kirby was doing damage to my son's wife, and I felt I had to do something about it. I couldn't let a member of my family be victimized like that. And there was no one to whom to turn. I couldn't turn to Everett, for obvious reasons. So when Carol left I followed her."

"But why did you take Ev's car?" Carol demanded.

Margaret Highland smiled ruefully. "Because mine was low on gas. I didn't think I'd be able to stop and buy gasoline and still follow you successfully, and I wasn't sure where the motel was on Roosevelt Boulevard. So I took Everett's car. I followed you there, Carol, and I watched you go inside. Then, after a while, you came out and drove away and then Mr. Kirby came out. I watched him go to this bar Mr. Murphy spoke of and come back later. Then, after he went inside his room, I went to see him. Everett's fishing club was on the front seat, and I took it with me for protection. I knocked on the door with it, and when Mr. Kirby came to the door, I tried to speak to him. I was going to offer him money, but he was abusive and rude. Finally I took the club from behind my back and just hit him with it. He was a vile, awful man, and I merely wanted to hurt him, to frighten him. He fell down, but he tried to get up again, so I hit him some more. Then he fell down and tried to get up again, and I hit him some after that. Then I ran out to Everett's car and drove home as quickly as I could. I'd forgotten that the door to Everett's bay was up. That was very careless of me, but I didn't realize at the time that the man was dead. I didn't mean to kill him."

There was silence for a moment in the room.

Murphy stared at Margaret Highland with a strange expression on his face.

"What did you do with the club?" Everett Highland asked.

Margaret looked at her son and shrugged, almost good-naturedly. "Oh, I threw it out the window on the turnpike. I don't remember just where. I just got rid of it, Everett. I wasn't thinking all that clearly."

Carol Highland sat in her chair, her face a mask of pure shock. She stared at her mother-in-law in horror. Everett Highland's complexion was the color of cottage cheese.

"Mother . . ." he said, his voice strained and weak.

Murphy shook his head and, despite himself, began to laugh. It wasn't a belly laugh, but it was more than a giggle. It was just the amusement he always felt when he'd iced a case, finally proven his theory beyond the vaguest shadow of a doubt. The Highlands turned their eyes to him in pure astonishment. Murphy held up a hand as he regained control of himself.

"Forgive me," he said, "I just couldn't resist it. Margaret, you're quite a woman. You truly are."

For the first time, Murphy saw Everett Highland's anger. It rather pleased him to see that Highland was capable of anger. It restored his faith in male hormones. Maybe this guy had a set of balls after all.

Red-faced, Everett Highland said, "I'm going to have to ask you to leave this house, Mr. Murphy. Immediately. I'm astounded that anyone could find humor in—"

"Just relax," Murphy said, his composure completely regained by now. "Your mother didn't kill anybody.

This is all a complete fabrication. Tell him why you lied just now, Margaret."

Margaret Highland glared at Murphy. "I told you what I did. Why isn't that enough? I'm confessing to the murder, Mr. Murphy. Lieutenant, are you going to take me into custody now?"

"Don't you get it yet?" Murphy asked Everett Highland. "She thinks you did it. The minute she figured out where I was going when I said the killer used your car, she was certain that you were the killer. Why? Because she knew it wasn't Carol and she knew it wasn't her. That left only you, Ev. Only she didn't know that you were the one who tipped me off to the fishing club, which you'd never had done if you'd really been the killer. She had no way of knowing that you weren't my prime target. Actually, we eliminated you for sure this morning. All it took was some deep thought, a phone call, and some luck. Look at your mother, Ev. Do you think she'd commit a murder to help Carol? She wouldn't walk across the street for Carol, for Christ's sake. Aside from which, her story about how Kirby kept struggling to get up is—you'll forgive me I'm sure, Margaret—pure, unadulterated bullshit. He was dead after the first blow. The medical examiner told us that. Of course, your mother didn't know that, either."

Margaret Highland gave a sigh of relief and sank back in her chair. The flush that had passed over Everett Highland's face began to fade. Carol Highland sat motionless in her chair, her eyes wide.

"Then who . . ." Everett Highland's voice trailed off.

Murphy looked directly at Carol. "She knows."

The Highlands turned their eyes to Carol. Murphy and Wilder stood up instantly, as if in marching formation.

"We'll be going now," Wilder said. "We have another stop to make. And you people have some talking to do."

Carol was trembling visibly. Murphy felt a surge of pity for her, although she didn't really deserve it. Murphy felt that Margaret Highland was absolutely right in her disdainful judgment about her daughter-in-law. Carol was his client, but Murphy didn't like her much, either.

She looked up at Murphy, eyes wide and pleading. "You're sure?"

He nodded grimly. "There's no real doubt. Not now."

"But how?" she asked.

"I'll give you the details later. When I came here, I had it all pretty well fixed in my mind. I just wanted to see what the reaction would be here. I did suspect you just a tiny bit, Margaret, if you want the truth. Maybe one percent. If you'd let Ev take the rap, then I'd have been less sure of the theory I'd put together. But you came through with flying colors."

"Thank you," Margaret Highland said. She and Murphy exchanged polite nods.

Then Murphy and Wilder left the house. It had gotten as hot as hell outside. They threw their suit jackets into the back seat, got into Murphy's Toronado and headed for the expressway, the air conditioner blasting them with frigid air. Philadelphia in the summer could feel like Murphy imagined summer in Nairobi to be like. If the guy who had invented air-conditioning hadn't gotten the Nobel Prize, then he'd gotten screwed, Murphy thought.

"I'm glad we got out of there when we did," Wilder said. "It's got to be one nasty scene back there right about now."

"Well," Murphy said, "maybe I'll get to handle the divorce. I could sure use the business."

"What divorce?" Wilder said. "They're not even legally married."

Murphy lit a Camel. "Don't be so sure. That's an interesting legal question. They've been living openly as man and wife. They thought they were married. In terms of a settlement of assets, a case like that could set a valuable precedent. Wouldn't that be good for my career?"

Wilder suddenly slapped his forehead. "Find me a phone," he snapped.

"What?"

"Pull over somewhere and let me get to a phone, quick."

"Why?" Murphy said.

Wilder eyed his friend suspiciously. "I just thought of something that might nail this down for good. Something you said back there just hit me."

Murphy was mystified. "What did I say?"

"Just find me a fucking phone. At least let me have one little thing to myself, goddamn it. Okay?"

"Touchy, touchy," Murphy said, pulling into a gas station.

CHAPTER TWENTY-SIX

Murphy's Toronado lumbered into the parking lot of the Grinch. As cars whipped by on the White Horse Pike, Murphy and Wilder got out and went inside the bar. It was past the lunch hour, and the place was sparsely populated. Murphy stood out because of his suit and tie. Wilder stood out because of his suit and tie and skin color. This was not lost on Wilder. He noticed being noticed when he walked into a place not commonly frequented by blacks. He settled into a booth while Murphy ordered two beers and went to the pay phone. Murphy popped a quarter into the slot and dialed a number.

A woman's voice answered. "Hello."

"Hello. Is Bob there?"

"Who should I say is calling?"

"It's Frank Murphy. He knows me."

"One moment, please," the woman said.

Murphy lit a Camel and waited, drawing the first drag deep into his lungs. He tapped his fingers on the little metal tray beneath the phone. He wanted this over with.

"Hello."

"Bob, Frank Murphy."

Bob Waterson's voice had a nervous quality to it.
"Hi, Frank. What can I do for you?"

"Shouldn't I have called you with your wife home?"
Murphy asked, knowing he shouldn't have.

"The timing needs some work," Waterson said.
Murphy knew that Waterson hoped his wife would
think he was talking about his GTO.

"I need to see you," Murphy told him.

"Well, could we set up a time for the appointment?"

Clever, Murphy thought. "We ought to do it right
now. I'm at that bar you took me to the day I stopped
by."

"I'm not sure the problem is that crucial," Waterson
said.

"This is crucial," Murphy said. "I'm going to be here
for another fifteen minutes. Then I'm coming over to
your house."

Waterson paused on the other end of the line. "Well,
I can bring it in right now, if you think this is the best
time."

"It is," Murphy said. "I'll see you here in a few
minutes."

Murphy hung up the phone and walked back to the
booth where Wilder awaited.

"Is he coming?" Wilder asked as Murphy sat down to
his beer.

Murphy nodded. "He'll be here."

"How do you want to play this?"

Murphy understood the question perfectly. He and
Wilder had spent years interrogating suspects together.
Sometimes Wilder would play the hardass, sometimes
Murphy. It depended on the suspect and the location of

335

the interrogation. Typically, Murphy had played hardass with black suspects while Wilder had been the sympathetic soul brother and the role had been reversed when the suspect was white.

"I honestly don't think we'll have to do anything but talk calmly to this guy," Murphy said. "He's a good guy, and he's probably too smart to buffalo. And we've got him dead to rights now, thanks to your phone call. I'd say we can play it straight, just lay it out for him."

Wilder shrugged. "Have it your way."

Murphy and Wilder drank beer and talked about baseball for the next ten minutes or so. They both knew the game cold, and their arguments on the topic were spirited. Murphy hated the Yankees, but he thought Mattingly was the best all-around player in the game. Wilder leaned toward Boggs of Boston, but he was willing to listen to reason on George Brett or Mike Schmidt. They were deep in a discussion on how Roger Maris had gotten screwed back in 1961 when he'd hit sixty-one home runs in fewer at-bats than Babe Ruth had hit sixty and still had that asterisk next to his name when Waterson came in the door. He was dressed in a knit shirt with an alligator on the chest and a pair of faded jeans. Murphy motioned to him, and he came over.

"Sit down," Murphy told him. "Beer?"

"A Lite," Waterson said, and Murphy motioned to the bartender.

Waterson stuck out his hand to Wilder. "Hi, I'm Bob Waterson."

Wilder took the hand calmly. "Jim Wilder."

"Actually," Murphy said as the bartender delivered

Waterson's beer, "he's Lieutenant Wilder, Philadelphia police."

Waterson's expression changed subtly as he sipped his Lite. "What's going on? Is Carol in more trouble?"

"No," Wilder said, "Mrs. Highland is pretty much off the hook."

Waterson smiled. The man had a nice, engaging smile. "That's great. So, what happens next."

"Well," Murphy said, "what happens next is that Jim here picks up the real murderer. You see, we've pretty much figured out who did it."

Waterson sipped his beer, keeping it up to his mouth, as he said, "Who's that?"

"You did it, Mr. Waterson," Wilder said. "We know that now. When we leave here, I'm afraid that you'll have to leave in my custody."

Waterson put down the glass of Lite. He looked first at Wilder and then at Murphy. Murphy only nodded to him. The gesture was clear. Murphy was with Wilder.

Waterson looked at the table. It was a wooden tabletop, and the dark stain matched the color of the old paneling in the Grinch. It was a dark, cool place, even though you could hear the cars whizzing by outside on the White Horse Pike. Finally Bob Waterson looked up at the two of them.

"I shouldn't say anything to you until I get a lawyer, should I?" he asked quietly.

"If I were your lawyer," Murphy said, "I'd advise you to say nothing, under the circumstances."

Waterson's lips tightened into a straight line. Then he said, "What makes you think it was me?"

Murphy lit another cigarette. "Partly process of

337

elimination. The police checked out all Kirby's known associates in Atlantic City. They weren't exactly wonderful people, but none of the ones they came up with could have done it. Everybody had a decent alibi. After a while, it became clear that neither Carol, her husband, nor her mother-in-law could have done it. You were the only person left, Bob. So then the question became: how could this crime be reconstructed under the theory that you're the killer? As it turned out, it wasn't tough. Let me tell you what I think happened."

Murphy turned to Waterson. He was sitting on the inside of the booth, next to him, while Wilder sat on the other side, alone and looking at them across the table.

"I think," Murphy said, "that after Carol told you she was meeting Kirby, you got worried about her. You wanted to be around in case she ran into trouble with this guy. He was a first-class scumbag, after all. Your family was out of town, so you could drive out to Paoli in the middle of the night without anybody knowing about it. You took the GTO, of course, because your wife had the new car. Remember, you told me that?"

Waterson said nothing. Murphy didn't blame him.

"So you drove out there," Murphy went on, "only when you got to Paoli the GTO was giving you trouble. It might even have quit one or twice on the way, the way it did when I rode with you. You saw Carol come out and get in her car and drive off down the street, and you were afraid to follow her in the GTO. First, it was making a hell of a lot of noise. You didn't get the muffler fixed until later. And the car was acting up besides. It was probably going to quit on you if you went after her in it. So when she left, you walked into

338

the open bay of the Highland's garage. You saw the keys in the blue Caddy, and you just took it. You're the guy who used Ev Highland's Caddy that night."

Waterson leaned back in the booth, away from Murphy and Wilder. His eyes were slightly wider than normal, and his expression was grim. But his voice was calm and well modulated. "That's nothing but sheer speculation, Frank."

"Yeah," Wilder said. "It's only speculation, all right. But we could dust the Caddy for your prints. We might not find any, because Highland has been using the car since then, and most of your prints have probably been obliterated by now. But maybe not all of them. You touch a car in a lot of places when you spend a few hours in it. The car has leather upholstery. You can get real good prints off leather. You might have touched someplace where Mr. Highland hasn't touched since you were in the car. If we find even one of your prints there—even a partial that we can identify—then that pretty much ices the case."

"But we don't even need that," Murphy broke in. "We can prove you went out that night. I called your neighbor Boynton today. I remembered how pleased he was when you got the muffler fixed on the GTO. I figured that the noise that thing made had caused him some problems. So I played a hunch and I asked him if he remembered hearing it that night Kirby was murdered. You know what? He was pretty sure that he heard your car go out and come in that night. He's not absolutely sure of the times, but the range is close enough. We can pretty much prove you went out, I think. It's circumstantial, but it's not bad circumstantial."

Waterson said nothing. Murphy watched the man. He could tell that Waterson was trying to decide what to do. Jumping up and running away was certainly high on his list of prospective plans, but Murphy figured he wouldn't do it. The guy was too cool. And besides, where would he run? He had a wife and kids and a whole life behind him. He had no place to go. Murphy didn't think the guy would try to split. He'd try to brazen it out. That's what Murphy would do in his place, and one of the things Murphy liked about Waterson was the suspicion that they were much the same sort of guy—with two exceptions. Murphy would never have carried on an affair while he lived with his wife. And Murphy would never have murdered anyone—not even Rhino Frost, no matter what Mary Ellen thought him capable of.

Then Waterson said, "If you don't have a print, you don't have zip."

Wilder smiled slightly. "Well, maybe we do, and maybe we don't."

Waterson fixed Wilder with an icy glare. "If I'd taken time to wipe the car down, you'd be in deep shit, wouldn't you?" he asked quietly.

"Did you wipe it down?" Murphy asked him. "You must have been in a pretty big hurry to get out of that garage when you put the car back. For all you know, Carol would be back any second. If you took time to wipe down the car, you must be a pretty cool guy under pressure. Cooler than most. Maybe you didn't do all that thorough a job. Maybe you missed a place or two you'd touched. It could happen, you know. There wasn't much time."

Waterson said nothing. From his expression, though,

Murphy got the distinct impression that he might, indeed, have taken the few extra seconds to wipe down the car. He'd had enough time driving back from the motel to Paoli to think of it. Or maybe he'd thought of it beforehand and worn gloves. It was possible, although not likely. Not many people carried gloves in their cars in such hot weather.

"Well," Murphy said, "maybe you wiped the car down and maybe you didn't. It doesn't make any difference, Bob. Prints or not, we can put you in that car at a specific location that night at a specific time. And you know how we can do that, don't you?"

Waterson blanched when Murphy said that. He kept his mouth shut, though, and good for him, Murphy thought.

"The speeding ticket," Wilder explained. "You got a speeding ticket on the way back from the motel. Ordinarily, we'd never have picked it up. But we got to thinking: you didn't know that Carol was going to have car trouble. You must have been in a hell of a hurry to beat her back to the house in Paoli. You probably went like a bat out of hell all the way back. And if you did that, there was a chance you got caught in a radar trap. It was near the end of the month. That's quota time."

"Actually," Murphy said to Waterson, "Lieutenant Wilder thought of that one. It didn't even occur to me. That's how far out of practice I am."

Wilder's smug grin was too much for him to hide. He felt he'd redeemed himself for trying too hard with Carol Highland. "We ran a computer check on Highland's license plates. The computer spit out the ticket. And guess whose driver's license number showed on the ticket? Yours. All we had in the

Pennsylvania computer was the New Jersey driver's license number, but that was in the Trenton computer. You got a ticket early that morning near the King of Prussia exit on the Pennsylvania Turnpike, and you were driving Everett Highland's Cadillac at the time. We've got you, Mr. Waterson. Even without the prints, we've got you. And, let me add, that even if you did wipe down the car, the odds are that you missed at least one print. The odds of you getting every print—on that steering wheel, on that seat, on that dashboard, on the power window buttons, on the outside of the driver's door—those odds are very slim. We've got you. Don't have any doubt about it. We've got your ass good. Believe it."

Waterson sighed suddenly, a huge gasp of air escaping from his lungs. His burly frame went almost limp, as though all his bones had dissolved at once.

"I didn't mean to kill him," he said shakily. "I saw Carol come out, crying, and I got furious. Then, after she left, I was all set to go after her and I saw Kirby come out. He was just a little shit. I was surprised. He went across the street to the bar, and I sat there in the car. I wanted to break his neck for doing that to her. I sat there, trying to calm down, and then he came back and went into his room. I went to talk to him, only he said some things that were too much for me. He was talking about Carol, about how he was going to soak her for every nickel he could get, about what a nasty bitch she was. I had the club I'd found in the car sticking out of my back pocket. I guess I'd planned to scare him with it, I don't know. I just lost it at some point and I pulled it out and belted him with it. He went down, and I belted him some more. When I left, I wasn't even sure he was dead. I thought he might be—

342

the thought of that scared the hell out of me, frankly—
but I wasn't sure. I knew I'd beaten the shit out of him.
But I wasn't sure he was dead. I thought about calling
an ambulance."

"It wouldn't have done any good," Murphy told him.
"You killed him with the first shot. By the way, are you
right-handed or left-handed?"

"Left," Waterson said dully.

All four of them, Murphy mused. He wondered what
the odds were on that.

"What did you do with the fishing club?" Wilder
asked.

Waterson shrugged hopelessly. "I just tossed it out
the window along the turnpike."

"Where?" Wilder demanded.

"I don't know. Somewhere along there."

"We don't need it, anyway," Murphy said. "Not
now."

Wilder leaned back. He eyed Waterson coldly. "No,
I suppose not."

"I'm not a murderer," Waterson said.

"Yes, you are," Wilder told him quietly.

"Well," Murphy said, "I don't know. You could
make a good case for manslaughter here. I've seen
worse."

Wilder's eyes glittered. This was not the old Murphy.

Waterson turned to Murphy. "Frank, will you
represent me? Will you help me on this?"

Murphy looked uncomfortable. "Well . . ."

"Oh, sweet Christ," Wilder said.

"I don't have a lawyer," Waterson said, his voice
beginning to fray at the edges. "Just get me manslaughter, please."

Murphy looked at Wilder. "Lieutenant, I'd like a

343

moment to confer with my client. Would you mind stepping outside?"

Wilder shook his head in exasperation and total astonishment. "Oh, fuck, Frank," he said.

Murphy held up his hands in desperation. "Hey," he explained, "it's a living."

Wilder waited in the parking lot, wishing he had a cigarette and saying words that had, in his childhood, prompted his grandmother to bop him upside his head. Murphy and Waterson came out ten minutes later.

"My client will surrender at the Roundhouse at precisely ten in the morning," Murphy said.

"Bullshit he will," Wilder said. "His ass is under arrest right now after this kind of shit."

Murphy sighed deeply. "Be a good guy, Jimmy. This guy has a wife and kids. He wants to break the news to his old lady tonight, before he turns himself in. I'll take the rap if he doesn't show. Look, we're talking about a plea here. Make this tough on him, and we'll be forced to go to trial. Why don't you check with Toddman first, okay?"

Wilder, steaming, stomped back into the Grinch.

Waterson stood next to Murphy in the hot afternoon sun. "I didn't really mean to do it," he said.

"I know that," Murphy said sympathetically.

Wilder came back out in a few moments, his brow creased. He glared at Waterson. "You be there at ten or I'm coming after you with a fucking regiment, you dig?"

"I'll be there," Waterson said. Then he got into his GTO and drove out of the parking lot and down the

344

White Horse Pike toward home. Murphy turned to the fuming Wilder.

"What's for dinner at your place?" he asked.

Graterford Correctional Facility, 1987

Bobbi said nothing about Bear.

She knew better than that. For starters, she knew how things worked—that nobody ever told The Man anything, that to tell The Man anything was to be branded a snitch, and that life for prison snitches was very bad indeed. Usually very short, too. The population might detest and revile a particular inmate who had performed a particularly reprehensible act—like hitting the likable and popular Bear over the head from behind and sending him through a machine that spit him out in ragged, bloody pieces—but the population would not condone going to The Man to turn in anybody for any crime or offense, no matter how heinous. A person who would turn in somebody for something particularly bad would also be likely to turn in somebody else for something far less bad. A person who would turn snitch was not a person to be trusted under any circumstances. A person not to be trusted was a person to be removed from the scene. And a person like Bobbi was particularly vulnerable. She was in no position to defend herself—not without Rhino there to take care of her.

So Bobbi kept her mouth shut about what Rhino had done to Bear. She not only failed to tell The Man, she didn't tell a living soul. She didn't confide even in one of the other queens because separate and distinct from the problem of how this would be received in the population there was the problem of Rhino. Bobbi now knew—had seen with her own eyes—just what Rhino was capable of doing. It made her blood run cold whenever they were together and much of the rest of the time when she was forced to contemplate being his company.

Bobbi knew how it worked. She would confide in someone and that someone would confide in someone else and pretty soon word would be around and then The Man would hear about it from some snitch who hadn't yet been dispatched to his eternal reward. Then, because The Man really and truly wanted to know who had stuffed Bear into the speed ironer, The Man would come and hassle Rhino, maybe even prefer charges against him. But it would take The Man a while to make a case against Rhino, and during that time Rhino would still be in the population. Where else could he be sent? They might send him to another prison, but Bobbi couldn't count on that. She'd been around long enough to know that in here you couldn't count on anybody—especially The Man—to do the right and proper thing.

And once The Man came to Rhino, he would know who had talked. Who else could have talked? And that would be all she wrote for Bobbi. No, Bobbi kept her mouth shut. She hadn't seen nothing, she didn't know nothing, she didn't want to know nothing. That's what she said whenever talk in the population got around to what had happened to poor Bear. Old Bear was history now, and Bobbi had to look out for Bobbi.

None of which did much for her nerves.

Rhino was sweet to her now. Bobbi stopped giving him any kind of guff and did everything she could to please him and keep him happy, and he was gentle with her and kind. He gave her two cartons of cigarettes for her birthday. Bobbi didn't smoke, but the cigarettes were used as currency, and a two whole cartons was an extravagant gift. She knew that Rhino had used his "white money"—real money from outside, money sent to him by his dead mother's lawyer—to buy the cigarettes. Ordinarily, she would have been touched by the gift, and she certainly pretended to be. But a much deeper and more profound emotion had suffused her very being since the incident with Bear.

That emotion was fear. Bobbi Hammond lived in utter terror of Rhino Frost. He would be out soon, she knew, and then she would be safe. With Rhino gone, there would be a few rough days or weeks, but then she would soon find herself another jocker to care for her and protect her, and her life would return to normal— the way it had been before that day in the laundry. She thought every day about Rhino leaving. Rhino, too, talked about getting out. It was very much on his mind.

"I got me some plans on the outside," he told her one night in the cell during his last week in Graterford.

Bobbi stroked his cheek. "What plans you got, baby?" she asked.

He gazed at the ceiling. "I got a guy I got to see. I been looking forward to seeing him for a long time now."

"Who's this guy?" she asked soothingly. "You never told me about no guy. You always told me that you were straight on the outside."

"I'm straight. I'll be straight again when I get out.

347

This guy, I got to see him about something else. I'm looking forward to seeing him."

Bobbi took her hand and put it on Rhino's crotch, feeling through his shorts for his remaining testicle. "Is he the dude who did that to you?"

Frost said nothing. But he pushed her hand away.

"You never told me who done that to you, baby," she pressed.

"I ain't going to, neither," Frost said.

"I tell you everything," Bobbi pouted.

"You shouldn't," Rhino said quietly. "You shouldn't never tell anybody everything. You dig?"

Bobbi dug. She felt a thrill of fear shoot through her. She said nothing. Saying nothing was a lot better than saying the wrong thing.

Rhino got up and walked over to the bars. He wore only boxer shorts, and he stood at the bars in silhouette, his hulking frame blocking out most of the light from outside. He was restless with so little time to go until his release. They would give him fifty bucks, some new clothes, and a bus ticket to anywhere in the state. In his case, that would be back to Philly. He would see that lawyer his mother had hired—Silver, his name was—and get some money and live for a few days in the house in which he had been raised. Then he would find himself a new place to live and have the house put on the market. He didn't need a house. He needed money. He needed money to pick himself up a new bike and maybe a car of some kind for bad weather. He would buy some weights and a good TV and maybe one of those VCRs he kept hearing about. He would find himself a woman, too—a real woman, not a fake one like Bobbi. He would meet his parole officer and maybe he'd have to get some kind of job until parole was up. He could go back to construction work for a while, just long enough to keep the parole officer happy. He'd be off parole in less than a year. Then he'd buy himself a new chain saw.

After that—when all that was finished—he'd look up Sergeant Murphy. Rhino really wanted to look up Sergeant Murphy. He'd been thinking about it for many years now, thinking about it almost daily. He had drifted off to sleep dreaming about it. Frost wanted to show Sergeant Murphy all his new things— especially his chain saw.

Rhino smiled through his beard at the thought of it. He wondered if Murphy would remember him. Maybe not. Frost was not a student of human nature, but he knew that most people forgot things as time went by. Not him, though. He never forgot. He'd never forgotten that time in the shower with Bear and the others. Bear had forgotten, but not Rhino. That had been Bear's mistake. Bear's big mistake.

Frost turned and looked down at Bobbi, who was stretched out on the bunk in just her shorts, her slim frame relaxing on the sheets. Her eyes were closed, but he knew she wasn't asleep. Pretty soon now he'd be gone and she'd be here looking for another jocker. And once she found her jocker, she would sooner or later tell him everything she had ever seen or heard or thought. She would do that because she was a dumb bitch.

Rhino knew she would do that because she had done it with him. Over the years, she had told him everything about her, everything that had ever passed before her eyes or through her head. All that eventually came out through her mouth. She wouldn't do it right away. It might even take as long as a year or two. But sooner or later she would tell her new jocker about Bear. And once that happened it might be years before word got to The Man.

Frost hoped it would take some time. He wasn't sure how much time he would need to get through parole and do what he had to do with Murphy, and his great fear was that Bobbi would spill her guts over that business with Bear before he could accomplish on the outside what he needed to accomplish. Once The Man heard about Bear, The Man would be after him. That part didn't bother Frost. He would never let The Man take him again on anything that would send him back here. He was perfectly willing to die before he would let that happen. But it would be better if he could just stay clear of The Man on the business with Bear long enough to conduct his business with Sergeant Murphy.

Then Frost would take what cash he had left, get on his bike and head south, maybe out west. Maybe he would go to California and try to join up with the Hell's Angels. That's what Frost had always wanted to be, a Hell's Angel. He wondered if they were really what they were cracked up to be or just a bunch of pussies with big reputations. That's what the Demons had turned out to be. As a teenager, Frost had paid to have several tattoos done. He liked one tattoo, the one that said "Passing for Human." He no longer liked the other one, though, which was the Demons symbol emblazoned on his chest. It was the face of a screaming devil with red eyes and the word "DEMONS" written beneath it. He wished now that he had not had himself decorated with the symbol of a bunch of pussies.

He had paid ten cigarettes here in Graterford to have another tattoo placed on his back six years earlier. This was a four-by-five-inch likeness of a Harley Panhead with Rhino in the saddle—a symbol of his own independence. That's the one he wished he could had had done on his chest, but the space had been taken.

Meanwhile, there was still the problem of Bobbi. The simplest and easiest way to deal with that difficulty would be to kill her. She could fall over the railing outside the cell down onto the floor of the cellblock, four stories down. She could have some other kind of accident. But if his cellmate died mysteriously, The Man would be curious about Rhino, since the nature of their relationship was well known. And somebody would be sure to remember Bear and put everything together. So killing Bobbi was out. What Rhino had to do was come up with some way to keep Bobbi from hooking up too soon with another jocker, and he had to frighten her so severely that it would be a long time before the business with Bear came out. Rhino had pondered the problem ever since Bear's death. He thought he had it worked out now. He was pretty sure that the plan he had come up with would keep her both unattached and quiet for some time after he got out.

"Bobbi," Rhino Frost said softly.

Bobbi stirred on the bunk.

Frost walked over to her, loomed over her. Bobbi's eyes opened and she looked up at him. Frost reached down to her, took her by the arms, and lifted her off the bunk, bringing her face close to his.

"Love you, baby," Frost said gently.

351

CHAPTER TWENTY-SEVEN

"Anything else, Frank?" Annabelle Wilder asked.

Murphy patted his ample belly. "I couldn't hold it, especially this late at night. Everything was great, Annabelle. Just terrific."

Annabelle smiled. She was a pretty woman in her late thirties with tan skin, lively brown eyes, and the body of a sixteen-year-old, and she had expressed no reservations whatever about feeding her husband and his best friend when the two of them had wandered into the house past nine. Where did women like this come from, Murphy wondered, and why couldn't he find one? Was there some sort of secret society that nobody was telling him about?

"It's nice to have somebody around who appreciates food," Annabelle told him. "Old skin and bones here never eats anything."

That was true. Jim Wilder's plate was still half full. Dinner had been a hearty salad, boneless chicken breast in a white wine sauce, potatoes whipped with cheddar cheese, and asparagus in butter and rosemary. Murphy had consumed it like a shark in a feeding frenzy. Wilder had only picked. Which might have explained why

Murphy had tended in his later years to run toward fat while Wilder was still whip lean. Of course, Murphy told himself, Wilder was a nervous sort, too. That was probably the real reason.

"How about some coffee?" Wilder asked his wife.

"It's already on," she said, clearing the dining room table of the Wilders' row house in Germantown. Murphy lit a cigarette and Wilder eyed it longingly. It occurred to neither of them to help Annabelle clear the dirty dishes. It seldom occurred to Murphy to clear dirty dishes when he ate alone in his own apartment.

Annabelle disappeared into the kitchen and Wilder said, "Are you going right up to the Poconos after Waterson turns himself in tomorrow?"

"Yeah. I'd like to go up tonight, actually, but I've got to hang around to see that this guy doesn't get weak knees tomorrow morning. I've got Catrelli up there, and I don't expect Frost to show until tomorrow night at the earliest. So I'm not all that worried about it. At least, I'm trying hard not to worry about it."

Annabelle returned with the coffee. "Here," she said, "regular coffee for you, Frank, and decaf for you."

Annabelle sat down. "So how's Mary Ellen, Frank? I haven't seen her in the longest time now."

Murphy shrugged. "She's still Mary Ellen. She has good days and bad days, just like all of us."

"You know," Annabelle said, "I keep waiting for the two of you to get back together."

"Well," Murphy said, "don't hold your breath. Mary Ellen gets along with me better from a distance—the further the better, as far as she's concerned."

"Oh," Annabelle said, "I don't believe that. Patricia is going away to college in a few weeks, and Mary Ellen

353

is going to be all alone in that big house. If she doesn't miss you now, she'll miss you then. Wait and see."

Murphy smiled ruefully. "She might miss me, but not enough to want to live with me again. For some people, it's a strain on the nerves to be amiable to the same person day after day. That's not just her; it's me, too. I like what Barry Weiner always says about marriage. He says that a man gets married because he's tired and a woman gets married because she's curious and both of them end up disappointed."

Wilder chuckled. "Barry ought to know. What's he gone through now, three wives?"

Annabelle frowned. "Yeah, that ought to make him a real expert."

"I remember a line I learned in college," Wilder said. "To marry once is a duty, twice a folly, and three times a madness. That's Barry. I never met a shrink yet who wasn't bonkers."

The phone rang. Annabelle went to answer it.

"Who is it?" Wilder called out to her.

Annabelle's voice came back from the kitchen. "It's my mother."

"She's good for at least an hour," Wilder told Murphy, glancing at his watch. "I can't figure out why her old lady can't call before ten. Let's go into the living room."

They took their coffee and settled in front of the television set. Wilder went around the dial and came up with boxing from Atlantic City on ESPN. Two tiny Hispanic guys were pounding hell out of each other. Murphy found an ashtray and settled back to enjoy the carnage. Twenty-five years before, for a period of several years while he had served in the Navy, Murphy had boxed. He'd been fairly good at it, too. He had a couple of medals from inter-service competition buried somewhere beneath a mound of soiled laundry back at his apartment to prove it. All these years later, Murphy still liked to watch boxing, although he preferred matches with bigger guys. In the lighter weights, action was so fast that he sometimes couldn't follow it, and these little guys never seemed to really be hitting each other with any force. That's how it looked on TV, anyway.

They watched the fight in silence for a few rounds. Murphy was full of food and would have been relaxed for the first time in weeks had it not been for the worry that beset him over Mary Ellen and Patricia.

As if reading his friend's mind, Wilder suddenly said, "I wonder where old Rhino is tonight?"

Murphy never took his eyes away from the television screen. "If my guess is right, he's sitting outside my apartment building waiting for me to come out. Come tomorrow morning, he'll realize I wasn't there. He'll go home to go to sleep for the day, then he'll hit my house tomorrow night. He'll find the directions on the table, figure out that's where I am, and head up to the Poconos. And Catrelli and I'll be waiting for him."

Wilder nodded. "How do you know he'll go up there?"

"I don't for sure. But he's got to be getting itchy now, especially after Catrelli and his boys jumped him the other night. For all he knows, I've got somebody coming after him now with guns. I think he's through waiting for me, and if my guess is right he'll be sort of pleased at the chance to come after me out in the boonies if he can, where there are fewer people and—

355

more important—fewer cops. This place is just about perfect to take him in, if the maps Harold showed me are accurate. The cabin is back in the woods, about a mile off the main highway. There's only one road in. All you've got to do is watch that road, and you've got him."

Wilder listened solemnly as he watched the fight. "How far are you going to let him go?" he asked finally.

Murphy understood the question perfectly. He had no choice but to let Frost take a threatening action before moving against him. The law was clear. You could use deadly force against an intruder only if you had reasonable cause to believe that the intruder was about to use deadly force against you and yours. Shoot a fleeting burglar, even in your own living room, and you were liable for civil and criminal action. Murphy thought it was a silly law, but he was stuck with it.

"I suppose I've got to let him get into the house," Murphy said. "There's no way out of that. Once he's inside, then I'm clear. What I'd really like to do is blast him out on the dirt road leading in, but that wouldn't stand up in court—even with his record and our history together."

Wilder said nothing for a long while. He sipped his coffee and watched the fight and wished he had one of Murphy's cigarettes. Only he didn't dare light up with Annabelle in the house. It would be worth his life. After a while, he stood up and stretched and yawned. "I'm going to hit the sack early. You know you way to the guest room, I hope."

Murphy said, "I won't be too far behind you. I just want to see how this fight comes out. After tonight, I don't figure to get too much sleep for a while—not until after he shows up."

"Frank," Wilder said evenly, "let me give you some advice. Don't give him too much of a chance. Do what you have to do and worry about the law later. This guy's real bad news."

Murphy drew on his Camel. "Tell me about it," he said.

CHAPTER TWENTY-EIGHT

Murphy's building was a three-story brownstone with two apartments on each floor. The building was constructed along the lines of a medieval fortress, which had created a particularly vexing problem for Rhino Frost.

How could he get in? There had to be a way to get in, he told himself.

Frost had cased the place carefully, and in so doing he had gone into the vestibule before dawn one morning, studied the mailboxes, and learned that Murphy lived in apartment 2-B, which he assumed to be the rearmost apartment on the second floor. The rear apartments overlooked an alley behind the building. Frost had briefly entertained a plan which would involve placing a ladder beneath Murphy's bedroom window and trying to sneak into the apartment unnoticed and unheard. But he had soon dismissed that plan as unworkable. If he tried it during the day, he would surely be seen. If he tried it at night, while Murphy slept inside, he would make too much noise.

The door from the vestibule into the first-floor hall

was made of heavy wood and thick glass and could be opened only with a key, which Frost did not have. And even if he could have cracked the door that opened from the vestibule into the building proper, he would still have no way to get into Murphy's apartment without making so much noise that somebody would be sure to call the police.

Frost had wracked his brain. He could think of no practical way to get into Murphy's apartment, so he was forced to consider how he might get Murphy out of his apartment at a time of Frost's choosing—and preferably without the gun he had taken to carrying again.

Finally Frost had hit upon a plan. It was not foolproof, but it posed no real danger to him even if it failed. That plan was in the forefront of Frost's brain at just after two in the morning, as Murphy slept soundly in the bed of Wilder's guest room many miles away, a situation of which Frost was utterly unaware. Frost walked up to the door of Murphy's Center City apartment building carrying a large metal can. He went through the front door and studied the mailboxes. Then, at random, he pressed a doorbell button for one of the third-floor apartments. He pressed it again, long and hard. Then a voice came through the intercom.

"Who is it?" the voice said. It belonged to a sleepy man with a slight accent.

"Sorry to bother you," Frost said. "This is Frank Murphy in 2-B. I just got home and I realized I forgot my key. If you'll just hit the door release, I won't bother you again. I've got a key hidden in the hallway outside my apartment door."

There was a pause. Frost felt a slight thrill of fear

shoot through him. No need, he told himself. He could always turn and run.

"You forgot your key?"

"Yeah," Frost said. "I don't know what was going through my head."

"And this is who?"

"Frank Murphy, apartment 2-B. You know me. I'm the heavyset guy with the gray hair. You know, the lawyer."

"Okay," the voice said.

The door release buzzer sounded, and Frost immediately opened the door. "Thanks," he said.

"You can do it for me sometime," the voice said, and the intercom switched off.

Frost climbed the stairs to the second floor. He had made it a point to hit the buzzer to an apartment above Murphy's, not one of the first-floor apartments. If he had hit one of the first-floor buzzers, the person he had disturbed would, he was sure, be at the peephole of his door looking out to make sure that it was, in fact, Murphy who was entering the building. But the man on the third floor would have to open his door, walk out into the hall, and look down the stairwell if he was curious enough. He might be, but Frost was hoping he wasn't. And he was lucky. No door opened on the third floor as he climbed the single flight of stairs.

He stopped outside Murphy's door. He wished he could have thought of a way to get in. He could probably have broken down this door, but the noise would have been unacceptable. As it was, he merely took the four-gallon can he carried and splashed gasoline on the door and all along the hall. He put the can on the floor next to Murphy's door. Then he lit a match and tossed it into the gasoline.

Flames erupted around Rhino Frost. The sudden intensity of the heat and light surprised and startled him. He turned and stomped down the stairs.

"Fire," he shouted. "The place is on fire."

Frost went out the door and sprinted across the darkened street. He reached his van and leaped inside. Then he peered out the window. They'd all be outside in a moment, every one of them in that building. And if Murphy survived the flames, he'd be out there with them. He'd be in his pajamas, startled and disoriented. He would be looking up at the burning building, and Frost could get behind him without difficulty, hit him from behind, drag him into the van, and take off. And maybe nobody would even notice. If they did, it didn't matter. Frost had nearly forty thousand dollars in cash in the van in the saddlebags of his Harley 1200. He had no intention of going back to his little apartment over the garage in Olney. He would drive to Fairmount Park and finish Murphy, and then he would head out to the house in Mount Airy and do that what he had long looked forward to doing. Frost ground his big teeth together as he thought about it.

Tonight would be the night, he knew. This would be the night. He fought back a deep-throated chuckle. Too soon, he thought. Don't laugh until you've got him. Don't blow this now. It's been too long to blow this.

Frost could see the light from the fire through the windows of the other apartments on the second floor. It was only moments before the first of them came running out into the street. Then the others came. There was a big dark-haired man and a woman, both in bedclothes. They stood on the sidewalk, looking up at the building. Inside the vestibule, smoke was forming and beginning to pour out. Another couple came out, the woman in a robe and the man in just a pair of underwear shorts. An elderly woman came out with a white miniature poodle clutched under one arm. Frost watched them as they came. He counted them. In less than a minute, there were nine people in the street outside the building, milling around on the sidewalk, watching the flames lick out the front windows on the second floor.

But Murphy was not among them.

Frost waited until he heard the fire engines coming. He heard the sirens and the bells and then he started his van, pulled out, and drove away down Schuylkill Avenue. He turned at the first corner and stepped on the gas. Frost was confused, and he didn't know whether to be elated. There were two possibilities. One, Murphy had been trapped in the fire. Two, he hadn't been in the apartment. In either event, Frost would be disappointed. He wanted Murphy dead, all right, but he wanted him to die face to face, eyeball to eyeball. If Murphy had been trapped in the fire, that wouldn't be enough for Rhino Frost.

He shifted gears on the van and headed for the expressway. His mind was working. He felt more alive at this moment than he had felt in many years, more alive now than he'd felt since entering Graterford. The incident with Bear had produced in him a flash of vitality, but it had been fleeting, and it had come after many years of a living death. Frost felt the blood move in his veins, and he felt a sense of power he had sorely missed.

And he wasn't finished yet. Even if Murphy was dead, Rhino Frost wasn't finished yet. He turned left on Spring Garden Street and headed toward the expressway.

Headed toward Mount Airy.

Frost moved through the darkness behind the Mount Airy house. He had parked the van a block away and walked here, trying to stay out of the streetlights. This was a quiet neighborhood, and he had moved quietly, being as innocuous as a man his size and his appearance could manage. Murphy's house was utterly dark tonight, and Frost wasn't sure what to make of that. He had watched this house off and on for several nights. Once he had even sat here in the backyard and watched through the window as Murphy had spoken to the girl and the woman as they sat at the kitchen table. He hadn't been able to make out what they were saying, but at one point—as Frost watched through the sliding glass door in the rear—he saw the girl pale and cover her breasts with one arm. Frost had only been able to guess at what Murphy had been saying then, but he thought he knew.

That night, however, the family had slept with the upstairs bathroom light on. They had done so the other night Frost had been here, watching from his van across the street. Tonight the house was a mass of dark shadows. Frost didn't like that.

He went up the steps onto the deck Murphy had agonizingly built on the back of the house two summers before. Despite Murphy's fundamental ineptitude at such tasks, it was a good deck. Its foundation posts were sunk into the ground, resting on several feet of concrete at each pressure point, and the deck itself was constructed of pressure-treated lumber, so it would last. Frost stood in the darkness in front of the sliding glass door and took a suction cup out of his pocket. It was from a child's toy he had bought in K-Mart and then taken apart, discarding the part he didn't need. He flicked out his tongue, licked the cup and stuck it to the glass, near the handle. Then he took out the glass cutter he had bought at the K-Mart hardware department and carefully cut the glass around the suction cup. As he came to the end of the circle he was making in the glass with a harsh yet relatively quiet grating sound, he grasped the cup with his free hand. He struck the cup lightly. Nothing. He struck it a bit harder, and he felt the satisfying sensation of the cut glass coming loose. He pulled the cup toward him, and it came away with a piece of glass attached. He threw it over his shoulder into the lawn, where it landed almost soundlessly.

Fingerprints? Frost didn't care about fingerprints. Let them try to find him. He would be riding with the Angels out west. Or he would be riding alone. Sometimes he thought it might be better if he just rode alone.

A huge hand worked its way through the hole in the glass and thick fingers found the lock. Frost flipped the lock, and then he slid the door open. He stepped into the kitchen. The house was silent and dark. Frost moved quietly toward the stairs.

This was, he knew, the point of greatest danger. If Murphy was alive and sleeping here, and if Frost had awakened him when he came through the back door, then Murphy might be standing at the top of the stairs, pistol in hand, waiting to blast him as he climbed toward the second floor.

Frost could see no way around it.

Without hesitation, he climbed the carpeted stairway as quietly as he could. He gained the upstairs hallway without incident, then he took out his knife. It was a survival knife he had bought at the Army-Navy store on Olney Avenue near his house. It was precisely the one Stallone had used in *Rambo,* complete with the compass Frost was sure he would never have use for. The door to all three bedrooms were open. Frost didn't know which one might house Murphy and his pistol. At this point, he simply didn't much care. He was too keyed up, too close, too wired to figure out anything else. He picked a bedroom at random, walked through the door quickly, and hit the wall switch.

The room was suddenly suffused with light from a lamp on the dresser. It was also empty. Along one wall was a poster of Tom Cruise. There was a stereo on a stand, a pile of beauty magazines, a neatly made bed littered with stuffed animals.

Frost killed the light immediately.

Nervous now, he went into the hall and stormed into another room. He lit the light. It was the master bedroom. Empty.

He raged into the third bedroom. It, too, was

unoccupied, flowered bedspreads blazing up at him under the overhead light. Frost slammed his fist against the wall switch, plunging the room into darkness. He stormed over to one of the guest-room beds and drove the survival knife into a bedspread, feeling the point rip through into the mattress beneath. He pulled the knife out and slammed it in again. Frost stabbed the mattress thirty-two times, swearing horribly in the darkness.

Then he turned and stomped out of the room and downstairs. He turned on lights as he went. It made no difference now. He had been cheated, robbed. They were gone. And he knew instinctively that Murphy had gone with them. He had not been in the apartment. He was still alive and breathing and laughing and talking and Rhino Frost was beside himself with frustration and rage. Nearly thirteen years he had waited. Tonight he had made his move and he had found an empty house and, he was now sure, an empty apartment. His anger was nearly uncontrollable.

"MOTHER-FUCK!" he bellowed as he stormed into the kitchen, slamming his fist against the wall switch and turning on the overhead light. He stood in the center of Murphy's kitchen, fuming and swearing. What now? What the Christ now? he wondered.

The sheet of paper on the kitchen table caught his eye. Rhino Frost picked it up, studied it, grasped its significance, and grunted to himself. Careless. Very careless. If, in fact, that was where they were. He stuffed the piece of paper in the pocket of his worn jeans.

Then, on the way out, he kicked in the television set, slashed the living-room furniture with his survival knife, and pissed on the kitchen floor. His only regret was that he had used all his matches and gasoline on Murphy's apartment house. He wished he'd thought to save some.

As he went out the sliding glass door in the back, Rhino Frost thought about how much he would have liked to have burned this house to the ground.

CHAPTER TWENTY-NINE

Wilder drove Murphy into Center City in time to get both of them to the Roundhouse at nine forty-five. Toddman met them in the Major Crimes section. He was smoking the first of the half dozen or so enormous cigars he would reduce to ashes before bedtime, and his creased face was pallid and grim.

"I hope your boy shows," he told Murphy. "I did you a favor on this one. Don't ask me why."

"Because you're a prince among men," Murphy assured him. "Someday they're going to put up a statue in your honor, Paul, and the pigeons won't even shit on it."

"I'm not kidding," Toddman said evenly. "If this guy took a powder overnight, Fletcher's going to have my ass on a stick."

"I thought he was going to run for governor this year," Murphy said. "Whatever happened to that?"

Toddman shrugged. "Somebody at the state committee must have spent a few minutes in conversation with him and found out what a total asshole he is. There's still the Senate race two years from now. Can you picture Fletcher in the U.S. Senate? Jesus, if that happens, I'm going to move to Canada."

"Save room for me when you get there," Murphy told him.

The three men sat there until well after ten, making small talk and all figuring the same thing—that Waterson was probably halfway to Mexico by now. Murphy mentally kicked himself for not hitting him up for a retainer. At least he'd have that. He could handle the legal part of private practice. He was a decent enough lawyer after dealing with the law and hanging around courts his entire adult life. But he freely confessed—to himself, at least—that he knew nothing about business. He was forty-five years old, and he'd never figured out how to balance a checkbook. Instead, he maintained three separate checking accounts with the same bank. He would switch from one account to the other every month and by the time he got back to the first one he could figure out how much money he had left in it. Lee Iacocca he was not, Murphy had to admit. Iacocca dressed better, too.

By ten-thirty Toddman was beginning to twitch nervously, and all humor had vanished from his conversation. Wilder was accusingly silent, and Murphy found himself carrying the conversation on his own.

"There's this guy," Murphy said, "he's going down the street and he sees this old guy—a guy of about eighty-five or so—and the old guy is standing on the street corner crying his eyes out."

"Is this a joke or what?" Wilder grunted.

"Shut up and pay attention," Murphy told him. "So the guy goes up to the old man, and he says, 'Sir, are you all right?'"

"Is this a Jewish joke?" Toddman asked. "Give it up,

Frank. You don't know how to tell a Jewish joke."

"He don't know how to tell any kind of joke," Wilder pointed out.

Murphy ignored them. He was going to keep them entertained until Waterson either showed up or they all were forced to deal with the fact that Waterson wasn't going to show up, a prospect which did not at all appeal to Murphy.

Without missing a beat, Murphy said, "So the old guy says, 'My wife, she died.' And the guy says, 'That's terrible. I'm so sorry.' And the old man says, 'No, you don't understand, she died twenty-five years ago. We had a terrible marriage. She couldn't cook. She wouldn't wash for me. We never talked. We had sex maybe six times in forty years. She didn't like it, so we didn't do it.'"

"I think I know this joke," Wilder told Toddman. "If it's the one I think it is, it really sucks."

"Up yours," Murphy said to him. "I'm telling this to Paul. So the guy says, 'If she died so long ago and things are so bad, how come you're so upset?' And the old man says, 'A year ago, I met this woman. Who would have guessed that this could happen to me at my age? She's about thirty-five, and she's gorgeous. We go out for a date and she falls in love with me. She moves in with me. We talk all the time. We talk about philosophy. We talk about literature. And cook? She cooks like a chef . . .'"

"Your dialect is really horrible," Toddman commented.

"Fuck you," Murphy said. "I'm telling this to Jim. So the old guy says, 'She washes for me. She scrubs for me. She works like a slave for me. And sex? Sex is wonderful, marvelous. We have sex six, seven times a week, and every time it's as though our souls have joined. It's so wonderful I can't describe it.' So the guy says to the old man, 'I don't understand. If everything is so terrific, how come you're standing here on the corner crying?' And the old man says—"

" 'I can't remember where I live,' " Wilder grunted. "I told you, Paul, the joke sucks."

"Where the hell is your client, Frank?" Toddman demanded.

Murphy said quickly, "Did I tell you the one about the three guys from the United Nations who are touring Kansas? There's a guy from Israel, a guy from India, and a guy from—"

Wilder's phone rang. He grabbed it. "Wilder. (Pause) What's his name? (Pause) Okay, send him in." Wilder hung up the phone. "Waterson's on his way in." He turned to Murphy. "That one sucks, too. I've heard it."

"Everybody's heard it," Toddman added sourly, but his tone carried a note of relief.

Waterson was wearing a suit. His face was the color of cottage cheese. A uniformed officer escorted him into the room assigned to the Major Crimes unit.

"I'm here to surrender," he said simply.

"And we're all glad to see you, too," Murphy told him.

Wilder stood up. "This is Mr. Toddman from the district attorney's office," he said. "You have the right to remain silent. You have the right to an attorney. Anything you say can and will be used against you . . ."

*   *   *

After Waterson was charged, fingerprinted, booked, and properly arraigned, Murphy dropped hurriedly by his office to check his messages. He was delighted to find waiting for him a check from Everett Highland for ten thousand dollars.

"When did this come in?" he demanded of Esmeralda.

"A man brought it in this morning, early. He said to thank you and that he hoped this would be enough to cover your services."

Murphy looked at the check, and he was suddenly suffused with a sense of well-being. Here was Patricia's next semester or two, at least. "Did he say anything else?"

She shook her head. "Not a word."

Murphy shrugged. "Maybe I won't get that divorce case after all. Listen . . ."

"I know," she said. "You won't be in for the rest of today."

"Tomorrow either," he told her.

"Soft touch you lawyers have," she said. Murphy signed the check and handed it to her. "Deposit this in the account, okay? And don't wrinkle or fold it or anything."

Esmeralda batted her eyes fetchingly. *"Moi?"* she said.

Murphy left the Fidelity Bank Building and went back to his apartment to get a change of clothes. He found the building a shambles. The hallway outside his apartment was charred and sooty and redolent of smoke. The door to his apartment was blackened but still intact. He let himself in—after wrestling with the key for a good five minutes—found what he was after, and stuffed it all into an overnight bag. On the way out, he banged on the door of Mrs. Froczek, a sixtyish widow with the build of Dick Butkus who lived in the other apartment on his floor. She checked him out through the peephole and then opened her door. She wore a flowered robe and clutched her Siamese cat, whom Winston had always despised. So did Murphy.

"What happened?" Murphy demanded.

"The building caught fire last night," Mrs. Fronczek told him. "We all got out just in time. I took Snookie with me and we just ran out into the street. Then the fire engines came and put out the fire. Doesn't the place smell awful, though?"

"Did somebody call the landlord?" Murphy asked her.

"I did. They're coming out to clean up today or tomorrow. You need a new door, Mr. Murphy."

"I noticed. Did anybody get hurt?"

She shook her head. "No. But Snookie won't use his pan anymore. He won't even let me put him down. Whenever I try to, he just howls and scratches at my leg."

"How did it start?"

"I don't know. Mr. Mancopov on the third floor said it started a few minutes after you came in last night. But you weren't here, were you? I didn't see you when we all ran outside."

"After I came in?"

Mrs. Fronczek nodded. "Mr. Mancopov said he let you in with the door release because you'd forgotten your key and that the smoke started right after that. Isn't that strange, though?"

"Sure is," Murphy told her.

"Do you think it was arson?" she demanded.

"Nah," Murphy said. "Who'd do something like that?"

Murphy virtually floored the protesting Toronado all the way out to Mount Airy. He hated to take the time out from his trip up to the Poconos, but he had to see if Frost had taken the bait. Had the dumb bastard been so stupid that he actually thought he'd gotten Murphy in the fire? Could he be that much of a moron? Murphy wasn't sure. And he wanted to know if Frost had gone to the Mount Airy house afterward.

Murphy pulled in the driveway, got out his keys and his pistol and entered the house cautiously. He came in through the front hall and headed straight for the glass door at the rear, which he knew was the most vulnerable and most likely point of entry. He found the hole in the glass. Then he carefully searched the house, his pistol ready. He surveyed the damage to the guest-room bed, to the television set, to the living-room sofa and chairs.

Murphy took in the damage with a combined sense of anger and personal violation. He remembered going out with Mary Ellen and buying that living-room set at Gimbels eleven years before. It had been on sale, but it had still been more than they had wanted to spend. Still, she had wanted it, so he had gone for it. Now it was trash. The TV set had been a gift from Murphy's sister, who had a few bucks. He looked over the damage with tightened lips.

You were pissed, weren't you, Rhino? he thought.

The paper containing the directions was, of course, missing from the kitchen table. Had Frost known it

374

was a trap when he took the piece of paper? Probably. Maybe, anyway. Frost was no genius, and he was seriously wound up now, if the damage to the house was any indication. That's how Murphy wanted Frost. He wanted him excited, angry. He did not want this man cool and calculating. Frost was dangerous enough when he was nuts; he would be immeasurably more so if he took time to think.

Murphy glanced at his watch. He had just enough time to get there before dark. And that's if he didn't get lost, which happened to him just about every time he left the city limits.

That would be all he would need, to get lost on his way to a rendezvous with a madman.

CHAPTER THIRTY

Early on a hot, vicious, nasty, sweltering August afternoon that made him feel like he was living in somebody's armpit, Harry Nelson looked up from his newspaper to see a battered Ford van roll into his gas station on Olney Avenue. Then a monster got out, and Harry Nelson frowned deeply.

A biker, he thought, putting down his copy of the *Daily News* and wiping the sweat off his lined brow. He could tell them a mile off, even when they weren't on their bikes. Look at him, for Christ's sake—all hair and dirt and big enough to wrestle elephants. Jesus, where did these guys come from?

"Come on, Elvis," Harry Nelson said, snapping his fingers. "You come with me for this one."

Elvis was a Doberman Pinscher with teeth like a mako shark. At the sound of his name, he wagged his stub of a tail. As Harry Nelson walked out of his gas station to the pumps, Elvis dutifully got up and walked out behind him, his muscles rolling in waves beneath his sleek black and tan coat. The dog's muscles and teeth were a total fraud. Elvis was a breeding blip, a gentle Doberman. He looked mean enough, but in

376

actuality he was eighty-five pounds of cuddly puppy, a collection of expensive canine genes gone awry—six hundred bucks down the drain. Harry had wanted a killer; he'd gotten a lover. Which had turned out to be his tough luck. When the dog's profound and disturbingly undesirable gentle streak had emerged, Harry had complained to the breeder, who had suggested that Harry perform an impossible sex act. Elvis was a born candyass, and Harry was stuck with him. Luckily, Harry Nelson thought as he walked out to wait on the biker, nobody could tell that Elvis was a candyass just by looking at him.

"Can I help you?" Harry Nelson asked the biker.

The biker was gigantic, and he was no kid, either. His gray-flecked hair and beard hung in tangled waves about his face. Harry—who was five foot six—realized that this guy was about a foot taller and had arms like tree trunks. Jesus, what a gorilla. Harry noted the two-inch square tattoo on the outside of the man's left bicep. It featured a crude drawing of a dragon with a legend around it. The legend said: "Passing for human."

"Fill it up," the biker said in a deep, rumbling voice. "Hey, you got a john around here?"

Harry motioned. "On the side—over there. The key's on a hook inside the door."

Wordlessly, the biker stalked off toward the door of the gas station. He wore a black T-shirt with a Harley emblem and worn jeans and Harry had never seen anybody so big up close. Harry had been to a couple of Seventy-Sixers games over the years and had seen guys that size from up in the stands. But he'd never seen a monster like this up close. Never a white guy that big, either. And he was the kind of nut who rode a motorcycle on city streets when he wasn't driving his van, Harry was sure. Only a maniac would ride a motorcycle on Philadelphia streets, what with all the traffic and the trolley cars and buses.

The thought of somebody that big and nuts besides made Harry nervous. As the enormous biker disappeared into the men's room, Harry Nelson screwed off the cap of the van's fuel tank and reached for a pump. Fill this mother up and get this guy out of here, Harry advised himself. Who needs this?

Harry Nelson was fifty-six. He'd run the Exxon station on Olney Avenue since it had been an Esso station. He had a wife who'd been lying in Holy Redeemer Cemetery for six years, a daughter unhappily married to a cocaine-addicted general contractor in Scottsdale, Arizona, a small row house with plumbing problems a few blocks away, sixteen thousand dollars in time deposits, a treasured collection of Glenn Miller records, and a big scar down the middle of his chest from a bypass operation fourteen months before. He needed bikers hanging around his gas station like he needed cancer. What he really needed was a buyer for the place. It had been listed for months now, and no serious offers. And Harry was willing to throw in the goddamned dog for nothing, too.

Elvis sniffed curiously at the van.

"Stay away from that," Harry snapped at the dog, who ignored him. Harry squeezed harder on the pump handle, pushing out the gas more quickly. He didn't like this guy's looks, not even a little bit, and he wanted the biker out of here and on his way. Who needs this, he thought? Who needs any of this?

378

Harry filled the tank, noted the amount showing on the pump, and went back inside the station. Elvis stayed by the pump, sniffing the van like it was a fire hydrant.

"Get in here," Harry called out the door to the dog.

Elvis only wagged his tail good-naturedly. Harry sighed and lit a Marlboro. Screw that heart doctor. Harry knew he should have bought a police dog. Who ever heard of a nice gas station dog? Gas station dogs were supposed to be mean. They were supposed to roll in grease and snarl at customers and keep the scumbags away. This goddamn dog even wagged his tail at niggers—at least at those few niggers who found their way into this neighborhood where everybody said nigger and made it clear that any nigger who wanted to do more than pass through had better buy a black-market M-16 and sleep with it next to his bed at night.

Harry sat down behind his desk and looked out over the rugged, urban street in front of him. He watched its motions, listened to its racket. He'd figured it out once. Every minute, on average, roughly forty cars rolled by in front of Nelson's Exxon. Yet he could go as long as a half hour before anybody pulled in for gas—sometimes more like forty-five minutes. He couldn't figure it out. He gave full service at the pumps. Nobody had to pump their own, and his prices weren't that far above those self-service operations. Why didn't he get more business? It was one of life's mysteries.

So was John Schulian, Harry thought, turning to Schulian's column in the sports section of the *Daily News*. How could anybody know so much about boxing and so little about baseball, he wondered?

He was deep into Schulian's column, shaking his

head over the latest attack on Mike Schmidt, when the biker came out of the john. Harry didn't see him, but the biker saw Elvis. He saw the Doberman, for reasons known only to himself, casually lift one leg and urinate over the van's right rear wheel.

Which turned out to be an immense error.

Frost was wired today. He was setting out on his journey for the Poconos, and he was about as wired as he could ever remember being. For a moment, the biker stopped dead in his tracks, watching almost in disbelief. Then, slowly, he stalked out to his van, next to the pump. The dog saw him coming and continued to perform the task he had carved out for himself. Elvis, oblivious to so much in life, had decided to leave his scent on this vehicle, and he wanted to make sure he deposited enough urine for the scent to take. He was concentrating all his meager brain power on this chore when the huge man drove a heavy boot straight into Elvis's face, catching him in midstream.

Dobermans are tough animals. Against most men, they can more than hold their own. But this hapless dog was roughly one-third of the biker's weight, off balance, and taken totally by surprise. The kick caught the dog on the side of the head and decked him instantly. Aside from which, the dog was a born sissy. Elvis slammed against the side of the van so hard that the sound brought Harry Nelson out of his reverie in short order.

What the hell, he thought.

He looked up to see the van's back door open, the huge biker reaching inside it for something, and his dog stretched out on the blacktop. Then he saw what the biker was getting out of the van. It was a Stihl chain saw, and the giant was yanking fiercely at its starter cord. The saw coughed into life on only one pull, just like on TV.

What the hell, Harry thought again—and this time with a sense of alarm. He stood up behind his desk and dropped the newspaper on the greasy floor.

"Hey, you!" he shouted.

Harry Nelson was just out the door when the biker reached down with one hand, grabbed the limp Doberman by the scruff of the neck, and lifted it, blunt claws weakly scrambling against the air, off the blacktop. The churning saw blade flickered in hazy city sunlight. Harry had made it almost to the pumps when the whirring chain links bit into the dog's neck. Blood and bits of flesh exploded in all directions. Elvis never made a sound; he just died. He was dead before his headless corpse hit the pavement with a dull flop.

And there was this giant, the cranking chain saw in one hand and the severed head of the Doberman in the other, looming up like a scene from a horror movie. He was splattered with blood and tiny bits of dog flesh and hair and he was looking with satisfaction into the blank eyes of his formerly friendly prey. From his expression, he seemed to be having a terrific time.

This was all a bit much for Harry Nelson, who was not a well man to begin with. His legs gave out. He sank to his knees in utter shock. The Doberman's headless corpse was gushing red blood all over the pumps, its heart still contracting a few more times, the most recent electronic signals from its missing brain still in transit along the dog's severed nerve endings.

Harry Nelson vomited.

The corned beef sandwich he'd consumed for lunch came roaring up out of his gut. So did the Rolling Rock beer he'd had with it and the soggy, sodden remains of the Lay's potato chips he'd eaten. It all exploded from his insides like a volcanic eruption.

As he barfed violently all over his blue work shirt and the steaming blacktop next to his pumps, Harry Nelson had the vague impression of the saw's motor dying, of the van's engine kicking into life and then roaring off out into Olney Avenue. Vaguely, as he emptied out his digestive tract, he heard brakes squealing as cars swerved and screeched to a sudden halt, of the stench of auto exhaust in the blistering summer air.

When his gut had stopped heaving, Harry Nelson gasped for breath and looked up. Elvis's head and body lay several feet apart in a pool of dog blood littered with ragged chunks of meat.

Good God, he thought to himself. Good, gracious, sweet Jesus Christ Lord God.

For Harry Nelson, that was what passed for prayer.

CHAPTER THIRTY-ONE

By the time he was halfway up Route 611, Frost had begun to calm down.

The highway was old and snaked through country-side once it got beyond the city and its suburban ring. Frost stopped several times at roadside stores to get food, to make sure he knew where he was going, and to help himself dull his nervous edge. He knew that the paper on the kitchen table had been all too convenient, but he was beyond the point of caring now. He would not sleep again until he had made his move against Murphy, and if that meant he had to travel to Canada to do it, that was fine with him.

As Frost moved into the Poconos, he noticed more cars with out-of-state plates, mostly from Jersey. This was vacation country, both winter and summer. He followed the road northward, through little towns like Riegelsville, Stockertown, and Mount Bethel. Frost had known a thief in Graterford who had come from Mount Bethel. He remembered the man telling him about a general store near the center of town. Frost found it, pulled up in front of it, and saw an old man in a straw fedora and a short-sleeved white shirt sitting on a lawn chair on the front porch. He was chewing a toothpick.

"I'm looking for the fastest way to a vacation development called Timberhill Estates," Frost said to the old man.

"What's it near?"

Frost consulted his stolen sheet of paper. "It's on a lake called Lake Lonely."

"Yeah," the old man said. "That's one of them new places up north of Stroudsburg. I know where that is. Still being built, ain't it?"

"Yeah," Frost said. "I suppose."

The old man chewed his toothpick. "You can stay here on 611 and cut off on 209 and then take 402. That'll take you in the front way. Or you can go in the back way on Barney Road. That cuts in up about two miles farther. Barney Road takes you back around to the other side of the lake, but there's a dirt road you can use to cut through the woods. Don't know what kind of shape it's in, though. It ain't used too much no more. Most people like 402 since it got repaved."

"Where's the turnoff to Barney Road again?"

The old man gestured with a thin arm. "Up past the Grand Union a mile or two or three up the road. You take a right on Beaumont Avenue and then, about a quarter mile in, you take a left onto Barney. Then just go straight. It's about fifteen, sixteen miles to the lake. Timber Hill is on the other side, off 402."

"Thanks," Frost said.

Barney Road was just as rugged as the old man had promised. Frost went about ten miles on it before he decided it was time to unload the van. He pulled it off the road and into a stand of woods. Then he wheeled the Harley out of the back. If he managed to do what he planned to do, he'd need to move faster than the van would permit. Besides, the bike could carry everything he really needed now that he had made up his mind to leave this part of the country. Just his money and his saw and some clean clothes. That was all he needed.

Frost kicked the Harley into life. It spoke to him in a throaty roar, singing him a love song. Frost loved the Harley's music. It was down deep and dirty. He wheeled the bike out of the stand to trees and back onto Barney Road. The bike made a little noise, but he doubted it would give him away. Trail bikes would be common enough around here. Besides, he would leave it in the woods when he got near Timber Hill Estates. He probably couldn't get it through the woods the old man had described without damaging it, anyway—especially now that it was nearing sundown. And Rhino Frost was not going in the front way, the way the directions Murphy had so conveniently left on the kitchen table called for him to enter the resort development.

He wasn't that stupid.

CHAPTER THIRTY-TWO

It had been a tough day.

Wilder had handled Waterson's surrender, then he had gone back to the more routine aspects of his job. He had supervised the interrogation of a yuppie-type Center City stockbroker who had been peddling cocaine to compensate for his faltering sales record. He had testified at a preliminary hearing in which a junkie was being charged with two counts of second-degree murder for taking out a North Philadelphia tailor and his wife who had been fatally slow in opening up the cash register. He had gone with a semihysterical mother to the morgue while she identified the butchered body of her thirteen-year-old son, who had wandered into the territory of a street gang with whom his own street gang had not been on friendly terms.

Wilder had come home battered and beaten and looking for a beer and for Annabelle's arms. Watching the mother's face as she had identified the kid had been a bit too much for him today. The mother had been no more than twenty-seven or twenty-eight. She must have had the kid in her early teens, when she was about the age of the bloody corpse on the slab.

When the phone rang, Wilder was lying on the sofa with his head on Annabelle's lap watching Steve Levy do the news and holding a bottle of Schmidt's Tiger Head ale loosely in one hand.

"I'll get it," Annabelle said, lifting his head and rising.

"Don't stay on long," Wilder pleaded with her. "Let's you and me go out to dinner tonight, what do you say?"

"Sounds good," she said. "Whoever it is, I'll get right off."

She went into the kitchen. Wilder sipped his beer and stared blankly at the TV set. This was one of those days when he wished he knew how to do something else that could bring in a buck.

Annabelle came back into the living room. "It's for you. Somebody named Zsa Zsa. You can explain that one to me over dinner."

"Shit," Wilder said. He got up, beer still in hand, and walked into the kitchen to grab the phone. "Hello."

"Hi," Zsa Zsa said. "Something came in here I thought you might want to know about."

"Yeah?"

"The DA's office just sent over a request that we pick up one Wendell Frost. Does that name ring a bell?"

Wilder was instantly alert. "On what charge?"

"Suspicion of murder two," Zsa Zsa said. "The authorities at Graterford have a statement from his former cellmate that implicates him in a murder while he was in prison. The witness claims he saw Frost conk a guy over the head and then run him through some kind of machine in the prison laundry about a month or so before he got out."

Wilder said, "There was an eyewitness?"

"That's what the DA's office says."

"The son of a bitch has been out a year now," Wilder exploded. "What the fuck took the people at Graterford so long to get the story out of the witness?"

"Look," Zsa Zsa said, "I just opened the mail and called up for more detail when I saw the name. Don't get sore at me, Jim."

Wilder wiped his brow. "I'm not sore at you. But this is mondo weirdo."

"According to what the DA's office has, the witness held back because he was afraid of Frost. The witness is apparently a queen. He's the Bo Derek of the prison, is the way the DA's guy put it. He wasn't going to say zip, only his new boyfriend insisted he do it. The queen was really scared. This guy Frost, do you know what he did to the queen before he got out? He bit off the guy's lower lip. The queen was terrified to snitch on him, but the new boyfriend made him."

Wilder was silent for a long moment. Then he said, "How would you like to send Rosario and O'Connell? We've got some traveling to do tonight."

Zsa Zsa said, "I'll send Rosario. He's still here. But O'Connell went home. I can come in his place, if you like. I wouldn't mind being in on this collar."

Wilder thought about it. There might, somewhere, be a woman tougher and shiftier and meaner than Zsa Zsa, but if there was he'd never met her.

"Come on with him," Wilder said. "And the two of you better bring overnight bags."

"Sounds kinky," Zsa Zsa said with delight.

Wilder hung up and pulled out his wallet, found his

address book, and found Harold Warren's home number.

Dial, dial, dial, dial, dial, dial, dial.

Ring . . . ring . . . ring . . . ri—

"Hello, this is Harold Warren. I'm not here now, so leave your message when you hear the beep, okay? Beep."

Click.

Wilder frowned deeply.

Dial, dial, dial, dial, dial, dial, dial.

Ring . . . ring . . . ring . . . ring . . . ring . . . ring . . . ring . . . ring . . . ring . . . ring . . . rin—

"All right, goddamn it," Harold Warren shouted into the phone. "Who is it?"

"Jim Wilder, Harold. I know you don't have an answering machine, and if you had one it would sound better than you did the first time I called."

"Well, I'm going to get one now," Warren snarled into the phone. "You may not care, Wilder, but you ought to know that you're interrupting a truly beautiful and meaningful human experience."

"Getting laid, are you?"

"I'm trying," Harold Warren said with profound annoyance. "How would you like to call back in 1995 or so? Would that be too much trouble?"

"Harold," Wilder said, "I need to find out how to get to that mountain cabin you sent Frank Murphy to."

"What for?"

"For good and substantial reason. Just tell me how to get there."

"I've only been there once," Harold Warren said, "and I didn't do the driving. The place belongs to a

389

client of mine. If I remember it right, you go up Route 611 to Stroudsburg and switch to Route 402 and you'll see the sign for the place a couple of miles out. It's on the right. It's called Timber Hill Estates. You go down a dirt road for about three-quarters of a mile and you'll come to the cabins all around this little lake. Murphy ought to be in the only one with the lights on. Nothing else is finished up there. What the hell is this, anyway?"

Wilder said, "I've gotten the all-clear sign to bust that psycho who's been on Murphy's tail."

"You're going to do it up there?"

"There's where Frank was going today, and he figured that the psycho would follow him up there."

"Jim . . ." Harold said.

"What?" Wilder said, anxious to get off the phone now.

"Listen, that place belongs to a client of mine. Try not to damage anything, okay?"

CHAPTER THIRTY-THREE

Murphy began to get the willies every time he got too far outside the city.

He was not comfortable without concrete beneath his feet. He found air difficult to breathe unless it contained a decent percentage of automobile exhaust. He liked the security and comfort of throngs of humanity around him—jostling and bumping into him and telling him that they were walking here. Murphy couldn't understand why anybody would want to get too far away from good restaurants and theaters and major league sports teams and public transportation.

Murphy was wary enough of suburban settings, where people just pretended they were living in the country, but he was downright distrustful of places where the most popular items of apparel were flannel shirts and bib overalls and where the hottest topic of conversation was the new gun rack on Orville's pickup. He suspected that a good many picturesque country houses contained at least one slavering and simple-minded adult with a cleft palate whom the family kept chained to a support beam in the basement because they were both afraid and ashamed of the fruit of their

incestuous relationships. They carried these relationships, he was sure, while the radio played twanging
guitar music performed by people like Mel Tillis and
Willie Nelson, who looked like a drug dealer Murphy
used to know and whom Murphy thought should be
arrested just on general principles every time he came
out in public.

Murphy also knew that while urban living indisputably had its dangers, the country had more and worse.
In the woods there were bears and wolves and the
occasional ill-tempered mountain lion. And even if
there weren't any animals like that in most forests
anymore there were always snakes. Nobody had gotten
rid of them. Whatever its other hazards, Murphy had
never seen a snake on South Broad Street. In the
woods, you also had to watch out for little insects that
could bite you and give you Rocky Mountain spotted
fever and Lyme's disease and God alone knew what
else. Not to mention all the rabid skunks and foxes.
Murphy would take a good, old-fashioned smack-
crazed mugger any day over a raccoon with rabies.

Murphy had seen *Deliverance,* and he knew what
went on once you go out in the country. And the hell
with it, was his point of view.

So it was that as he drove up Route 611 watching
civilization slowly fade, Murphy grew increasingly
nervous. Part of it, he knew, was the impending clash
with Rhino Frost. But no small part of his unease was
the setting of the upcoming confrontation. He'd been
able to think of no other place where he could both
isolate Mary Ellen and Patricia for the few days he had
needed to wrap up the Highland case and, at the same
time, set up a proper trap for Frost. He wished he'd

been able to get off a little earlier in the day, but if he stepped on it he could make it to Timber Hill Estates before it got too dark. Murphy pushed down the Toronado's gas pedal. The big car slurped gas and picked up speed.

Murphy went through Stroudsburg a few hours out of Philly and switched to the other highway. Not far up the new road he found the entrance to the development. It was a dirt road back into the woods, and it was marked by a large, professionally lettered white sign with black and red letters. It said:

TIMBER HILL ESTATES
Luxurious resort living
at affordable prices

Beneath that was another sign. It said:

GRAND OPENING
MAY 1st

Murphy took a right down the dirt road. It was rugged and worn, beaten down by heavy equipment rolling in and out. Ordinarily, heavy equipment would be rolling in and out today. Murphy knew, however— because the developer was Harold's client—that construction on Timber Hill Estates had come to a sudden halt due to a pending divorce in the developer's family. Namely, his own. The developer was up to his ass in debt, and he wasn't about to take on any more to finish the development of sixty vacation chalets and cabins around the lake until he had some idea of how badly his wife was going to gouge him in the settlement. Harold said this was a reasonable precaution on the developer's part, since his wife had caught him, pants around his ankles, with the roommate of their college-age daughter in the backseat of his bronze-colored Seville, and had been unimpressed when the developer had asked, "Well, Norma, are you willing to listen to a reasonable explanation or are you just going to jump to conclusions?"

Murphy slowed the Toronado to a crawl and proceeded carefully down the road. He had gone several hundred yards and rounded a turn when he saw Catrelli, armed with a pump-action shotgun, move out from behind a tree. Murphy stopped the car and got out.

"I see you're taking care of business," he said.

"Not a sign of nothing since I got here yesterday afternoon," Catrelli told him. "This is the most boring job I've ever taken. I'm glad you're here. I haven't slept a wink since I got here."

"This'll wake you up," Murphy said. "And he took out his checkbook and wrote Catrelli a check for a nice amount. Catrelli took the check, looked at the figure appreciatively, and stuffed it in his jeans.

"Now I feel better," he said. "I kept wondering when I was going to see some bread. Not that I didn't think you were good for the money, Frank, but I wasn't sure just when, you know."

"Nice gun," Murphy said, motioning toward the shotgun.

"Yeah, ain't it? I stole it from the department about six years ago. Twelve gauge, ten shells, and it's got a kick like a motherfucker."

"Listen," Murphy told him, "let me spend some time with my wife and kid and maybe get something to eat.

Then I'll come out and relieve you, and you can crash for a while."

"Sounds good to me. Bring me a sandwich or something when you come out, okay? I had some lunch, but it's getting toward dinnertime now."

"Fair enough. See you about dinnertime. Listen, I checked the maps of this place and everything, but you're sure this is the only road in here?"

Catrelli nodded. "I cased the place pretty good when I got here yesterday. This road here is the only way in, unless you're fucking Daniel Boone, which most people aren't."

Murphy looked down the dirt road where it turned and led out to the highway. "I guess you can hear anything coming in before it hits that bend there."

Catrelli nodded. "Yep. I got me a nice deck chair over there behind that tree. Nobody can see me, and I can hear pretty good anything I want to hear before the car comes around that turn. That goes double for a bike."

"Look," Murphy told him, "you know we can't just blast him. He's got to do something first."

"Hey," Catrelli said, "I've been at this a long time, remember? If anything happens to Frost, it'll be because he waved a gun at somebody."

Murphy studied the little man. "And you've got just such a gun to stick in his hand afterward."

"Is the pope fucking Polish?" Catrelli said. "I got it with my stuff over behind the tree. If you get to be the guy in the shooting gallery, just remember not to touch it without a cloth. It's wiped clean, and the only prints on it will be his."

"Where'd you get it?"

"A leftover," Catrelli said, "from the Jorgenson bust four, five years ago. Remember that? Jorgenson had more guns than the fucking PLO. Nobody missed this one. It's a nice, sweet little thirty-two with a pearl handle. Nice touch, eh?"

"Impressive," Murphy said. "See you in an hour or so."

"Don't forget the sandwich," Catrelli said as Murphy got back in the Toronado. "And a beer would be nice, too."

"You got it," Murphy said, and drove off.

Timber Hill Estates consisted of about a half mile of crudely raped forest wrapped around a small, pine-shrouded lake. The land was occupied by the naked, partially finished frames of houses—in some cases, just their foundations—and strategically protected trees girded with red plastic ribbons to protect them from the bulldozers and backhoes that had cleared the building sites. In the dim light of early evening, one house stood out conspicuously against the new development and the still waters of the lake, which it faced. That was the chalet with the lights on, the only completed sample house. That was where Mary Ellen and Patricia were staying. Murphy pulled into the driveway at the rear of the house and got out of the car with his overnight bag, wondering as he gazed about at the surrounding woods when the bats would come out and how many of the little buggers would be foaming with hydrophobia.

Mary Ellen, in cutoff jeans and Murphy's Seventy-Sixers T-shirt, came out around the house on the wraparound deck. She looked good, Murphy thought. Then again, she always did.

"I thought you might be here last night," she said, walking down the steps toward him.

"So did I, but it took a little longer than I'd figured."

"Did you wrap up the case?" she asked as she reached him.

"In a gold ribbon. My client is off the hook, and the killer is in custody."

Mary Ellen smiled broadly. "Good for you. Congratulations." Then she said, "Did you collect your fee?"

Murphy said, "I haven't even sent the Highlands my bill yet."

Which wasn't a lie. He was not about to tell Mary Ellen about the ten grand. If she knew about that, she'd never rest until she got her hands on it. Murphy loved Mary Ellen desperately and always had, but he was aware that she was as avaricious as any human being he'd ever met.

"I'll collect something nice, though," he told her reassuringly, "enough to get Patricia through her first year and then some. Speaking of that, where is she?"

"Swimming out front. You hungry?"

"Funny you should ask," Murphy told her.

Inside, the chalet was impressive. The first floor consisted of a large living room that overlooked the deck and the lake beyond through a pair of sliding glass doors. That floor also housed a kitchen/dining area, two bedrooms, and a bath. Stairs next to the fireplace led to a loft in the rear of the building. The half-open basement, which was finished into a recreation room that stretched the width and breadth of the entire house, also opened out into the beach area through a pair of sliding glass doors. Since this was the model

397

house, it was professionally decorated in very nice style.

"Nice," Murphy told Mary Ellen, looking around.

"Go out on the deck and wave to your daughter," she instructed.

Murphy went out through the sliding glass doors and saw Patricia—in a shamelessly scanty bathing suit which made him frown even though no one else was in sight—swimming back and forth in front of the house. Murphy had never learned to swim, and he looked out at his daughter enviously. He wondered absently if there were snapping turtles in the lake. Or water moccasins. You never knew, out in the woods like this.

"Having fun?" he called out to her.

Patricia heard the voice and waved in midstroke. "I'll be in in a minute," she called out.

"No hurry," he called down to her. "I'm going to change my clothes."

When Murphy went back in, Mary Ellen was at the stove. "Cheeseburger and fries okay?"

"Fine, if you've got a beer to go with them. Make something up for Catrelli, too. How's he been, by the way?"

Mary Ellen shrugged. "We've hardly seen him. He showed up just after we did and made me cook him some dinner. Then he went out to the road. We didn't see him until lunch today. He just came in around noon and got some food and went out back to wherever he's hiding out there on the road."

Murphy grunted absently. "Just as well, with Patricia running around in a bathing suit like that. Catrelli's a friend, but he's also sort of a pig with women. And he doesn't care whose women, either."

398

Mary Ellen looked over her shoulder at him with a bemused expression. "Gee," she said, "I never knew you had friends like that."

Murphy frowned. "I want to get out of this suit. Which room is mine?"

"The one furthest back."

Murphy went into the bedroom. Like the rest of the house, it was lavishly furnished. He left his suit, dress shirt, and tie in a heap in the corner on top of his wingtips and got into a maroon Temple University sweatshirt, jeans, and sneakers. He debated bringing his .38 out to the main room with him, then he dismissed the idea. The sight of the pistol would surely unnerve Mary Ellen, who was acting as though they were all here on a vacation of some sort. He would get it later before he went out to relieve Catrelli. Murphy went back out into the living area just as Patricia, dripping and wrapped in a towel, came in from the dusk wrapped in a towel. She kissed her father.

"You're soaked," Murphy told her.

"I'll go change," she said, and disappeared into one of the bedrooms.

Murphy sat down at the counter separating the kitchen from the living room. Mary Ellen reached into the refrigerator and got him a beer, then she went back to her cooking.

"What the story with our friend?" she asked.

"He'll be here, I think. Probably tonight."

Murphy watched her pale slightly, although she said nothing.

"Catrelli and I will be ready for him," he told her.

"I hope so."

So did Murphy, although he didn't say so. What he

did say was, "I haven't seen you cook for a long time."

"It's not exactly a spectator sport with most people," Mary Ellen said, but she smiled slightly.

"It always was with me. Remember when I used to sit at the kitchen table and watch you cook dinner?"

"When you were home."

"When I was home," he agreed. "I always liked watching you, though."

"And I liked the company—when I had it."

Murphy lit a Camel and sipped his beer. "How do you like it, just the two of you?"

Mary Ellen flopped the burger into a bun and loaded his plate with formerly frozen french fries from the toaster oven. She put the food beside him and sat down on a stool on the other side of the counter.

"I've gotten used to it. I don't sit around waiting for you to come home anymore."

Murphy ate and looked at her over the food. "Well, when I came home I usually didn't get the impression that it was particularly important to you. Besides, there was always the question of making a living. I had to keep the place afloat, after all. And I couldn't do that too efficiently from the kitchen table."

"That's right, Frank," Mary Ellen said in a tone that had always made Murphy feel like going for her throat. "you kept the place afloat. Tell me, how much cash do you have in the bank? How much money did we have when you left?"

"When you threw me out," he corrected.

"When we agreed to separate," she compromised. "How much was there? What did we have to show for all the time you spent away and doing God alone knew what out on the street at all hours of the night?"

"Police work isn't exactly a nine-to-five occupation, Mary Ellen. You could have been married to an obstetrician and had me buzzing out of bed at four in the morning to deliver babies."

"In which case we'd have had money set aside for Patricia's education, wouldn't we?" she countered.

Murphy felt himself beginning to lose it. All this had such a familiar ring. Mary Ellen had been born with an imposing array of talents. She could sing like a bird, and nobody could tell a better joke. She had a money sense he sometimes envied. She was meticulously organized in every aspect of her daily life, right down to keeping her outfits for school arranged in her closet in order with the date she had last worn something in the pocket. But her greatest talent—the one that surpassed all others by a considerable margin—was her talent for pissing him off. It wasn't just that she had a knack for it. It was more like a gift, or a genius.

"You know," he told her testily, "you're doing it again. You've been doing it from the time Patricia was born. Did I ever tell you that? I'm sure I did."

Mary Ellen sat back coolly. "You did. New Year's Eve—in front of everybody we knew. Remember that? Of course, you might not, because you were shit-faced at the time. I remember it, though."

"I was wrong to do that," Murphy said. "I've apologized for it time and again, and I won't bother to do it again here. You're not interested anyway."

"You're right. I'm not."

Murphy chewed angrily as he spoke. "But just because I made an ass of myself in saying it doesn't mean it isn't true nonetheless. From the time we had her, you've conveyed to me the very clear impression

401

that I no longer fulfilled any role in your life except bringing home the cash. That became my sole function. Go out, catch the scumbags, pick up the check, and come home to listen to you complain. You had no time for me in conversation. You were always too tired, too worn out, too distracted—too this, too that. When we were first married, Mary Ellen, there was nobody you wanted to be with—no person whose companionship you valued more—than me. But that seemed to go right out the window once I'd given you what you really seemed to want—a child. Once I'd fulfilled my stud duty, it became very clear to me that my usefulness to you was over. I became nothing more than a necessary annoyance to you. I somehow lost my capacity to make you laugh, even to smile. And now that I'm out of the house and sending monthly checks, I'm not even a daily annoyance, am I? You've got the best of both worlds. You've got the money, and you don't have to put up with me."

Mary Ellen's lips tightened as he spoke. He knew she was furious, but Mary Ellen was controlled, and he knew she wouldn't erupt. She would just turn on the ice now. Mary Ellen was the original ice queen. Nobody knew that better than Murphy.

"You're such a jerk, Frank," she said finally. "You're just about totally and completely self-absorbed. It never occurred to you that I was running a household, holding down a teaching job, and raising a baby all at the time you were out doing whatever it was you did to earn that paycheck. You always seemed to think that somehow, when you came in the door, all that was going on in my life was supposed to come to a screeching halt just because you were home. And when

402

that wasn't possible, you just stopped coming home. That was your solution. You went to college. You went to law school. You went to the ballgame. You went to those silly poker games. You went where you wanted to go. Meanwhile, I was teaching classes and raising our daughter—"

"Somebody mention me?" Patricia said, coming out into the living room in a royal blue sweatsuit.

Murphy held out his arms to her. "Give me a hug," he said.

Patricia complied. The embrace made Murphy feel better. If the first woman to whom he had given his life no longer loved him, at least the new one did. He wondered absently if Patricia was still a virgin at eighteen. Then he shut out the thought. If there was anything in life he didn't want to know . . .

Mary Ellen got up and turned on the radio near the sink and began doing dishes. Patricia said, "I'm going to finish that book I bought. I've gotten into it, and I can't put it down."

She went back into the bedroom, and Murphy sat there finishing his meal in silence. When he was done, he lit another cigarette.

"Do you have any coffee?" he asked.

"Instant."

"That's fine," he told his wife.

Mary Ellen filled a cup with water, put it in the microwave over on the counter—this place had every imaginable convenience, Murphy realized—and got out the coffee while the microwave did its work. Murphy watched her move in the kitchen, saw the fine lines around her eyes, and realized how the years had changed them. All the years they had been together . . .

403

and the months they had not. He remembered the early days—the passion, the closeness, the laughter. Did Mary Ellen still know how to laugh? Not that he could tell.

Over the radio, Diana Ross and the Supremes sang, "Baby love, my baby love . . ."

"Hey," Murphy told Mary Ellen, "turn that up."

"What, this?" she said.

"Remember this?" he asked her suddenly.

"What about it?"

"Jimmy and Annabelle's wedding. Remember that?"

She looked at him suspiciously. "Remember what?"

"The band," Murphy said, all anger suddenly evaporated. "Remember they had these three girl singers, and they did all the Supremes songs. We danced so much that night that neither of us could move the next morning."

Mary Ellen nodded, smiling slightly in recollection. "I remember," she said, turning up the radio.

The Temptations came on and sang, "I know you want to leave me, but I refuse to let you go . . ."

"Hot damn!" Murphy said, jumping up. "I remember that one. Come on, let's dance."

Mary Ellen shook her head as Murphy moved away from the counter into the living room.

"Frank . . ." she began.

"Oh, shit," Murphy said, smiling. "Come on."

Mary Ellen smiled and shook her head. "All right."

Mary Ellen, in her cutoffs and T-shirt, came around the counter and moved within a few feet of Murphy, who had already begun moving in the twisted gyrations of the Philly Dog.

"Let's get with it," he told her.

Mary Ellen got with it. The Temptations sang, "If I have to beg, plead for your sympathy, I don't mind 'cause you mean that much to me . . ." Mary Ellen moved her hips to the music.

"You still got it," Murphy told her.

"So do you," Mary Ellen said, laughing. "In fact you've got a lot more of it."

"Up yours," Murphy said, throwing some more action into the dance.

Patricia came into the room. "What's this?" she demanded.

"We're dealing with the feeling," Murphy told her. "We're bound to the sound."

"It's in my feet. Oh, yeah!" Mary Ellen chanted as she danced.

"And ain't it neat? Oh, yeah!" Murphy chanted and danced in response.

Patricia rolled her eyes and went back into the bedroom.

"It'll happen to you, too," Murphy called after her.

Then came Sam Cooke. He sang, "Yoo-o-o-o-o-o-o-o-send me. Darlin', yoo-o-o-o-o-o-o-o send me . . ."

Murphy looked at Mary Ellen standing before him, looking gorgeous.

"Slow dance," he told her softly.

She came into his arms. He held her. They clung to each other, moving only slightly to the music. His senses were filled with the fragrance of her hair. He felt her warmth and softness against him. There was no one but Mary Ellen. No one. Time stood still. They were young again. They would be young forever. Tomorrows stretched over the horizon, so many of them that they defied counting.

The announcer said, "And now, the news. Governor Casey said today that . . ."

Murphy stepped away from Mary Ellen. He looked at her. She looked at him. The announcer droned on about a clash between the governor and the Milk Marketing Board—big news around here, Murphy figured. Murphy felt suddenly awkward and exposed, and he didn't like it much.

"I've got to go out and relieve Catrelli."

Mary Ellen looked at him. "I didn't make him anything to eat."

"I'll send him back. You can feed him when he gets here."

Mary Ellen looked away and went back to the kitchen to resume cleaning up. She flipped off the news. "Fine."

Murphy went back into the bedroom and got his navy blue nylon jacket and his pistol. He stuffed extra shells into his left front pocket. He couldn't conceive that he'd need more than the five shots he habitually carried in the pistol but who knew for sure? He came out as Mary Ellen was wiping off the counter with a dish towel.

"See you later," he said to her.

Mary Ellen looked over at him. "Keep your eyes open."

"I always do," Murphy told his wife.

CHAPTER THIRTY-FOUR

Catrelli sat in his deck chair behind the big oak in the dark woods, his Remington pump-action twelve-gauge across his lap, the plug to his Sony Walkman in his ear. The sports announcer was going over the field for tomorrow at Liberty Bell. There was a horse in the sixth named Dad's Mustache. If ever there was a hunch bet, and here he was. Fuck, Catrelli thought, stroking his own luxurious mustache.

Which did not mean that Catrelli was not watching the darkened road. He was making it a point to do that as the light diminished. He sat silently and unmoving, and—radio or no radio—his eyes were glued to the road. His other ear—the one that did not contain an earplug speaker from the radio—was turned slightly toward the road as well. He had a big flashlight handy next to his chair. He had several pistols near him. He had with him a sap, a set of cuffs, and a set of brass knuckles that had served him well in the past. What he did not have was food.

No one would ever guess it from his small size and wiry, almost emaciated frame, but Catrelli habitually ate like a mule. He'd never been able to put on an ounce. He was just a natural-born skinny Guinea, he supposed, just like his old man had been. Catrelli's first wife had once told him he could pose for concentration camp pinup posters. She'd been a million laughs, he thought sourly as he recalled her, and he put her immediately out of his mind. Today he had eaten very little, and faint gurgling sounds were issuing from his trim midsection. His stomach was talking to him, saying, Hey, what is this shit? Where's the food? Let's go.

Be cool, Catrelli told his stomach. Any minute now.

Actually, Catrelli didn't plan on eating much. Just enough to ease the hunger pangs. He didn't want to get bloated. He wanted to be able to move easily when the time came, which it would, he was sure, before dawn. Already it was so dark that he could see only blurred shadows instead of complete shapes. He figured they had some hours yet. Frost wouldn't come in after midnight—perhaps not until well after—when most people would be asleep or their bodies would be pushing them to sleep even if they were trying to stay awake, when they would have lost their mental edge, when reaction times would be a hair slower. That's how Catrelli would play it in Frost's place.

Gurgle, his stomach said.

Catrelli heard Murphy coming down the road behind him before he actually saw him. Catrelli heard the sound of shoes on dirt and gravel and turned around. He saw Murphy's shadowy form moving up the road toward him.

Gurgle, Catrelli's stomach said again.

"Christ," Catrelli said, "I'm fucking starving. You got the beer, too?"

"Yeah," Murphy said, moving toward him in the darkness.

By the time Catrelli realized that it wasn't Murphy, it was far too late. The big, dark shape was upon him, looming over him, and Catrelli tried to whip the shotgun into line, but strong hands—huge hands—grabbed it and tore it away from him and Catrelli reached down for one of the pistols, but the hands had him by the throat and pulled him fully out of the chair, his fingertips only brushing the cold, reassuring metal of the pistol on the ground and fingers closed on Catrelli's throat and he felt his air supply cut off totally and his face suddenly redden and his eyes bulge.

All this in just the briefest fraction of a second. All this so quickly that it took Catrelli a moment to try to drive a foot into this guy's nuts as he hung there in the air. Catrelli felt the toe of his shoe strike Frost's enormous thigh. He kicked again. His hands were on Frost's hands, pulling and scratching vainly at them. He kicked wildly at the giant's torso.

How long could he go without breathing, Catrelli wondered? A minute? Two minutes? That gave him plenty of time. That gave him time to think of something. Meanwhile he would kick at this guy's body and scratch at his hands and he would wiggle and flip around in his grasp and something would come to him. The important thing was to stay cool. That was the thing. He had to stay cool.

After thirty seconds or so of this, however, staying cool was becoming something of a challenge. Frost's hands were on his throat—all the way around his neck, actually—and Catrelli had scratched all the flesh off the back of them without seeming to have made a dent in the giant's resolve to strangle him. Catrelli had kicked fiercely, but the kicks were growing weaker, and they seemed to have no effect anyway. Frost had him completely off the ground, Catrelli's feet perhaps a full twelve inches off the dirt surface of the road, and there seemed no way to fight free or break loose before he blacked out, which was an event coming up in the not too distant future, Catrelli was sure.

Well, he thought, if you're going to black out anyway, why not let him think it's already happened?

Catrelli went completely limp in Rhino Frost's grasp.

For a moment, Frost maintained his grip, even intensifying the pressure. But by then he had been holding one hundred and thirty-five struggling, kicking pounds a foot off the ground and had done it all at arm's length, and his big, thick arms were protesting. And this dude was gone. Frost dropped the corpse.

Catrelli's body hit the ground the way a cat's body hits the ground. He hit on his feet and came up instantly as if on springs and drove his right fist in a vicious uppercut directly into Rhino Frost's remaining testicle.

"Uuuuh!" Frost said, and fell directly on top of the little man.

Catrelli tried to move to his right, but Frost managed to fall across his thin legs. Frost was a deadweight across the legs, and that weight was one hundred and fifteen pounds more than Catrelli's total weight. He felt as though his legs had been pinned beneath a tree. Catrelli struggled while Frost grunted in pain. Catrelli knew he had about five seconds—ten, at the outside—to work himself free. He could still feel those hands on his neck. He struggled frantically, pounding on the giant's torso.

Then Frost stirred.

He moved slightly and slowly, but the move he did make was not at all to Catrelli's liking. He reached underneath himself and dug strong fingers into Catrelli's thin leg. Then he pushed himself into a kneeling position over the smaller man and reached up with the other hand, clutching again at Catrelli's throat. Catrelli saw Frost's eyes flicker in the darkness. Catrelli struck at the hand, tried to push it away.

And failed.

Rhino Frost's left hand closed on Catrelli's throat, and then Frost leaned on it, pinning the little man beneath him. Catrelli felt his air cut off again, felt his face flush and redden as though it were being pumped full of hot fluid, felt the great weight settle on him, driving his thin back into the dirt.

"Now . . ." Frost grunted.

Frost took his right hand from Catrelli's thigh and drove it into Catrelli's groin, big fingers finding their target, closing on them, squeezing with inhuman force, mashing, tearing, ruining. Catrelli tried to move, couldn't. Just couldn't. The pain was unimaginable, agonizing. It was worse than the choking.

They stayed there unmoving for a long time, it seemed to Catrelli, Frost on top squeezing mightily at both ends and Catrelli on the bottom, helpless and in pure torture. A very long time, it seemed to Catrelli. Centuries. Eons. Far too long a time to endure what Catrelli was enduring and still stay cool about it.

In fact, if he could have gotten out the sound, Dominic Catrelli would have died screaming.

411

CHAPTER THIRTY-FIVE

That was another thing Murphy hated about the goddamned woods. No streetlights.

When he came out of the chalet, walking out the side door and off the deck to the ground, he missed a step in the blackness and came very close to tumbling over the side and breaking his neck. He clutched at the railing and said something extremely inelegant. Then he started down the long, black tunnel of the road to Catrelli, who was waiting several hundred yards out toward the highway.

Murphy walked cautiously as his eyes adjusted to the stygian night. He heard the gravel crunch under his worn white leather Nike sneakers. From the woods on either side of the road, he heard wind gently rustling leaves and grass, and he heard as well the sounds of life—of owls hooting, of creatures moving. He heard dull cracks as the prey animals moved across twigs, as the hunting animals stalked them. He heard a chorus of several million crickets. He wondered idly if crickets could get rabies, too.

If he strained—but only if he strained—he could hear the sound of traffic on the highway. He could hear the rumble of an occasional and distant ten-wheeler moving along pavement, gears whining and diesel engine churning and burning. By the time he reached the spot where Catrelli was supposed to be, Murphy could still see almost nothing. It was a moonlight night. Only the stars shone, gleaming points of brightness in the moonless sky, and while they offered some light it was hardly sufficient to make a city dweller feel secure.

"Dom," Murphy said. "Hey, Dom?"

Nothing.

"Goddamn it, Dominic," Murphy said, "where the hell are you?"

With his next step, Murphy tripped over something. He threw out his hands and broke his fall nicely as he hit the dirt. Then he felt for what had caught his foot. When he realized with a start that he had tripped over Catrelli, he immediately drew his service pistol and lay perfectly flat in the road, scanning the blackness of the woods on either side. He lay there for a solid minute, feeling his heart pump wildly but letting his breath in and out only in short, quiet gasps.

After the minute had passed, Murphy waited another minute. Then he decided that Frost was gone. Murphy had made a fair amount of noise coming down the path. He had made more when he had called out for Catrelli. He had made more still when he had tripped. If Frost had been around to nail him, he would have done so at any one of those points. That's what Murphy would have done in his place. Murphy would have been hiding along the road waiting, and he would have pounced under cover of darkness. It was, he knew, an exercise of only limited utility to make judgments on what Frost might do by putting himself in Frost's place, since Frost was crazy and Murphy was not. At least, he didn't think he was. But he couldn' stay here all night lying in the dirt.

Slowly, cautiously, he climbed to his feet, his pisto ready, and moved toward the dim shape of Catrelli': oak tree only a few feet away. Murphy moved behind the tree and felt with his hand in the grass. His hand closed on the .32 pistol Catrelli had brought along and discarded it for the moment. He felt in the grass until he found the big flashlight. Then he stood up and walked back over to Catrelli, lying in the road. Murphy flashed the light on him. Catrelli's face was purple, his eyes wide open and staring into the night sky. His mouth was a wide "O" of surprise and shock beneath his treasured mustache. Marks made by thick fingers stood out on his crushed throat, above the top of his T-shirt. Murphy satisfied himself that Catrelli was dead, and noted to himself that Catrelli, despite his small size, was not a man to go gently into that good night. He had left some mark on Frost at least, Murphy was sure. Frost had not gotten this one for free.

Murphy's mind worked quickly. How had this come to pass? Frost might have left the bike on the highway and sneaked in through the woods that lined the dirt road. He had probably sensed a trap—a deductive exercise that would have required no particular genius on his part—and come in very slowly, quietly, and cautiously through the woods. Murphy wondered, though, how such a big man—and not one accustomed to moving in forest—could have come up on Catrelli so quietly that the alert little man would not have heard him. Murphy knew Catrelli. He knew that confronted with a strange noise Catrelli would have blasted with his shotgun first and worried about who and what he had hit later.

All this planted in Murphy's mind several disturbing possibilities. To check the first of these, he went back to Catrelli's oak and flashed the light around its bole. He saw the Walkman in the dirt, surrounded by Catrelli's little arsenal, the earplug speaker still attached. That might explain part of the mystery. Catrelli had been sitting here for almost twenty-four hours by this point, and his mind must not have been as sharp as it had been when he was a working cop.

Also, Murphy thought, it was possible that Frost had not come in from the highway at all. It was possible that he had found some back way into the resort development, some path that allowed him to reach the road someplace between here and the chalet instead of between here and the highway. If he had done that, he would have come upon Catrelli from behind, and that might have given him just enough of an edge in darkness like this.

If that's what Frost had done, Murphy thought, then he would be moving back the same way, probably in the woods off the road. And he would have been a fair distance off the road, because he knew he would make noise. It was even possible that Murphy had heard him as Murphy had walked down the road to relieve Catrelli and not been able to distinguish between the distant sound of a big man moving slowly through forest and the normal sounds of the woods at night. Murphy was, after all, no Tonto. And if Frost had come in somehow from the back, that meant he would be moving back in a direction that Murphy knew would put him disturbingly near the chalet—the chalet

415

that stood out at night because it was the only building in the development with lights.

Murphy picked up the .32 and stuck it in a rear pocket. He found Catrelli's prized Charter Arms .44 Bulldog and stuck that in his belt. He also slipped the brass knuckles in the other rear pocket of his jeans. He left the sap and the other gear behind the tree.

Then, with great caution, he started back along the road, hunched over with his pistol out and the flashlight off. He moved much more slowly than he would have liked, but the more Murphy thought about it the more he was certain now what had happened and what was happening, and he didn't want to walk into any traps. He couldn't afford that. He was acutely aware that Catrelli's shotgun had been nowhere to be found.

Murphy didn't know how good Frost might be with firearms—probably not very good, given his background—but with a shotgun you didn't have to be very good to make very big holes in people.

And that's the sort of thing Rhino Frost enjoyed doing.

Smokey Robinson sang, "People say I'm the life of the party, 'cause I tell a joke or two . . ."

Mary Ellen didn't know what radio station she had on, but she liked it. She wiped down the kitchen counters and moved with the music, swayed with it. Good stuff, she thought.

From the rear bedroom, Patricia called out, "Mom, could you turn that down a little? I can't concentrate on this book."

Mary Ellen called back, "This is the sort of stuff you ought to listen to instead of that Rod Stewart crap. Come on out and listen to this. I'll show you how to dance to it, too."

"I'm reading," Patricia protested. "Come on, I'm almost finished with this book. Just a few more pages."

Mary Ellen frowned. "All right, but you close that door, then."

Mary Ellen turned down the radio slightly as she heard Patricia's door slam shut. Mary Ellen's hips swayed. Smokey Robinson sang, "So take a good look at my face. You'll see my smile, it looks out of place . . ."

Mary Ellen caught her own reflection in the sliding glass door that looked out over the lake. The giant sheet of tempered glass was like an enormous mirror, and she watched herself as she swayed with the music, moving to it, humming along with it. When she got back home she'd have to get out her old albums and maybe have them converted to tape. She knew she had this album somewhere. Mary Ellen had always liked Smokey Robinson and the Miracles better than just about any other group.

She moved and swayed with the music. Frank had gotten her into this silly mood, she knew, but she didn't mind. It was about time that he had sparked in her some emotion other than anger. How long, before tonight, had it been since they had danced together? A long time, for sure. Could she still do a full swivel, she wondered? Sure she could. She leaned to her right, put her weight on her left leg, and swiveled to her left just like she had when she was sixteen years old, just like she could always swivel—

—face first into Rhino Frost's chest.

"AAHHH—" Mary Ellen began to scream.

But Frost's huge hand, its back torn and bleeding, clamped over her mouth, stifling the sound. Mary Ellen felt strong arms enfold her—incredibly, inhumanly strong arms, tightening around her—and she felt the cold hardness of the shotgun run along her spine from shoulder blades to behind.

Frost looked down on her face and its huge wild eyes above his dirt and blood-encrusted hand. His yellow, horselike teeth showed through the ragged beard.

"Hel-l-o-o-o-o-w, Bay-bee!" he said in his best Big Bopper style.

Mary Ellen had made very little noise—had been permitted to make very little noise—but she had made enough to rouse Patricia's curiosity. Patricia, clad in her blue sweatsuit, came out of the back bedroom to find her mother firmly in the grip of one of the biggest men Patricia had ever encountered. In his worn jeans and his black T-shirt with the Harley emblem on the chest, Frost loomed up in the living room of the chalet like a monstrous statue. He was covered with dirt from rolling in the road, and his arms and the back of his hands were ragged with cuts and scrapes. Patricia felt her heart leap into her mouth. The shaggy giant holding her mother pointed the shotgun at her with his free hand.

"Come on over here, little lady," he rumbled.

That's close, Patricia thought.

Patricia dropped the paperback novel and pulled a butcher knife out of its wooden platform sheath on the kitchen counter. She held it firmly in her hand, blade pointed toward Frost.

418

"Let her go," Patricia said with a calmness that belied the panic she actually felt.

Frost laughed.

"They're out there," Patricia told him. "You can't go anywhere. Let my mother go."

Mary Ellen struggled, but Frost merely tightened his already ferocious grip. "You come on over here and we'll talk about it," he said.

"Forget it," Patricia said, brandishing the knife.

"Have it your way," Frost said.

Then he pulled the trigger.

Murphy was still some distance from the chalet when he heard the shotgun go off.

"Jesus," he said aloud.

Murphy broke into a frantic sprint in the darkness. He ran the last hundred yards or so as best he could in the darkness. Frantic though he was, he still didn't dare turn on the flashlight. Especially now, he didn't dare turn on the flashlight. Frost would be looking for it. The flashlight would make a beautiful target in the darkness.

It seemed to take him forever to reach the chalet, ablaze with light against the inky waters of the lake. Murphy tore up the steps to the deck and stopped suddenly, chest heaving, just outside the open door. He flattened himself against the exterior wood paneling, pistol ready, gulping quick breaths while he listened to—

—nothing. There was nothing from inside, not a sound, not a goddamned peep. Only Smokey Robinson. He was singing, "Since you left me, if you see me

419

with another girl, seemin' like I'm havin' fu-u-u-u-nn . . ."

Murphy launched himself into the room, rolling as he hit the floor, pointing his .38 all around, aiming it, getting ready to fire at—

—nothing. The living room was empty.

Cautiously, but quivering with panic and rage, Murphy got to his feet and moved shakily into the kitchen. He found his daughter stretched out face down on the floor beside the counter with a butcher knife clutched in her hand.

He felt his heart sputter like a failing car engine. Murphy said, "Patricia . . ."

Then she leaped up and into his arms, weeping uncontrollably, the knife clattering to the linoleum floor beside her discarded novel. Murphy glanced behind her at the mortally wounded refrigerator, which sported a hole in the door through which he could have put his whole arm, had he been so inclined.

"You all right?" he demanded.

She nodded vigorously. "He-he shot at me, but Mom bit him, and he didn't get me. I ducked down here, and—"

"Where's your mother?" Murphy demanded.

Patricia looked up at him, wild-eyed. "He must have taken her," she said, her voice breaking.

Murphy looked at the open door. They could be gone only seconds. He turned back to Patricia. "I'm going after them. I can't stay here with you. You get out of here in case he comes back. Just get out of the house and get into the woods and hide somewhere. And don't move until daylight unless you hear me calling you. Just dig in somewhere outside and stay there.

Understand? And don't move a muscle."

She nodded.

Murphy pulled Catrelli's .44 out of his belt and pressed it into her hands. "Take this. Use it if he finds you and comes at you. Don't get fancy with it. Just point it at him and squeeze the trigger until it's empty. And don't look away when it goes off. Keep your eyes on him when you fire. You got it?"

Patricia nodded numbly.

Then Murphy was out the door. He got to the bottom of the steps and stared out into the darkness.

Where? Which way?

"Frank!" he heard Mary Ellen call out from some distant spot.

"Fra—"

Over there. It came from that way.

Murphy started for the sound. He moved in a crouch, the way he had learned at the police academy so many years before and, before that, in combat training, courtesy of his Uncle Sam. He moved as quickly as he could in that position, the .38 in one hand and the big flashlight, still dark, in the other. He strained to hear.

There, he could hear. Footsteps in the darkness. They were ragged and awkward. Only one set. Where was Mary Ellen? There, he heard two sets. Then one, breaking through the brush, moving not all that fast, straining.

He was dragging her or trying to carry her, Murphy realized. Only Mary Ellen wasn't cooperating. That was Mary Ellen, all right, he thought, and thank God.

Murphy followed the sounds. He followed them into deep woods surrounding the development. He heard them grow louder as he followed. It took him only a minute—two at the outside—to come close to them. He was, after all, moving by himself, and Frost was clearly half dragging, half carrying a struggling woman.

"Frank!" he heard Mary Ellen call out.

Murphy flipped on the flashlight and scanned the woods ahead with it. The beam of light cut through the darkness. There! He caught a flash of Mary Ellen's white T-shirt not thirty feet ahead and the looming shape of Frost beside her, pulling her by the arm. As the light hit him, Frost turned toward Murphy, eyes wide.

The shotgun went off in a booming explosion of fire that blinded Murphy. He immediately dived to the right, knowing it was pointless to do so, since the shotgun pellets moved with considerably more speed than he did, but doing it anyway, just out of reflex. He had the misfortune to hit a tree as he dived, bouncing off it painfully and into the dirt. He was aware of pellets ripping through leaves and into tree trunks.

High. The dumb bastard had fired way high.

The shotgun explosion was embedded on the inside of his eyeballs now, and Murphy could see nothing but its residual glare. He had no choice now but to use the flashlight again. And he did. The light flashed into the woods, creating ghostly shadows. Murphy fanned with it until he had them again. He aimed his pistol over it, praying silently. Murphy had many skills, but he was not the world's greatest shot. Only once before had he fired at another human being, and on that occasion he had missed by a considerable margin, blowing out a

422

Mercedes Benz windshield instead of hitting his man.

"Down, Mary Ellen!" he called out.

Instantly, Mary Ellen collapsed into the undergrowth as though her bones had turned to rubber. Frost still had her by the arm, but if Murphy aimed high . . .

Murphy fired twice. He did aim high, of course, and he had no chance of hitting Frost. But if he could frighten him, startle him—

—which he did. Frost released Mary Ellen's arm as the bullets whizzed through the trees several feet above his head. He fired back with the shotgun, but Murphy flattened himself behind a tree—he wished it had been a bigger tree—and the pellets passed by harmlessly. Then Murphy spun and aimed again and—

—no Frost.

What the hell, Murphy thought.

"Mary Ellen?" he called out.

"Here," she called back.

Murphy moved quickly and as carefully as he could manage to his wife's side. She was scratched and bruised, but otherwise seemed unhurt.

"Which way?" he demanded.

Mary Ellen pointed off into the woods to Murphy's right.

"Can you walk?" he demanded.

She nodded silently in the darkness. Shaken, Murphy thought. And understandably, too. He pressed the .38 into her hand.

"You've got three more shots left in this," he told her. "Use it if he comes back. Meanwhile, you stay right here."

"You're leaving me?"

423

"I've got to get him."

"Don't leave me, Frank."

For only the briefest of moments Murphy was torn. "You'll be fine," he said finally. Then he stood up and moved off into the dark woods in pursuit of Rhino Frost.

CHAPTER THIRTY-SIX

Rosario the diabetic had gone through his last Snickers bar somewhere around Stroudsburg, and his humor was not good.

"Hey, *Jefe,*" he said to Wilder, "you really know where you're going?"

"Almost there," Wilder said, at the wheel. "The turnoff is along here somewhere."

"This is really the boonies," Zsa Zsa offered, gazing out at the darkened woods along either side of the highway. "I came up to the Poconos on my honeymoon a few years back. I didn't like it then, and I don't like it now."

Rosario the diabetic grunted. "Which honeymoon?"

"Second, I think," she said.

"Hey," Rosario said, "how come you get married so much?"

Zsa Zsa turned in her seat and looked over at him in the darkness of the rear of the car. "My mother always told me never to go to bed with a guy unless I was married to him. I'm a good girl; that's why I get married so much."

Wilder saw the sign. "There it is."

He turned the city Dodge onto the dirt road, which was pitted with holes and marked by bumps.

"Nice fucking public works department they got up here," Rosario the diabetic commented.

They rounded the turn and found Catrelli's corpse in the middle of the road. Wilder stopped the car, and for a moment no one said a word. Then the three of them got out of the car, pistols drawn, and Wilder looked down at Catrelli.

"I knew I'd see that sooner or later," he said quietly. "He was a good guy, but he was never as tough as he thought he was. Come on, help me move him."

The three of them moved Catrelli off to the side of the road. The little man was already stiffening in the night chill. They laid him down as gently as they could manage. Wilder went back to the car and killed the lights and the engine.

"We'll walk in the rest of the way," he said.

They moved through the darkness along the road with great care. Wilder and Rosario held their pistols in their hands while Zsa Zsa kept her hand in her purse, her fingers tight on the grip of her Beretta nine-millimeter. It was her private gun. She wasn't supposed to use it on duty, so she wasn't anxious to let Wilder see it unless she had to use it. She liked it better than the city-issued Smith & Wessons. The Beretta was easier to handle, held more shells, and had more punch. The medical examiner had more than once overlooked the fact that people collared by Zsa Zsa who had required some persuasion had been wounded or killed by a nonregulation firearm. Zsa Zsa sometimes thought that maybe Weinberg sort of had the hots for her, in his dirty-old-man way, and that was why he looked out for her like that.

The three police officers reached the chalet in just a few moments, and all three of them liked the sight of electric lights burning out here in the wilderness. As they went up the steps to the rear of the deck, Patricia came out of the woods.

"Lieutenant . . ." she said.

All three of them whirled as one and leveled pistols at her.

"Drop it or you're dog meat," Zsa Zsa ordered crisply, spotting the .44 in Patricia's hand.

Patricia dropped it.

"She's okay," Wilder said, putting away his own pistol. "That's Frank's daughter. Come here, Patricia. Everything's cool."

Patricia ran from the woods to Wilder, who took her in his arms. He felt the girl give as he held her, felt her tears.

"It's okay, it's okay," he told her. "Where are your parents?"

Patricia motioned to the woods. "There. That man—Frost—took Mom, and Daddy went after them."

"How long ago?" Wilder demanded.

"Five, ten minutes."

Wilder virtually handed Patricia to Zsa Zsa. "You take her inside. Watch her. And stay alert. That's a nonregulation firearm, Zsa Zsa. Don't let nobody but me catch you with it."

Zsa Zsa stuck the Beretta back in her purse without a word. Then, all sympathy now, she wrapped her arm around the weeping Patricia. "You stick with me sweetie," she said, and they went inside.

"What now?" Rosario the diabetic asked Wilder.

"Let's go after them."

Rosario the diabetic looked apprehensively at the dark woods.

"Hey," he said, frowning, "did we ever make the peace with the fucking Indians around here?"

CHAPTER THIRTY-SEVEN

Frost was beside himself.

He had been fine, everything had been going just fine, until he felt those bullets whiz over his head. Then he'd done what he'd sworn he wouldn't do. He'd rattled. Frost had rattled and let go of the woman, and he was furious at himself and furious at Murphy.

Mostly at Murphy.

Frost had bounded off into the woods after the shots had come his way and after he had blasted indiscriminately with the shotgun. He wished he had never picked up the goddamned shotgun, which was getting in his way now as he tried to move through the woods. He didn't know from guns. He wished he had just waited there in the house for Murphy. He wished he had had more time with the woman, some time to love her up a bit at least. They never forgot it after Rhino loved them up. That was something they always remembered. That's what Frost had been after tonight. He had been going to love them up, both of them, but he had gotten into the house and they had both been there and Murphy hadn't, and Frost hadn't counted on that. What he had counted on was catching

Murphy and then loving them up while he made Murphy watch and then doing something that would keep them all quiet until he'd been able to get on his bike and make tracks out of there.

And he knew what he would have done to do that. He knew that he couldn't have left any of them alive. He hadn't wanted to leave any of them alive.

Only now they were all alive—except maybe the girl back in the house, the one he'd shot at—and Frost had blown his chance, and he was furious with himself. He was moving through the woods in pitch-blackness, bumping into tree branches and scraping himself up, and he was positively foaming. Plus he didn't know where he was or where he was going.

Frost was moving now, he knew, in the woods somewhere near the lake. That was all he knew. He thought he was moving toward the spot on the lakeshore where he had stashed the bike and the chain saw, but who knew? Even in daylight he might have had problems finding the trail again. At night? At night, it was just about hopeless. He felt a sense of true desperation setting in. He couldn't leave without the bike.

He lumbered through the underbrush and suddenly found himself on the water's edge. He stopped, trying to determine his position. Which way to the bike, right or left? He had no idea. In the end, he just guessed.

And he guessed correctly.

Frost came upon the bike, hidden in a stand of poplars, only a few minutes later. He put his hands on it, almost caressed it, and began to move it out to the trail. Then he stopped.

What was that?

He heard sounds coming from his right, someone coming through the woods. Frost stepped away from the bike and dropped to one knee in the darkness. The sound was moving toward him, crashing through the woods. He smiled. Murphy was making more noise than Frost had ever made out here. Frost made it a point not to move, to hardly breathe, for several minutes. It paid off.

He could pinpoint the sound now. It was over there, at the edge of the lake. He saw a dim shape moving against the backdrop of the water, perhaps forty feet away. Slowly, Frost raised the shotgun. He aimed it as best he could. He followed the dim shape as it moved. There were trees in the way. He couldn't be sure. Then the shape passed between two trees, in the open for a moment.

Frost fired.

The light from the explosion blinded him. He could see nothing. He crouched, waiting for return fire, but none came. Slowly, Frost stood up, moved toward the spot where he had seen the shape. Then he saw Murphy's outline on the ground not ten feet ahead. Murphy had the pistol. He was lying on the ground, struggling to rise to a sitting position, trying to point the pistol.

Frost grinned in the darkness. He brought the shotgun up to his shoulder. He pulled the trigger. The explosion deafened him. Did he hit Murphy? Frost couldn't tell.

So, just to be sure, Frost approached the dim shape on the ground and emptied the shotgun into it, pumping shells into the firing chamber after every blast.

Boom!

click.

Boom!

click.

Boom!

click.

click.

click.

Empty.

Frost tossed aside the empty shotgun and moved like a flash over the few remaining feet to lean over the corpse on the ground. The open area near the beach was not as dark as the woods, but it was still very dark, and his eyes were suffering from the explosions they had witnessed at such close range. Frost couldn't see. He rubbed his eyes. Then, after a few moments, things began to come into focus. In the shadows, he looked down at the man lying in the shadows next to the lake. And, as he did, his face took on a queer expression. He didn't know who this was, but it wasn't Frank Murphy.

Frost knew this because from behind him, at the edge of the woods, he heard a voice. It was Murphy's voice.

It was saying, "Wrong guy, Rhino."

Wilder heard the shots. How could he have not heard the shots? He moved toward them in the darkness, catching his suit jacket on tree branches, on bark, on leaves and twigs.

And he used to think North Philly was an inhospitable environment.

He moved toward the sound. Then he heard some

movement, a rustle, to his left. Wilder pointed his pistol toward the sound.

"Jimmy?" he heard Mary Ellen say.

Frost turned toward Murphy. The two men were no more than a dozen feet apart. Frost looked down at the corpse at his feet.

"Another one of your buddies?" he asked.

Murphy glanced at the body. "I think so. It looks like a cop I know named Rosario. That means there are other cops here in these woods looking for you. It's time to give it up, Rhino."

Frost pondered the situation. Then he said, "Yeah, I guess you're right. Guys are looking for me. But you're the one who found me."

And he launched himself straight at Murphy.

Murphy had expected that, and while he had given away both his .38 and Catrelli's .44, he still had the brass knuckles, which he had fitted over his right fist, and the big police flashlight in his left. As Frost charged, Murphy flipped on the light and shined it directly into the giant's face. Then, at the last second, Murphy dropped the flashlight and watched Frost's eyes follow the beam of light as it fell to earth.

And as Frost leaped toward the light—which was all he could see, after all—Murphy stepped to the right, turned quickly, and unloaded with the brass knuckles squarely on Frost's jaw. Murphy felt teeth crunch and break off beneath his blow.

He also felt Frost's huge arms wrap around him and bear him to the soft dirt.

For a moment, Murphy came close to panicking.

433

But then he realized that the blow had stunned the giant, and he scrambled out from beneath him and to his feet as Frost lumbered up, towering up against the lake, huge. Murphy hadn't realized how huge this bastard was. He'd forgotten. He hadn't stood close to him since that day on the street outside his office and not for many years before that. This son of a bitch was immense, enormous.

But did he know how to fight? That was the question.

Frost shook his head, clearing it from the blow, and then came in at Murphy, big hands reaching, clutching. Murphy danced back, dropping into a boxing stance. He flicked out a hard, stiff jab—a jab designed to stop a big man and hold him upright momentarily while you went down low with the right for his vitals.

That was the theory, anyway.

In this case, Frost came right through the jab, grunting and roaring. Frost felt Murphy's sweatshirt beneath his fingers. He grasped it, pulled on it. He had Murphy now. Frost felt as though he had died and gone to heaven.

Only then, suddenly, he had only the sweatshirt. Murphy had ducked down, stepped to one side, and then pulled away, letting the giant pull the sweatshirt off his back, leaving him naked to the waist in the cool summer night, and that was okay because it gave the big man less of a hold when he reached and grabbed and that was fine with Murphy. Murphy threw a hard, brass-knuckle-covered right, and it drove straight into the side of Rhino Frost's forehead, like a baseball bat striking home. Murphy had a good right. He'd always had a good right. When he'd been boxing in the Navy, he'd always been able to count on the right to keep

434

opponents off him. When he'd been able to get it in cleanly, it had worked unfailingly.

Except this time, that was.

Frost took the blow without a sound and reached for Murphy's arm. Murphy moved back. He remembered that fight at Shea Stadium years ago when Chuck Wepner, a boxer, had taken on a professional wrestler named Andre the Giant. Wepner had been a big enough guy, bigger than Murphy, but Andre had been over seven feet tall and had weighed in at over four hundred pounds. Wepner had turned the guy's face into raw meat the first two rounds. But in the third, Andre had caught Wepner and picked him up and thrown him out of the ring, breaking his arm, and that had been all she wrote.

Murphy remembered that bout. He remembered seeing it on closed circuit at the Spectrum. And he remembered thinking that Wepner had been operating at a disadvantage. He hadn't been able to kick the giant in the balls. Murphy could—and did.

Frost took the blow on the thigh, just to the left of home plate. He lumbered toward Murphy, clutching and grabbing, and Murphy danced back, popping in jabs that he knew had to hurt, but he couldn't figure out why they seemed to have only negligible stopping power against this monster. Murphy crossed with a few rights, with the brass knuckles, and he saw blood gush from Frost's nose and from gashes in his forehead and his cheeks, but there seemed to be no stopping this guy. Murphy pounded and bobbed and weaved and pounded and bobbed and weaved some more, but nothing much seemed to be working. Murphy knew he was well ahead on points, but he wasn't sure how much all that counted for in a clash like this. Murphy wasn't frightened yet, but he was beginning to worry a bit.

The two men circled each other for a moment, Murphy in classic boxing pose and wishing he had another set of brass knuckles for the left, because this guy could easily be hit with a left.

Frost, eyes gleaming, said, "I'm going to take your head off, motherfucker. I'm going to make this one last for a while."

Murphy wasted no breath talking. He was finding breath tough enough to come by at this point. He just drove in another left.

Which turned out to be a terrible mistake.

Murphy was tiring now. He was, after all, forty-five, and he was not exactly in prime shape. The mistake he made was to paw with the left instead of snapping it in, and Frost used both huge hands to grab his left wrist and to pull him close. Faced with no other alternative, Murphy stepped inside and drove a hard right to Frost's midsection. Nothing.

Then Frost had him. He had both arms around him, pinning Murphy to his huge body. The man's strength was awesome. Murphy felt his breath pushed out of him as though his lungs were some sort of huge bellows. Then Frost lowered his head and drove his teeth into Murphy's naked shoulder.

Murphy cried out.

Frost pushed him back against a tree. The rough bark tore Murphy's flesh. He struggled to break free, but the left arm was pinned between them and he didn't have the angle with the right. Frost's big teeth dug into his shoulder. Murphy could think of no way to break free, felt the huge weight pinning him against the tree, felt the tree's surface turning his back into stewing meat.

So he kicked Frost in the kneecap.

It was a hard kick, a vicious one. Frost grunted, and one leg went out from under him. He fell backward, and Murphy fell with him. The two men went down, rolling. And as they rolled and struggled and punched and kicked—

—Murphy broke free.

He rolled free of Frost and gained his feet, shaky but more confident now. Frost lumbered up, standing unsteadily, one leg useless. Murphy wondered if he had broken the giant's kneecap. He hoped so.

Murphy moved in then. He seemed to have his second wind. Blood poured down his left shoulder, arm, and chest from the bite mark, and that seemed to infuse him with a new sense of fury. He danced about Frost, nailing him with the jab, driving him in the right with the added power of the brass knuckles. Murphy hit the big man hard, as hard as he could. With blow after blow, he slowly began to make Rhino Frost's face disappear.

Frost groped for him weakly now, desperately. Murphy caught him high in the face, slammed blow after blow into the beard, into the now broken and bloodied teeth. Murphy took his time. He would not be caught again. He worked over Rhino Frost carefully and methodically.

And he enjoyed it, too.

In the end, it took a hard kick against Frost's remaining kneecap to bring him down. Murphy had the impression that he could stand there all night bouncing the brass knuckles off that thick skull

437

without accomplishing his end. So, after a while, he faked with the right, and when Frost's big arms went up, covering his head, Murphy turned and drove the sole of his right Nike directly into Frost's knee. He heard it pop, a satisfying sound.

Frost hit the ground hard.

Murphy stood over him, blood pouring out of his shoulder wound and mixing with the sweat dripping off him, the contents of an entire brewery pouring out of his pores.

"You're going back again, Rhino," he said, gasping. "This time it'll be for a long, long time. Two murders they've got you for this time."

Frost's chest heaved as he lay there. "I'll get out again," he got out. "I don't care if I'm fucking ninety years old, I'll get out again."

Murphy started to turn to retrieve his sweatshirt, but as he did Frost somehow summoned up reserves of strength that seemed unnatural. He rolled and clambered to his feet and half staggered, half crawled down the lakeside. His knees were gone, and he could hardly move. Murphy, about to slip on his sweatshirt, watched him in the darkness. Murphy knew Frost wouldn't go far in that shape. He started after him at an almost casual pace.

But Frost did make it to the bike, which Murphy hadn't realized was nearby. And as he made the bike, Murphy saw what was happening. He tossed aside the sweatshirt and tried to run toward him. But Murphy didn't have all that much left, either, and he'd never been much of a sprinter to begin with. He finished covering the forty or so feet between the scene of the fight and the bike just as Frost's chain saw kicked into life, starting up with a roar and a whine. Frost swung it weakly in Murphy's direction, and Murphy dodged back, the blade missing his face by inches. Murphy did not dodge with much grace, however. He tripped and fell into the shallow water.

Frost came at him with the chain saw then. Murphy struggled to scramble to his feet, but the churning blade of the saw was swinging toward him. Even over the sound of the saw's motor, Murphy could hear Frost's triumphant roar.

Murphy rolled in the water, digging in his back pocket with frantic fingers. He found Catrelli's pearl-handled .32 in his back pocket and emptied five rapid shots at point-blank range into the giant, howling shape looming up over him.

Three of the bullets went right through the face of a demon.

CHAPTER THIRTY-EIGHT

Wilder took Mary Ellen back to the chalet.

It wasn't easy, but he found his way back through the woods, in the process ruining a pretty good suit, one of the ones he'd bought at Boyd's when he'd made lieutenant just after the first of the year. He left both Mary Ellen and Patricia in the care of Zsa Zsa, who was making coffee and talking a blue streak trying to cheer everybody up and keep them calm. Then Wilder went back out into the woods.

He heard the shots from Catrelli's .32 and followed them. He found Murphy standing, dripping sweat and blood and chest heaving mightily, standing over the body of Rhino Frost. Murphy motioned to the right.

"Rosario," he said simply.

Wilder moved off in the direction Murphy had indicated. He used his flashlight, flipped it on for a brief moment before killing the light, then he came back to Murphy's side, his face grim. "Rosario would never have gotten taken like that on the streets. He was a good man."

Murphy was furious, Wilder could see. He was trembling with rage, even now when it was over. He motioned toward Frost.

"He wasn't," Murphy said. "He was about the worst I ever came across. We should have just killed this asshole when we had the chance, all those years ago. If we'd done that, Catrelli would be alive now and so would Rosario."

"Yeah," Wilder said, "well, there's this little loophole in the law, you know."

Murphy ignored the remark. He merely picked up Frost's chain saw, which lay in the shallows of the lake, and pitched it angrily out into deeper water. Wilder heard it hit and sink with a loud splash. He turned his light on Murphy, who looked terrible. He was bruised and soaked with sweat and blood, some of it Frost's but most of it from the bite wound on his shoulder.

"You look like shit," he told Murphy. "Come on, let's go back to the house."

Murphy shook his head. "Mary Ellen and Patricia are out here somewhere."

"No, they're not. I've got them both back at the house. Zsa Zsa's with them. They're both okay."

Murphy felt an enormous sense of relief—to go along with his enormous sense of utter exhaustion. He took a deep breath, then his gaze fell on Frost's Harley. Murphy's eyes narrowed.

"You go on ahead," he said. "I'll be along."

"What are you talking about?" Wilder demanded.

"Hey," Murphy said, his voice harsh, "are we friends? Do this one thing for me, okay? Go on ahead. I'll be there in a minute."

"What's this all about?"

"Don't ask," Murphy said.

Wilder studied his friend in the darkness. He'd never

441

seen Murphy's face so tightly set. Then again, he knew, Murphy had never killed anybody before—not in all those years of police work. Wilder had never killed anybody, either, and he wondered if he would be as upset about it as Murphy seemed to be now.

"All right," Wilder said finally. "You've got five minutes after I get to the house. Then I'm coming back out after you."

Murphy stood in the darkness, watching Wilder move off. When the light had disappeared along the lakeshore, Murphy let his eyes adjust to the darkness again and went over to the bike. He studied it in the shadows. A new Harley 1200. Big bucks for one of these babies.

Then he dug into the saddlebags until he found what he was after. The money to pay for Patricia's college education. Let Quick Silver and the others figure out where Rhino Frost's forty grand had gone. He wrapped the saddlebags in his sweatshirt. He could hide them in the woods near the house and retrieve them on his way out of this godforsaken place. Murphy figured he'd earned it.

Before he left the beach, Murphy took the time to push Rhino Frost's Harley into the lake, where it sank with a pleasurable sound.

CHAPTER THIRTY-NINE

Early on a Sunday morning at the end of August, Murphy pulled the Toronado into the driveway of the brick house in Mount Airy. He killed the engine—and his Temptations tape with it, the one Mary Ellen had made from her old albums using her new box with the two heads—and went inside. Mary Ellen was in the kitchen.

"Is she ready yet?" Murphy asked, lighting a Camel in the doorway.

"She's just finishing packing up," Mary Ellen said. "Give her a few minutes. Want some coffee?"

"Yeah," Murphy said, and sat down. The Sunday *Inquirer* was on the kitchen table. He leafed through it. It was just past nine, and he hadn't gotten up in time to both look through the newspaper delivered to his apartment and to get ready for the trip to upstate New York. Mary Ellen served him coffee the way he liked it, with cream and Sweet 'N Low. He sipped it and smoked as he went through the sports section. Mary Ellen sat down across from him.

"How long do you think the drive will take you?" she asked.

"About four or five hours, I think. Longer if I stop. Then I've got to come straight back. I've got to be in court at ten tomorrow morning."

"That's a long haul for one day," she said. "You're sure you don't want me to come along to keep you company?"

He shook his head. "I can handle it. I don't want to have to come way out here and then drive all the way back to Center City when I hit home territory. She's taking her own sweet time, isn't she? Give her a holler, will you, Mary Ellen?"

Mary Ellen went to the bottom of the stairs. "Your father's here, Patricia. Get a move on, will you?"

"Any minute now," she called down.

Mary Ellen came back and sat back down. She watched her husband go through the newspaper, the cigarette dangling from his lower lip. She wished he'd quit smoking those things. She wished he'd quit a lot of things, though, and he wasn't likely to.

"What happened in the Waterson case?" she asked him.

"He pleaded Friday to manslaughter two. He'll do some time, but not all that much, everything considered. He can kiss good-bye to his education career, though. Poor bastard."

"Well," Mary Ellen said, "he did kill a man, after all."

Murphy looked up. "Oh, I know he did. I'm glad he's getting jail time. Don't get me wrong. The fact is, I think that manslaughter two is a bit light for what he did—even though I got it for him."

Mary Ellen smiled slightly. "Always a cop, aren't you? Always the moralist."

"There are worse vices," Murphy told her. "Liberalism, for example. That's a worse vice, don't you think? Where the hell is she?"

"Patricia," Mary Ellen called out.

"I could have done that," Murphy pointed out.

Then he heard Patricia's footsteps on the stairs. She came skipping down. Murphy knew she was happy to get away. College ought to be a big adventure for a kid. He'd gone at night, during his off hours, first to undergraduate school and then to law school. It had been no fun. He had no idea of what it would be like to attend college as a kid, living away from home. If it had been him in this situation, he suspected, he'd have flunked out in the first semester. Murphy hoped she didn't. He'd paid enough for this first year—both semesters up front—and he didn't have all that much of Frost's money left. His conscience had gotten the better of him, and he'd sent ten grand in anonymous cashier's checks to the widows of both Rosario and Catrelli. Tuition and board for the first year at Skidmore had pretty much wiped out the rest of what he had taken from the saddlebags. He had no idea of what he'd do to pay the freight for next year, although the newspaper publicity about what had happened up in the Poconos had brought him some new business. It had helped, at any rate.

Patricia came into the kitchen. She was grinning ear to ear.

"Close your eyes," she told her father.

He frowned. "What's this crap? Come on, we've got a lot of miles to cover."

"Close your eyes, Frank," Mary Ellen said.

Murphy gave up. He closed his eyes. A moment

passed. Then Patricia said, "Now, open them."

Murphy did. Standing on the kitchen floor was a bulldog puppy—a small, incredibly ugly little dog who didn't really walk. The puppy more or less ambled, its gait eerily familiar. The puppy wandered the kitchen for a moment, sniffing here and there. Then it walked over to Murphy and snorted, spraying his feet with saliva and spittle and dog slime. Murphy bent down and gathered the little animal in his arms. The puppy turned its wrinkled, pushed-in face toward him and a pink tongue flicked out, catching Murphy on the cheek.

Mary Ellen and Patricia stood side by side, grinning co-conspirators. Murphy thought for a moment that he might weep, but he contained himself.

"What are you going to call him, Daddy?" Patricia asked.

Murphy cuddled the bulldog puppy in his arms, holding it close to his big chest.

"What the hell do you think?" he asked in a hoarse voice.